Praise for Matt Manochio

"A real page turner. Matt Manochio has constructed a very real and believable force in Krampus and has given it a real journalistic twist, and he has gained a fan in me!"
—David L. Golemon, *New York Times* bestselling author of the Event Group Thriller series

"A riveting tale of a community under siege by a grotesque, chain-clanking monster with cloven hooves, a dry sense of wit, and a sadistic predilection for torture. Manochio balances a very dark theme with crackling dialogue, fast-paced action, and an engaging, small town setting."
—Lucy Taylor, Bram Stoker Award-winning author of *The Safety of Unknown Cities*

"Beautifully crafted and expertly plotted. A clockwork mechanism of terror that blends Freddy Krueger with the Brothers Grimm! Highly recommended!"
—Jay Bonansinga, *New York Times* bestselling author of *Shattered*

"Matt Manochio is a writer who'll be thrilling us for many books to come."
—Jim DeFelice, *New York Times* bestselling author of *American Sniper*

"In *The Dark Servant*, Matt Manochio has taken the tantalizing roots of Middle Europe's folklore and crafted a completely genuine modern American horror story. This is a winter's tale, yes, but it is also a genuinely new one for our modern times. I fell for this story right away. Matt Manochio is a natural born storyteller."
—Joe McKinney, Bram Stoker Award-winning author of *The Savage Dead*

The Dark Servant

Matt Manochio

To Katie,
Thank you!
And be good!

SAMHAIN
PUBLISHING

Samhain Publishing, Ltd.
11821 Mason Montgomery Rd., 4B
Cincinnati, OH 45249
www.samhainpublishing.com

The Dark Servant
Copyright © 2014 by Matt Manochio
Print ISBN: 978-1-61922-660-9
Digital ISBN: 978-1-61921-972-4

Editing by Don D'Auria
Cover by Scott Carpenter

First Samhain Publishing, Ltd. electronic publication: November 2014
First Samhain Publishing, Ltd. print publication: November 2014

Dedication

This book is dedicated to Daniel Dickholtz, my boss and friend, who in December 2012 asked me if I knew about Krampus. I didn't. That morning led to *The Dark Servant*.

Chapter One

December 5

Travis Reardon drove his Mazda CX-5 out of his parents' three-car garage and met the foggy darkness typical of his early morning drive to high school—yet the odor, slight but detectable even with the windows up, gave him pause.

The eighteen-year-old senior lowered his window to identify the smell. His new crossover's headlights were all that guided him down the windy driveway to Winchester Road. Streetlamps didn't exist in this densely wooded stretch of Hancock Township. It was one of the few places in rural New Jersey where light pollution didn't ruin starry skies.

"Gross" was all he said as he raised the window and continued his fifteen-minute commute to school. He reached into his book bag on the front seat for his iPhone and dialed his girlfriend. He put the phone on speaker and placed it on his lap.

"Hey, baby," a female voice answered.

"You miss me?"

"Parts of you," she purred. "You on your way?"

"As we speak. How 'bout you?"

"In my car, in the school parking lot. Waiting. I'll wander on over in, oh, just a little bit. I'll be cold, baby. My legs especially."

"You minx. Any tests today that I can take your mind off of?"

"English, some Shakespearean Othello nonsense. God forbid we learn something that can actually help us succeed in the real world. Since when does knowing a few lines from some old play make you well-rounded? It's not like quoting Iago will help me land a job."

"Unless you become an actress."

"Hardy har. Any tests on your horizon?"

"I play football, honey. Tests don't mean dick. My throwing arm does. That's all Virginia Tech cares about right now."

"So, it's Virginia Tech today? What happened to Boston College?"

"I go back and forth. It's a nice luxury to have when multiple schools offer you free rides. Christ, it *stinks!*"

"Excuse me?"

"Not *you*, baby. I've been on the road for like five minutes and there's this awful smell all over the woods. It keeps getting worse. Like something died."

"I hope it doesn't stick to you. Sweaty can be sexy. Smelling like roadkill? Not so much."

"It's just, I can't describe it. I hope whatever it is died quick."

"Let's not end things by talking about dead animals, big guy. I'll leave you with this. I'm going all Anne Hathaway today. It's a good thing the paparazzi aren't waiting around to photograph me stepping out of my car. It would be quite the naughty picture in the school paper."

"You are such a tease—I love it. See you in ten."

"Bye, sugar." And she was gone.

Travis pumped his fist. He'd reach second base in the morning and throw touchdowns that night. Howard Stern prattled on satellite radio in the background and Travis noticed the temperature outside was in the thirties, appropriate December coldness. Dirty remnants of a freak Thanksgiving snowstorm littered the landscape. There'd be no respite from the white stuff. A blizzard was set to blanket the tristate area come evening.

What a gyp, Travis thought. *Why couldn't the damn thing wait to start Sunday night? It'd wipe out school on Monday, maybe Tuesday too. What a waste.*

The road was clear, save for the occasional salt stain, and he stayed under the forty-miles-per-hour speed limit. He wasn't going to let a deer leap from the shadows and smash into his early graduation present from Daddy. *Maybe a dead deer's stinking up the place?* They infested northern New Jersey and he regularly hunted them with his father and uncle. It wasn't a skunk's scent, the lingering kind that eventually dissipates. This alien reek intensified.

He decelerated when the first of two stoplights that punctuated his journey came into view, and that's when the shriek shattered his ride. The Mazda's closed windows blunted what seemed to be the screams of prey being mauled by a pack of beasts.

Just put it out of its misery, please, he thought.

And then the wails ceased. Travis stopped at the red light and turned off Howard Stern. Curiosity led him to lower his window and he was arrested by the odor and silence, broken only by his breathing. He counted five Mississippis of quiet before an anguished scream rippled through the air and then devolved into a growl. Travis swore he heard a chain clanking every time the thing drew breath to resume its gnarling.

"Some kind of guard dog that escaped?" Travis asked aloud. His nerves spiked the way they did the first time he saw police lights in his rearview mirror—his dad was mayor—no speeding ticket that day.

"Turn green. Turn green already," he commanded the light.

The snarling persisted from afar, but from where? Travis fumbled through his glove box and found his emergency flashlight. He acted like a high school quarterback and scanned the forest to his left. Eyes darting back and forth, the beam danced from here to there, and instead of finding an open receiver he spotted huffs of condensed breath puncturing the darkness, as if some unseen bull was preparing to charge his red Mazda.

The light turned green and Travis floored it. He had to trust that no deer ahead of him would jump into his path. A pickup truck passed him going the opposite direction, as did a couple of school buses out to retrieve their loads of kids. He'd traveled ten miles since leaving home, and his headlights illuminated the final stoplight, meaning he was five minutes away from school.

The howling resumed and grew louder as Travis approached the light.

"Jesus *Christ*, what *is* that?" he blurted.

He looked in his rearview and swiveled his head over his shoulders, looking for something trailing him. Nothing. But the howling, brewed deep in the bowels and belched skyward, would not die, nor would the smell.

Travis had to slow down. The cross street always had some school traffic this time of morning and he'd be crazy to blow through the red light that greeted him.

"Just keep it together," he told himself. He scanned left and right and saw a school bus in the distance, traveling toward the light from his right. Travis despised this signal because of the length of time it took to change. The bus would pass him, and perhaps another would too, before the light turned green. He'd felt on edge before, when two-hundred-pound linemen were bearing down on him. But that was a game.

His shaking grip on the steering wheel at the ten and two positions made it appear as if he were bending an iron rod. He wanted to be at school. He wanted his green and white football jersey that he wore under his varsity jacket to broadcast to the world that he and his teammates were superior specimens within a sea adrift with regular students. He'd even French-kiss and cop feels off his girlfriend—who admitted she wasn't wearing a *shred* of underwear—before the homeroom bell, all of it five minutes away.

The school bus headlights approached. He kept his window down despite the putridity. He neglected to turn on Howard Stern. He wasn't in the mood to find out how old the Kardashians were when they all lost their virginity. Instead, he heard earthmoving footfalls and a growl erupting into an otherworldly roar.

Travis turned to his right to see through the passenger's window a dark mass burst through the forest. *Screw the light,* he thought. *Just go!* But it was too late. The thing barreled into the side of the Mazda, lifting it off the ground. The bellowing thing repeatedly rained down a heavy chain with watermelon-sized links—the kind that could lower drawbridges—onto the Mazda's hood, crushing the vehicle's engine into a stall.

Travis went to unbuckle his seat belt but again was too slow as the creature's hairy right hand smashed through the window and began to thrash and grab. The Mazda's headlamps and dashboard lights still worked and illuminated dark tangles of grimy fur attached to a log-thick forearm.

A meaty, calloused hand with crescent-shaped talons raked though Travis's seat belt. The hand grasped through Travis's jacket and jersey, talons slicing into flesh on his chest. Its grip firm, the thing pulled Travis across the passenger's seat and out of the window. It disregarded the pain Travis felt as it dragged his body over jagged edges of the remaining window glass, its shards wedging into his thighs.

Now fully extracted, Travis remembered a long tongue waggling around fangs, and his six-foot-two-inch body reduced to being a rag doll's, tossed by hand *over* the beast's head and into what Travis surmised was a wooden crate strapped to its back. His skull cracked against the crate's base, dazing him. Now he knew what a notebook felt like in a backpack.

Jesus, how big is this thing?!

And then running. Travis's legs jutted out of the crate and his head smacked against wood as his kidnapper bounded through the forest's dead leaves and snow. And the running stopped, but not the movement. *Gliding?* His stomach churned as if he were plunging on a rickety amusement-park ride.

Besides the beast's howls, the last bit Travis remembered before losing consciousness was the smell that started the nightmare: the odor of a malevolent force that invaded New Jersey twenty days before Christmas.

Chapter Two

"You're going to school today, buddy. No doubt about it." Tim Schweitzer stood outside the open bedroom door and spoke to his younger brother, Billy, as if he were their father.

Tim, himself an eighteen-year-old Hancock High School senior, as well as the football team's running back, was jacketed and ready to go when Travis Reardon's drive to school ended.

"I'm not feelin' good. I have a fever." Billy, a year younger than Tim and a junior, remained in bed with his blankets held chest high.

"A fever? Really?" Tim strode into the room and put his palm on Billy's forehead before he could duck under the sheets. "Cool as ice, kid. You're not fooling anyone."

"What do you care if I go to school?" Billy flapped the sheets away from his body and sat amid his failed ruse. "We're not in any of the same classes. We don't have the same lunch or gym periods. You're in your cool world and I'm in my shitty one."

"Oh, quit the sob story, Billy." Tim checked his watch. He had a few minutes to try to inject sense into his brother's head. "Every guy gets rejected by a girl at some time or another."

Billy was incredulous. "Have *you*?"

"Well, *no*. But you're missing my point. I could ask out any number of cheerleaders on the squad and I guarantee you at least one of them would say no."

"That's supposed to make me feel better? Only *one* hot girl out of fifteen would shoot you down? Come on, Tim. You're popular, you play four sports. Christ, you've never had a pimple. You have no idea what this feels like."

Billy still reeled from rejection's sting doled out the previous evening by Maria Flynn, a comely redheaded junior he'd pined for since fish crawled out of the sea, and whom he'd finally summoned the courage to ask over the phone to the movies.

"You told me that Maria said she was already seeing someone, so it's not like she was repulsed by the suggestion. I guarantee you she was flattered you asked her out. And how were you supposed to know she's dating some guy from outside the school? I'm sure you did your homework, asked around where you could, thinking that if she was with anyone, the guy would be at the same high school and you'd have found out."

"She probably already told all of her friends and they're all going to be giving me those giggles and glances when I walk by their lockers."

"First of all, I sincerely doubt that. Second of all, so what if they do? Don't pay attention to any of them. Now get out of bed and stop feeling sorry for yourself. Play the field, man. Maria's not the only girl in your grade, you know. And you don't even know anything about her. She could be a real bitch."

"That's not true," Billy spat back. "I've gone to school long enough with her to know she's nothing like that. And from what I've seen, she's not like one of those stuck-up cheerleaders who theoretically might reject you."

"Fair enough, you're probably right. You're smart, you'd know if she wasn't worth the trouble. All I'm saying is you've got to get her off this pedestal of yours. And you've got to go back to school sometime. So why not today?"

Tim sat on the edge of his brother's bed, knowing he was hurting. The two had become closer during the last couple of years in the wake of their parents' divorce.

"I feel like I have a boa constrictor squeezing my brain." Billy looked down at his sheets, not wanting to meet his brother's eyes. "I feel sad. *Really* sad. Am I supposed to feel like this?"

"Let down? Sure, that's only natural—you're not the first guy to go through this." Tim patted Billy on the shoulder. "How would you feel if a girl you weren't really that in to asked you out and you turned her down?"

Billy's eyes darted upward to mull it over. "I don't know."

"Would you feel terrible?"

"I don't think so."

"Maybe a little happy and possibly a little upset that you hurt her feelings by saying no, even though you never intended it?"

Billy considered everything and whispered, "Yeah. I would."

"I know you would. And I know that because you're a good person. And if Maria is anything like you are, that's exactly how she felt after you hung up the phone last night."

"I hope so."

"She did. Trust me. And you can't avoid her or her friends forever. So let's just go."

Tim rose from the bed and retrieved from his jacket pocket the keys to his dad's hand-me-down Ford Ranger. It had 175,000 miles on it but was serviceable for ferrying Tim and Billy to school, which stood ten miles from their home on the other side of town.

"I've got to get going. So it's me, the bus or Dad in his cruiser. But one way or the other you're going to school today. And believe me when I say you're *not* talking your way around Dad. So, last chance. Come on and get ready."

"I'll take my chances with Dad. I don't feel up to it," Billy said before slumping into his mattress and pillow, and bringing the blankets up to his chin.

"Fine. Have it your way." Tim turned for the front door of their one-story, three-bedroom home, but before he left he made clear that Billy would attend school that day.

"See you, Dad!" he called to Hancock Police Chief Donald Schweitzer, who was donning his uniform. "Billy's faking sickness to try to skip school today! Don't let his skinny butt get away with it."

The elder Schweitzer, forty-five years old and a lifelong Hancock resident, graduated from the same school his sons now attended. He stood a cop's build of six feet four inches tall, and had the same blond hair and blue eyes as both of his sons. Sure, his ex-wife had something to do with it. However, only Tim wound up the same height. Billy's five-foot-nine-inch frame carried wiry strength.

"I'll deal with him" was all Tim Schweitzer heard from behind his dad's closed bedroom door. Mission accomplished. Tim grinned and practically heard Billy mutter *"dammit!"*.

Gotta get off the mat sometime, kid, Tim thought. He was tired of seeing his brother depressed, and this was *before* Maria Flynn rejected him. Billy failed to make the junior varsity baseball team during his sophomore year. He spent the summer moping when he should've been bulking up in the weight room and strengthening his throwing arm. Billy played a good second base and he was a jackrabbit around the bases, but he needed more practice and could make the team the next season if he put in the effort. But he didn't, and he'd spurned Tim's offers to help him train.

Tim was on the road when Billy got out of bed. He stood and pulled the cord to the overhead light. He grabbed a stick of deodorant off his dresser and smeared his armpits before donning a white T-shirt followed by a black hoodie he pulled from the drawers. He then surveyed the wrinkled clothing strewn across the floor and used his right foot to scoop up a pair of jeans. There was no use delaying the inevitable. The chief was involved. Billy thought he should've forced himself to vomit instead of claiming a fever. At least then he'd have had a puncher's chance. There was no knock on his bedroom door, just a "we're leaving in five minutes, I'll be in the car, waiting" as his father marched down the hallway and out the front door.

"Let me find my shoes, Dad." Billy kicked the shirts and pants on the floor until striking something hard, his sneakers. He slipped them on and then walked to his desk, which had transmogrified into a drafting table. The architecture project wasn't due until next week, still plenty of time. Billy slipped his hand underneath scattered sheaves of oversized paper and charcoal pencils to retrieve his wallet.

A piece of scrap paper poked out of an unoccupied credit card slit. Billy's stomach heaved upon seeing it, for it contained the numbers, two different sets of them, hastily scrawled for future reference. Maria Flynn was listed on the Zabasearch website, along with the family's home phone number, which he'd scrawled on the paper. More digging could've unearthed her cell phone number but he feared the move might send off stalker vibes.

They were Facebook friends, and he could've sent a private message asking her out, but the move seemed too impersonal. So he did it the way kids did in the 1990s: His dry runs included pacing before his iPhone, picking up the phone, dialing her number, ending the call before the first ring and setting the now-sweaty phone back on his desk, waiting for the nervousness to subside. He repeated the process twice more until mustering the courage that kept him on the line.

Hi, is Maria there?

Who may I ask is calling?

And so went the evening Billy would forever remember.

He had scribbled a second set of digits unrelated to Maria's underneath her phone number. He'd recorded these over a prolonged period of time in the shadows when those who were supposed to be vigilant let down their guard.

Billy tore off the bit of scrap with Maria's number and dropped it in the tin New York Giants trash can next to his desk. Billy flicked the remainder of the sheet like a playing card onto his desk and tugged out the light before heading to the kitchen for some Pop-Tarts he didn't care to eat. Nothing saps the appetite like dashed romantic desires.

Gray clouds filtered a distant sunlight through Billy's bedroom window to grimly illuminate the remaining string of numbers.

Donald Schweitzer kicked a bundle of tied kindling sticks off the house's front steps to make sure his youngest boy didn't trip on them like he almost did.

Irresponsible boy, I asked him to bring in the wood last night, the chief internalized. *At least Tim's got his head on straight.*

He sat in his idling cruiser facing the home where he and his ex had raised the boys together until a few years ago. Billy's shadow slipped in and out of sight behind dimly lit curtains.

"Let's go, kid. It's not hard to toast something." The chief drummed the wheel, thinking. Always thinking.

At first Diana came home later than usual from her finance job in New York City. Reasonable enough, the chief thought at the time. The commute was ninety minutes with typical morning traffic on good days.

But after a while the infrequent, going-through-the-motions sex waned to the point of not even making up excuses of headaches to avoid it, just "I don't feel like it", usually from her. Their conversations always culminated with one of them walking away angry. And her late nights reached deep into morning.

He never cheated on her, never thought about it. But he wasn't stupid. He didn't become the chief by pulling a prize from a Cracker Jack box. And he didn't raise his kids to be stupid. They knew. Something had to give.

"What's his name?" he asked more than two years ago.

She told him, and added that she wanted a divorce. Their love, once genuine, had declined in value the way a new car's does when it rolls off the lot.

A really good car makes it fifteen years before it's time to junk it, he thought. *The same can be said for mediocre first marriages.*

It wasn't terrible, the chief reasoned. Meet at Rutgers University, get hitched, churn out the grandkids to make the folks happy and then grind out daily life with hopes of a nice vacation every few years. Fortunately, her New York City income allowed for more good moments than bad, until the last few years.

The divorce never went before a judge. She was prudent and knew she would come out on the short end because she'd started the affair.

"Keep the house, Don, and I won't contest you taking full custody of the kids. Let me visit with them a few times a month and it'll be peachy. I'll take my stuff and will be fine with the new guy, his apartment overlooking Central Park and the emotional support he provides that you no longer could because of that police job of yours. Let's just pretend like the whole marriage never happened."

But it did happen. Schweitzer was glad it happened. Now he spent his days wishing he could've prevented it from ending. Billy broke his train of thought when he opened the car door and sat next to him.

"Let's go," he told his father.

The chief's unmarked Crown Victoria hummed down his driveway and turned left onto Winchester Road. The high school was on the way to police headquarters at the municipal complex, so it wasn't an inconvenience to drive Billy there. Still, the chief didn't like having to walk into school to deliver his boy, but he'd do it, in part to embarrass him, hoping Billy's classmates would see that even the chief's son didn't have get-out-of-jail-free cards.

"You're doing sixty in a forty-five," Billy observed. "Better not let the cops catch you."

"Watch it, smart-ass. I know what I'm doing."

"You could at least make it official looking and put on your flashers, Dad."

The chief glanced sideways at his boy, who caught the *I am not amused* expression and decided it best to focus his eyes forward.

The elder Schweitzer had no clue Billy was torn up because of a girl, among other things, but he saw something was wrong.

"Look, whatever you're going through, I can tell you we've all gone through it. Was it that you didn't want to take a test today?"

"No, Dad. Don't worry about it."

"I *will* worry about it if you keep trying to cut class."

"It's not like I do this all the time. Hell, I've never really tried to skip school before. I just had a rough couple of days, that's all. I thought I could use a mental health day." Billy chuckled.

"I don't think that's funny," the chief replied. "Mental health is a real concern among kids these days, not something to be taken in jest."

"'Not something to be taken in jest'? Who the hell talks like that, Dad? I wasn't making fun of any—"

"When do I get to see your next report card?"

"Wait, you're suddenly concerned about my schoolwork? Did a teacher call you to remind you to ask me? I know Mom didn't."

Ah, strained relations with the kids. Another casualty of divorce. At least Tim had handled it with more maturity than I expected. I can't blame Billy, though. Only fifteen when things went kaboom. He has every right to be pissed off and confused.

"Leave your mother out of this and drop the attitude. I *do* care and that's why I'm asking. When do you get your report card?"

"Well, soon, I suppose. Winter break's coming up."

"How are your grades?"

"I'm doing fine in everything except English, algebra, social studies, science and gym."

Another glance from the chief.

"I'm kidding, I'm kidding. Jeez. They're fine, my grades are fine. Bs, I'm guessing. Maybe a C in math, but all the other ones are good."

"What's your elective?"

"Drafting. You know, like architecture. I'm pretty good at that."

"I know. I've seen your drawings. You know, when I do my drug sweeps." One of the rules of living with this police chief was all bedrooms could be searched at any time and doors were never to be locked. Billy accepted it and knew his father was cracking what the chief considered to be a joke.

"Thank you. My best grade's probably in that class. A solid A."

"Excellent. Architecture's a respectable field, Billy. You could start your own firm."

"Oh good, we're here!" He did not want to get roped into a conversation with his father about his plans for college and life.

The chief turned into the high school complex and looped around to park in front of the doors by the central office.

Billy wanted this shaming to be over, so he scooted to the two-tiered building's entrance, his father trailing him, and pressed the buzzer for admittance. The school resource officer, Patrolman Dennis Pena, pushed open the door and smiled.

"Hello, Billy. Good morning, Chief."

"Officer Pena, please be so kind as to walk this young man to homeroom." Chief Schweitzer saw hallways bustling with students heading to their classrooms.

"I don't need a police escort, Dad. I promise I'll go to homeroom. You've made your point, see?" Billy directed his father's attention to the dozens of kids gawking at the two police officers hovering over the solitary, fully humiliated student.

"Sir, I will if you want me to, but I don't think it'll be necessary, if you don't mind me saying so." Pena, twenty-three, came fresh from the Academy to the school because he could better relate to the kids in his charge. He wore his gun belt around his dark slacks but wasn't attired in his official uniform. The Hancock Police Department crest stitched onto the breast pocket of his blue golf shirt helped identify him to anyone there.

"Okay, Officer Pena. I'll overlook this blatant example of insubordination just this once." He winked at the young cop. "Get going, Billy. Oh, and the next time I ask you to bring in firewood, please just do it."

Billy attempted to rebut his father, but both Pena's and the chief's radios crackled with the same message of a one-car accident on Winchester Road with a possible ejection. The two lawmen looked at each other and had the same dire feeling. A car accident this close to the school, at the time of day when it's still dark outside, meant a student in all likelihood.

"Officer Pena, I'll be in touch." The chief grabbed his shoulder mic to respond he was en route.

"Please do, sir," Pena said, and then went to address Billy, who had already slipped away and blended into the swirl of students.

Chapter Three

Brittany Cabot heard the homeroom bell from across the grassy field that led to the rear of the school's football-field bleachers, the spot where she and Travis Reardon always met for a passionate pre-homeroom make-out session.

Like most pretty high school girls, she was ill-dressed for the cold weather—all the better to taunt the boys with what they couldn't have, and also to remind the self-conscious girls that they *wished* they could look this awesome. Her arms crossed her chest, holding her sides for warmth. Her slender leather jacket didn't provide comfort, and her bare thighs were exposed to the chill. Shivering was the price she paid for knee-high boots and a short leather skirt.

Brittany's teeth chattered. The first snowflakes of the day flittered into view. She looked from side to side—her long blonde hair swishing across her shoulders—hoping her boyfriend would arrive. The sun, indecipherable through gray clouds, helped give her a clearer picture of the campus. Travis always parked his car in the main lot, snuck around the side of the high school and strolled across the field to his sweetheart, who stood underneath the bleachers that provided her shelter from the elements.

Her singsong voice broke the silence: "Travis, I'm late for schooo-oool. Hell, Travis, we're *both* late for schooo-oool. One more late-to-class after this one and I get detention. That's not cooo-oool."

Her voice was joined by a loud creak on the bleacher steps behind her. She turned and saw a figure through the bleacher's slim gaps in the slats, the kind that prevented children from falling through. Daylight barely illuminated the figure, which lingered halfway up the wide stands' thirty tiers. It stepped up another deck, its weight denting the aluminum stairs downward. It continued its climb, sending squeals of bending metal echoing across the barren field to the forest encircling the campus.

"Travis? What the hell?" she called through the slats to the shadow that now hovered above her. "Go all the way up to the top so I can see you."

Deep sniffs were all she got in reply. The shadow scrunched itself into a stoop and smushed its nose against the gap between the slats. This time she got a drawn-out sniff, as if it were inhaling a pizza pie fresh from the oven.

"Um, Travis, it's freezing out here. Yes, I am wearing that perfume you like, but it'll smell better indoors where it's warm. Let's just get inside, we'll fool around later."

A fragrance of decay overwhelmed her senses. The shadow expressed a contented "Mmmmmmm" followed by the sound of a wet tongue licking lips.

"That's disgusting, Travis. And you *better* be Travis and not that creepy custodian with the lazy eye. I'll report your ass to the principal for sexual harassment and you'll be mopping up shit in some nursing home for the rest of your livin'-in-a-trailer-park life!"

The shadow rose from its crouch and bounded down the bleacher steps.

"You fucking pervert!" Angry and repulsed—Travis wouldn't treat her like that, not if he wanted to get to second base again in his lifetime—Brittany let her bulky purse slip off her shoulder and she sprinted underneath the stairs to the bleachers' entranceway. This letch needed to be confronted, lateness to class be damned.

She marched into the football complex and saw nothing. She walked lengthwise along the field's sidelines and ascended the bleachers to the area where she was being ogled. She surveyed the misshapen steps and dented seats. A viscous brew of drool and snot puddled where the creep got drunk off her scent. It oozed through the crevices leaving strands of saliva dangling over the spot where Brittany stood moments earlier.

She shook her head to snap herself back to reality. She was late for school, her boyfriend had stood her up, and some sick freak was on the prowl. She had to warn the principal for the sake of every girl in the school. Brittany descended the bleachers and exited the football complex and grabbed her purse. She crossed through the underside of the stands and spotted the drool drips.

Brittany missed seeing the huge open hand that sprang from the darkness of the bottommost rungs. The palm swung through the stringy goo, batting it into Brittany's face, causing her to respond with an "ugh!". She stepped backward and instinctively raised her hands to wipe away the splattered gunk. She never saw the entirety of the black mass rising from underneath the bleachers. She blindly swung her handbag at her attacker but it slipped from her grip and sailed toward the school. The same hand that had slapped the drool onto her now cupped her face. She felt the strong grip of long fingers on her skull and the sting of talons nicking her scalp. Her screams muffled, the thing swung Brittany's head, ramming it against one of the thick metal beams supporting the bleachers. Her body went limp but did not hit the ground. The thing lifted her barely five-foot figure and placed her headfirst into the wooden crate strapped to its back, reuniting Brittany with her boyfriend.

Chapter Four

"What do we know?" Police Chief Donald Schweitzer asked Patrolwoman Amanda Fryer, a ten-year veteran and the first officer to respond to the scene. Schweitzer, fifteen years her senior, respected her no-nonsense demeanor and trusted her judgment. Multiple police cruisers, lights flashing, were parked along the road's shoulder as officers directed traffic around the wrecked Mazda.

"This was no accident," Fryer said as she and the chief circled the vehicle, taking in the damage. "No skid marks anywhere. It's not like the car was T-boned and came to a stop here." She pointed at the spot. "I can't find a point of impact to suggest another vehicle was involved. In theory it could be a hit-and-run, but you can see for yourself: the only place this vehicle was hit was on the hood and side." She waited for the chief to observe the wreckage. "Does it look like a car did that?"

"No it doesn't."

"But something had to have hit it. Check this out." She maneuvered the chief to the vehicle's battered hood. "Rust. It looks like some kind of residue to me." She moved her latex-gloved hand over a portion of the bent metal and held up her pointer finger, now covered with black and brown specks. "It doesn't belong to this vehicle."

"Get a good sample of it and have the state police lab do a rush job."

"I already bagged some."

"Good." The chief surveyed the wider accident scene. "So, if there was no impact or crash from another vehicle, that means there was no ejection. So where'd the driver go?"

"That's the other thing, Chief. There's no body. We can't find one anywhere. There's blood, not a lot of it, around the passenger seat and the broken window, and some drops on the ground directly outside the passenger door, leading into the woods. A bus driver on her way to school called it in. She pulled over, grabbed her fire extinguisher and blasted it on the hood just in case. She said the driver was already gone at that point."

"At least there are some good people left in the world. Is she still here?"

"No, she wanted to deliver her kids, get them out of here. She said she won't leave the area and knows we'll want to talk to her again. I've got her cell phone number."

"She didn't see another car speeding away?"

"Nossir."

The chief's gaze went from the hood to the passenger door. He cocked his head.

"There's snow and mud right next to the car. So where are the footprints?"

"Yeah, that's been eating at me," Fryer said. "There're no footprints anywhere. None that we can find. But, if you look closely, there are hoofprints."

"Beg your pardon?"

"Hoofprints, Chief. Big ones. I'm talking Clydesdale big."

"A horse did this? Impossible."

"Sir, I grew up on a horse farm in Sussex County. I know hoofprints when I see them."

"You can't expect me to believe that a horse reared up and smashed its front hooves onto this car's hood. Let's have a look-see at these hoofprints, please, Amanda. Point them out to me. I need to see what Clydesdale hoofprints look like."

"I'm not sayin' for certain it's a Clydesdale, sir, just that something with big hooves made them." Fryer directed the chief to a line of marks leading up to and next to the Mazda. "If you look into the car, you'll see the seat belt is broken—it's buckled in, but the straps were cut through."

He peered inside. "Someone took the driver. Great. Say, Amanda, I probably should know this, but did the town ever get the money for those traffic cameras we've been asking for?"

She eyed the traffic lights above her. "You mean the ones that would've probably already helped us figure out what happened here? Nossir. But I'd like to tape off this area, if you agree that we're dealing with a crime scene."

He let the hoof impressions ruminate before responding.

"Do it. And do it quick. Before our evidence gets a foot of snow dumped on it. Put up tarps if you have to. Did you run a check on the

24

plate?"

"Yeah, this is gonna get messier than it already is. It's registered to Travis Reardon."

"Paul's kid?" The chief was on a first-name basis with Mayor Paul Reardon, who graduated with Schweitzer from the same Hancock High School class eons ago.

"Yessir."

"*Shit.* Has he been told?"

"We were waiting for you to decide the best approach."

The chief had called parents and relatives many times before, usually after deadly car accidents involving young drivers prone to simultaneously speeding and texting.

But what was he going to tell the mayor? *Hi, Paul, bad news. We found your son's crashed SUV on the side of the road and there's no trace of your boy, and we think he might have been kidnapped and carried away on horseback.*

"Call the prosecutor's office. They'll want to know about this. And the sheriff's office, please tell 'em to bring that bloodhound of theirs."

"Yessir, but there's one more, well, observation that's been bugging me. Please don't think I'm crazy."

"I won't, Amanda. Enlighten me."

"Well, like I was sayin', I grew up on a horse farm. It's that those tracks—" she jabbed at them from afar, "—they're bipedal, if that's the right word. Like left-right, left-right—the kind that you and I make. We have a limited batch, but I can't find a single set of rear and front hoofprints anywhere. My point is that nothing was galloping around here."

The chief acted like Fryer had asked him the final question on the math part of the SAT.

"I'm not crazy, Chief."

"Never said you were." He shook his head, unable to process what he'd been told. *It makes no sense.*

"Come to think of it, Chief. Those aren't horse prints at all because horses don't have cloven—"

"Give me a second, Amanda." The chief politely waved her off and dialed his cell phone. "Go do what you need to do. I have to make a call."

Chapter Five

The hallways thinned out of students, Billy among them, finding their ways to first period. He'd gotten a couple of good-natured taunts from some of his peers—*"Selling crystal meth in school again, Billy?"* It would've been worse had he been late and frog-marched into homeroom. Billy swiveled the lock, opened his locker and grabbed his science and German books. He shut the door, turned to leave and was met by Maria Flynn's stares from across the hall.

Billy swore his heart pumped a gallon of blood into the pit of his stomach, flooding his insides with warmth. There stood this heavenly creature who on her worst day without makeup would outshine an airbrushed Aphrodite. They'd attended the same elementary school and had always been friendly with one another. They'd grown up less than a mile away from each other and had gone to the other's birthday parties when they were kids, that time of adolescence when grubby boys and pigtailed girls were beginning to choose their core groups of lifelong friends and had yet to be cast as a jock, popular, Goth, tough, band geek, nerd or the student who didn't fall into a category, the latter slot being where Billy and Maria both felt they belonged.

They were the type of classmates who knew each other, not well, but were friendly nonetheless. Each carried their own impressions of the other. She considered Billy a nice guy (a description Billy would abhor), one of the kind kids she'd grown up knowing while passing through different grades and school buildings. Billy could write *The Brothers Karamazov*-length volumes extolling what he believed to be her unassailable virtues as well as her physical attributes. She had green eyes! Well, blue eyes bordering on turquoise—emeralds when bathed in soft light. And those eyes now expressed a mix of sweetness and pity.

"How are you, Billy?" Maria, who shared his age of seventeen, tried making him feel at ease with a handwave. "Is everything okay? I saw Officer Pena and your dad talking to you."

Don't make an ass of yourself. Don't make an ass of yourself.

"Oh hi! Hi there, Maria." His voice slightly elevated, Billy glanced to see if any of Maria's friends were feasting on his discomfort. Only Maria stood by. "Yeah, uh, thanks for asking." His brain and mouth worked rapid-fire. "My brother left home before me and my dad this morning and I missed the bus and I really don't like taking the bus anyway because the older you are when you take the bus the lamer you are in the eyes of students who don't even know you so my dad had to bring me here even though I really wasn't feeling that good and wanted to stay home today but it's probably for the best that I'm here, right?" He took a breath. "And you look nice today." *Oh God, did I just say that?*

Maria blushed. "Thank you, and that's—wow!—a lot to digest! I know what you mean about the bus, and I'm sorry you're not feeling well. I'm sure it will pass."

"I hope so." Billy's monologue had drained him of his energy, although he didn't show it.

"Look, I've got to get going. I just wanted to make sure you're all right. Really, thank you for calling me last night. I hope you understand why I can't, that's all."

"Oh completely!" Billy forced a smile. "I totally get it. And that *Texas Chainsaw Massacre* remake isn't really a good first-date movie anyway." *Stop talking immediately.* "So, yeah, I get it."

Maria chuckled. "Okay, I'll see you in algebra later." She gave another little wave and walked to class.

Billy had kept his black hood up the entire time and that made him feel even more ridiculous. He wasn't sure why.

The first-period bell rang and he sighed, again reminded of what he wanted but could not have.

Let's go to gym. Billy's thoughts wandered to the accident report he'd heard from his dad's and Officer Pena's radios. Pena's office was on the way to the boys' locker room, so Billy decided to stop by to see if there was anything he could learn about the apparent crash. It probably was a student, Billy knew. Hopefully nothing serious.

Pena had his own small office, big enough for a desk, its chair and another chair usually seating a troubled student. Billy entered the main office and was about to turn a corner and knock on Pena's open door when he heard what he knew was Principal Elliot Clarkson's voice.

"The mayor just called me. His son was involved in that accident on Winchester this morning and nobody can find him."

Billy hung back, trying not to make his eavesdropping apparent. Fortunately, the administrative workers were too busy going about their chores to notice him. *Holy crap! Travis Reardon is missing?*

"My chief just called me with the news," Pena said. "It's only a matter of time before the kids start finding out. And not to complicate matters, but have you looked outside recently? The snow's starting."

"Early dismissal?" Clarkson knew where Pena was going.

"We're in the sticks out here. If it gets bad early, we might want to consider sending them home before the roads get slick."

Yes! We might get out of here early! Billy smiled for the first time that day. Algebra with Maria Flynn wasn't until seventh period. Normally he loved getting to class, eagerly waiting to see what Maria decided to wear that day. Some guys were put off by the creamy-white skin so typical with redheads, but Billy adored it and the way Maria's scarlet hair draped over her shoulders and down her neckline. *Goddess* wasn't a strong enough word for Billy. But he could no longer have Maria catch him stealing a glance, without risking her thinking he was some type of degenerate. His smiles at her would now be forced facial movements void of emotion.

"Let's hope the snow holds off until school ends and then the kids are their parents' problem," Principal Clarkson said.

Pena looked at him.

"I'm sorry, that didn't sound right." Clarkson shook his head. "Many things going on at once, Officer. Know what I mean?"

"Don't worry. I do."

Clarkson saw Billy waiting outside of Pena's office, catching the principal off guard. "Billy, may I ask what you're doing here?"

"Yes, you may, Mr. Clarkson. I heard about a car accident on Officer Pena's radio this morning and wanted to check in with him to see if it was a student."

"Officer Pena doesn't know, nor do I, Billy. I appreciate your concern but I believe it prudent for you to simply go to class," Clarkson said. "Now, if you'll excuse me."

The principal walked away as Pena emerged from his office, arms crossed. He waited for the headmaster to be out of sight before he spoke, "I'm not dumb, Billy. How much of that did you hear?"

Chapter Six

"Why? *Why*, boy?" the voice echoed.

Travis Reardon awoke to dim flames. He counted twelve burning candles hovering in rocky crevices in an area he couldn't define. He rested facedown, his cheeks pressed against cool rock. A cave? Hancock ceased being a mining hub a century ago. Plenty of abandoned shafts hid in and amongst the forested hills. Being subterranean seemed logical. He couldn't move his hands, bound by scratchy rope behind his back, or his feet. The fiendishly knotted cord cut his skin when he moved his wrists and ankles.

"Why?! Sit up and say!"

It can talk! Travis blinked and widened his eyes to focus on his captor.

"I can't sit up!" The echo pinballed around rock walls.

"You are strong, boy! Sit up against the wall!" Travis could not place the accent attached to the brooding voice that pronounced Ws as Vs. He guessed European. *It's a guy! It's gotta be. And he can't even pronounce* wall *right. Crazy foreigners!*

"Okay, fine! Give me a second."

"Do it now!"

Candlelight flickered as a darkened mass paced back and forth before Travis. The smell he associated with the creature vanished. *It's immense,* he thought. *Maybe five hundred pounds.* And the way it walked! The ground rumbled with its every step. Despite the pain, Travis rolled onto his back and produced enough momentum to seat himself upright. Using his hands to balance his body behind his back, he brought his knees up to his chin and pushed his feet against the ground, propelling himself backward. He inchwormed his way back until his head bumped against rock.

"There! You happy, you son of a bitch?!"

Travis played baseball and regularly heard the ball whiz past him when he stood in the batter's box. He heard a similar sizzle, only it was generated by the thick switch the thing used to slash Travis's left side.

One rib cracked, then two.

"Why?! Answer, boy!"

Travis screamed as the creature thrashed the stick with the ferocity of a deranged butcher chopping meat on a block.

"Speak, the Master commands it!"

"Please stop!" He squeaked because it hurt to catch his breath. He mustered enough strength to say, "Why are you doing this? Who are you?"

"The Master is not pleased!" The thing ceased its abuse. It had beaten Travis onto his side, leaving exposed his left rib cage, much of it now cracked. "You will tell me why! Later!"

"Fine, we'll try later," Travis whimpered.

Its husky voice taunted Travis. "You do not mean it, boy." The thing gave Travis a tsk-tsk-tsk finger wag. "Insincerity, boy, you reek of it. And later, I will rid you of it."

"Who put you up to this? My dad has money, he'll pay you."

"Money?" The thing chuckled in grunts. "Boy, do I look like I carry a wallet?"

"Then what the hell do you want?" Travis stayed on his side, doing his best to sound peaceful. "Do I even know you? Like, if you're pissed that I slept with your girlfriend, you've got the wrong guy. And why are you dressed like that?"

The thing backed away from Travis and dropped its switch. Travis then heard rustling. Candlelight again flickered as the thing moved to the brightest flame in the center of the room. Travis followed it, and more of the place came into focus.

Christ, are those skulls on the floor?

Candlelight bathed three human skulls, all of them complete and displayed in a row.

They once sat where I am now, he thought, and then other bones— ribs, femurs, tibias—emerged in the light.

The thing clutched a scroll in its left hand and let the bottom drop out of it. Travis heard the parchment unrolling on the floor. A head with pointy goblin ears bobbed in and out of the candlelight, examining the scroll.

"Ah, Travis Reardon."

It has my name!

The thing's illuminated face contorted into a wicked grin. Leathery, brown lips stretched to reveal fangs jutting every which way. It slathered its long tongue around its cheeks, nostrils and chin. The creature's eyes, soulless black orbs wreathed in white, as if two solar eclipses burst from its skull, glared at Travis. The thing exposed its right-hand palm to Travis. It dragged its index talon from the bottom of its palm, slicing up to the base of the same finger. Blood gushed from the slit. The thing dabbed the same talon in the blood and then scratched a red line across the parchment. It took its time rolling up the aged scroll before securing it in a leather pouch fastened to the crate on its back.

"Travis Reardon, accounted for. But there are others. So many of them."

Travis forgot the pain that coursed throughout his body and became engrossed by the thing cutting open its hand. Could it be some guy in a fancy monster suit? Conceivably, but...

"Look, I don't know what the hell you are. Maybe you could tell me why you're doing this and I could help you in return by—"

"Boy, do yourself a favor: be silent and think." It waited for Travis to heed its words. "Think hard. Do so, and maybe death will not be a foregone conclusion. Because right now, in my mind, it is."

Travis couldn't speak. *It plans on killing me!*

The thing scanned the floor, mumbling gibberish to itself: *"Jetzt, wo ist mein...?"*

It made a happy noise and picked up its switch and stowed it like a samurai sword in a leather sheath nailed to its crate. It then grabbed an end link to the thick chain it had coiled in the far corner of the cave. Ready for conquest, it inhaled and blew a stream of air around the cave, extinguishing the candles, exiling Travis in darkness. It left Travis with the lunatic shrieks it had visited upon him hours earlier. Soon its screams, plods and chain clanks faded.

"How many others?" Travis mumbled.

"Travis! Travis, where are you?! Speak up!"

"Brittany?!" he rasped, a surge of unexpected energy buoyed him. "You're here?! Are you all right?"

"Under what fucking scenario would me being stuck in a pitch-black cave translate into me being all right?!" Her voice careened around the walls.

"Baby, I'm not doing too well here. It literally hurts when I talk."

31

"What the hell is that thing?!"

"Can you move?" Travis could not pinpoint how far away Brittany was from him. She was a voice floating in darkness.

"No, I can't move! That thing tied me up good."

"Are you hurt?" he croaked.

"My head's killing me. And I feel like I'm gonna puke if I can't wash my face in the next ten minutes. You've got to come over here and cut me loose."

"I'm fine, Brittany, thanks for asking. I'm assuming you—" Travis had to catch his breath in order to speak, "—you must have heard that thing beating the shit out of me, right?"

"I'm sure you've been through worse playing your stupid football games. Now, where are you?"

The blip of strength vanished. *What do you see in that girl?* his mother had asked him.

An eminently fuckable body that makes up with tits and ass for what it lacks in compassion and decency. He of course didn't tell his mother the truth: Brit was awesome to look at, but beyond that she could be a real…

"I'm going to close my eyes now, bitch—I mean, Brit. I hope that thing doesn't do to you what it did to me."

"I hope it doesn't either." Only it wasn't Brittany who responded.

"Oh God no," Travis replied. "I know that voice."

Chapter Seven

Russell McDonald knew he was pushing it by allowing his gym class to play touch football outside. The snow wasn't *that* heavy, and there was enough turf for his juniors to gain some traction to run, the phys-ed teacher reasoned. Of course, the girls hated being in the cold, despite the heavy sweat suits they wore. They huddled, sides clutched, halfheartedly running when their team's quarterback yelled "hike!".

Billy Schweitzer didn't mind. He could run a fast route and the cold air invigorated his lungs. The exercise pumped his endorphins, helping to clear his mind.

Each class had at least three or four varsity football players who knew what they were doing. One of them always played quarterback. McDonald's class had twenty-six students, thirteen per side—two more than were allowed on the field during regulation games, but this was touch football, so who cared?

Indeed four varsity players, the biggest juniors in their grade, were evenly divided among the teams, but they were preoccupied. News of Travis Reardon's car accident had spread. Officer Pena pleaded with Billy not to broadcast that Travis hadn't been found, and Billy'd obliged. But truth and rumors circulate high schools the way the plague spread across medieval Europe. Nothing could stop the concerned Tweets and Facebook posts.

"So, like, Travis went through his windshield and was impaled on some tree limbs?"

"You're way too smart to believe any of that bullshit, Mike."

Billy's best friend, the equally lanky but not-so-sullen Mike Brembs, had been by his side since kindergarten. Brembs had made the baseball team, resulting in Billy being jealous of his brother's athletic prowess and his best friend's ability to throw an above-average high school fastball. Still, they were friends, always would be. Both boys lined up for the same team, waiting for the ball to be snapped.

"How the hell are you gonna play football tonight?" Billy and Mike heard one of their classmates, Roy Fowler, ask one of the varsity team's defensive backs, Neil Washington.

"I mean, it's the last game of the season and Travis is the team's best player. Who are they supposed to play? Jefferson High? Maybe the Jefferson kids are behind this."

Oh for Chrissakes, Billy thought.

"Hey, strange shit happens," Fowler continued without waiting for a reply from Washington, who gave him a crooked eye. Mike and Billy stayed bemused. "I read about this wacko woman in Texas who wanted to hire a hit man to take out some chick to open up a spot for her daughter on the school's cheerleading squad. So, like, Jefferson sends a few of their goons over our way and cripples the team by taking away the Division One-bound quarterback. It's brilliant."

"Hike!" called the touch-football quarterback, sending Billy, Mike, Neil and Roy scrambling downfield toward the football complex. Nobody stepped foot on the football field's turf before game time, so the teams lined up perpendicular to it. The four boys chugged toward the bleachers.

Billy played wide receiver and hugged the invisible sideline delineated by the small orange cones placed on the makeshift field's four corners. He bounded, snowflakes whooshing by his face, in the direction of the bleachers and cut left, easily outrunning the pudgy boy wearing a *Lord of the Rings* sweatshirt who was covering him. Billy crossed the goal line created by two orange cones and waved at the quarterback, who heaved the ball. And then Billy tripped over something and tumbled face-first onto the frigid ground.

"What the hell?" He winced as the thrown football thumped next to him. *I was wide open too.*

Billy pushed himself up to stand and realized that something had wrapped around his right ankle. He'd tripped over a girl's pocketbook, with his leg now tangled in its strap.

He righted himself and picked up the bag, hoisting it above his head for all to see.

"Did any of you drop this?!" he called to the huddled girls. "Why the hell didn't you leave it in the locker room?"

The girls all glanced at one another, and gave *nope* headshakes.

"Give it here!" Russell McDonald, gym teacher extraordinaire for the past twenty-five years, waddled his stocky frame toward Billy and the boys who'd followed him into the end zone.

Billy handed it over and McDonald examined the unzipped white

34

bag—a chameleon in the fresh snow—looking for a driver's license without trying to invade the owner's privacy.

"Let's see, cigarettes, lighter, phone, lipstick. Ah!" He found it in a wallet sleeve and flipped it frontward and backward. "Brittany Cabot. She's in one of my later classes."

The students remained quiet.

"Any of you girls seen her today?" McDonald called to the gaggle. "Come on, one of you has got to be friends with her. Where is she? Back in my day, girls weren't caught dead without their purses and that sure has hell hasn't changed today."

The little brunette, Joyce Radinsky, whose family lived next door to the Cabots, answered, "She gave me a ride to school this morning, Mr. McDonald. So, yeah, I've seen her, but that was hours ago when we first got here."

Billy, still catching his breath from the fall, wandered around the area where he found the bag, not far from the bleachers, to see if anything had fallen out of it. A mass of saliva clouded by a mucous yolk sprawled before his feet. Odd indentations encircled the puddle, along with Brittany's boot prints. Growing up a policeman's son had helped Billy learn to identify things not obvious to most civilians.

He grimaced and looked above the slime to see bleachers dented downward. Mike joined him.

"Did you puke?"

"No, Mike. I didn't do that."

"Maybe Brittany did. Why would she come out here to vomit? Maybe it's embarrassing for a hot girl to puke in the presence of lesser girls?"

Billy, ignoring his friend, saw McDonald speaking with Radinsky and quickstepped toward the football field's entrance, Mike tailing him.

McDonald turned toward the bleachers when he heard someone charging up the steps.

"Who's in there? Get your ass back out here or else it's detention for you!"

"Mr. McDonald!" Billy responded. "You better come up here quick!"

Chapter Eight

Hancock Township, like most of the municipalities in Morris County, New Jersey, derived its name from one of the country's founding fathers. (Washington Township, as you might expect, took the name of the nation's first president, who bunkered in Morristown as a general when fighting the Revolutionary War during the brutal winter of 1779-80.) Hancock, at forty-four square miles, ranked among the most bountiful iron-mining communities in the northwestern part of the state for two hundred years, with operations ending in the early 1900s. The township's southernmost tip borders Lake Hopatcong, New Jersey's largest lake, as do four other municipalities in Morris and Sussex counties. Many of Hancock's twenty thousand residents concentrate themselves in the southern wedge of the township, which, aside from the sliver of shorefront land, consists of hilly terrain covered with dense forests. Four of the state's four hundred fifty abandoned iron and limestone mines hide underneath forests of evergreens, oaks and maples.

Despite the state's well-earned reputation of being nothing more than a jumble of highways, Hancock lacks a major one running through it. (You have to leave Interstate 80 at either the Jefferson or Rockaway exits to get to Hancock.) Some of the town's residents work at nearby Picatinny Arsenal, the US Army base that designs hi-tech weapons of war. A majority, however, of those living in Hancock travel out of the municipality to get to work in New York City (roughly fifty miles east) or head to one of the larger towns housing pharmaceutical companies, for instance.

Hancock's middle and high schools, located off Winchester Road, are joined by four elementary schools sprinkled throughout the municipality. And the logistics of getting the district's thirty-six hundred students home before the brunt of a blizzard burdened Superintendent Geraldine Rapuano.

"That snow's not slowing down," Rapuano said during a morning conference call with the six schools' principals. "I loathe doing this, but

I keep coming back to early dismissal as being the best option. Had we not burned so many snow days after Hurricane Sandy hit I would've canceled classes yesterday. I took a gamble thinking the snow might hold off until this evening but that's obviously not the case. This shouldn't come as a surprise, but the football game has been canceled. I don't want to risk having the buses on those roads deep in the middle of nowhere during this thing. That's what's driving my decision. Thoughts?"

The high school's Elliot Clarkson spoke first.

"Geraldine, I know your hands are tied but I must remind you that one of our students apparently was taken from the scene of a car accident, and another student's missing. Her car is parked here, but the only thing we can find of her is her pocketbook. The police are already here."

"I'm aware." The superintendent, a tall, middle-aged woman with her graying hair tied in a bun, hunched over her office's table, her arms keeping her erect. She examined an oversized map of the township before speaking into the receiver centered on the table. "I just can't get around the possibility of a bus skidding off the road and getting stuck, especially in the parts of town where it takes police at least twenty minutes to get to when the weather's good."

Harding Elementary School Principal Kristine Meyerson's voice sounded next.

"You're also dealing with a lot of my students heading home to empty houses, Gerri. Parents will not be happy when they learn their six-year-olds are locked out of their homes in the snow. Stay-at-home moms are practically extinct. They're working, trust me."

Rapuano sneered at the speaker, wishing she had mental powers that could make it implode. *It's not the speaker's fault that Kristi's right.*

"I'm going to consult with the police chief in the next ten minutes to get his opinion. You'll hear back from me within the next thirty minutes. I think you know where I'm leaning, though. Talk to you soon." Rapuano punched the button to end the call.

The district's main office was located on-campus within a small building centered between the middle and high schools. She walked through a courtyard to the high school to speak with Chief Donald Schweitzer. No doubt she'd get an earful from the principal too. But she didn't blame him. The car accident, if that's even what it was, unnerved her. But the Cabot girl missing downright frightened her.

Chapter Nine

Mike and Billy looked out one of the gymnasium's windowed exit doors at the police officers erecting tarps over the bleachers and the putrid plot of land.

"Maybe they eloped?" Mike said. "I mean, they were dating."

"You need money to elope, Mike. Women usually keep it in their purses. Brittany wouldn't leave without hers. And you usually skip town in an automobile. Last I heard, Brit's was in the parking lot and Travis's car is broken down."

"Maybe she's wearing a money belt?"

Billy turned, his voice raised: "Would you please be serious? Do you honestly think they ran off to get married in the middle of their senior year at high school?"

"You're right, Billy, sorry. Christ, you're so right. I mean, Travis is on the verge of accepting a coveted scholarship and getting more grade A pussy in four years than you or I could ever get in our lifetimes squared and—"

"I don't need this right now, Mike." Billy rested his forehead against the exit door's cold glass.

Mike continued undeterred. "Come to think of it, he's probably already *gotten* more grade A pussy with Brittany than we'll ever get—"

"Would you shut the hell up?!"

"Whoa, calm down, man." Mike stepped back, thinking Billy might reach back for something extra and pound him. Then he realized the obvious. "Oh, I'm sorry, man. Maria Flynn. You don't need to hear me talking like that. My bad." He attempted to switch gears. "At least my eloping theory makes a lot more sense than some of the other bullshit floating around here. And it's a lot more pleasant than—"

"Reality, Mike. This is reality we're dealing with. Someone took those two. If you can't see that—"

"Excuse me, boys." A police officer politely shoved his way between the two kids and opened the double doors leading to the bleachers.

"Dad?!"

The chief, halfway out the door, snow blowing in, did a double take.

"Sorry, Billy. I didn't see you there."

"You couldn't recognize one of your own sons from five inches away?" Billy said.

Mike took it as his cue to get the hell back into the locker room to change out of his gym clothes. "See you in German class!" And he disappeared. Mike knew Billy had an ever-increasing rocky relationship with his father.

"Billy, please don't be like that. I've got a lot going on and have to find out if the guys outside have what they need or if we need help from other towns. In case you haven't noticed, it's been a busy morning."

"No fucking shit," Billy mumbled, looking downward.

"What did you say to me?"

"Sorry, *sir*. No disrespect intended."

The chief gritted his teeth and closed his eyes a purposefully long time before addressing his boy.

"You're better than this, Billy. I raised you to be better."

"Really? You raised me? Strange, Tim's been more of a dad to me over the last year than you've been. I know I have Mom to thank for part of that. Maybe you didn't pay enough attention to her, either. Maybe that's why she ditched us."

"I can't do this right now. One of my men is going to ask you some questions about what you were doing out there when you found the pocketbook. I'd do it myself but I can't stand the sight of you right now. Excuse me."

"Yeah, have fun looking at hoofprints."

The chief stopped.

"What did you say?" The chief focused on the policemen working fast in the snow.

"Come on, Dad, I didn't even swear that time."

"No! You saw hoofprints out there?"

"Yeah, I mean, I think that's what they were."

"Come with me, show me. Walk where I tell you to walk and don't touch a goddamn thing. I'm not playing here."

Billy eased his hands up and down. "Calm, stay calm. I'm coming. Sorry I've been a dick lately. I know I was out of bounds there."

"Apology accepted. Now get out here."

Billy followed his father's directions and showed him the tracks that the other police officers had found and marked for reference. They photographed what they could before the snowfall buried them. Billy ran through the scenario that led him to finding Brittany's bag.

"And it looks like someone dropped a boulder on the bleachers, Dad."

"You didn't touch anything when you found all this?" The pair stood behind the flapping yellow tape the police strung from one end of the bleachers, around some portable sawhorses, to the other side of the stands.

"I know well enough not to. Why are you so interested in the hoofprints? Your antennae went up when I mentioned them. Did you find them by Travis's car too?"

"You know I can't confirm or deny that." The chief arched one of his eyebrows. His son couldn't miss it. "And you won't bring that up again around any of your friends, right? I mean it."

"No, sir. I won't say a thing, promise."

"Go to your next class. Have Officer Pena write you a late slip. Mum's the word. Got it?"

"I do."

Billy ran ten minutes late for German class and it would've been less time had he remembered to go to the school library instead of Frau Rebecca Barker's regular classroom. *Class project, I completely forgot.*

Mrs. Barker—her students formally addressed her in German as Frau Barker—had taken her students to the library to do Internet research on obscure German holidays. The rule: browse only German websites.

Billy and Mike nestled themselves in a corner of the media center where computer stations were clustered together. They kept their voices down. It *was* the library. Nobody there focused on anything remotely related to schoolwork. The news of Brittany's bag made its way around the halls. It began grating on Billy when all he heard around him were students concocting one absurd Travis-Brittany theory after the next.

"Two kids taken on one day, that doesn't happen by chance." Billy opened Google Germany and searched for *Fröhliche Weihnachten—*

Merry Christmas in German—and opened a resulting page in case Frau Barker wandered by to see if he was working.

"That moron in gym class who thinks this was all about throwing a football game was right about one thing. This happened for a specific reason, but not over football," Billy said. "So is there something else special about today?"

"Holy crap!" Mike cupped his mouth and looked around to make sure he wasn't bothering anyone other than Billy. He leaned in and whispered, "You're right! Today's the anniversary of Pearl Harbor. But nobody here is Japanese, so it doesn't make sense."

Billy sighed.

"You're two days early, genius. Pearl Harbor happened on December 7. Today's the fifth. I can't think of anything hugely historical that happened on today's date. Maybe it's Hitler's birthday or something?"

"Nah, man, that's April 20."

"Yeah, silly me for not being able to creepily recite it as if it's common knowledge. Just be quiet for a second."

Mike gave an *excuuuuuse me* look as Billy typed December 5 into the English Wikipedia site that he had opened on a separate page. A list of holidays and observances, none of which Billy had ever heard of, popped up near the end of the encyclopedic entry.

"Let me help you there, buddy." Mike opened the same page and replicated the search to narrow Billy's list. "Saint Abercius, a martyr of the Christian Church. His feast day's today."

"I don't think that's it," Billy replied. "Looks like the Episcopal Church in the United States observes Clement of Alexandria."

"Ditto with Sabbas the Sanctified, some Greek dude that founded a bunch of monasteries."

"That's probably not it. Haiti and the Dominican Republic celebrate Discovery Day today."

"Nah, man, do you really think someone would go around kidnapping people on something called Discovery Day?"

"That's logical, Mike." Billy meant it as if to say "next!" the way a casting director dismisses lame dancers. "It's the king's birthday in Thailand. Next we have Faunalia, in honor of Faunus the Roman god—I have *no* idea who that is. Oh, and it's International Volunteer Day for Economic and Social Development."

"Workers of the world, unite," Mike said, adding, "and it's Saint Nicholas' Eve in several parts of Europe."

"Krampus," Billy said.

"No, man, it says it's celebrated in Europe, not in Krampus."

"Jesus Christ, Mike. Have you ever heard of a continent called Krampus? It's a holiday or something."

Both Billy and Mike saw the same line underneath the list of December 5 events: *Krampus (Austria)*.

They clicked the hyperlink and were met by a Wikipedia page worded in German.

"Dude, where's the American version?" Mike said.

"I can't find a link on mine either."

Mike leaned toward Billy's ear. "I can't stand reading German!"

"Your test scores bear that out, Mike. But I know what you mean." The boys scanned the first of many paragraphs:

Der Krampus ist eine Schreckgestalt in Begleitung des Heiligen Nikolaus des Adventsbrauchtums im Ostalpenraum, in Ungarn, Slowenien, Tschechien, Teilen des außeralpinen Norditalien und Teilen Kroatiens. Während der Nikolaus die braven Kinder beschenkt, werden die unartigen vom Krampus bestraft. Der Krampus ähnelt somit in der Funktion dem Knecht Ruprecht, es bestehen aber Unterschiede zwischen beiden Figuren: Während Knecht Ruprecht einzeln auftritt, treten die Krampusse meist in größeren Gruppen auf. Die Gruppe aus Nikolaus, Krampus und anderen Begleitern wird als Pass bezeichnet.

"Would you look at that?" Mike said. "German Scrabble must come with ten thousand tiles. And *größeren*? What the hell kind of letter is that in the middle? Did the Germans invent one and not tell anybody?"

"I'm more interested in the picture." Billy clicked on the black-and-white rendering underneath the first paragraph to increase the size of an artist's 1886 depiction of a hairy, cloven-hoofed creature with goat horns sprouting from its head. The beast descended on two screaming children. The youngsters' parents watched the attack, delighting in their children's suffering.

The picture's caption contained more German gobbledygook, but one phrase enticed Billy.

"*Krampusnacht*," he said. "I suppose when the sun goes down, it'll be the night of the Krampus."

"That can't be good," Mike said. "The only other German *nacht* with a *K* that I know is *Kristallnacht*, and it was anything but festive for a whole lot of people."

The two returned their attention to the picture, imagining the creature's lolling foot-long tongue drenched in blood.

"Oh good!"

Mike and Billy flinched in their seats at the sound of Frau Barker's voice, unaware she'd been standing behind them.

"You found the Krampus! You *were* paying attention, Billy," Frau Barker continued. "And even more miraculously, so were you, Michael." She gestured to Mike's computer. "There was a reason I picked today's date to send you on this little hunt. Nobody else has figured it out yet. I'm quite impressed."

Even though Rebecca Barker had moved with her family from Köln when she was eight years old and had resided stateside for the past fifty-five years, she still retained a slight German accent. A portly woman prone to wearing nondescript dresses that fit like muumuus, she tied her naturally blonde hair in a ponytail.

"Yeah, Krampus looks...fun," Billy said.

"*Auf Deutsch*," she chided.

"Um, *ja, Krampus sieht gut aus*?"

"Tell you what, I would prefer you each write about different observances, but since you found the Krampus, I suppose it is acceptable for you both to report on him. You will submit them to me Monday, providing we have class, *ja*?"

Billy eyed the pajama-clad children, their faces frozen in fright, clinging to their parents as the monster shambled through the front door to savage them.

"Frau Barker, *Ich habe keine Ahnung* how to ask auf Deutsch, so when you were growing up in Europe, was Krampus some kind of big deal?" Billy asked. "I have to be honest, I really have no idea what it is I'm lookin' at."

"That's not that hard to ask auf Deutsch, but I'll let it slide this one time. As for your question, the Krampus was so scary! It takes me back so many years when I was a young girl. I constantly teased my little brother, Klaus. He was a couple of years younger than me.

"One time he was working on a puzzle of a dog chasing a cat; it probably had about fifty pieces, nothing too complicated for a five-year-old boy. He was putting the last piece in the center of the puzzle to complete it, but I kicked the whole thing"—the Frau steadied herself on one leg and gave a wobbly kick to illustrate her point—"across the room before he could finish, just to be, I don't know, mean. And it *was* a mean thing to do.

"Klaus cried for hours. My parents could not console him. So my father told me the Krampus would be coming for me. That was in…November of 1950? I don't remember the year, but I was seven because it was a year before we moved to the United States. So I was impressionable still, ja?

"On *dem Vorabend des Heiligen Nikolaus*, my parents brought me and my brother out to the center of town along with all the other families." Frau Barker rubbed her palms together in excitement. "We all lined the main road. We were told a parade was coming with *der Heiligen*."

"Who is der Heiligen?" Mike asked.

"I'm not going to make your report easier for you, Mr. Brembs. It defeats the purpose, and it's not that difficult to figure out. Be grateful I'm reminiscing." She bowed her head to the level of the seated boys' ears and lowered her voice. "But there was no parade."

She sprang up and blurted, "Just this hairy monster that came out of nowhere!" She quashed her volume before continuing. "It scrambled down the street like a rabid animal. It had a devil's face and horns and jumped from side to side of the street, screaming at the top of its lungs and grabbing children and swatting their backsides with a tied-up bundle of sticks.

"I was one of those children! I tried hiding behind my father's legs, but it found me and pulled me out into the center of the road and gave me a few swats, and then brought me back to my parents. I couldn't stop screaming. Neither could my brother! He ran back into our home shrieking! He didn't even have time to see der Heiligen walk down the street, following Krampus. It sort of calmed me down to see der Heiligen. He waved at me, which brought a little comfort, but not much that evening.

"All of the children the Krampus grabbed started kicking and screaming to get away from it. And the parents all smiled to each other. I never understood why until later. You know, looking back, the Krampus didn't hit me at all. They were exaggerated, playful slaps, and it never was rough with me."

"Did it have hooves?" Billy asked.

"Hooves? Goodness no! It was a man in a hairy suit wearing a mask! Like one of your sports mascots. I later found out that it was a friend of my father's who had dressed up as the Krampus. He knew what I looked like and that's why he found me so easily. I suppose it didn't hurt that my father was waving at him to help get his attention. But, I do digress. I expect roots and origins in your Krampus report, Billy. Auf Deutsch. You too, Michael."

"*Natürlich*, Frau Barker," they both said in unison.

She gave a pleasant nod to the boys and went to check on her other students.

Billy turned to his friend. "Those were hoofprints outside by Brit's pocketbook."

"Gimme a break, Billy. There were footprints all over the place."

"From us playing football, from us walking around where I found the pocketbook. There were *none* other than Brit's around that pile of puke. Just hoofprints, deep ones."

"You sure you didn't hit your head on the ground when you fell? Like, do you want to see the nurse? Because you're starting to sound crazy—no offense."

"So you don't find it a little bit coincidental that Travis and Brittany go missing today? Like, it's December 5 and we find out that this Krampus thing has hooves and—"

"Okay, you're officially losing it, dude. Coincidences happen, like on that 9/11 anniversary when one of the New York lottery drawings came up 9-1-1. Was it a little freaky? Yeah, but nothing more than that. You've got to take this a little more seriously. I mean, who the hell thinks December 5 is anything special? Only people who have birthdays today, that's who. You're making that loser who thinks that the other football team took Travis sound like Sherlock Holmes."

The bell rang, signaling the end of the period. Mike closed his browser and scooped up his books. "And that's a wrap, Jack. Text me later when you're slightly less insane. Peace."

Billy knew how he sounded. Before he logged out he did an image search for *cloven hoof* and printed out a couple of different up-close images of a deer's hoof divided into two toes. He also enlarged and printed the Krampus picture from the Wikipedia page. He grabbed the Xeroxed papers and examined the deer hooves the entire time as he walked to his ethical studies class trying to remember how they matched up against the ones he discovered that morning.

Chapter Ten

Kelly Flynn sat in the back of Catherine Jensen's Thomas Jefferson Elementary School's fourth-grade classroom listening to the other nine-year-old children rattle off the (sometimes) correct state capital names. It'd soon be his turn.

Maria Flynn's younger brother despised his name. He thought of it constantly. *It's a girl's name! What the heck were my parents thinking?* Fortunately for Kelly, the big kids never abused him over his perceived-feminine tag because he *was* the biggest kid in the school. Every grade level has that one freakishly large boy who towers above his peers. He stood five feet two inches tall, with a fleshy face and squinty eyes. His light-brown hair distinguished him from his sister's red, making the giant child appear more like a hostile Hummel figurine than the cute little cherub he once was. He scowled more than he smiled, and his friends believed he'd be a much happier person had he been named Jake or John, or any number of other normal boys' names.

But he was Kelly. Kelly Carroll Flynn. The indignity of it all. Two girl names for one boy. *Curse the guy who played Archie Bunker! Why'd that have to be my dad's favorite goddamn show! If we were Italian instead of Irish this wouldn't have happened! I'd be Paul, Vincent or Tony.*

"Mr. Flynn, Nevada?" Mrs. Jensen, keen to the boy's sensitivity, formally addressed him.

"Carson City," he said without looking at her. Kelly slouched over his desk in the back of the classroom next to the windows. He planted his right elbow on the desk and rested his head sideways in the palm of his hand, looking out at the falling snow.

"Very good, Mr. Flynn. For extra credit, Vermont?"

Unseen, he rolled his eyes. *Give me something harder, please.* "Montpelier."

"Outstanding." Mrs. Jensen, a young blonde teacher who wore dark-rimmed glasses, moved on to the next student. "Raquel, New York?"

"New York City, Mrs. Jensen."

Kelly smiled and mouthed *Albany* simultaneously with Mrs. Jensen as she corrected the girl. And on went the litany of states.

Hancock's never-ending forest border stood ninety feet away from Kelly's window. He longed to be outside making snowmen he could domineer with brute force.

The little black blur first appeared in the distance, bobbing up and down as it ran. *A bear cub!* Kelly felt a welcomed jolt of euphoria upon seeing genuinely dangerous wildlife his parents told him never to go near. It bounded out of the forest, saw the wide one-story school building and stopped, skidding on all four paws in the snow. The bear spun around after a split second of thought, leapt and clung to the thick trunk of a one-hundred-foot-tall oak on the forest's lip, and skittered midway up the tree to catch its breath on a sturdy limb.

Kelly sat upright to see his classmates' reactions but nobody had witnessed it but him. He was on the verge of making social studies infinitely more interesting for everybody by shouting "Mrs. Jensen, there's a bear outside!" but refrained, to enjoy his discovery a few moments longer. *It's not a baby bear but certainly isn't an adult,* Kelly observed of the juvenile bruin.

A small black object arched like a comet through the treetops and struck the limb holding the bear. Enough snow had fallen on the branches so that when the black bear cub fell, a cascade of white powder followed it to the ground. The animal landed with a bounce while the black chain—Kelly could see it now—crashed next to the bear.

This exciting silent movie transpiring behind the windowpane became more surreal when the chain withdrew into the woods. It moved haltingly, slithering and stopping ten feet at a time until vanishing into whiteness. Kelly had snow-globe vision, his eyes centered on the injured bear as thousands of flakes swirled around it. And in the distance, trudging its way through the trees, the bear's mother materialized.

Two of them! Kelly couldn't believe his luck. He'd never seen a bear outside of the Kodiaks at the Bronx Zoo. It was one thing to see a deer when you were a kid—that was enthralling enough—but two bears in one day would be a tale Kelly would pass down to his grandchildren.

Wind-whipped snow stuck against its dark-furred body as it slid in and out of Kelly's sight, weaving its way around the trees to reunite with its cub. *That's one big bear,* Kelly thought, the picture becoming clearer with each of its steps. *And don't they normally walk on all fours?*

Yes, yes they do. What kind of bear—

The realization that it wasn't the bear's mother overwhelmed Kelly when it emerged from the forest, the wind gusting away enough snow to reveal the creature's full monstrosity. Its slobbering mouth agape, the creature breathed heavily as it towered over the cub that rested on its side, its back to the thing. The cub lifted its right forepaw as if reaching for help.

Are those antlers, or am I just seeing tree branches funny? Kelly thought in the same instant the monster plunged both of its clawed hands into the helpless animal, lifting it up like a baby, with its feet dangling and its head jerking from side to side. The monster thrust its fangs into the bear's neck, bulging jaw muscles driving teeth through skin. Kelly quivered as the monster tore out the bear's throat.

The monster's eyes met Kelly's as its talons bored into the bear's soft belly. It then clutched the eviscerated bear in its left hand and violently jabbed its bloodstained right forefinger at Kelly.

Kelly disgorged the falsetto scream of a housewife hopping atop her kitchen table as sewer rats swarmed the floor. His fifteen startled classmates turned toward him as Mrs. Jensen scampered to the back of the room. He jumped from his seat and his screams intensified as he saw gobbets of ragged meat tumble from the creature's mouth.

"Kelly! Kelly, what's wrong?!" Mrs. Jensen abandoned all formality, stooped to meet his eyes and gently grabbed his shoulders. "Are you hurt? Tell me, what's the matter, honey?!"

"It ate the bear!" Kelly pointed out the window. "The monster ate the bear!"

"A bear's outside?!" one of the students shouted. "Where?!"

His classmates rose in unison and rushed the windows to steal a glimpse.

"Children, please!" Mrs. Jensen knew she'd lost control but focused more on the hysterical child who'd wrapped his arms around her and pulled her in tight for a hug. Mrs. Jensen, only a few inches taller than Kelly, was taken aback by the kid's strength. She patted his back as he nuzzled his head against her for comfort.

"It's all right, Kelly." She said it softly. He continued sobbing, his tears staining the top of her sweater. "I won't let anything hurt you."

"What bear? There's no bear!" Mrs. Jensen heard one of her disappointed students say but kept Kelly's head pressed against her chest to keep him from looking outside.

She didn't see it either.

"Kelly, there's nothing there," another student said. Almost all of the students fixated on trying to spot the phantom bear. A lone student, Bryan Welles, a scrawny, bespectacled boy of normal height for his age, sat in his chair, watching Kelly's breakdown, cackling to himself, unable to conceal his perverse enjoyment. Kelly wiped away tears while spotting Welles's amusement and pointed. "Stop it, you shit-face!"

"Kelly!" Mrs. Jensen scolded.

"Your attention, please," a voice over the intercom interrupted. "Your attention, please. Due to the snowstorm, there will be an early dismissal today."

Except for Kelly and the teacher, the classroom erupted in cheers that drowned out the rest of the announcement. Kelly mewled as Mrs. Jensen eased him back into his seat.

"I didn't see any bear out there, honey." She spoke as comfortingly as she could.

"I don't want to go outside," he pleaded through sobs. "Please don't make me go out there."

Chapter Eleven

The news of the early dismissal set abuzz Hancock High School's hallways.

"You wanna go snowmobiling?" Mike Brembs watched Billy Schweitzer pick through his locker for the right books to bring home for the weekend. "Don't forget the English-to-German dictionary. We'll both need one."

"Mine's already at home," Billy said. "And I'll wait for the snow to stop falling before hitting the trails, but thanks anyway."

"So you're just gonna sit around? We'll be home before noon, man. I can be at your house in no time."

The boys lived on parallel blocks separated by two miles of woodlands rife with trails for snowmobiles and all-terrain vehicles. Although illegal in New Jersey if done on public land, the police usually turned a blind eye to both activities the day after severe snowfalls. Sometimes both were necessary forms of transportation and preferable to multiton cars swerving down icy roads without guardrails. Billy had loved snowmobiling with his father when he was a little boy. Both the Brembses and Schweitzers had snowmobiles for the winter and an ATV for whenever.

"You know what? I just want to relax," Billy said while zipping up his backpack. "If I had my way I wouldn't even be here today."

"Look, I know you're down in the dumps over Maria, but how long are you going to be moping around like this? One week? Two? Listen, a couple of days, I'm talking this weekend, should be enough time to get this out of your system, but any obsessing beyond that is an exercise in self-defeat. I can't take this sullen-Billy routine."

"Sorry for the inconvenience, pal. How 'bout this: I'll bury myself in schoolwork. That should take my mind completely off my self-defeatism. Maybe I'll be up for the snow on Sunday."

Billy's Maria Flynn radar tripped without him having to catch sight of her. Her voice roiled his insides just as effectively. He zoned out Mike's prattle and concentrated on Maria's confusing conversation with one of her friends whose locker stood on the opposite hallway behind Billy.

"What's he flippin' out for? It was probably a bear," the friend, Carrie Riccardi, said.

"Kelly insists it wasn't. He kept saying it was a monster. Over and over—'Maria, a monster ate the bear!'—I swear to God. I mean, the kid has an imagination but it usually involves Pokémon. And they're not eating each other."

"When'd you talk to him?"

"Just five minutes ago. I was called down to the office and spoke to him and his teacher over the phone. He's terrified to go outside. It sounded like he was scared enough to piss his pants *and* the kid's next to him. His teacher wanted to know if my parents could pick him up."

"Do bears even eat other bears?" Riccardi asked.

"How the hell should I know? They eat meat, right? I guess they could be cannibals."

"You mean to tell me a hungry bear can't find one single deer to eat in this festering-deer Petri dish of New Jersey and has to resort to going all Hannibal Lecter on Winnie the Pooh? That's twisted."

"It would appear," Maria said.

"What about your folks? Can they get him?"

"I doubt it. They work in Pennsylvania. It'll be at least an hour, probably more, if one of them left right now. And with the snow falling? You're looking more at two hours in this mess."

"Looks like it's the bus," Riccardi said. "That's not so bad. Maybe you can meet him over there somehow? That school's not far from here. Heck, doesn't your bus pass it on the way home? Just ask the driver to drop you off there so you can wait with him. You could probably even walk home with him from there."

"He doesn't want to leave his *classroom.* I don't see how I'm going to convince him to walk a couple of miles with Bearzilla out there. Hang on a minute, Carrie."

Billy, intrigued, was upset the conversation ended, but froze upon hearing, "Hey, Billy, can I talk to you?"

Maria Flynn stood behind him. Mike, realizing his presence instantly had become even more unwanted than it already was, slipped away. Billy calmly closed his locker door and turned.

"Sure, what's up?" He managed a pleasant smile through his

nervousness. His jumpiness began receding into resignation, which wasn't such a bad thing, Billy rationalized. He had a year and a half left in school with her. Tim was right. He couldn't wall himself away from reality.

Maria filled him in and explained that his father, the chief, was in the office when she took the call from the elementary school.

"He's going over there now to see what happened, but before he went he asked me to tell you to get a ride home with your brother and just stay there until you hear from him. He's going to have a late night, although you didn't need me to tell you that, right?"

"I'm guessing I won't see him until midnight." The conversation flowed easier than Billy had expected it would.

"He said he'd have taken you home himself, but with him going to my brother's school, and not knowing how long he'll be there..." She trailed off, knowing Billy understood.

"Thanks for letting me know. I'll find Tim for a ride. I was going to, anyway. Say, I hope you don't mind me asking, but what exactly did your brother see?"

"Not at all. Kelly has it in his head that some kind of monster attacked a bear while he was in class."

"A monster?"

"He said it sort of looked like Chewbacca, but bigger and fatter."

"An overweight Wookiee from *Star Wars* killed a bear in Hancock? The day keeps getting stranger. Is he all right?"

"He's freaked out of his mind. I know this is probably really weird, and I wouldn't put you in this position if I didn't have to, but would it be okay if I caught a ride with you and your brother? Kelly's school's on the way, and I think it'd really cheer him up if I waited with him for his bus."

"Just let us drop you both off at your home, Maria." It wasn't because Billy wanted to continue torturing himself by sitting next to her on their way to the elementary school. He wanted to help, and expected nothing in return.

"Doesn't your brother drive a pickup truck? It'll be a really tight fit."

Dammit! Why couldn't Dad have handed down a stupid passenger car?!

"I can sit in the bed of the truck."

"Um, it's starting to become a blizzard out there."

Billy again barreled into reality. "Tell you what, Tim can take you to Jefferson, and then take you and your brother home from there. I'll take the bus. It's absolutely not a problem."

"It's a lot for me to ask. I'm not just saying that."

"I know you're not."

"Are you sure? I really don't want to intrude."

"Don't give it another thought. Let's go tell my brother."

Billy, his backpack slung over his shoulder, scooted from the western wing of the school to the east side of the building where the seniors' lockers were situated. Maria kept pace behind him. Dismissing the high school students first proved easiest. The seniors and the few juniors who could drive would do so when the roads would still be navigable for amateur drivers. The school buses were based on the campus and would first empty out the high school then middle school, and then spread out to the elementary schools. The entire process would take hours, and the administrators feared the worst for the kids with each passing minute. The students knew this and moved to get the hell out of there for early freedom.

Billy and Maria reached the senior wing and found Tim's locker open, with a kid in a varsity football jacket obscuring the interior.

"Oh hey, Billy, how's it going?" said Tim's lockermate, Ray Schwartz, the football team's kicker. Ray zipped up his jacket and grabbed his book bag, ready to leave.

"I'll tell you in a minute," Billy said, waiting for Ray to move aside. "Dammit! It's never easy!"

"What's wrong?" Maria stood behind Billy.

"We missed him. We must have just missed him. His jacket's gone. You ready to run to the parking lot? He'll be in spot 203."

"Not unless you know something that I don't," Ray interjected.

"I'm sorry?!" Billy cocked his head.

"Didn't he call out sick today? His truck's not there. I showed up late today, like I do most days. And his truck's always here when I get here. It wasn't today. And he sure as hell wasn't in trigonometry with me today. I'm glad the game's canceled tonight. Travis fuckin' disappeared, Tim's sick. We'd be screwed."

"Tim's not sick." Billy's uneasiness around Maria vanished. He now feared for his brother. "Tim left for school way before I did today. I need to call my dad."

Chapter Twelve

The chief inspected the vicinity of the Thomas Jefferson Elementary School, four miles from the high school and closer to where the Schweitzers lived, for anything suspicious as he pulled in front of the building. He deployed his officers between the two crime scenes at Winchester Road and the high school, and hoped a third one wouldn't be necessary here. There'd be overtime for someone should there be anything to the Flynn kid's story.

Schweitzer squatted to gauge the blood slick now layered with a snowy sheen. Catherine Jensen, Kelly's teacher, wrapped herself in her winter coat and stood back from the chief after showing him where Kelly said he witnessed the attack.

"Is that a lot of blood?" she asked.

"It's more than I'd care to lose at one time. It'd be nice if whatever lost it was still here." The felled limb that Kelly described rested nearby. Bits of chewed meat pockmarked the snow like bad acne. "You didn't see what did this? None of the other kids did?"

"Only Kelly, and I believe him."

The chief stood and faced her. "It's kind of hard not to, miss?"

"Mrs. Jensen."

He nodded. "Thank you for looking after that boy, Mrs. Jensen. Is he good most of the time? Not prone to making stuff up?"

"He's smart, on the quiet side. I think he feels a little bit like an outsider because he's such a big kid. Can we go back inside?"

The chief saw her shivering. "Of course, yes. Thanks for bringing me out here. And, for the time being, please make sure nobody disturbs the area. Not that they would, but—"

"Is it like a crime scene?"

"After you." He extended his arm and escorted her back to the building before answering, "At this point, no, it's not. I don't mean to sound flippant, but it's not illegal for a wild animal to attack another animal, even if it *is* in a school zone." He smiled. She got the joke. "But I'm going to call for some of my men to come out here. I'll hang around until they arrive."

They walked around the corner of the building and he held open the main door for her. "Please go be with the children. Get them ready to go home. I'll want to speak with Kelly, and soon, while things are still fresh in his little head."

"Have you ever seen anything like that before? That kind of mauling, if that's what it was?"

"Honestly, no. But in fairness it's not really all that common to stumble across fresh animal kills like that. Dead deer on the side of the road? Hit and killed by a car? Sure. But I can't recall ever seeing what supposedly happened to a bear that nobody can find."

They stood in the lobby.

"What should I tell the kids?"

"That they're not in danger," he said. "And they're not. Tell them they'll be going home soon to their parents. I'm going to take one last look out there before leaving."

"Sounds good, thanks, Chief." She walked to be with her kids.

"Anytime." He then radioed his police station.

She didn't see them, the chief thought. *Or if she did, she didn't think very much of them. Hell, they were right there in front of her. Maybe we do have a crime scene. It's the third one today featuring hoofprints and not much else.*

The chief returned to the attack site to put his finger on something that had eluded him while speaking with Mrs. Jensen.

No blood trail. How can a mortally wounded animal dripping with blood not leave any speck of it while stumbling toward death, or even being carried away?

The chief skirted the outline of the carnage and stood at the forest's border. He found the bear's tracks leading to the tree where it took refuge. He stepped over twigs and branches, moving into the woods and following the odd tracks that pursued the bear, but they vanished. Only pawprints remained.

"So where'd it come from?" the chief asked out loud, and then lowering his voice, "And where did it go?"

The chief doubled back to reexamine the bloodstained area. A large set of hoofprints was set deep in the snow, inches from the slaughter.

Where's the turn? The pivot to leave, to get the hell out of here?

None existed. It was as if whatever had caught the bear had

teleported from the spot after gorging itself.

"Chief! Hey, Chief!"

Donald Schweitzer greeted his trusted captain, Jim Sherwood, followed by a couple of the department's newest patrolmen.

"Thanks for getting here so quick. One of the kids in that classroom"—he pointed toward the room rife with children whose noses were pressed up against the glass as they watched full-fledged police activity—"saw a small bear apparently killed by—"

"Chief, forgive the interruption," Sherwood said, arms raised to ease Donald into silence, "but something's happened. A woman walking her dogs on Winchester found your pickup truck. It'd been driven off the road, down a hill and head on into a tree."

The chief, not prone to excitable blurbs, absorbed Sherwood's words and kept his steely veneer.

"Is Tim all right?" he said sternly.

"God, I hope so. We haven't found him yet."

Chapter Thirteen

"Dammit, would you work!" Billy vented on his iPhone. He stood outside of the school's front entrance, unable to get reception. Hancock's remote geography played against him.

Maria Flynn returned from the row of idling buses parked at the curb and stood next to the school's main doors to avoid the students flooding through them into the storm.

"Billy, I just asked the bus driver, he'll drop me off at Jefferson."

"I can't get through to my dad," he replied. "I'm going to ask Officer Pena to reach him directly, if I can *find* Officer Pena."

Billy had jogged to his brother's parking spot and confirmed it was empty.

"Okay, so, let me find Pena." Billy thought out loud while standing next to Maria. "Hell, I'll just go to the office and have them page him. My dad needs to know."

They each sponsored worried expressions. The long, flat awning covering the front doors sheltered them from the snowfall.

"Are you going to take the bus home?" Maria asked. "Or wait here for your dad?"

"I don't know. I haven't really thought it over. I don't suppose I can do much good here. My dad would probably want me to wait for him, but I think I'll go nuts if I have to." He tilted his head from side to side, weighing the options. "I'll go with you, make sure you get to the school all right, and then take the bus home and wait for my old man. Who knows? Maybe Tim's home?"

"Did you try calling him?"

Billy balefully looked at his iPhone's call history.

"I called his number right before my dad's—nothing." He didn't let his frustration linger. "Maria, get on the bus, and please don't let the driver leave without me."

"I won't, promise."

Billy waded into the school through throngs of students eager to leave.

Chapter Fourteen

Hancock Township resembles any other modernized, picket-fenced place in America that offers an excellent school system—"That's why we moved to Hancock!"

The township lacks rustic general stores where the codgers gather to use the same spittoon. There's no town drunk who's on a first-name basis with the cops. In New Jersey, Hancock and places like it have Walmarts, Dunkin' Donuts, ShopRites, IHOPs and Pizza Huts. Neighbors might know each other, or not. Hancock, like its brother towns, experiences its share of mayhem and death.

Every winter some poor soul whose sense of invincibility rivals his lack of common sense rides his snowmobile—it's always a guy—onto what he thinks is a frozen slab of Lake Hopatcong. Sometimes they fish the body out of the same crack through which it fell, other times spring must bloom for the corpse to surface. Hancock's military heroes, star high school athletes one or two years earlier, have been killed in Iraq and Afghanistan and all the wars dating back to the Revolution, their names chiseled into the war memorial stone by the municipal building.

Murders happen too. Every town has them. A local housewife and her lover rendezvoused a year earlier at the Bryerson apartment complex a mile from her home. Her husband followed her. First, one shot. Then two. Then three. He spared their child, whom he'd left with the teenage babysitter next door. But murder-suicides, or murder period, are not Hancock's norm. One every decade seems like a lot for this lily-white suburb in Northwest Jersey. But they happen.

More typical are the occasional perverts caught in kiddie-porn sweeps, or spates of car burglaries. Route 15 intersects with Interstate 80, which leads east to the drug haven of Newark. Heroin, crystal meth, ecstasy, guns, all of them forty minutes away. Those desperate for fixes routinely break into cars lining Hancock's curbsides as their owners dream. Loose change, wallets, GPS systems, CD players or anything the thieves can hock, they will for drug money. Nothing sets Hancock Township apart from any other Morris County town. No long-abandoned, dilapidated house that once held dominion over unspeakable acts, only to have the horror reoccur decades later when a stranger comes to town. That happens, but not in New Jersey. Not really.

But clerks killed for $10,000 in computer equipment? A janitor murders a priest in the rectory? A stranger found dead facedown in a stream next to a dive bar, his body stripped bare for what little valuables he had? Yes, that happens in New Jersey, just pick the town.

But what occurred early on December 5 in Hancock?

"Three kidnappings. I can't believe this." Chief Donald Schweitzer stood on the shoulder of Winchester's westbound lane, looking down on his crashed pickup truck, unable to conceive that someone had snatched his son from it. The Ranger left the elevated roadway and smashed headfirst into a centuries-old oak at a forty-five degree angle. The truck, its grill crushed inward, came to rest in front of the tree. And similar to Travis's Mazda, someone had obliterated the driver's side window to grab Tim.

"The air bag deployed, and he *was* wearing his seat belt." Captain Jim Sherwood had accompanied the chief to the scene, leaving the two junior officers to scour for whatever evidence could be found at the Jefferson school.

"Let me guess, the seat belt was cut?" Schweitzer spoke barely above a whisper.

"It was. There's no damage to the rear. He wasn't bumped off the road. There are fresh skid marks that we believe the truck made. He swerved, Chief, probably to avoid hitting something. In fact, we *know* he collided with something."

One of the county prosecutor's best accident-reconstruction experts scuttled around the pickup, speaking his observations into a digital recorder. Law-enforcement vehicles lined the roadway.

The chief adjusted his navy-blue, round-top hat. Snowflakes stuck to its brim.

"Jim, I know it's clichéd, but me and my ex-wife always told each other we could never comprehend how parents of dead children could go on living without them. Now we are those parents. I haven't called Diana yet to tell her."

"Whoa, hold on! Don't sound like that. There's nothing suggesting Tim was seriously injured. The only blood we found was on the air bag, and that was just from impact, probably bloodied his nose a little. Until we learn otherwise, Tim's alive."

"You're right. Sorry. Of course you're right." The chief shook his head to refocus. "You said he hit something. What was it?"

"If you face the truck, you'll see the right-hand side of where the windshield meets the frame is dented inward and the windshield's cracked, right at Tim's eye level. The prosecutor's guy said it wasn't a result of hitting the tree. We don't know what made the impact, and it's still all preliminary, but that's probably what caused Tim to swerve off the road and crash *into* the tree."

The chief shuffled down the embankment with Sherwood. They both stood far enough away so as not to impede the investigator. Schweitzer squinted to see where the Ranger was struck.

"So, what, did a condor swoop in front of Tim and smack the windshield? I don't see any dead animals around here. Speaking of animals..." The chief trailed off and glanced downward toward the driver's side, his eyes following a path of snow turning salty and dirty up to the roadway.

"Do those look like hoofprints to you?" The chief repeatedly pointed to and fro.

"We haven't really analyzed them yet but—"

"They're hoofprints, Jim. At least that's what Officer Fryer says. They lead right up to Tim's door. I've been seeing a lot of them lately."

"Chief, let us do our work. You don't have to be here. Go call your ex and be with Billy. They'll need you."

"And the tracks go only in one direction," the chief continued. "Downhill from the road. I don't see any heading back up to the street, at least not in the immediate area."

The chief walked a wide perimeter around the site and into the woods.

"But there's no trail leading into the woods from the other side of the truck. Can you explain that?"

"I can't," Schweitzer said. "Not unless the perp retraced his steps to the millimeter back up to the road."

"Unlikely."

The forest expanded exponentially every time Schweitzer surveyed the amount of ground they'd need to cover.

"Tim's somewhere out there," Schweitzer said.

The snow intensified.

Chapter Fifteen

"So, I'm driving to the high school, nothing seems out of the ordinary, and that thing jumps out in the middle of the road and then *into* my lane, swings a big chain at me, smashes my windshield, and I swerve. That's all I remember until waking up here with you guys." Tim Schweitzer guessed he, Travis and Brittany were all in the same cavern, but spaced a distance apart.

"Did it beat you up yet?" Travis groaned.

"No. But I heard what happened to you. I'm assuming you're in no position to try to free yourself."

"It hurts to breathe, Tim. I just want to sleep."

"Tim!" It was Brittany. "Can you come over here and untie me?! Travis can't. I'll keep talking so you can follow my voice?!"

"I don't think that's gonna happen anytime soon. I can't budge." The thing had bound Tim's wrists behind his back, and did an equally merciless job knotting his ankles together. Only stillness eased the bristly rope's grip on his skin.

Tim's echo faded into silence, intermittently broken by unseen drops of water.

"I sincerely doubt it's trying to ransom us." Tim tried generating conversation.

"I just want to get out of here!" Brittany whined.

"So do I, Brit. So do I." Tim shifted his attention away from her. "Travis, I saw light flickering from where I'm guessing you are. Can you describe anything?"

"I remember a lot of candles in crevices," Travis replied. "A bunch of skulls and bones on the floor. It's not like it's got a Justin Bieber poster hanging on the wall. You?"

"I haven't seen anything since that thing blew out the lights and left you. Brit?! How about you?!"

"Fucking nothing!"

"Okay, well, let's look at the bright side. Our folks, the police, have got to know we're missing by now and are looking for us."

The walls amplified their voices and made shouting unnecessary.

"Yeah, well, where the fuck are we?" she said.

"Obviously one of the mineshafts."

"Obviously," Brittany mocked.

"Well, yeah, it is obvious."

"No shit, genius. There are like a thousand goddamn caves all over Hancock. I doubt that thing left a trail of breadcrumbs for the cops."

Tim rested facedown on the cool earth.

"Why aren't we dead?" Travis wheezed.

Nobody answered. Travis figured Tim and Brittany had both thought the same thing.

"It could've finished me off but didn't," Travis continued. "Look, for all I know it still might. But it said we'd try later, whatever the hell it meant by that."

"Travis, it asked you why you did something. What was it talking about?"

"I have *no* idea."

"It seemed pretty insistent that you did."

"Who the hell's side are you on here? Ahh Christ, that hurts!" Travis's effort to speak devolved into moaning.

"I'm on your side, man, but maybe that thing meant it. You must've done something to piss it off, that's why you're here, apparently."

Travis followed up some labored breaths with, "And if I don't remember?"

"Then maybe that thing finishes you off, and then kills Brittany and then me."

Chapter Sixteen

Billy Schweitzer dreamed of moments when he could talk to Maria Flynn about anything and everything important and not, but right now, sitting next to her on the bus traveling to Jefferson Elementary, he didn't utter a peep. His brother's disappearance had to be connected with the two others, and it consumed Billy.

"Are the people at school going to call your dad?" Maria asked.

"Officer Pena said he would. He had a real grave look on his face. I mean, something was really wrong, but he wouldn't tell me." Billy clasped his hands in his lap and looked down at the floor. "Whether my dad can get through to me is another matter. Reception has and always will suck the farther we move into the sticks."

A scene Billy had grown accustomed to at school diverted his attention: Jason Nicholson picking on the shorter and heavier Eric Halberstrom, both boys juniors along with Billy and Maria.

"Just because we're getting out of here early doesn't mean I'm done with you." Jason sat in front of Eric, but he hunched over the back of his seat, looming like a vulture over the weaker boy. "So, you gonna go home and jerk off earlier than usual, right?"

"Go to hell," Eric meekly said.

Jason replied with a hard right punch to Eric's left shoulder, deeply bruised by similar hits. "What'd you say to me, you fat shit?"

"Why are you picking on him?" Maria asked. Billy looked at her for the first time on the bus and then across to Jason for his answer.

"You care about this little shit?"

"Just, I want to know what he did to you. That's all."

"Nothing," Jason replied nonchalantly, followed by an arrogant grin.

"Is it because he doesn't fight back?" Maria probed. "Like, if he did actually fight back you'd find someone else to pick on? I'm just curious."

"This little shit wouldn't fight back even if he could."

"Oh, okay, so you've proved my point. You pick on him because he doesn't resort to your type of juvenile behavior. Interesting." She thought for a few moments and asked loudly: "Are you trying to overcompensate for something? Like, do you have a small dick?"

Eric burst into a belly laugh. Jason, not expecting the pushback, looked around like a frightened prairie dog. The kids sitting near him laughed. Billy, too, snapped out of his gloom to chuckle.

"What's a matter, Jason? Oh, you're not used to someone actually taking it to you. I get it. Completely understandable."

"You think she's bein' funny, you fat fuck?" Jason raged at his usual target.

"Yeah, actually." Eric felt emboldened. He knew it would get bad later when the cute girl couldn't defend him. He wished to one day summon the strength to do it himself.

"Hey, Jason, concentrate! He's not the one asking you if you've got a small penis! I am," Maria continued, drawing the attention of everyone in the bus, including the driver. "I'm the one accusing you of probably sporting a small pecker."

She spoke as if making friendly conversation with the other kids. "I mean, I really don't want to know, and fortunately for me I will *never* be in the position to find out for myself, seeing that I have standards, regardless of pecker size."

Maria elicited well-timed laughter with each barb.

"But don't worry, Jason, I'm sure some lucky lass will take pity on your shriveled pickle. Just remember to bring lots of cash and a bag to put over your head to spare her one of two gruesome sights."

The students exploded into guffaws.

Jason, sporting a golem's face, pounded Eric's sore shoulder three times and then snapped at Maria.

"I pick on this fat shit because I can. And I'm not stopping because of you."

Maria prepared to continue her lopsided repartee when the swirl of blue and red police lights on the horizon captured everybody's attention.

The bus driver, already traveling slowly along the snowy road, decelerated. Billy looked out a window to see five police cars lining the street opposite the bus. He absorbed as much as he could as the bus drove by.

"That's my dad's cruiser," he said to Maria, who looked out the same window. "He's there! Oh my God!"

Maria mouthed the same phrase. She could identify Tim's pickup, even with its front smashed.

"Stop the bus!" Billy yelled to the driver.

"Kid, I can't! I can't just drop you off in the middle of the road by an accident scene. I don't care whose son you are. We're almost to Jefferson, we'll be there in five minutes."

Billy watched the police cars fade and then slumped into his seat.

"That must've happened a while ago," he said to Maria. "Tim didn't even make it to school, so we're talking like almost four hours ago. I didn't see an ambulance. Maybe that's good? Nobody injured, right? God, now I know why Officer Pena looked so upset."

"Billy, I'm so sorry," she said.

"Pena should've just told me. It would've been better than finding out about it like I just did." He tried again to call his father but knew, correctly, the spotty reception would kill the call.

The school bus made it over one of the large humps highlighting the ebbs and flows of Winchester Road and began descending the steepest hill on its journey. The driver, Devin McTiernan, a retired policeman for twenty years and current part-time driver, eased down on the brake to slow the bus if it gained too much momentum. The driver ignored the fifty-miles-per-hour speed limit and drove below forty.

"The second I get home, I'm taking my snowmobile to meet my dad," Billy said. "This is getting ridiculous."

With a sucker punch's suddenness, every kid on the bus lurched forward as McTiernan slammed on the brakes.

"Jesus Christ!" he yelled. The bus, despite its slower pace, traveled fast enough to fishtail. McTiernan turned the steering wheel to prevent the bus from entering the opposite lane, but the slick road made it impossible. The bus skidded across the road toward the guardrail. It crumpled like aluminum foil as the bus drove over it, heading downhill.

"Everyone hold on!" McTiernan yelled over the shrieking children. "Here we go!"

Billy first heard and then felt the loud creak of the bus tilting over and then plummeting down the slope. The bus didn't continually flip like a race car that had lost control on a track. It landed on its left side, bringing the children with it, and slid twenty feet down the slope before stopping.

"Is everyone all right?!" McTiernan yelled. "Check the kid next to you!"

The shrieking settled into a few cries, as well as a murmur among students who were checking themselves for broken bones.

"Billy, are you hurt?" Maria wound up lying on top of him, and he didn't have time to think about the awkwardness of their embrace.

"I don't think so. Can you stand? Just watch out for my hands."

Maria gripped the bus seat for leverage and stood on cracked passenger windows. Billy did the same.

"Billy!" McTiernan called. "Can you make your way back to the emergency door and pop it open?"

He and Maria stood three rows from the emergency exit.

"Give me a second." Billy walked along the stretch of curved metal above the passenger windows to get to the rear exit. He held on to the seats for balance and reached the rearmost seat, which was built into the bus's interior. The emergency exit hovered above him to his right. He grabbed the back of one of the seats and pulled himself up enough to successfully grasp the red emergency handle and wrench it clockwise. The door swung outward and down and banged against the bus's rear exterior.

"I want one big kid outside of the bus and another big kid in the bus to help guide out the smaller students!" McTiernan took charge. "Everything's going to be fine. If you're hurt and can't move, then stay right where you are. I'm not leaving this bus until you do. And once you're out, stand a good distance away from the bus, just in case there's a fire!"

"Did you call for help?!" one of the students yelled.

"Radio's busted! The fall must've screwed it up and dislodged something. And my cell phone fell out of my pocket. We'll call 911 after we get out of the bus. I don't think it's on fire but I'm not risking it. Now move!"

Fifteen students needed freeing. Billy'd never considered himself a big kid, but sufficed as one and stayed inside to lend a push to students struggling to lift themselves out of the bus. Richard Blount, a junior, manned the outside of the bus and lowered to safety the students who needed it. Jason Nicholson raced over Eric Halberstrom, Maria and everyone else in his way to be one of the first kids out of the bus.

"You're as chivalrous as you are decent, Jason. How unsurprising," Maria said. He scowled at her while lowering himself out of the bus.

"Get your fuckin' hands off me," he barked at Blount.

All the kids abandoned their book bags, except for Billy, who wore his over his shoulders. The girls kept their purses, of course. McTiernan and Maria helped the younger students get their bearings and herded them toward Billy. Eric Halberstrom didn't exit until all the girls and the lowerclassmen had preceded him.

"Go ahead, Maria, please," Halberstrom said to the last girl on the bus. "And thank you."

Her wholesome smile expressed *you're welcome.* She grabbed the lower edge of the doorway, crouched and then jumped to give her the momentum to deftly swing her left leg over the rim.

"Give the little lady a hand, kid," McTiernan said. "I smell fuel."

Billy detected a noxious aroma. "He's right."

Maria straddled the frame like a saddle, and without thinking, Billy held her arm and pushed her knee upward so she could get over the edge and let her weight slide her to the ground.

Blount, his hands outstretched ready to assist, shadowed her graceful descent.

"You got this?" Billy asked Halberstrom, nodding his head toward the exit.

"Yeah, no problem. Thanks." With a little effort Halberstrom managed to up-and-over.

Billy and McTiernan, who first tossed a handheld fire extinguisher to Blount, then escaped.

"Gimmie that." McTiernan, red-faced and huffing, grabbed the red extinguisher from Blount and shooed the kids thirty feet away from the bus.

McTiernan then doused the area around the fuel tank, grumbling obscenities under his breath, followed by, "Any of you kids get a reception?"

The students collectively flashed *oops! we forgot!* facial expressions and whipped out their mobiles to hit the emergency call buttons.

"Jesus Christ, they needed *me* to tell them?" McTiernan lumbered toward the teenagers.

One of the sophomore girls chirped, "I got through!"

"Tell them we're on Winchester in between Green Lake and Ironside Roads," McTiernan said.

McTiernan bent over and placed his hands above his knees to rest himself.

"Mr. McTiernan?" Billy cautiously approached the old-timer, worrying he might keel over in the snow. "What happened back there?"

"I'll tell you what happened." A few labored huffs later: "What happened is the biggest goddamn bear I've ever seen in my life ran right in front of my bus."

Chapter Seventeen

"Jesus, what the hell's happening?" Donald Schweitzer heard static dispatches describing the bus crash over his radio. Helplessness browbeat him at the site of his eldest son's disappearance. "That bus passed us not five minutes ago."

Captain Jim Sherwood, standing alongside of him, gulped when he asked his distracted friend a pressing question, "Chief, was Billy on that bus?"

And he was off. Not even a "you're in charge here, Jim, I've got to go!". The chief sprinted to his cruiser and floored it into a U-turn. Wheels spun and snow and gravel blew backward as Schweitzer swerved but regained control of his car en route to the crashed bus.

First to arrive, he pulled another U-turn to park parallel to the flock of school students standing clear of the bus. He left his cruiser's lights flashing and jumped from the shoulder to the accident site below where he hugged Billy off his feet.

"Dad, put me down!" Billy hissed.

"I just needed to know you're all right. I can't have both of you missing." He placed his hands on his son's shoulders and couldn't help but look at his young face. Regaining his composure, the chief turned to the bus driver.

"What happened here?"

Devin McTiernan told him everything.

"And everyone's all right?"

"Bumps and bruises, some shaken nerves. But that's it," McTiernan said. "And I can't believe how big that bear was, Chief—bigger than Governor Christie."

"Leave Chris out of this, I like the guy. My union might not, but I do."

"All kidding aside, Chief, that bear was frigging huge. Five hundred pounds at least. Just zoomed across the road." McTiernan pointed uphill and ballparked where it'd crossed.

"Great. Now we have a Goliath to worry about." The chief scanned the woods for any movement, seeing none but swirling snow.

Billy, who'd been listening in, figured it was as good a time as any to ask.

"Mr. McTiernan, you sure it wasn't a deer? Like, did you see antlers?"

The driver eyed Billy as if he'd asked him in Swahili.

"Son, I know what a bear looks like. They don't have horns."

"Okay, just asking."

It was a long shot, Billy thought as he stepped backward toward the pack of students. He patted his hoodie's pocket containing the printouts he'd taken from the library. *An absurd long shot.*

A Hancock Township Fire Department pumper, sirens wailing in concert with its flashing red lights, rumbled into view.

"I want everyone to pay attention to my voice!" the chief called out, waiting for the students to hush. "I'm going to make sure another bus gets here soon to get you all home. You're just going to have to wait here a little bit longer. So in the meantime, I want you to stay right where you are and do not go anywhere near the road or into the woods!"

Billy approached his father and spoke quietly, "Anything on Tim? I saw what you guys were doing back there."

"Not yet." The chief took equal discretion. "I wish I could tell you different." He reassessed his son. "Thank God. Just, thank God you're all right. I'm gonna call into headquarters and let them know nobody's hurt."

The chief returned to his cruiser, leaving Billy with Maria, who felt compelled to be by his side. She sensed his emotional fragility but also appreciated his genuine concern for her brother, and she reciprocated the feeling for Tim.

"Dad, wait!" He motioned for the chief to rejoin him. Billy explained that Maria was headed to Jefferson to be with Kelly before the accident happened.

Donald Schweitzer knew Kelly Flynn was a basket case because of what he'd witnessed, or thought he'd witnessed.

"Can you take us there, Dad?"

"Why do *you* need to go?" The chief seemed puzzled, not knowing if Billy regularly hung out with this girl.

"Uh, I guess I don't, but I want to make sure they both get home all right, and it's really not far of a walk to our house."

"I could just drive you home myself. I don't like the idea of you being out there on your own with us still not knowing what's goin' on around here. I'm already missing one of my boys."

"Well, I figured that would be taking you out of your way, especially with the weather getting worse."

Maria stepped up from behind Billy. "He can stay at my house."

The chief expressed surprise. Billy? Shock.

"No, really, Chief Schweitzer. At least he'll be around me and my brother, and he won't be sitting alone in your house worrying about Tim—I'm sorry to hear about the accident, by the way."

"Thank you."

The pumper parked on the shoulder to reach the bus below. Its crew worked to ensure no hotspots flickered within the bus's crevices. An ambulance had followed in case students needed treatment.

"Another officer should be here any minute," the chief said, mulling the proposition. "Once one arrives, I'll take you both to Jefferson and then to your home. Go wait by the car. I'll be there in a minute. I want to check on something first."

Billy and Maria walked toward the cruiser as the chief jogged along the shoulder of the road, past the pumper, toward where the bus began its slide. He spotted the zigzagging tire marks.

"Where'd you come from, big boy?"

Whatever crossed the street had left a snowy crater in the middle of the lane, running opposite the bus. No pawprints, but rather an indented pathway defined by smatterings of black hair poking out the snow, like it'd glided across the road.

The chief walked to the shoulder's edge and looked downward.

That's one big bear, he thought.

Its supine carcass rested underneath a thin shroud of snow, as if waiting to be autopsied at a zoo morgue. The chief shuffled down for a closer examination and drew his Glock just in case. Its mouth produced no breath and remained agape with its tongue frozen in place, not touching a single tooth. The bear's eyes were open. Eyes of the dead, the chief could spot them anywhere. He holstered his gun.

McTiernan must've hit the poor bastard and broke its back. But something ain't right. Something...

Schweitzer trudged uphill and walked past the crater to what he knew would greet him on the other side of Winchester Road.

It did not run.

Billy watched his father shaking his head in disbelief from afar.

"Excuse me, Maria," Billy said. "I have to make a call."

He wandered along the shoulder to a point where he felt comfortable nobody could hear him and dialed Mike Brembs. *Please work, please work.* The call went through and Billy told him about his brother's accident.

"Still no sign of Tim or the others. But I actually called to ask a favor."

Billy explained what he wanted and knew how his friend would react.

"You seriously want me to research this Krampus thing when I could be outside in freakin' fresh snow on my sled tearing up the trails? Had you called five minutes from now that's exactly what I'd be doing."

"The snow will be there all day today and tomorrow and the next day, Mike. I need all the help I can get at this point." Billy attempted discretion by cupping his hand over his iPhone while listening simultaneously to Mike and for student eavesdroppers. He knew he sounded off his rocker.

"Today's date, the hoofprints—it cannot be a coincidence. I haven't had a chance to look any of this stuff up for those reports we're supposed to do."

"Screw those reports! Your brother's a little more important than some stupid German project. I'm pretty damn sure a missing sibling negates you having to do any homework."

"This isn't about homework, Mike. I'm not asking you to believe me. I don't blame you for being skeptical, honestly. But please humor me, do me this favor. Find out whatever you can. I'd do it myself but my phone's battery is low and I left my charger at home. You've got the Internet right at your fingertips. Come on, do me a solid."

Billy heard the *Jeopardy!* theme music playing in his head as he waited for his friend's answer.

"All right, you win," Mike said. "I'll call you in an hour or so. Borrow someone's charger, genius."

A second police car arrived as the chief returned. He made a beeline for the bus driver, who was performing a student headcount.

"Chief, I think we're—"

Schweitzer couldn't wait.

"Did you hit the bear, Mr. McTiernan?"

"Excuse me? Uh, no. No. At least I don't think I did. Is it over there? Dead?"

"It is and it is."

"Big, wasn't it?"

"Just like you said it was. You sure you didn't hit it?"

"Something big like that? I sure as hell would've felt *something*."

"Yes, I suppose you would have. Anyway, you wanted to tell me something?"

"We're down one student."

"*What?!*"

Billy and Maria directed their attention at the chief. This disappearance was news to them too.

"I counted them, Chief," the driver said. "Fifteen kids. I counted each one of them leaving the bus. There were fifteen of them. I just head counted them three times now. There're fourteen of them. I'm positive."

"Who?"

"What's the kid's name?!" McTiernan called over his shoulder to the students while still meeting the chief's worried gaze, and then addressing him alone, "I know their faces, Chief. But I can't put names to all of them."

"I get it."

"It's Jason." Eric Halberstrom stood before the two men. "His name's Jason Nicholson. He was first off the bus, well, after Richard Blount."

"Oh, *that* asshole," McTiernan blurted without thinking. "I mean, that's the nickname I gave him. Blount's a good kid. Jason's the asshole. What I mean is—"

"That's not very appropr—"

Eric interrupted. "Don't be mad at him, Chief Schweitzer. Mr. McTiernan never calls him that. *Never*. Go ask anyone on the bus. And, honestly, Jason's one gigantic asshole. I can attest to that. Where's a Bible? I'll put my hand on it."

"Did any of you kids see Jason?" the chief called to the students, who used their phones' cameras to record the firemen milling around the bus.

"Hey! Put those goddamn things down and pay attention!"

The startled kids looked at one another and then shook their heads or murmured "no".

"Jason Nicholson! Who last saw him? He was right here! Got out of the bus just like you all just did!" The chief looked at Eric, recalling what the boy just told him. "All right, where's Richard Blount?! Step up!"

Blount slipped through the middle of the pack and raised his hand.

"I'm right here." He stood five feet in front of his classmates, who didn't know whether they'd get yelled at if they resumed recording everything.

"Okay, Rich, try to think, where'd Jason go when he got off the bus? And don't say 'I don't know' because I'm pretty damned sure you saw the direction he walked."

"Can I go stand where I was standing when he got out of the bus?"

The chief turned to the firefighters lingering around the wreck.

"Is it safe over there?"

They all agreed it was, and Blount sauntered to the rear of the bus, established where he'd based himself when helping lower out the kids, and then turned 180 degrees.

"Mr. McTiernan said to get back at least thirty feet," Blount reminded the chief. "So..." If Blount was standing at the six o'clock position, he pivoted slightly and instead of walking straight to noon, he diverged and ambled to ten o'clock.

The chief walked to Blount's spot.

"I can't say for sure he stayed here, or that this is exactly where he waited," Blount said. "He walked in this direction. Most of the girls stood closer to the road."

The chief saw footprints where Blount said he'd seen Jason, but the kids had created a hurricane of prints around the snow. Discerning whose were whose, while not impossible, would prove difficult as the snow continued to fall.

"Thanks, Richard, please go stand with your classmates." The chief clapped him on the back to send him on his way.

"Mr. McTiernan?" the chief called. "Could he have just walked home from here?"

"Not a chance. He's the last one on my route. You're talkin' ten stops until his."

The chief scanned the ground around the woods beyond where most of the students waited, looking for any telltale signs of movement. Much like the crater made by the bear in the middle of Winchester Road, the chief spotted an impression of disturbed snowy ground. A few droplets of blood stained the snow crimson.

So this is where he fell...and was dragged.

The depression stretched into the woods the way a smashed Mischief Night egg oozes yolk down a window.

"Stay there!" he commanded, a little harshly, the students who began inching nearer to see what he'd uncovered. "Please. I mean, please don't come any closer." He waved them away and they complied.

The chief walked parallel to the path over which Jason Nicholson was dragged from the scene. For once he didn't see hoofprints, probably because whoever was pulling Jason had covered his own tracks by dragging the body directly over them. And then everything vanished about sixty feet from where Richard Blount had directed the chief. The marks ended atop a wide, flat rock that emerged from the ground. The snow on the stone appeared spread around, as if the perpetrator used Jason's body like a rag to wipe the area before departing.

But to where? No further signs of disturbance availed themselves to the chief, just a panoramic snowscape that the guy with the big beard and Afro on television teaches you how to paint.

"Jason!" Gusts of wind and snow muffled the chief's voice from carrying through the trees. "Jason Nicholson!" Nothing.

He double-timed it back to the students, making certain not to blemish the drag marks, and spoke to the Hancock policeman who had arrived on-site.

"Where are we on getting these kids out of here?"

"The superintendent said she's sending an empty bus, Chief. It should be on its way."

"Confirm that. Tell whoever's driving to hurry the hell up. I want these kids out of here." He leaned in closer to avoid frightening the kids. "This is a goddamn crime scene. Someone *took* that boy... Cameras."

"What, Chief?"

"Cameras!" The chief jerked around to address the students, some of whom, indeed, were recording the situation.

"Turn those damned things off and listen!" He waited for the kids to obey.

"How many of you, right when you got off the bus until now, used your camera phones to, I don't know, record the moment for posterity or put it on Facebook?"

Seven hands went up.

"Okay, now, I know you'd probably hire a civil rights lawyer if I demanded you give me your phones so I can see what you recorded. I could do that but I honestly don't have the time or sanity right now. So here's what you're gonna do. Everyone one of you who recorded something or even snapped one digital picture of what happened either on the bus or after the accident, you're going to email it to this address: dschweitzer at hancockpd dot gov."

He spelled it out for them twice.

"Punch that into your phones now so you don't forget it. And if the file's too big, break it up and send it in waves. This is important!" He let that sink into their skulls. "One of you might have seen what happened to Jason and not even know it. So please start sending me stuff." The chief had transfixed the students. "Do it now!"

The children furiously click-clacked phone buttons as an empty school bus descended the steep hill on which McTiernan had lost control. The chief's smartphone buzzed in his pocket with the kids' emails.

"Mr. McTiernan, thanks for looking after them and handling things the way you did. Get on that bus with them." The bus broke to a stop.

McTiernan ushered the children up the shoulder to board the bus.

The chief again spoke to the patrolman, who understood the instructions and shook his head to affirm it.

"You saw where I was walking, right?"

"Yes, Chief."

"Okay, that's where you need to direct the detectives. Got it? If they give you any trouble about getting someone out here, call me immediately."

"I will, Chief."

Schweitzer turned. "Billy! Girl whose name I can't remember!" the chief addressed his son and his friend who stood by his cruiser.

"It's Maria," she said.

"Maria, sorry. Let's get you to Jefferson." He opened the rear door like a gentleman. "You too, Billy. Let's go." Billy followed and the chief shut the door.

"Chief, real quick." Eric Halberstrom, who'd be the last student to board the bus, approached Schweitzer. "I'm sorry that Tim's missing. I really am. Spend your time looking for him and not Jason. He's not worth it."

"What did you say? Look, asshole or not, you're talking about someone's son. How could you say that?"

"Here's how." Halberstrom unzipped his coat and unbuttoned the top of the golf shirt he wore. He didn't care about overstretching the fabric. Eric yanked the shirt down by the left side of the collar to expose his bum shoulder, revealing an amorphous mass of bruised skin. "Tim would never do anything like this."

He sensed the boy's humiliation and attempts to withhold the tears beading in his eyes. Eric released his shirt, hiked his coat back into place and zipped it up. "Go find your son, Chief. He's one of the good ones. Jason can freeze out there for all I care. Fuck him." Eric disappeared into the bus.

The chief, aghast, started his cruiser, did a U-turn and drove to Jefferson Elementary.

Chapter Eighteen

Jason Nicholson rocked from within the crate. His face ached when any part of it pressed against the wood trapping him. It wasn't fresh-cut lumber from the Home Depot, Jason knew, because his father was a building contractor. It felt and smelled of mold but remained resilient, no rattling or loose planks. This timber box gave the aura of outlasting ages of pestilence and surely would survive centuries more.

He remembered bolting away from the school bus toward the forest. He turned his back to the bus for one second, only to be smacked in the face by something heavy and cold. A quick crunch, some hurt and then blackness. At one moment his captor crazily charged through the woods and then Jason felt a gentle rocking in his stomach as if aboard a ship at sea.

His body twisted into an L shape within the box and his legs poked out of the crate the way feathered arrows rest in a quiver. And then with a thunderclap's suddenness, the kidnapper landed on the ground, momentum scrunching Jason into the crate's base, forcing him to cough up whatever sputum remained in his body. He then descended into darkness as whatever it was trundled over rocky earth, leaving clip-clop sounds in its wake.

"Here we are, boy!" A hand wrapped around both of Jason's legs and squeezed with the force of a thousand blood-pressure cuffs.

The thing—not a man, Jason knew it couldn't be—flipped him in the air like a juggling pin and grabbed him by the nape of his neck, bringing his face inches from a maw spewing rancidity and contempt.

"Hold still, boy!"

"Who are you?!" Jason shouted at the unseen face.

"I ask the questions!" Hot spittle splattered onto Jason's head, searing skin as the thing berated him. "Such a pity someone with a name so close to the Master's could be so vile. You disgrace his very existence!"

"What the fuck are you talking about?!"

The thing clutched Jason in one hand and with the other nabbed the boy's right arm, stretching it as if to floss its teeth with the appendage. It bit through the length of the arm, snapping bones as easily as uncooked linguini.

Jason's shriek spooked sleeping bats and sent them darting in all directions. The thing opened its mouth, allowing Jason's limp arm to slide from fangs, making a sloppy sucking sound as flesh dropped from teeth. The thing savored Jason's blood.

"Tasty, boy! Quite tasty. But I have eaten better. Do you wish to keep your other arm?"

"Yes!" Jason cried. His mangled arm swiveled in ways that healthy bodies would never permit.

"Now, you want to be visited by the Master, right?!" He gripped Jason around his ribs with both hands and rattled him with a deranged au pair's zeal. "The Master is most displeased with you, Jason."

"Your master can go fuck himself."

A deafening howl silenced Jason, followed by another round of shaking. His limp arm flapped in the air as if it held no bones. The thing drew Jason close to its mouth.

"Please don't eat me!" Jason weakly thrashed to break its grip.

"Then do not encourage me! The Master's disregard for you seems most warranted. So, you will stew on why you are here, and you will feel me coursing through your wretched body. And you will become sickened. And I cannot wait to see you writhe."

The thing pulled a length of cord from its crate that Jason didn't recall being there. It nimbly tied together Jason's ankles and then twirled the rope around him, knotting the rope by Jason's neck. It then tossed him away like a bagged newspaper on a porch. Jason's cries drowned out the sounds of unfurling parchment and surgical scratching.

"You best sleep for a bit, boy. We will talk later with your little friends. Remember what your Good Book says: 'Death and life are in the power of the tongue'." It kicked Jason in the gut and then sprinted away.

"Jesus, *what* friends?" Jason asked, not expecting an answer.

"I don't know who you are, Jason," Travis Reardon's voice echoed. "But there are three kids in here other than you. And up until you got here, I thought that thing was pissed off at me the most. Do yourself a favor, when it comes back, just keep your mouth shut and try not to piss it off, for all of our sakes."

Chapter Nineteen

"We're getting calls from the newspapers, Chief, both the *Ledger* and the *Record*, whadda we tell 'em?" Patrolwoman Amanda Fryer spoke over the chief's radio as he drove his cruiser from the school to the Flynn home. Kelly's eyes had darted in all directions earlier when he walked from the school to the chief's car. He, Maria and Billy now all rode in the cruiser's rear.

"Good question. Is the prosecutor's office handling the press on this one? Rather, has Vincent Di Renzo insisted upon it?" The chief couldn't veil his disdain for the well-tanned county prosecutor, who wouldn't partake in the Apocalypse unless attired in a thousand-dollar suit. "Most of his guys are probably up here anyway."

"Yeah, their mobile command center's parked in front of the municipal complex."

"Great, the circus is officially in town." The chief realized what needed to be done, and that he and his family would be part of the story.

"Amanda, there's a photograph of Tim in my office on the bookcase. Please scan it for distribution. Call the mayor and get one for Travis, and please contact the parents of Brittany Cabot and Jason Nicholson. Jesus, wait! I don't even think the Nicholsons have been told. Can you send me their number? I'll call. It might be easier coming from me. Contact the Cabots in the meantime and get a headshot of their girl. Use a yearbook if you have to."

"Yessir. So, we can release three identities and hold off on the one until I get the say-so from you?"

"Yes, thank you, Amanda. Remember the phone number. Out."

Billy and the Flynns said nothing. Pleasant discussions seemed impossible.

What if I never see Tim again? the chief thought. *I didn't even get to say goodbye to him this morning. What if I see Tim when he's no longer my boy? You just assume you're going to see your children after you leave them for the day and come home at night. You expect a vibrant, smiling face one minute and then confront the possibility of having to identify someone under a sheet: your dead child. I've been next to parents in the morgue when that sheet's lifted and their knees buckle and they see that final image of their baby before the closed-casket funeral. Life cannot ever be the same.*

The chief met Billy's eyes in the rearview mirror. He regarded his father the way he might while caring for him during his golden years. Anything Billy could do to help his old man, despite their flare-ups, he would.

"He'll be okay, Dad." What else would his father think about? "I know it."

Billy meant it. He'd heard those reassuring phrases before, and his bullshit radar always buzzed when people who meant well insincerely said them to comfort those in need. He hoped his father's bullshit radar knew the difference.

The chief broke his gaze and reminded himself of the three lives in his charge, and he wouldn't fail them.

"Are you kids sure you want to stay at your home?" he asked. "I mean, yes, I can drop you off, but I'd feel much better if there was an adult there. No offense to you, Maria, but you know what I mean."

"I do, Chief. None taken. I can take care of myself and my brother. My parents are on the way home. They both have four-wheel-drive SUVs and are good drivers. I'm guessing we'd be without them for hopefully no more than an hour."

"I'm sure you could, honey, but I'm going to throw caution to the wind on this one. Judgment call. You know Officer Pena, from the high school, right? I'm going to station him in your driveway until your folks get home. You know him. He's a pro."

The chief summoned dispatch to get Pena. As it happened, the officer had remained at the high school making sure the kids left safely, and to keep tabs on students who couldn't go home lest they wait in the snow.

"Are there enough administrators there to replace you?"

"Plenty, and some live close by so they don't mind staying."

"Good, here's the address. See you soon."

The chief disengaged the radio and made a right off of Winchester and then a left into a cul-de-sac to pull into the Flynn's driveway, parking in front of the garage doors.

"Thank you, Chief," Maria said, then nudged Kelly from his stupor.

"Thanks," he whispered without looking up.

"No problem," the chief said. "Maria, I appreciate your offer to let Billy hang with you guys in the meantime, but I'd rather he stay with me. But I want you to call him if you need anything. Billy, give her your number, please, and if you don't mind, Maria, can you give your phone number to him in case we want to check on you?"

"Um—" Billy's stomach became the county fair's Tilt-A-Whirl powered by jet fuel. *That won't be a problem, Dad. Funny you should bring it up because...*

"Sure, that's a good idea, Chief!" She rattled off her number. "Go ahead and enter it into your phone, Billy." It saved him the embarrassment of not having to reveal it was already there. "And what's yours?"

Billy got the idea and tried not to sound defeated when reciting the ten digits.

The chief exited his cruiser and opened the rear door so Maria and Kelly could leave. Billy slipped out to sit next to his dad in the front.

"I hope Tim's all right, Chief. Thanks for taking the time to look after us," she said before turning from the chief to his son. "And I appreciate you helping to make it happen, Billy."

He felt a glimmer of happiness to have assisted. "From both of us, you're welcome," the younger Schweitzer said.

Patrolman Pena's cruiser's lights whirled to a stop as he pulled into the driveway next to the chief.

"Go on and get out of the cold, kids. Billy, climb in." The chief opened the front door for him. "I need to have a word with Officer Pena."

"I'll walk Maria and Kelly inside while you guys talk."

"That'd be nice, Billy." She pleasantly nodded and passed him with her arm around Kelly. Billy followed.

"Interesting day, huh?" he said once the adults were out of earshot.

"Interesting *morning*," she said. "It's not even noon. How are you holding up?"

"I'm worried about Tim, obviously, but also my dad. My mom's probably buggin' out of her gourd right now. She's on her way to the municipal building. That should be a reunion for the ages."

Maria knew his folks were divorced and said nothing.

They ascended the five-step brick stairwell—holding tight to the banister because the steps held two inches of accumulation—leading to the two-story house's front door. Regardless, Billy's foot caught underneath some carelessly tossed, snow-covered sticks on the second step. He nearly toppled into Maria, but braced himself by clenching the railing, ceasing his forward momentum, but not enough to prevent him from inhaling whatever sweet scent emanated from her red hair.

She didn't see the near fall, only Billy catching himself.

He regained his balance and dexterously kicked the wood up to his hand like a skateboard. "You might want to move this." He held it out to her and she cautiously accepted.

"Yikes. I thought I got rid of that. It was on the front porch when I left this morning. Good thing I put the porch light on or I'd have wound up in the bushes." She poked the sticks over his shoulder to the shrubs across from the steps. "I just tossed it onto the lawn but Kelly or my folks must've brought it back."

Kelly lifted his shoulders into an *I don't know* shrug.

"We don't even have a fireplace," she said.

"We do." Billy examined the two-foot-long bundle of freshly snapped birch tightly tied in knots he'd never seen in his life. "Can I see that?"

"Keep it. You probably can use it tonight."

"I suppose, it's just that—" A salt-and-pepper Labradoodle recognized the Flynns and barked down at them from the casement bay window.

"Don't mind Casey, he's just happy we're home. Right, Kelly?" She patted her brother on the back, hoping to prompt some type of conversational exchange. He stared at her as if he were starring in a hostage video. Billy brought his hand to his hoodie pocket, pressing against the paper within it, wanting to show Kelly the photo but knowing nothing but chaos would follow.

She pulled the house keys from her pocketbook and unlocked the front door.

"Go ahead, Kelly. Put on some hot choc—" And he disappeared, shutting the door behind him. Maria let the moment pass. White flakes stuck to Billy's wavy, blond hair and his black hoodie.

"How are you not freezing?" Maria chuckled, not understanding why some boys have no concept of how to dress for the cold. He smiled through it all.

"I'm fine. And all awkwardness aside, you can call me if you need anything—I mean, if your brother needs anything."

Maria reopened the entrance and stood behind the glass storm door.

"Billy, things will only be awkward if you let them be. I don't think they are. Please think about that when you can. Now"—she nudged her head toward the driveway—"go be with your dad and your mom. She'll need you too."

Billy felt the chief and Officer Pena watching him.

"I will," he said, buoyed by her kindness. Tim was right—he always was—about how she'd behave around him. He backed down the first step and held up the bundle of sticks, indicating farewell and thanks.

She waved and closed the door.

Billy ruminated over what she'd said, turned and jogged to the police cruisers.

"Let's go!" he told them and slipped into his dad's car.

Chapter Twenty

"You sure you don't want to drop me off at home?" It was the first time Billy or his father had spoken since departing the Flynns' home as they rode toward the municipal building. "You can still turn around."

"I think your mom would find a way to divorce me again if I left our youngest child home alone on the same day our oldest and only *other* child went missing. No father-of-the-year awards there."

"You divorced her, Dad. She started it."

"We don't need to get into that, Billy. Thanks all the same."

The cruiser's windshield wipers thumped at a furious clip. The snow wasn't blizzard strength yet, but the chief didn't want to risk anything. He knew how to drive in the snow and was making good time.

"Well, that Maria seemed like a nice girl."

Uh-oh, I don't like where this is going. Billy spoke cautiously, "She is."

"Have you considered asking her out on a date?"

As much as I want to throw myself from this police car, that ain't happening. May as well just come clean.

"I did, Dad. She has a boyfriend." He hoped his curtness would compel his dad to talk about anything else.

"Oh." The chief focused on the road, and after a few seconds passed: "*Ohhhhhhhh.* Now I get it.*"

"I hope so. You *were* a detective at some point."

"I'm sorry, Billy. But it doesn't change that she's obviously a very nice young woman. I hope you're not taking it too hard. At least it explains why you've been down in the dumps lately."

"As much as I enjoy talking to my father about my failed fledgling ascent into manhood, can we *please* talk about something else?"

"Of course. You're right. It's none of my beeswax. I guess I wish I could focus my mind on something other than Tim right now, because that's where it keeps wandering."

"That's precisely where it should be, Dad. I'm sick over this too.

But I really believe that wherever he is, he's fine. I mean, healthy. Not hurt. Don't you ever get gut feelings about these things?"

"Yeah, sometimes."

Billy knew his father had seen ghastly things during his time as a municipal policeman. Even Mayberry has car wrecks and worse. Idyllic towns are bullshit. With life comes death, and police officers see more of it than anyone should before retiring. Billy feared his father's gut portended the unspeakable.

"What was that thing you tripped over, slick?" the chief, his turn to switch subjects, asked.

"I'm sorry?"

"You almost took a fall on those stairs back there because of it. You hopped in the car so quick with it I didn't even see what it was."

"Oh! Oh this." Billy had placed the taught bundle on the floor by his legs and now brought it up for a look. "It's firewood, I guess. It was on her doorstep and she said she didn't need it, so— Dad!"

The chief had taken too long a look at the sticks and drifted from the right lane almost over the shoulder. He quickly corrected the wheel. "I'm sorry, Billy! My fault! That's on me!"

The cruiser straightened out. Billy waited a few moments until he could feel the tires consistently spinning safely over the snow. "What the hell's wrong?!"

The chief, both hands gripping the wheel ensuring its steadiness, breathed hard.

"Your left arm isn't hurting, is it?" Billy said. "Do you need to take aspirin?"

Billy caught the chief's manic glances at the object. *He's seen this before.*

"One of those exact same things was on our porch this morning," the chief said. "Exactly the same. *I* almost tripped over it."

Billy maneuvered the bundle in his hands, examining all aspects of it. "Okay. You sure it wasn't something—"

"I scolded you earlier for leaving the firewood on the porch. *That's* what I was talking about. And no, it's not something else. It was tied up with the exact same rope."

Billy ran his finger over the smooth brown braids. He didn't know much about rope—really, who does? It was old, nothing like the hardware store's bright-yellow rope that's unnaturally slick to the touch.

"I mean, except for the rope, there's nothing that unusual about it, I think," Billy said. "The wood looks fresh cut. I don't know what kind."

"It's birch." The chief timed his glimpses from the road to the sticks every five seconds. "I gathered that stuff for kindling all the time when I was a kid. You see how its bark is white?"

"I'll take your word for it."

"Those aren't just a bunch of twigs thrown together," the chief said. "They're almost the same length. You can see how they've been cut—torn from the tree, by the looks of them, and whittled at the ends. It took time to do that."

The chief pushed the button on his steering wheel to activate his Bluetooth phone and voice commanded the number he wanted dialed.

The phone rang. Billy hushed and took out the papers folded in his hoodie pocket.

"Hello?" answered a hesitant voice expecting terrible news.

"Paul, it's Don."

"Jesus Christ, have you found them?" Mayor Paul Reardon had stayed at home, per the chief's request, in case someone phoned with a ransom demand for Travis.

"No, I wish that's why I was calling. A third boy went missing not long ago. But that's not why I'm calling, either. This is going to sound odd but did you find anything out of the ordinary on your front porch this morning?"

"I'm sorry?"

"Paul, go to your front doorstep and just tell me if there's anything there that shouldn't be."

"Just hang on."

The chief heard the phone smacked down on what he assumed was a table. Billy mouthed, *He's pretty mad,* and grimaced.

"So am I," the chief replied.

Paul picked up. "Two yellow-bagged phone books. Who the hell uses them anymore? Waste of money and trees. Is that what this is all about?"

"No. You keep firewood on your porch?"

"Christ, Don, *no.* We use a gas fireplace! I don't—"

"Listen to me!" The policeman's voice shut the mayor down. "We're both going through the same thing here, and I know this might sound

90

like bullshit to you, but it's not. I need you to go back outside and scour your front porch for a bundle of tied-up sticks. They'd be no longer than a few feet. Don't question. Please look."

No words, only a louder smack. He returned in less than ten seconds.

"Okay, what about them?" Paul said.

"It's tied on both ends by worn threads?"

"Why does it matter, Don?"

The chief explained where the other two were found.

"And you think there's one of these things on the Cabots' porch, and whoever else's?"

"I do. I don't know why just yet, but it means something. Please put it aside, just in case there are prints on it. I'll have someone pick it up. Can your wife wait by the phone? I'd like you to meet me at the municipal building. Prosecutor's already there. Maybe we can better marshal our resources."

"Yeah, she can stay. And I'll put this thing in a garbage bag and bring it with me, okay?"

Billy pocketed the computer printouts while his father concluded the call. He expected the chief to say something but the old man kept pensive.

"Dad?"

"Yeah?" The chief watched the road, half hearing his son, half lost in his own world.

"Back before we left the bus crash, you went up and looked at that bear, right?"

"Yes."

"Right before you came down the hill and we took off, you were looking at something in the ground, on the other side of the road from where the bear wound up dead."

"That's right."

"You were looking at hoofprints." Billy didn't ask. He knew the answer.

Chapter Twenty-One

Casey, the Flynn family Labradoodle, panted expectantly before Maria. Pena, who stood next to her after being let inside, held out his hand to Casey's nose. It sniffed and allowed the officer to pet him.

"He kinda looks like a lion, an emaciated lion, actually," Pena observed.

"Nah, he's healthy. There was a woman in Florida who deliberately groomed her Labradoodle to look like a lion. She let it outside and people called the cops thinking a lion had escaped from the zoo. He hasn't had a chance to do his business in a while, so if you'll excuse me."

Maria patted her leg to get the dog's attention. "Come on, Casey, out we go." The dog followed her to the kitchen. She slid open the door leading to the deck, allowing Casey to slip into the snowstorm.

"You sure you don't want any water, Officer Pena? We have a Brita, nothing but the best at the Flynn house. Or we have soda and iced tea?" she called from the kitchen to the officer who paced behind the front door, moving the frilly curtains to peek outside every few minutes.

"Sure, Maria, water would be nice."

"For once! Thank you! You ever notice that when you offer a drink to someone who you didn't expect to be in your house, they always say no? Like it would be too much of a hassle, when it only takes about ten seconds? I make it a point to accept a drink—it could be seawater, I don't care—whenever one's offered to me. It's a habit of mine. Weird, I know."

He heard the clink of the ice cubes in the glass and the slow pour. She brought him the drink with a smile.

"I'm happy to have destroyed your stereotype." He gave her a head nod of thanks as he took the glass. "How's your brother?"

"Preoccupied, which is good. He's in the family room, watching *Phineas and Ferb*." She gestured to the room to their left, from which came sounds of preteen squawking and maniacal screams of "Curse you, Perry the Platypus!".

"That's a funny show. I'm an adult. I watch. I'm not afraid to admit it."

Kelly was curled into a ball on the couch, watching the flatscreen television hanging on the wall in front of him. The cartoon flashed in his eyes like Morse code signals. Pena and Maria doubted the unsmiling, almost-unblinking boy registered anything.

Pena's smile faded after seeing the girl's concern. "Maria, how is he?"

"He's scared out of his mind. I just want my parents to get home. Maybe he'll cheer up when they get here."

Pena checked his watch: 12:30 p.m.

"You heard from either of them recently?"

"About an hour ago. Traffic's slow on Route 78. Honestly, I think Kelly's holding it together because you're here. Do you want to take your coat off?"

Pena wiped the residual snow off his heavy leather jacket. "I'm fine. I'm pretty comfortable, actually. I'll just hang by the door, if you don't mind."

The loud thump against the thick-glass deck door drew their attention down the hallway. Then the rapid-fire barking, *Arf-arf-arf-arf! Arf-arf-arf-arf!*

"I guess Casey's done," Maria's reticence made it sound like a question.

Arf-arf-arf-arf! Arf-arf-arf-arf!

"Usually he sits against the door until we notice him."

Arf-arf-arf-arf! Arf-arf-arf-arf! The dog's yelps came across as screams.

Thump!

She sped into the kitchen with Pena to see Casey ramming his head into the glass door.

Thump!

Casey stumbled back and peered wide-eyed to his right. He couldn't build much momentum due to the deck's limiting confines. Regardless, he launched himself full bore into the barrier. He wanted in.

Thump!

Arf-arf-arf-arf! Arf-arf-arf-arf!

He reared on his hind legs, standing almost as tall as Maria, doggy-paddling his front paws against the glass door as if swimming for his life.

"Casey, hold your horses!" Maria scurried to pull the door handle sideways.

Arf-arf-arf-arf!

Her eyes met Casey's desperate gaze. She yanked and the dog squeezed through the entrance like Plastic Man. He practically ran in place, toenails clattering on laminate flooring, and caught his footing to scramble out of the kitchen.

"Please step aside," Pena said.

Maria pulled the door open. Snow found its way through as Pena zipped up his coat and ventured outside.

The house's rear, like almost any other Hancock dwelling, faced a maze of trees. Log fencing with wire mesh outlined the half-acre-backyard's perimeter. The deck stood bare, save for the circular table— the four chairs, grill and umbrella were all housed in the backyard storage shed for the winter.

Pena descended the eight feet of steps and ducked underneath the deck to see if anything had taken shelter. He kept his right hand on his still-holstered service pistol. Nothing but an old push lawnmower without the bag.

He'd never seen a dog frightened like that.

A few fir trees and maples stood at opposite ends of the backyard. Its vacant middle begged to have volleyball played there. By now, the snow had layered the ground with three inches. Pena, his eyes squinting through whipping snow, followed Casey's prints and small crevices of urine-stained snow from the deck stairs to the rear of the yard. Save for the dog's feet and his, nothing had crossed the premises. Pena looked beyond the fencing into the gauntlet of crooked trees and snow-covered pines.

Squinting as snow stung his eyes, he turned his head from side to side with robotic precision to catch anything unordinary. He inhaled cold air through his mouth, puffing out steam, waiting for the eerie serenity to break.

That dog ran from something out there, Pena thought.

Pena turned to face Maria, who was watching him through the glass door. Kelly, a brown chenille blanket draped around his shoulders like a cape, stood by her side. Pena shrugged his shoulders and raised his hands to signal he couldn't see anything.

A Douglas fir worthy of Rockefeller Center and standing thirty feet from Pena behind the fencing began to shuffle, so much so that Kelly and Maria, even from their distance away, turned their attention from Pena to it. He followed their lead. Snow began falling from the fir's higher branches to the ones below, triggering a massive cascade.

Pena heard clinking and then saw a thick black chain plummet to earth with a thud, sending snow plumes aloft. He stepped backward, his eyes following seven grounded fat links connected to ones dangling skyward into the pine branches, as if a sickly umbilical cord led to an ungodly newborn. Pena drew his weapon. Maria and Kelly pressed their faces to the glass.

The chain snapped back, its links vanishing into the forest, only to rocket forth like a striking asp, the two front links smashing into Pena's face, dropping him like a marionette freed from its strings.

It leapt from the fir's midsection, through the air, roaring, *screaming* its presence, and trembled the earth when it landed in a squat in the backyard. The black chain, gripped in the thing's right hand, crashed around the creature in a perfect circle. It drew its darkened eyes upward to devour the glorious image of two children screaming behind thick glass.

Chapter Twenty-Two

"Kelly, listen to me!" Maria shook her brother to distract him from the creature plodding toward their home. "Get your sneakers on right now!" She pushed him into the family room where he'd taken them off.

It's toying with us, she thought. *It's grinning! That thing's enjoying this!* It was eight feet tall, maybe nine, even taller when considering the two twisted horns that reached from its skull as if trying to escape hell.

The creature turned his back to Maria and descended on Pena's body.

Anger overcame her as she ripped open the glass door. "Leave him alone, you bastard!"

It disregarded her and knelt over Pena, obscuring its deeds from Maria.

I can't watch this! Please, God, may he not suffer.

Maria locked the deck door and ran into the family room where Kelly had finished lacing his sneakers. "Kelly, it's gonna come inside! Pay attention! Look at me!" He did, shaking his head yes. She spoke calmly but forcefully, "I need you to go to the basement. Stand by the back door. Don't open it until you hear it enter the house. When it does, run to Officer Pena, find the keys to his police car and then meet me by his car, crawl underneath it and don't come out until you see me. You understand?"

He squeaked out a yes.

"Get your coat!"

He grabbed the winter coat he'd tossed on the family room's rocking chair when he got home and bounded down a stairwell leading to the basement. Maria was ready to roll. She hadn't removed her shoes and ran to the kitchen to get the coat she'd draped on one of the chairs. Nothing in her house could be used to fend off whatever was coming. Even so, she wanted to wield something in case she had to go down fighting.

She ran to the hallway closet by the front door and pushed aside musty coats and shoes without matches, until finding her aluminum softball bat. She let it rest on her shoulder like a rifle, hoping to God she could summon strength when the time came to swing it.

Methodical plodding ascended wooden steps.

It finished off Pena, she thought as she squeezed the bat's handle, and then turned toward the kitchen. *Okay, come and get me.*

Kelly was all that mattered now.

A sharp talon sliced across glass to raise every hair on her body.

She entered the kitchen to see the hulking thing looming outside.

It stepped back and stooped so it could see inside. Its strength was no match for the locked door. The beast effortlessly slid it open, ripping from the frame the turn lock still fastened to the now-detached latch, letting in a gush of Arctic air that whooshed around Maria's body.

Kelly, please tell me you heard that. The thing obscured any view of Kelly running to Pena.

She believed in God, celebrated Mass regularly and ate the Host with reverence. The unfathomable presence of this giant in her kitchen bolstered her belief that Jesus Christ was her Savior, for if something like this abomination lives, then He *must* exist. But Jesus came second to her brother.

"Brave of you, girl, but I'm not here for you." It crept halfway into the spotless white kitchen, making the full-sized refrigerator look like one that might be seen in Maria's college dorm room if she survived to attend. The thing dropped the chain and retrieved a neatly tied scroll of parchment from the pouch on its crate. It plucked loose the twine allowing the list of names to drop and unroll across the kitchen floor, eventually stopping where Maria stood.

Kelly Flynn—her brother's name, calligraphically inked in black, was the last full name she saw among countless more still wound in the scroll.

She stared at the name while simultaneously hearing, "Surely you know why I have come to collect him. Little boys these days, so much more insolent than from bygone ages. You are watchful of him, but not enough. However, you can be forgiven. It is hard to be everywhere at once to correct his behavior."

Hitting the creature with the softball bat would be about as effective as using a pool noodle, she thought, and then ran her fingers up her unzipped coat to retrieve the necklace pendant tucked underneath her shirt. She held out the small crucifix and walked toward the monster.

"Get out of my house!" she screamed.

Amused, the creature fully entered the kitchen, Maria for the first time seeing a swaying lionlike tail that the monster used for balance. The thing dominated the kitchen and resorted to hunching because standing erect would send its horns through the ceiling.

"Flattering, girl, but do I *look* like a vampire to you?" It drew the unfurled parchment toward its body. Maria saw Kelly's name sliding across the floor. "I was out in daylight before and did not go *poof* into dust. That should have been your first clue. And I did not need to ask for your invitation to enter your lovely dwelling, now did I? So why you think some trinket of Christ would repel me is a bit confusing to me. Ah, but where I do have something in common with the vampire is this—I enjoy blood."

It disgorged its wormlike, forked tongue and he drew a talon down it, letting the blood flow. It dabbed a pointy nail in the fluid and scratched through Kelly's name before retying and stowing the scroll.

"Now, has your brother successfully reached the police officer outside?"

Maria's face sunk.

"I have been doing this long enough to know when someone is scheming to flee. You know you cannot outrun me, so you did not even try. And I respect that. But you think you can escape me inside one of those wheeled horses with the twinkling lights. I understand your brother needs to get that special treat from the policeman's pocket that you apparently feed to the horse to get it to run!

"My how things have changed over the years! Horses were so much simpler back then. I liked it better when you rode on them and they could breathe. And they were tastier.

"And yet, some things have not changed at all. You split up, try to distract me, hoping to gain the advantage. But here I am, and you do not want to see what happened to the other children who thought they could run."

It brought up the index finger and twirled it like a centrifuge. Maria realized the small object orbiting the creature's talon was Pena's key chain, and the means of her escape.

"We shall go find your brother now, ja?"

Bang!

The creature grunted and lurched forward.

A succession of loud claps followed, bringing the thing to its knees.

Kelly stood in the broken doorframe behind the beast. Tearfully, he aimed Officer Pena's gun at the creature's head and emptied the clip of bullets. The monster fell forward, its hand flying forth and sending the keys across the kitchen and hitting the wall next to Maria. The beast landed facedown, its horns penetrating the wall in front of it. She snatched the keys.

"Kelly, come on!"

The boy dropped the gun, and the pair sprinted out the front door and climbed into Pena's cruiser. Maria had completed three of her six driving lessons and knew the basics. She started the car and nervously waved her hands over the wheel, getting a feel for the gearshift, while finding the brake and gas pedals with her foot.

"Maria, it's got him!" Kelly pointed to the casement bay window where they were being watched.

The creature tauntingly waved at them with one hand and with the other brought up a writhing Casey.

"I thought I killed it!" Kelly screamed.

The monster's eyes glowered. It howled at the two kids, fogging the window. It waved the pane clear so they could see it shove Casey face-first into its mouth and chomp off his head like the top quarter of a Snickers bar. It chewed with relish.

Kelly's earsplitting screams matched the tires squealing as Maria pulled the gearshift into Reverse and fed the cruiser too much gas, launching it out of the driveway and across the road. The rear wheels hit and rode over the sidewalk on the opposite side of the street as the car's undercarriage ground against the curb's lip. The kids' bodies flopped forward and back before the vehicle stalled.

Maria and Kelly gasped as they got their bearings.

"Your seat belt better be on," she told Kelly while turning the key, but the cruiser responded only with clicks.

"Start it!" Kelly pulled his seat belt strap across his shoulder but refrained from buckling.

"I'm trying, it won't turn over!"

Kelly had none of it. He let loose the strap which zipped back into place and he opened the door and ran.

"Kelly, no! He'll catch you! It's what he wants!"

The frightened boy refused to become a canned sardine, knowing that the monster could easily rip off the cruiser's roof. He ran through the snow, at times slipping and catching his balance, toward the home of Claire Price, their elderly neighbor on whose yard a police cruiser now rested.

"Mrs. Price! Please open the door!" Kelly yanked open the storm door and hammered his fist against the wooden front door. He turned and could not see the creature. He pounded the door, causing the metal door-knocker handle to flap and clank with each hit. Dollops of powdery snow shifted from the roof, falling onto him, sneaking into his collar onto flesh. He ignored the cold and continued the racket.

Maria abandoned the cruiser and ran halfway up the yard before stopping.

Kelly spotted her peripherally and turned to wave her to his side.

Clumps of snow plummeted and stained Kelly white. He ceased his attack on the door and still the snow drenched him.

Maria's fear registered upward.

Kelly snapped his head up and was greeted by enormous animal hooves dangling above him, as if the thing was lollygagging on the edge of a dock. Those hooves, Kelly thought, chipped and frayed around the edges from traversing inhospitable, long-forgotten lands.

And then it poked its head over its hooves, looking at the little guppy it was preparing to hook. It dropped the black chain on top of Kelly, the front few links striking the top of the boy's head, knocking him down.

The thing pushed itself off the rooftop, bringing with it an avalanche of snow, and crushed the ground between Maria and Kelly, facing the dazed boy.

Maria charged, trying to protect her brother, but the thing anticipated the move, swinging its right arm without looking, backhandedly smacking her face. She landed flat on her back.

"Time to go, boy." It plopped Kelly in the wooden bin and then ran toward the road, past Maria. She flopped on her belly to see her brother, his little fingers gripping the top edge of the crate, his head peeking out, screaming for his sister until his cries died in the forest.

Chapter Twenty-Three

The Hancock municipal building, like most on the planet, posted placards above office doors, denoting, among others, the sewer department, building inspector and clerk. The hard carpets were colored the same shade as the walls: bureaucratic gray, the Crayola of choice for children of public servants.

But today the building buzzed not with residents seeking variances or permits, but with terrified parents. Mayor Paul Reardon, whose wife was keeping vigil over the home phone in case the ransom call came, arrived first. Reardon graciously accepted all the warm regards from the staffers who'd gotten to know him over his two terms. He conferred with the prosecutor and then secluded himself in his office after learning nothing new had transpired.

Brittany Cabot's sunken-eyed parents arrived next. The mother, a young, trim blonde like her daughter, gave birth to her when she was twenty years old, making her a MILF in the eyes of the boys who'd sell their souls for five minutes in the sack with her daughter. Brittany's dad, a big man who worked at the rock quarry one town over, had shaggy, brown hair and a few days' growth on his chin. He resembled his daughter's missing boyfriend: a high school football player with seemingly limitless physical potential. If only his Achilles hadn't snapped during his first college game, perhaps he wouldn't have been stuck in the quarry for two decades. The Cabots sat with detectives in one of the meeting rooms.

Jason Nicholson's father met with police in the building's kitchen area. The municipal worker bees knew not to interrupt. A man in his late forties with thinning black hair, wire-rimmed glasses and a hot temper, he could be heard down the hallway asking what the hell were police doing to find his son.

Newspaper reporters from the *Daily Record*, *Sussex Herald* and the Newark *Star-Ledger* loitered in the lobby, seeking comments from distraught adults who scurried into the building. The journalists, a slovenly bunch sporting sneakers, stubble and girth, who ran the age gamut but not a fifteen-minute mile among the lot of them, knew something was up. Social media rumors had spread word of three disappearances, and now a fourth one began making the rounds on Facebook and Twitter, but those weren't official sources, as much as the media wanted them to be.

"Is it true, Chief?! Can you confirm Tim was in an accident?"

"No comment. The prosecutor will have a statement."

"Mayor, is your boy missing?"

"Not now. I'll have something to say later."

"Mrs. Cabot, has Brittany disappeared?"

"Have some class, fellas," Mr. Cabot said.

"Mr. Nicholson, what can you tell us about Jason?"

"Fuck off, every goddamn one of you."

Photographers fired their digital cameras like machine guns. It was all part of the job and the officials tolerated it. They felt the pitying stares from the cadre of low-level bureaucrats scuttling papers from here to there. Soon the press would get what it craved: a carefully controlled show.

Vincent Di Renzo, the county prosecutor, directed Captain Patrick Todd, his chief of investigations, to set up the podium in front of the municipal council's dais, which also served as Hancock's judicial chambers during the day.

"American flags flanking each side of the podium, but toward the back, and leave enough room for the lineup of officials behind me. You know the drill," Di Renzo said. "The police chief and the mayor will be directly to my left and right. They're the faces of this disaster, well, after the missing kids. Are the damn networks anywhere near here?"

Chief Donald Schweitzer stood in the back of the chambers, slouched against the wall, shaking his head at the pre-preening.

"Are the printouts ready? Or are we still waiting on that Jason kid's parents for his photo?" Di Renzo spotted the chief. "Hey, Don, when did you call them?"

"About an hour ago, after I dropped off the Flynn boy. The mother emailed me the photo. The dad's here. Your guys are putting it all together now."

"You get the photo of your boy back?"

"Yes, thank you."

"Good." He then addressed Captain Todd, "Have our own video

camera placed on the table in front of the podium. And make sure you remember to hit the Record button this time. It's not hard to do."

Todd gave a *yes, master* head bob and continued his monkey work.

Billy Schweitzer entered the chambers to check on his father.

"How are you doing?" The chief asked before the boy got a word out.

"I just answered a bunch of questions about Tim for one of those detectives. I can't see how any of it's going to help."

"You'd be surprised. Sometimes the littlest detail can lead to the big break."

"Are you going to talk to them?"

"I was answering the same questions when you were, just with a different guy. I finished up a few minutes ago. The mayor went through the same thing. Now we're just waiting for the dog-and-pony show to start." The chief nodded in the direction of the media choreography.

"A couple of the newspapers already sent people," he continued. "They're just waiting on all that matters now: television cameras that will drench the New York market. I think someone's angling for a judgeship when his term expires." He smirked while watching Di Renzo adjust his tie and smooth his hair in his reflection on the framed George Washington portrait.

"There you are! Billy, your father and I need to talk." Diana Applewood, who'd dropped the Schweitzer name after the divorce, regarded her ex-husband with her typical disdain. She dusted the snow off her mink coat and long black hair.

"Oh good, your mother's here. Let's not fight in full view of the prosecutor and his merry men. Follow me to my office so she can hang up that dead animal she's wearing, which I'm sure was another wonderful token of love from that hedge-fund guy. Oh, and please at least express your concern to Billy."

She grabbed her son—they were the same height—and pulled him close. "Thank goodness your father didn't lose you too."

"Diana—" the chief tried before Billy defended him.

"Mom, Dad didn't *lose* anyone."

"Of course, take his side as usual." She said it loud enough so that the prosecutor and Todd paid attention to them. "But I am glad to see you, and that you're safe, honey." She pecked the top of his head, and drew him closer again, genuinely hugging him.

"You know that girl you like, Billy?" the chief said. "At one point I felt the same way about your mother. Be forewarned that *this* can happen to you."

"Billy, you didn't tell me you have a girlfriend."

"I don't! Can you please both control yourselves?"

Diana realized the imprudence of creating a scene and changed course. "Anything on Tim?"

The chief told her what he couldn't say publicly. She kept her mouth shut.

"It's like they disappeared off the planet," he continued. "We've got recruits from the Academy and volunteers helping our guys comb the woods and haven't kicked up a thing at any of the abduction sites. And the goddamn snow isn't helping."

"Why aren't you out there? He's your son too, you know. And how can you be so calm?"

The chief closed his eyes before reengaging with a growl. "You think I don't know that? I'd give anything to be in those woods right now, but the prosecutor over there wants me here as a prop for his press conference. I sort of have a conflict in investigating my own son's disappearance, which is bullshit because I had—" he pointed to Billy, "—*we* had nothing to do with this. I'm doing what I can to help coordinate the other investigations, assigning resources. Would I be out there if I could? Hell yes! And I still hope to.

"And then there's this guy." Again, he motioned to Billy. "I can't let him out of my sight. And as for my emotions, I *have* to be calm. What kind of example would I, the fucking *police chief*, be setting for these parents if I was pacing around the building, all *woe is me*, looking as if I'm about to lose my shit?

"I've got to show strength! Someone has to tell them, both in words and appearance, that they shouldn't lose hope, and they goddamn well *shouldn't!*"

Diana digested it all.

"I believe you, Don." She caressed her boy's back as a tear slid down her cheek. "And you're right. Keep this little bugger where we both can see him."

"Why don't we go into my office? You can say whatever you want to me there."

"No. I'm not at my breakdown point yet." Diana sidled up to Billy. "Nobody's threatened you, contacted you over the phone or the Internet and harassed you?"

"Like I told the detective, Mom, no. Absolutely nothing like that has happened to me, and I doubt it happened to Tim."

"Then *why*?"

"That's what a bunch of policemen are trying to figure out, dear." The chief called her "dear" out of habit, with nothing sentimental attached.

Billy's phone vibrated in his hoodie pocket. He identified Maria's number and his pulse raced. He ducked away from the powder keg that was his parents having a conversation.

"You've got to calm down! I can't understand a word!" He kept his voice low as he paced the corridor, and she explained everything.

"Maria, can you log on to the Internet somehow?"

"Why?"

"Just do it."

"Okay, give me a second," she replied in a shaky voice. "I have to look it up on my phone. I'll call you back if we get disconnected, but I should be able to talk and browse at the same time."

"Log on to Google when you can." He waited until she acknowledged she was online.

"What am I looking for?"

"Do an image search for Krampus." He spelled it for her and tensely waited for an array of images to load.

"That's it." Her voice expressed disbelief and certainty. "I mean, it's not the exact same one but it's—Billy, *what* is it?"

"I'm still trying to figure it out, myself. But, look, are you in your house?"

"I'm at my neighbor's house." She gave him Claire Price's address. "Right across the street. I didn't want to go back inside and see whatever was left of Casey. Holy crap! Officer Pena! I'm not even sure if he's dead. Jesus, he's been lying out in the snow all this time."

"Go check on him, I'll tell my dad."

Billy ended the call and ran to the chambers. He told his father the basics. He wasn't sure how to explain the monster, so he didn't, only that Kelly was gone, Pena was down and Maria had seen it all.

News crews from the ABC and CBS affiliates walked into the

municipal building for the 1:30 p.m. media brief. They had twenty minutes to spare. The prosecutor directed them where to set up.

"Sorry, Di Renzo, the presser's going to have to wait or you'll have to have it without me. I've gotta go. Have one of your guys follow me."

The chief, not thinking, said it loud enough for the reporters to hear. They snuck out to their cars without trying to make it look too obvious.

"But what about my press conference?" the prosecutor said. "This is really disappointing."

An ambulance and three cruisers, including the chief's with Billy tagging along, roared down Winchester.

Chapter Twenty-Four

"Officer Pena! Can you hear me?!" Maria shook the officer, whose face was buried sideways in the snow. Most importantly, he was alive. His slow breathing had cleared enough snow for him to have airflow. His body rose slowly with each breath.

Maria tried dragging him but the body was too heavy, and she realized his neck or back could be broken and that moving him could worsen things. She crouched into a ball and hugged her knees together.

"I thought that thing was going to kill you. Keep breathing." She didn't know what else to do other than try to comfort him. The snow absorbed the blood that flowed from the head wound made by the chain.

Why didn't it kill him? It could have stomped and split open his head like a pumpkin when it took his keys.

"He let you live," she told Pena's unconscious body. "He let *me* live." It dawned on her for the first time. She stood and paced backward, heeding Billy's caution to not walk where the creature had been.

Captain Jim Sherwood, who had been looking for evidence at the bus crash, arrived first and rushed to help his fallen comrade. The officer brought a first aid kit and stabilized his neck with a padded brace after finding a pulse. He gingerly brushed the snow off Pena's body.

"Who did this? You'll need to tell us so we can put out a BOLO," he said to Maria, referring to a be-on-the-lookout alert, while focusing on Pena. "Come on, who did this?" He turned to see Maria running from her yard to Claire Price's house.

She wanted to be away from her home and didn't know how she'd ever be able to go back inside.

Mrs. Price, a matronly woman in her eighties, let her in and handed her a hot cup of cocoa. Maria sat on a couch within a family room that carried the musty odor that lingers within all homes of the elderly. She sipped her cocoa for ten minutes as Mrs. Price sat with her. Maria's eyes focused on black-and-white photos of Price's family members framed in faux gold, until the police cars arrived, reinvigorating her.

She ran outside and found the cruiser with Billy and the chief.

"I was on my back in the snow. It ran right by me." She grabbed Billy's arms and excitedly blurted the rest, "It could've snapped my neck easy as pie. Just as easily as it could've killed Kelly. But it *didn't*. It wants them alive! That means Tim is alive too. They all are!"

"All right, hold on," the chief intervened and spoke to Maria before Billy could respond. "Don't get ahead of yourself. I need to check on Officer Pena and then you and I are going to have a talk about who did this."

"Not who, Chief," she said. "It's a what."

Chapter Twenty-Five

How does it light the candles? Tim thought. *Something with fingers the size of kielbasas can't flick a BIC or fidget with a flipbook of matches.*

Somehow, ember pinpricks evolved on wicks into solitary flames and lifted the room from darkness.

Tim thought the thing whimpered as it summoned flame, but then saw hovering above the crate two beady eyes reflecting fright in the firelight.

"Now, boy, we can do this one of two ways," it spoke in a raised voice, and Kelly's whimpers ceased. "That is better. Now, as I was saying, I can tie you up like the squealing piglet you are." The creature shambled around the cavern, collecting its captives to huddle them together before the wall of candles. "Just look at your friends gathered down there."

Kelly saw the beaten, roped bodies of Travis Reardon and Jason Nicholson, and the unscathed but still bound Tim Schweitzer and Brittany Cabot. He knew none of them, only that they'd all suffered under the thing's oppression. He gasped upon seeing skulls illuminated by candlelight.

"Or, and I think you would much prefer this, Mr. Flynn, I can take you out of there and you can freely sit on the ground like a good boy." It then prompted the boy. "Well, answer, please!"

"I'll be good," Kelly squeaked.

"I thought you might. Hold on!" It reached into the crate and pinched Kelly's winter coat between its forefinger and thumb and popped him out like a Kleenex. It placed him on the floor between Tim and Brittany. Travis flanked Brittany while Jason slumped next to Tim.

Kelly looked up, his eye-line barely reached midway up the thing's hairy shins. Candles unevenly glowed around the cave, leaving pockets of darkness hiding skeletons of things human and not.

"A warning, boy. You could try to get up and run, but trust me when I say that if you attempt to slip by me, the only thing left of you will be your bat-chewed skeleton crawling for sunlight that you will never find. Look around and see what became of the ones who did not listen. So stay put, ja?"

The remains littering the cave ensured Kelly's cooperation.

"Do as it says," Tim whispered to Kelly, and then refocused on the creature. He was taken, as they all were, by its size, but also by the height and breadth of the cave. Tim couldn't see the cave's ceiling. For all he knew, it was either flat or dripping with stalactites. Tim guessed stalactites, if for no other reason than the creature probably would enjoy tossing bodies skyward, hoping they'd stick.

"Yes, listen to the smart boy," it said. "I will deal with him last. Now, as for the rest of you..." The creature, standing before the kids who formed a semicircle around it, stroked its chin with one hand and performed an "Eeny, meeny, miny, moe" with its other.

Four sets of eyes followed its halted finger, and then to the kid on its receiving end.

"It fuckin' figures," groaned Jason Nicholson, his face sweaty with a cadaverous pallor. His head dipped back and forth with each labored breath.

"You must be burning up, right, boy? That bite must look like vultures picked over it by now." It reached into its crate and approached Jason. "You are weak. You cannot fight back."

"Please don't beat me!" Jason screamed.

"Beat you? Oh, you thought I was reaching for—you silly boy. No, no. I am not going to beat you yet. I am simply hungry and I imagine you are too. Would you like a bite?" It yanked out Casey's half-eaten body, extending toward Jason a mangled mix of ribs and intestines. Kelly's eyes rolled into his skull and he tipped sideways onto Brittany's lap.

"What the hell is that?!" she screamed.

"What, not hungry?" The thing jiggled the offal under Jason's nose.

"I'll pass." Jason didn't have the strength to feel repulsed.

"All the more for me, then!" The creature snapped back the body and in four bone-crunching bites devoured Casey: midsection, hips, meaty thighs and paws down to the toenails. It pumped its fist to its chest and belched, and then wiped its gooey fingers against its fur before picking up Kelly's languid body. It tugged more rope from its crate and spool-wound Kelly.

"You said he could remain untied," Tim carefully stated.

"I suppose I did. Prudence would dictate I not leave him unbound the next time I take leave of you. After all, we would not want him trying to untie any of you, which I am certain you would encourage him to do. I figure the child's had quite a day, and to bind him while he was awake in this place might be a little much for him to take, ja?"

"I thought you didn't care about things like that," Tim continued. "I mean, Travis and this guy next to me have had quite a day too. And you don't seem to be as considerate with them."

"That is one way of looking at it, boy." The creature placed Kelly's knotted body back in between Tim and Brittany. "Another way of looking at it is that I am letting the child feel a little more at ease by presenting palatable options, lulling him into a false sense of security. And then, when he thinks you all will be receiving the brunt of my wrath, I punish him worse than any of you."

"He's just a kid! You're going to torture a little boy?!" Tim thought his outburst would result in his first whipping.

"Torture? Admittedly, my methods differ depending on the child and the circumstances that brought me into that young one's life. But let me put it into terms that you might better relate to. Some of your people consider something called 'waterboarding' torture. Now, I do not know what this waterboarding is—I imagine it consists of a bucket of water and wooden planks of some kind—but I am still not quite certain how you torture someone with a wet stick. Well, actually..." the thing contemplated the possibilities, almost losing its train of thought, "...never mind that. My point is that your definition of torture might be my definition of motivation. But there are differences between the two. One tortures another to extract information. One motivates others to better understand information already available to them, and react to it."

"You'll have to forgive me, but..."

The thing finished Tim's thought: "You do not understand me."

"Not at all."

The thing groaned as it squatted in front of Tim, who pushed himself against the stone as the thing's hairy knees brushed by his cheeks.

"Boy, I believe you will understand by nightfall, if not a bit later. It has yet to play out the way I think it will. I still think there is hope for you, Mr. Schweitzer. I know what your plans were. And maybe they

111

continue to slink around in that sick mind of yours."

"Wait, *I'm* the one with the sick mind? You're the one who tied up and flogged a defenseless kid!" Tim recalled the old adage about never getting into a shouting match with a fool.

"Do not question me! And yes, your mind is polluted! It is probably the dirtiest among you all! You think cowardly and selfish thoughts. I should pop off your head like a dandelion simply for thinking them. I will indeed save you for last."

"What are you—"

The thing sprang backward, landing on its hooves with a thud that silenced all sound and thought, and stood before Jason.

"And now I will beat you."

Jason had no time to react. The creature snatched the switch from its sheath and swung into Jason's right side, his bad side, where he was certain his arm was becoming gangrenous.

He screamed for his life, screamed to pass out to end the pain, screamed for mercy. "Stop! Stop! *Please* stooooooooop!"

"Stop? But you did not stop? So why should I?"

"What the fuck are—" Jason bit his lip, knowing not to question it. "I don't understand you!"

"How can you be so ignorant to the fact that the pain you feel is the pain you cause?" It again whacked the boy. The rope barely absorbed the blow, not enough to prevent Jason's humerus from breaking.

The snap clattered around the cavern, causing the conscious occupants to groan in unison, *"Ugh!"*

It stopped and grinned. "Tell me, boy, what does it feel like to be so small, so weak, so unable to fight back against something so unprovoked? Answer!"

Jason gasped, reeling from the pain. "It hurts!"

"Of course it hurts! But you surely knew that when you were doling out the pain and you disregarded it! So why did you keep doing it?!"

"I don't know!"

"Oh, 'I don't know'?" It reared back and swatted. Jason's body convulsed. "Ha! 'I don't know' is a child's most transparent lie! You know very well why you cause pain to others. Because it makes you feel good! You experience tyrannical power that masks your insecurity.

112

The Dark Servant

You lust for power over insecurity every moment of your pathetic life, so you attempt to satiate it by inflicting more pain! Well, now who is the tyrant, boy?! But the good news for you is you still have a chance for the Master to visit!"

"The master? I'm not a Satanist! I'm not some devil worshipper like you!"

"Satan? The *devil*?!" The thing crushed Jason's side with the switch, launching his body onto Tim, who tried scooting sideways to escape. "How dare you insult the Master! Does Satan ever visit you?"

"What?"

Whack!

"Ow! No! Satan never visits me!"

"Then why would Satan start visiting you now! Has there been some offer to sell your soul to Satan? I have not heard of one. This has nothing to do with Satan. Do you not want my Master to visit you?! Answer, boy! Yes or no!"

"What?!"

"Not what! The Master is a who!"

"Okay! Who?"

"My Master, Nikolaos of Myra! Saint Nicholas! Santa Claus!"

"*Who?!*"

Jason's last question unleashed the monster's full fury. It grabbed him by the head and flipped him away from Tim. Jason landed on his broken arm and screamed as the creature beat him until his left arm snapped.

Chapter Twenty-Six

Billy answered a phone call from Mike Brembs as Maria spoke to the chief inside the Price home. The chief had asked Billy to wait in the cruiser. Billy told Mike about Kelly Flynn's abduction but held off on what Maria said did it.

"Did you charge your phone?"

"I got a little bit less than fifty percent, so I should be good," Billy replied. "Whaddya got?"

"Apparently this Krampus of yours is part of some European pagan ritual dating back thousands of years—we're talking before the time of Christ. The townspeople would dress up as horned beasts during the winter solstice and get drunk off their pagan asses to blow off steam. So, Saint Nicholas, our Americanized Santa Claus, back in the day in Germany, Austria, Switzerland or wherever the hell else in Europe, he focused solely on giving gifts to the good kids and he farmed out the bad ones to his dark servant, Krampus, who'd stuff them in a barrel on his back, haul them away to his hidey-hole, beat them with a ruten. Oh, it's a bunch of birch branches tied together—"

"Yeah, I know." Billy twisted and examined the wooden bundle given to him by Maria. "We found them at my house, Travis's and Maria's." He said it in a *so what do you think of that?* tone.

Mike didn't hint that the morning's events and the subsequent revelations had unnerved him.

"Leave it to the goddamn Germans to terrorize Christmas," he said. "Even the name Krampus, it derives from a German word for claw. Makes sense to me. Anywho, Krampus would swipe the kids and eat them, or he'd drown them. He'd do all sorts of wicked shit to them. I guess it all depends on his mood. It's like Santa had an enforcer to do his bidding. How messed up is that? Like, you've been bad, so instead of Santa putting a harmless lump of coal in your shoe, he unleashes a pissed-off demon on your ass."

"You've got to admit, that's a much better incentive to be good."

"Well, it would explain this chain that Maria supposedly saw."

"She saw it, Mike!"

"Don't be snippy, pal. I'm the one doing you a favor. Anyway, the chain that she *saw* represents the one that locks Krampus in hell. That's where the cloven hooves come into the picture. It's some kind of devil. I guess he becomes unlinked when Saint Nicholas comes a calling: 'Here's the list, Krampus, go have at them.' Oh, since you already know about the birch switches, let me ask you this: did Maria mention anything about bells?"

"No. Why?"

"According to some of the stories I found, Krampus announces his presence to the world by clanging bells. Again, how depraved is that? You're a little kid sitting in your house churning butter, you hear jingling bells, run outside thinkin' it's the ice-cream man, and bam! You're totally screwed."

"I'm pretty sure they didn't have ice-cream men back then, Mike. But point taken."

"And, as it happens, Krampus is still pretty popular in Europe. There are huge parades in cities over there where men dress up as Krampus—you should see some of these costumes on YouTube, Billy, they're terrifying, and they run around the streets and spook the kids. They did the same thing eons ago when Frau Barker was a little fraulein, just like she said.

"The Americanized Santa Claus dropped any pretense of religion held by Saint Nicholas, who'd wear a miter and other bishopy things. Our Santa took on the dual role of determining who's been naughty or nice. I guess that's why we don't really know much about Krampus. I mean, seriously, have you ever heard of him before today? I haven't."

"Neither have I."

"And that's what's surprising to me. Christmas is so commercialized these days, so how could some company *not* capitalize on Krampus and smear his ugly mug all over the United States? I'm thinking plush dolls, action figures, T-shirts, a line of hair-care products. You name it! Hell, you could have shopping-mall Krampuses! Think about it, tell your bratty kid you're taking him to the mall to see Santa, and instead plop him onto some demon's lap and scare the shit out of him. *And* you can have Krampus's little helper—I don't know, maybe a hobgoblin?—photograph the whole thing and charge ten bucks a picture. I'm serious, Billy. This is money waiting to be made."

"Let's backtrack, Mike. Focus." Billy's exasperation knew no bounds when dealing with his best friend. "First, I'm pretty sure corporate America wouldn't risk unleashing the wrath of a predominantly Christian nation by marketing some child-abusing devil during the exact same month when they're preparing to celebrate the birth of Christ."

"I don't know about that," Mike mumbled.

"*Second,* you mentioned something about pagans. That might have something to do with this."

"Now you're starting to sound reasonable, Billy. Maybe there's a bunch of pagans hiding in the woods and dressing up like some—"

"No, that's not what I meant. Doesn't paganism have something to do with witchcraft?"

"Now you're suggesting a bunch of witches hovered over a caldron and conjured up a Krampus?"

"I don't know what I'm suggesting. This has been hands down the most surreal day of my life. Five kids vanish off the face of the earth, hoofprints in the snow where human tracks should be but aren't, people seeing flesh-and-blood monsters. I'm examining all possibilities."

"You're thinking of Wiccans, Billy. And based on some of the things I've read, Wiccans, at least some of 'em, believe in a goddess that associates with the moon, the stars and fate, and another god, a horned one representing forests and animals and, if you believe the Internet, the realm beyond death. So maybe that's where Krampus gets some parts of its origin. But I haven't read anything about witches trying to summon one of these things from the great beyond by chanting nonsense over a bubbling pot.

"Krampus is old, older than Jesus. From my point of view he's a story rooted to a bunch of European drunks who played dress-up. Stories get handed down from one generation to the next, a few details get added here and there—Krampus is chained to hell during its off-hours, it rings bells—and that makes for good times around the campfire."

"Do you believe in Jesus Christ, Mike?"

"Don't do that to me."

"Well, do you? I do. I believe in God. I believe He is good. And if He exists, then so can His counterpart and its evil acolytes."

"Look, Billy, I believe man certainly is capable of evil things, just look at the Nazis and the Holocaust, or the slaughter that happens almost daily in any number of African nations. Men are compelled to do evil things, and their actions usually are driven by greed and selfishness. But I can't say I'm sold on some dark and unholy force prompting them to commit atrocities.

"People's brains become screwed up because of genetics and shitty upbringing, or they live off drugs and alcohol, or they're just losers who are stupid and impressionable. All of those things can breed evil actions. I don't believe that some wicked puppet master controls any of those things. We're ultimately responsible for what we do, and that includes pinning the blame on someone or something else to try to avoid the consequences. People have murdered millions, all in the name of God, Billy. Committing atrocities in the name of a God who's everything good and decent? That's evil. Did the devil make them do it? No. Warped beliefs and simple minds did. That's probably what's going on here."

"*Probably?* So you've left some wiggle room?"

"Put it this way: I'm inclined to believe in what offers the most realistic explanation. And you're not."

"That's just my point, Mike. I've yet to come up with anything close to a realistic explanation for what happened to my brother, and especially to Brittany. Crushed bleachers, globs of goo around her abduction site. Jason Nicholson vanishes, and standing fifteen feet away are a dozen people who don't see a thing? It makes no sense. But I keep telling myself there has to be a logical explanation to all of this, but I'll be damned if I can think of one yet."

"I've got to admit, it sure seems weird. Hell, it *is* weird."

"Anything else?"

"I'm still looking."

"Good. Just humor me a bit more and keep at it."

"How's Maria doing?"

"Shaken up, what you'd expect."

"How is it around her, if you don't mind me asking?"

"Truthfully, before Tim went missing, I felt shitty, but I can't say I'm focused on that right now," Billy said. "It's not even second or third or fourth on my mind."

"That's good. Priorities, my man. I'm praying for you."

"Even though you don't believe in God?"

"Maybe I'm leaving some wiggle room after all."

Mike concluded the call by dispensing a few more bits and pieces from his fact finding. Billy exited the cruiser and sought out the girl whom hours earlier he'd hoped to avoid at all costs.

He knocked on Claire Price's front door and the kindly woman allowed him to enter. He looked up the staircase leading to the family room and the kitchen. He climbed it and spotted Maria sitting on a sofa, looking around like she was in a doctor's waiting room. Billy had a few minutes to sound delusional and sat next to her without asking.

"Maria, we need to talk."

Chapter Twenty-Seven

Claire Price set a steaming cup of tea before the chief, who sat at her kitchen table with Maria and wrote down everything she said. Billy sat next to her. Captain Jim Sherwood stood behind the chief, also listening.

The chief rhythmically tapped his pen on his notepad before speaking. "You cannot expect me to broadcast to every police agency in New Jersey to be on the lookout for a nine-foot-tall, brown, furry monster weighing six hundred pounds, with horns on its head and hooves for feet. Oh, and it uses a chain for a weapon and stores kidnapped children in a big wooden box on its back."

"And it speaks English but with a slight German accent, at least I think it's German," she added. "And it's wounded! Kelly shot it a bunch of times with Officer Pena's gun."

The chief sighed and turned to get his captain's opinion. Sherwood shook his head, not knowing what to make of it. Schweitzer then refocused on the girl.

"Your nine-year-old brother emptied a Glock clip into this creature of yours?"

"It's not *my* creature or anyone else's—it exists! Chief, why would I make any of this up? What purpose would it serve? It has my brother. It has your *son*. I wouldn't lie about something like this."

"I believe her, Dad."

"You stay out of this, Billy," he snapped. "And I never said I thought you were lying. It's just a little hard to believe, that's all. Kelly said he saw a bear and—"

"No! No he did *not*! He said he saw a monster that *ate* a bear! And it ate my dog too. You'll find what's left of his body in the family room."

"Jim, get ahold of whoever's over there and ask them about the dog, an empty gun and bullet casings in the kitchen, and anything else that might be out of place."

The captain left the room holding his shoulder mic.

"I never found a dead bear at Kelly's school, Maria." He measured his tone. "There was some blood, I'll admit that."

"I can understand you not believing my brother. Hell, I didn't believe him at first. I mean, he's just a scared little boy. But I saw the exact same thing that he did!"

"Well, I believe you saw *something*. But—"

"Please don't patronize me, Chief. You found hoofprints at all of the other scenes. Billy told me."

The chief scowled at his son, who flipped his hands in the air as if to say, *What'd I do?*.

"Chief, it's all right. There are hoofprints in my backyard."

He sat back in the chair. "I know. I saw them."

Sherwood returned to the kitchen. "You want to talk in private, Chief?"

"Do we need to?"

"I guess not. First, we didn't find a dog anywhere in that house."

"Blood!" Maria shouted. "There has to be—"

Sherwood raised his palm. "We found a blood trail starting on the couch and leading out on the deck and into the snow. So maybe it got injured and walked—"

Maria looked at Billy. "I told you they wouldn't believe me."

"Anything else, Jim?"

"Yes. The gun was there. We found a clip's worth of spent casings *and* impacted bullet heads lying on the kitchen floor. All over the place."

"That's impossible! My brother was less than five feet away from that thing when he shot it."

"Maybe it was wearing a bulletproof vest because the slugs definitely hit something, but there was no blood on the bullets or on the floor where they landed, just what I am assuming is the dog's blood on the floor," Sherwood said.

"Did you find any holes in the wall?" Maria asked.

"Yes, two bullet holes, but—"

"They're *not* bullet holes! It's where its horns hit. Go dig into the walls, I guarantee you will not find a single bullet."

Maria's phone broadcast the *Benny Hill* theme across the kitchen and she ripped through her purse to find it.

I knew there was a reason I liked this girl, Billy thought.

"Sorry about that." She found it and answered.

"Is it your parents?" the chief whispered. "I need to talk to them."

"No, excuse me." She got up and walked into the adjoining family room. Then Billy realized who had called, which served as a reminder that reality continued to suck for innumerable reasons today.

"I'm fine. Yeah, they let us out early. You too?"

Billy stared blankly at his father and mouthed, *It's him.*

She tried keeping her voice low, with so many different ears potentially listening. "How is it up by you?...Your parents make it home safe?...Mine? No, they're on their way...I wish I could be with you too."

The chief and Billy exchanged uncomfortable glances until, "Listen, things are kind of crazy around here right now, so can I call you later? No, everything's fine, I think. Just crazy. I'll fill you in later." She returned to her spot at the kitchen table.

"Thank you for the discretion, Maria. There's no sense in spreading panic, although I sense that's inevitable."

"He doesn't need to worry about me. He's got his own little brother to watch."

What's his name? Billy thought. *What does it matter anyway, no sense in further self-defeat.*

"Well, he sounds like a considerate young man," the chief said.

"Thanks, I met him at church; he goes to Morris Catholic High School."

Ah-ha! At least that clears that up, Billy thought.

Maria had flustered herself by describing her own fledgling foray into the dating scene and steered the conversation back to what mattered.

"And I didn't feel quite right telling him about what I saw less than an hour ago."

"Maria, put yourself in our position," the chief said. "We need to be able to tell the public that five kids are missing, along with some details about the abductor. At this point I'm willing to say that the suspect may be wearing some kind of costume—"

"Wasn't a costume." Maria trilled the last word.

"Jim, leave us a minute," the chief politely commanded his obliging officer. He then resumed. "Maria, what if I told you that I believe you saw something that had hooves? I can't deny what I saw out there or any of the other places. So, yes, I believe there's someone running around out there wearing hooves."

Billy butted in, "Dad, *why* would anyone wear hooves while running around in the snow and all those hills out there? It'd slow you down."

"Because some people are deranged, Billy. Some people are crazy. In fact—" the chief leaned back in his chair and called to Sherwood, "—Jim, call up the area psychiatric hospitals and find out if anyone's gone missing. Anyone really large."

"On it, Chief!" Sherwood replied.

"Dad, you just hit on it. It might not be that hard for some sex pervert to make off with a kid like Kelly—" he turned to Maria, "—which I don't think happened, the sex-pervert part. But what I'm getting at is this thing took Tim and Travis. They're practically grown men. Think about the effort it would take to carry them off, even if they weren't able to fight back. Whoever did this would have to be freakin' huge. Almost super... super..." Billy laid it out, "...supernatural."

The thought hung over them.

"Or it's a team of kidnappers, Billy. We have to consider that," the chief said.

"I think it's a Krampus, Dad. Its name is Krampus. It's some kind of creature that comes out of the mountains in Europe on the Eve of Saint Nicholas, which, by the way, is tonight. It takes away bad kids to, well, punish them, drown them or in some cases eat them, to get them to be good in order for Saint Nicholas to bring them presents. Although I don't know how you can redeem someone by killing them. It kind of defeats the purpose. Anyway, he uses a chain, maybe the one that binds him to hell, for effect. That explains what both Maria and Kelly saw."

The chief thought his son had briefly gone insane. "Saint Nicholas as in..."

"Yeah, *that* guy. That's Europe's version of him, from what I've been told. This Krampus puts a *ruten* on the porches of the houses he plans to visit. That's what you found this morning, Dad. That bundle of branches. They're called rutens. Krampus was telling us it was going to take Tim, and Kelly. And it apparently also uses them to beat kids."

"Billy, listen to what you're saying! My God! The prosecutor will never go before television cameras and say anything close to this," the chief said. "But it lends to someone being deranged and really caught up in this myth of yours."

"It's not a myth, Dad. For something like this to happen, the way it's happened, it's real. It has to be real. Just look at the evidence. That's what you always say, 'look at the evidence'."

"The evidence tells me that Tim cannot be a bad kid worthy of whatever that thing might do to him," the chief said.

Maria interrupted them, "I think I know what Kelly did." That silenced them. "He's been pretty bad recently."

Maria's phone rang and she answered it.

"Chief, this is for you," she said.

Chapter Twenty-Eight

"I feel terrible that I just informed your mother that her son's missing, especially while she's out driving in this." The chief still sat with Maria and Billy around Claire Price's kitchen table. The mother had called to tell her daughter she'd soon be home and to see how everyone was doing.

"Now you can use Kelly's picture, right? I want it out there," Maria said.

"Yes. If your mom doesn't get back here by the time I leave, Captain Sherwood will stay at your home until she arrives. We'll be processing your house for a while. Now, tell me about your brother and why he's been..."

"Bad, Chief. He's been a really mean kid recently," Maria said. "It started a month ago when Bryan Welles's mother called my mom."

The chief scribbled notes as Maria spoke. Billy listened in silence.

"Bryan's a classmate of Kelly's, and as it turns out, Kelly misinterpreted Bryan making fun of Kelly's name because it sounds like a girl's name. Bryan apologized, but Kelly kept picking on Bryan, I guess because he could. Well, Bryan told his parents and that's when we got the call about what Kelly had been doing to him.

"He'd wrench Bryan's arm behind his back, make him scream 'I'm a pussy! I'm a pussy!' until Bryan cried. He'd haul off and just punch him in the stomach, one of those blows that knocks the wind out of you and you can't breathe for like five minutes. One more slipup by Kelly and the school said it would suspend him for a week. It's the no-bully policy. I'm surprised the school didn't pick up on it sooner, but kids tend to hide that they're being picked on. Shame, I guess.

"At any rate, when we picked up Kelly today, he mentioned that Bryan just kept laughing and laughing at him when he was crying today. I told him it didn't matter. If he touched Bryan, he'd be out of school, and if it continued, expulsion. That's how bad it got."

The chief stopped writing. "Zero-tolerance policy or not, kids get bullied. Sad fact of life, but it happens, and, honestly, what Kelly was doing to that kid sounds tame in comparison to some of the stuff I've read about. I'm not excusing it. I'm just saying."

"Dad, I agree, but—and Maria witnessed this today with me—Jason Nicholson was treating Eric Halberstrom like crap today, and that's been going on for a while. I've seen it in the halls at school, not just on the bus. Jason's remorseless when he goes after Eric. And now Jason's gone."

The chief felt tired and it wasn't even three o'clock yet. His son's vanishing and its circumstances, and the other disappearances, had caught up to him. He needed a second wind. "I suggest we go, kids. Maria, I asked Mrs. Price if you could stay here until your folks show and she's fine with it. There'll be police officers outside to keep an eye on things, and I know your parents want you to be here when they get home. It's not going to be easy for them."

"I know. I'm staying. I'm not looking forward to telling them what I saw. They'll believe me about as much as you do, Chief."

"Maria," the chief spoke so that only Maria and Billy could hear him, "let me tell you what I believe. That bear, the one that ran in front of your school bus? I believe that bear was already dead before it crossed the road. I believe that bear was thrown across the street, tossed like a sack of laundry, perfectly timed, so it would slide in front of your school bus and cause your driver to crash it, all with the express purpose of taking Jason Nicholson.

"Now, I believe that because I didn't see one footprint to indicate that *anything* ran across Winchester Road into the woods. No disturbances except for tire tracks right where you'd expect to find them. I believe that bear's neck was snapped as easy as a wishbone. And here's what really bothers me—I believe that whoever killed and hurled that bear is bigger and stronger than any police officer on my force. And I believe that whoever did it is still out there and that this town's children—because that's what it's apparently after—are in a lot of danger if we don't put a stop to it. That's what I believe."

The chief sat back and closed his notepad. "Now, as for a monster? I'm not there yet, Maria. I'm just not. I'm more inclined to think it's a lunatic strung out on drugs that, I don't know, maybe gets your adrenaline pumping so you can move heavy things. That's more logical, at least to me, than some type of Bigfoot with horns and a wooden backpack. That's what I believe."

Maria gulped, somewhat chagrined. "I didn't mean any disrespect."

"I don't think you showed any, dear. Now I'm going to go try to find your brother and my son."

"Please stay in touch." She turned to Billy. "Please call me and let me know how things are going out there. Any updates you can give. Anything."

"We will, Maria," the chief said. "I promise."

The chief's radio crackled: "The mother's home."

"Be right there." He got up and left the kitchen.

Maria sheepishly looked down and away from Billy. "Do you believe what I saw?"

"Without a doubt," he said. "After we go, and I don't know how you're gonna do this—maybe you know someone?—try to think about what Travis and Brittany might've done that really pissed someone off."

"You think they've been bad like my brother, like that Jason asshole?"

"Yeah, it would make sense. And unfortunately it means that Tim must've done something awful, and for the life of me I cannot figure out what it might be."

She nodded. "Me neither. I mean, I don't know him well, obviously. But you hear about people in the halls, you know? And I've never heard anything bad said about your brother."

"Precisely, that's why I'm hoping you know someone who might've heard something about those other two. Maybe it will lead back to Tim somehow."

"All right, I'll get on it," she said.

"You probably should go and be with your mom right now."

Chapter Twenty-Nine

Dolores Flynn stood outside of her old Caravan and shook, and not because of the snow. The chief explained everything he could about the kidnappings—he'd only told her about Kelly over the phone. He placed his hand on her shoulder to steady her, and reinforced the notion that she needed to be strong, and to let the police work to figure out who might have done this. He wasn't prepared to tell her stories about the boogeyman.

She should probably be sitting for that, he thought.

"Your daughter helped us pick out a photo we could use, I hope that's okay," he said.

"Maria! Where's my daughter?!"

"Mom! Mom! Over here!"

Maria ran into her mother's arms and did her best to absorb her sobs. She couldn't help but cry too. "Let's go into Mrs. Price's house," Maria said. "It's all right."

"When can I go back into my house?" Dolores addressed the chief. Billy had wandered next to him.

"It's a crime scene for now, so we sort of need you out of there. Probably closer to evening. If there's anything in there you need, we can get it."

"Where's Casey?"

The chief and Maria exchanged grave glances, which tipped off the mother.

"He's dead?!"

"Yes, but we don't think Kelly is," Maria answered.

"Chief, do you think my boy's okay? Do you think your boy is alive? And those other children?"

"Mrs. Flynn, I have no reason to believe otherwise. I mean that."

"I hope so."

"My men will take care of you and ask you some questions, and time's sorta of the essence here. Why don't you go into your neighbor's house with your daughter, who has been really helpful to us, by the way."

Maria smiled.

"I gotta get going back to the station, maybe make a stop along the way."

Billy reiterated his promise to keep Maria and her mother informed, and they parted ways.

Billy strapped himself into his dad's cruiser and clutched his book bag on his lap. The chief drove out of the development.

"You said we might make a stop along the way? Where?"

"Hopefully to Eric Halberstrom's house. I know his dad, Jack, somewhat. He used to work for the water department before going to the power company. And he lives near the municipal building. But I'm sort of guessing the prosecutor is hot to trot for me to get back there with what Maria said."

"You gonna tell him everything?"

A snowplow barreled past them, pushing mountains of salt-stained snow off the street.

"Yeah, I'm just trying to figure out how I'm gonna say it. I sort of wish the plows and salt trucks weren't doing such a good job on the roads, otherwise I'd have longer to think about it."

Chapter Thirty

"I think he's dead, Travis. Does he look dead to you?" Brittany Cabot, dismayed that she might be next on the menu, nudged her tied-up boyfriend with her forehead. "Do you see his chest moving at all?"

Travis Reardon leaned forward with effort and squinted. "I can't tell," he said before relaxing his body against the wall. "I'm pretty sure that's what I'm gonna end up looking like after it's done with me. It already got a head start."

Still bound and displayed horizontally on the floor, Jason Nicholson's body moved involuntarily with its breaths. The creature had left the kids to their thoughts of premature death and hadn't said why. It'd decimated Jason with its switch and positioned the body in the center of the cave to make it look like a sacrificial offering in the candlelight.

"I'm still trying to come to grips with that thing somehow being on Santa Claus's payroll," Travis continued. "Do you believe what it said? How anything even remotely associated with jolly ol' Saint Nick can be responsible for *that*"—he tilted his head toward Jason and didn't complete the thought.

"I don't know what to make of it, either," Tim Schweitzer interjected. "I'd have an easier time accepting it if this was Christmas Eve or something."

"Do you realize how crazy you both sound?!" Brittany screeched. "Everyone wants to be famous these days. I bet you anything it's some psychopath in a costume who's got us on video and is live-streaming it across the Internet so some sick fucks in Russia can get their rocks off."

"Live-streaming our torture over cyberspace, that I could believe," Tim said. "There are some twisted people who would pay to watch innocent people suffer, unfortunately."

Travis chuckled before saying, "Yeah, one of their names is Brittany."

"Go to hell," she hissed.

"It's real, I believe it," Kelly Flynn, sitting next to Tim after regaining consciousness, said. "Why would Santa send a monster after us?"

"I'll tell you why, and I can't believe I'm about to say this," Travis replied, "but which do you think would do a better job kidnapping and tormenting us: that thing, or that geezer snowman that sings and plays the banjo?"

"Yeah, that makes sense!" Kelly meant every word. "It all makes sense."

"You doin' okay, kid?" Tim asked Kelly, who couldn't stop staring at the body. "Why don't you lie down? You don't have to look at that."

"I'm sorry," Kelly mumbled.

"You don't need to apologize to me, I just don't think it's doin' you any good to look at him, that's all."

"I should never have done it."

"What the hell are you talking about?" Brittany butted in. "Stop feeling sorry for yourself, you little snot. We're all in the same damn boat."

"Brit, lighten up," Tim snapped. "He's a kid. Leave him be."

"Oh sorry, *Dad.*"

Kelly ignored her and continually whispered, "I'm so sorry."

Intense thudding in the distance twisted their stomachs, except for Jason, who seemed comatose. The ground trembled and they braced themselves for the thing's schizophrenic rage.

The candles flickered as it emerged from blackness to assess them all. Its eyes darted from one body to the next. Satisfied no one had fled, it reached with both arms for what Tim took to be four long, thick logs jutting from the crate. It grunted while gathering strength to pull out and throw a deer at the cave's far wall. It slapped against rock and plopped to the ground, eyes open, neck snapped. The thing took pride in its kill.

"Hungry? I guess the dog wasn't enough." Tim kept the snark to a minimum. "I ask because you could've saved yourself a trip and eaten Jason over there."

The thing's laugh grumbled in its chest. "Trying to figure out what I am going to do to you? Nice try, *Herr* Schweitzer. Keep stewing. But since you ask, I prefer my humans to be on the meaty side—lean meat, mind you, not the blubbery flesh that seems to cling to the bones of the children in this age." It pointed at Kelly. "That one, for example, spends his sheltered life either looking at a big glowing box hanging on a wall, or a smaller glowing box on his desk, or even at a tinier glowing rectangle he holds in his hands. Does he play outside? No. Does he even bother to *go* outside? No. Kelly's life revolves around glowing squares and eating triangles covered in black specks and orange dust."

Tim, confused, mulled it over: "You mean Doritos?" He looked at Kelly, who emphatically nodded yes.

"Whatever you call them, Kelly seems to subsist exclusively on them. The boys and girls of times gone by, they worked outside, either milking the cows or scything the fields. They played hide-and-seek in the woods when not laboring with their parents. The last place they wanted to be was indoors, and only then so they could sleep in order to go outside early the next day. *Those* were the children who tasted good! And they did not eat these Doritos of yours. They ate normal things: beef, chicken, pigs, even fruits and vegetables! And if they ever got wide around the hips and stomachs, their outdoor activity quickly melted it away!

"Today's winsome brats have bellies so big they can't see the tips of their toes when they look down. Nothing but jiggly fat as far as the eye can see. So, to answer your question, no, I will not be eating Kelly, or Jason, for that matter, as he barely has enough edible flesh on his bones to begin with. You and Herr Reardon, on the other hand, are the closest things here to what I consider to be tasty. So I would behave if I were you."

"That's comforting." Tim erred on the side of being polite. "About not eating Kelly or Jason, I mean. But what are you going to do with Jason? He's dead, and if he isn't, he will be soon. You just gonna let him rot before our eyes?"

The creature ripped a deer leg out of its socket and chewed its flesh before deigning to respond. It ambled over to look at Jason's ashen complexion. Shreds of slobbery deer meat fell on his face.

"It seems I may have been too rough on Herr Nicholson, ja? I do not think he will learn if he has not already."

It knelt over Jason and gently maneuvered the boy's comparatively small head with its other hand.

"Wake up, boy," it spoke softly, then roared, "Now!"

Jason's eyes opened smooth as a vampire's upon sunset and saw the thing's taunting grin. Jason's eyes reflected indifference. The

131

creature sealed his fate, and Jason would greet it, hoping at worst for a painless death.

"That is more like it." The creature whispered words intended only for Jason. No matter how hard Tim tried, all he heard were rambling shooshes and shushes.

Jason inhaled deeply and widened his eyes.

"You will remember everything I have said?"

Jason bobbed his head forward.

"Do you believe me, boy?"

He repeated the gesture.

The creature pulled Jason up by his feet and flipped him in its crate. The thing devoured all the deer meat from the leg and then tossed the bloodstained bone, which clattered before Tim's feet.

"Eat before you go! Ja?" It turned its back to the foursome and tore into the deer's belly.

It finished eviscerating the carcass and faced its captives, grinning as blood and entrails rained from its mouth.

It raced into the darkness but not before jubilantly roaring, "The day becomes more interesting as Krampusnacht approaches!"

Chapter Thirty-One

Vincent Di Renzo, resplendent in his blue Dolce & Gabbana suit, his thick black hair perfectly coiffed, tried not to appear nervous when adjusting his silk tie before a bank of television cameras whose On lights prepared to glow red. He checked his Rolex: three o'clock. Two hours later than he would have liked. All the major news networks from New York City waited for his cue.

The county prosecutor counted seven unwieldy cameras on tripods spread across the Hancock council chambers' public seating area, all lenses trained on him. The broadcast journalists, a few prickly veterans perturbed to be out in Bumblefuck, along with some college graduates eager to make their bones, sat ahead of the cameras in chairs typically occupied by cranky senior citizens pissed about their property taxes. Photographers from the newspapers clicked away as print reporters stood to the side of the chambers, pens in hand, ready to scribble on notepads. The reporters had placed their microphones and digital recorders on the podium, which normally carried nothing on its front, but today displayed the state seal of New Jersey (Di Renzo toted one everywhere just in case he caught wind of a possible press conference).

Di Renzo, in his late forties and with aspirations bigger than being the county's chief prosecutor, always felt smooth in his own skin when preening before the networks. Never a drop of sweat or a tight collar, and he'd been doing this for years. This time he fidgeted, his sweaty hands gripped both sides of the podium. He'd gotten the orchestration he desired: A phalanx of business-suited officials and uniformed lawmen, including the mayor and the chief, stood behind him on both sides.

Di Renzo cleared his throat and took a final sip of water from a tiny Poland Spring bottle on the podium before glancing over his shoulder at the chief, who nodded in the affirmative.

Yes, everything I told you during the briefing was true, so get on with it, the chief thought.

The chief's ex-wife, Diana Applewood, stood in the back of the chambers along with the other missing children's weary parents.

Billy Schweitzer had foregone the festivities and stayed in the chief's office scouring the student-emailed videos sent to his father's account from the site of the school bus crash, hoping to spot anything related to Jason Nicholson's abduction.

"Okay, let's begin," Di Renzo said, and then rattled off the typical roll call of identities of the people behind him.

"Our departments are jointly investigating what we believe to be the orchestrated kidnappings of five Hancock Township children." He rattled off their names and ages, and the places of their disappearances, and methodically plodded through the boilerplate language identical to what was typed on the press release given to each reporter. He recited the approximate times of the abductions, and referred to the color photographs of each child on separate handouts. Di Renzo then hesitated before delving into the nitty-gritty.

"We have no suspects at this time. An eyewitness described one potential suspect as being"—he coughed into his hand to delay the inevitable—"somewhere between eight to ten feet tall and dressed in a brown, hairy costume."

Di Renzo heard murmuring from the Fourth Estate, and saw journalists giving each other odd glances.

"This suspect was reported to be wearing some type of rubber Halloween monster mask with pointy horns, and is using a chain for a weapon, and wearing a wooden carrying crate on its back. And there is the possibility that this suspect has traveled on horseback in and around the abduction sites. We ask anyone in the public who saw someone riding a horse along Winchester Road at any point this morning to contact police immediately."

The prosecutor let a moment pass so he could survey the assembly of cameramen and reporters, all dumbfounded over the tale being spun.

"Obviously we believe there might be psychological issues at play here and—"

"That's the understatement of the year," he heard one of the gruff veterans loudly whisper to a contemporary.

"And we believe this individual to be physically strong, dangerous and not to be approached. Anyone who sees this individual should call 911 immediately and not attempt any sort of heroics. Anyone with any information about the abductions is being asked to call 1-800-COP-

CALL. Now, I will take a few questions but please be aware I am limited to what I can say, given the ongoing nature of the investigation."

And then began the descent into absurdity.

Reporter: "Is the person in the monster suit a man or a woman? You left that part out."

"We believe it is a man who speaks English with a slight German accent."

Reporter: "Can you ballpark how old the monster man might be?"

"No, but given the fact that we believe this man to be incredibly strong, he likely is in his twenties or thirties. We don't believe this is an elderly monster." The prosecutor almost smacked his forehead with the palm of his hand. "I mean man. We don't believe it's an elderly man."

Reporter: "Were any of the kids injured by the German-speaking monster?"

"Would you please be serious?" the prosecutor chided. "Please don't forget that the fathers of two of the abducted children are standing right behind me, and I'm certain they don't appreciate your irreverence. As for injuries, I can't comment other than to say we believe all the children were alive when they were taken."

New York tabloid reporter: "Do you suspect the Jersey Devil might have had something to do with this?"

A few chuckles and then another reporter answered before the prosecutor could respond, "Nah, the Jersey Devil's supposed to have wings and lives in the Pine Barrens. Excuse me, Mr. Di Renzo, did the German monster have wings?"

"No," he said tersely.

Reporter: "How do you know that this isn't part of some elaborate hoax on the part of the kids? You must admit this all sounds very far-fetched."

"We believe the abductions are real and not part of an attempt to fool police."

Reporter: "We've heard that you've found footprints at the sites of the abductions, can you say whether they've led anywhere, any specific direction?"

"I won't get into specifics as to what we might or might not have found, but it goes without saying that we are fully investigating all avenues."

Reporter: "Have there been any ransom demands? Either notes or phone calls?"

"We have received no communications, but if the person responsible for this is hearing me right now, please contact us. We want to resolve this so that no harm comes to you or to the children."

Reporter: "Did any of the abducted kids or their families receive any threats that you are aware of?"

"I can't comment on that."

Reporter: "Was any surveillance footage of any kind taken of the monster man that you can release to us?"

"I can't comment on that."

Reporter: "You mentioned a chain. What kind of chain?"

"The description we've been given is it's big and it's black and it's long."

One of the African-American cameramen chuckled and quickly composed himself.

Di Renzo stared laser beams through his skull.

"Excuse me, Mr. Di Renzo, may I please?" It was the chief, accurately sensing the media wasn't grasping the gravity of the situation. The prosecutor wordlessly acquiesced and switched spots with Schweitzer. A tidal wave of digital camera clicks followed.

"My name is Donald Schweitzer. I'm Hancock's police chief, and my son, Tim, is a straight-A student. He loves his younger brother very much, looks after him when I'm not around, which is a lot sometimes. He's a good football player and he's never had any disciplinary problems at school. He would never willingly cause harm to anyone. Rather, Tim would be the first to defend someone who needed it, even if he didn't know the person. I raised him to be responsible for his actions, and he always has been. He prides himself on that.

"And today he's missing. My boy's gone right now and I have no idea where he is or who has him. Neither does his mother, who is a wreck right now." The chief noticed his ex-wife in the back of the room, appreciatively nodding in agreement with his description of Tim.

The chief resumed, "And neither does his younger brother, who's holding up all right in the face of all this, trying to be strong for his mom and dad, but who's also frightened by what we all cannot comprehend.

"I was at the scene of Tim's accident this morning. None of you were. None of you saw the reality of his truck having crashed into that tree. None of you saw my son's blood on the air bag. It wasn't much, but it was indeed the blood of the little boy who I once cradled in my arms eighteen years ago."

The chief let that settle in the reporters' minds and continued commanding the room with his deep, authoritative voice, "My son realizes what we, the police, do for a living, and he would never participate in something that would make us spin our wheels during a blizzard when our resources should be deployed to help people affected by the storm. Now, I can't speak for our mayor, Paul Reardon, who's standing behind me, but I know what we both are experiencing is brutal, and I sincerely hope it's something that none of you ever have to go through, because maybe then you wouldn't be so quick to be flippant over what is genuine suffering, a terrible pain also felt by three other families.

"So, with all due respect, you have been given what we can release at this point. You've been given what are real photographs of children who want nothing more right now than to be reunited with their families. Please be responsible when writing your articles and broadcasting your stories. We will give you updates when and if future developments warrant them.

"Thank you, Mr. Di Renzo."

Mayor Reardon expressed similar sentiments to the press with his own spin on them. The prosecutor then wound down the news conference by asking the reporters to be respectful to the families of the missing children, and then he made himself available for one-on-ones with each network that wanted an interview.

The chief declined any further comment. "What I said up there pretty much covers it," he told the reporters. And then he slipped away to check on his younger boy.

Billy boringly looked at the chief when he walked into his office.

"I take it the videos are—"

"A spectacular waste of time," Billy finished the thought. "Don't get me wrong, it was a good idea, Dad. But all of the clips pretty much depict the school bus. And the only times they weren't focused on the bus was when the photographer flipped the camera around to take a selfie."

"Did you see Jason in any of them?"

"Not a single one. Maybe you can get some people with that fancy video gear to enhance the images?"

"Like on *Law & Order*?" The chief chuckled. "That'd be nice, but it's not wrapped up in ribbons in sixty minutes. It'll take a while. I'll still send them out to the state police in Trenton or the FBI's forensics lab in Newark, but I wouldn't bank on getting results anytime soon."

"Have the people searching the woods updated you?"

"They haven't found squat, the wind and snow are making certain they won't, at least for a while."

"How'd the press conference go?"

"Someone essentially asked the prosecutor if the Jersey Devil was a suspect. That's how it went."

"The Jersey Devil has wings, Dad."

"Yeah, so I've heard. But now you see why this is a problem. The media's gonna minimize a serious story with references to the Jersey Devil or Bigfoot or whatever."

"They can't minimize the fact that five kids are gone, Dad, especially if they interview the Cabots, the Nicholsons or whoever wants to talk about their kids."

"I hope you're right. But it's been my experience lately that facts take a backseat to what makes for the media's desired narrative. Maybe I'll be pleasantly surprised."

"So, now what?" Billy said. "We can't just sit around here."

"Damn straight. We're going to Jack Halberstrom's house to have a talk with his boy, Eric."

"Dad, not that you want my opinion on this, but Eric Halberstrom somehow being involved in all this...?"

"I didn't say he was involved. I just want to make sure I'm not missing anything. Maybe Eric will have something to offer."

The overhead lights, desk lamp and computer monitor all flickered for a second but didn't go dark. Both Billy and the chief instinctively looked upward at the panel lighting and could hear collective groans coming from various departments.

"At least the lights stayed on." Billy stood, flipped up his black hoodie and grabbed his book bag, ready to go.

The lights again shut off for ten seconds, increasing the dismay among the administrative worker bees, before flashing back on.

"Shit. That's the generator kicking on." The chief likewise grabbed his coat. "It's the rest of the town I'm worried about now. The wind's picking up. The snow'll get heavy on tree limbs and bring them down onto power lines. And I trust what the electric company says about as much as I do Baghdad Bob. Just fantastic."

"Well, it's still daylight." Billy paused and looked out the window. "For now."

"Yeah, for another couple of hours. Then the darkness really comes."

Chapter Thirty-Two

Jack Halberstrom, a balding, beefy, bushy-mustached man with a fleshy roll of a neck, stood with his hands at his sides, tapping his foot on his family room's hardwood floor. Eric Halberstrom occupied the center spot of a three-seat sofa, with Billy seated to his left.

The chief, earnestly clutching his hat in hands, finished recounting the press conference and what led him to want to speak to Eric. He placed a copy of the prosecutor's press release and a sheet with the missing students' profiles on the glass coffee table.

The Halberstrom home stood in a cozy neighborhood off of Winchester Road like Maria Flynn's house, practically a cookie-cutter version of it, complete with the same casement bay window. Only this house was less than five minutes from the municipal building. The Halberstroms, like thousands of residents who lost power for two weeks in the wake of Hurricane Sandy, had bought a power generator that loudly chugged outside, almost keeping in time with Jack's foot tapping.

"The notion that my son somehow orchestrated the kidnapping of this bastard bully of his, I find it beyond ludicrous, and, frankly, insulting. My wife and I raise our boy the right way." Jack Halberstrom kept his simmering anger below the boiling point. "And if she wasn't visiting her mother in Virginia, she'd tell you the same."

"I am not accusing Eric of anything unseemly or illegal. But the fact is, and I am sorry to say it, Jason Nicholson apparently was pretty vicious to him. Eric showed me that bruise on his shoulder—"

"What bruise?!" Jack, his rage mixed with concern, glared at his boy.

Eric buried his face in his hands. "We'll talk about it later," came Eric's muffled reply.

"Jack, please listen." The chief drew the father's attention back to him. "Something really bothered me about the way Eric so blatantly told me to not even bother finding Jason. I know this whole situation sounds weird. It does! But I have to do my due diligence and—"

"First of all, my son makes minimum wage pushing carts at Walmart." Jack's raised voice quivered. "Second, any money he does make goes right into buying one of those Xbox games where you shoot zombies in the face, and *not* toward hiring some Scooby-Doo monster to seek revenge.

"And for Chrissakes, Chief, it doesn't take a genius to figure out all these kidnappings are related! My son had nothing to do with any of them! Not with Jason, not your son. None of them! Not to sound callous, but bullied kids these days don't contract hit men to take out their enemies. They walk into school with a gun and do it themselves! And I'll be goddamned if my son would even consider doing something like that!" Jack quickly looked at Eric. "You *wouldn't*, would you?!"

Eric negatively shook his head, still buried in his hands, and croaked, "Never!"

Billy scrambled his mind to think of some way to console Eric, whose shoulders flinched up and down as he silently sobbed. An arm around the shoulder would make the situation even more uncomfortable.

"I don't think he would do any of those things," the chief reassured Jack. "What I'm getting at is perhaps Jason picked on other kids too. Not just your son."

The chief then turned to the boy on the couch.

"Was that the case Eric? If it is, maybe you heard some of those other victims talking about getting even with Jason. It's not a leap to think that's possible."

Eric lifted his tearstained face and looked to his father.

"It's all right," Jack said. "Talk to the man."

"I don't think so, Chief." Eric righted himself and cleared his throat. "None that I know of. But then, I'm not in all of his classes. I guess I'm just an easy target for him. That's what they look for. And that's why I'm not backing down from what I told you earlier today."

The younger Halberstrom's posture improved. He puffed his chest out, widened his shoulders—just thinking about his tormenter and the fact that he was now gone emboldened him. "You could comb every inch of this earth and never find Jason and I'd be doin' the Snoopy dance all the same. You want me to say I hope you find him? I don't. Fuck him and whoever turned him into the twisted piece of shit that he is— Pardon my French, Dad."

Eric continued his extemporaneous outburst without giving his father a chance to scold him, "Chief, I'd sooner throw a lifeline to Jerry Sandusky than I would to Jason Nicholson, but that doesn't mean I did anything to hurt him or make him disappear, as much as I might want to. That's what separates me from an animal like him. I know there are consequences, potentially bad ones, for my actions. Jason doesn't. And if his vanishing today is somehow payback for never taking responsibility for all the shit he's put me through, or anybody else for that matter, then I couldn't be happier."

The chief, Jack and Billy stayed quiet as Eric eyeballed all of them. Eric gave off an unmistakable *you gotta problem wit dat?* vibe. Eric's breathing slowed and he came back down to earth.

The sound of crunching metal killed the generator's chugging, and the lights in the room went dark.

"I just put gas in that damn thing," Jack sighed. "This is the first time we've used it since putting it in. That damned warranty better hold up." Jack tossed his arms in the air and got his coat from the hallway closet. "First my son's getting bullied, now this shit."

"That didn't sound like it ran out of gas," the chief said. Perhaps his nerves continued to fray as the day wore on, but Donald Schweitzer reached for his gun.

Billy and Eric went rigid when he did and Jack became the voice of reason.

"Chief, it's just a generator. Shit happens. I'm gonna go check it out."

"I'll come with you," Schweitzer insisted. "Lead the way."

The two men stood in whirling gusts of snow in the backyard off to the side of the house, where the 8,000-watt, automatic-standby Generac generator was tipped on its side, the cord connecting it to the house's circuit panel crudely yanked off and tossed into the snow.

"That thing weighs three hundred fifty pounds, Chief." Jack held out his hands. "That cost me twenty-two hundred bucks, and I'll be goddamned if the wind is strong enough to blow it over."

"Or disconnect the wiring from your house." The chief crept closer to the destroyed cord, its end a bouquet of tangled wires. The generator was dead so he knew the wiring wasn't live. Still, they were both technically standing in water, and Schweitzer didn't want to risk anything.

The chief then realized he might be stepping on evidence and scanned the snow. The tracks leading up to the generator could've been made by anything. The wind had its way with the snow so that any holes in the ground were practically filled an instant later.

"Someone must've taken a sledgehammer to it, Chief." Jack ran his fingers into the deep indentation on the generator's side, which now faced skyward and had begun filling with snow. Jack hushed and listened. "Can you hear my neighbor's generator going? I can. Hell, I hear another one too. They've all got their own distinct sounds. Why mine? Holy Christ!"

"What?!" the chief shouted, slapping his hand on top of his police hat to keep the wind from blowing it off.

"Do you smell that?" Jack Halberstrom said.

The chief inhaled the stink and gagged. He then drew his gun.

Chapter Thirty-Three

Billy and Eric sat next to each other on the sofa in the Halberstrom family room, wondering whether either should take the initiative to force a conversation neither wanted to have. The cacophony of generators rumbling around the homes surrounding Eric's pushed Billy to break the monotony.

"I don't blame you for what you said. I'd probably feel the same way."

"Thanks." Eric said it sarcastically. "And you *would* feel the same way, I guarantee it." He then looked at Billy and didn't turn away. "I wish I had an older brother like yours. Do you think Tim would let a dickwad like Jason treat you the way he treats me? I can't recall one time I've ever seen anyone push you around."

Billy couldn't disagree. He'd had a scrape or two in the past, nothing more than inane misunderstandings between kids which had led to shoving matches that quickly resolved themselves. But nobody had ever verbally or physically pummeled him on a daily basis.

"Tim would catch wind and put a stop to it," Billy confirmed.

"Why don't others?"

"Whaddya mean?"

"Other kids have seen him push me into lockers, or take a cheap punch at me, and they do nothing. They watch and keep walking, like helping a kid being brutalized would somehow take them down a notch from whatever ridiculous social peg they think they're on. I'm glad Maria stuck up for me earlier today."

"I'm sorry that I didn't, Eric. I stayed quiet. I shouldn't have."

Eric turned and practically pleaded, "Why didn't you?"

"I could say I don't know, but that's bullshit. I know full well why. I've got my own problems and just as soon not add any new ones to them. That's probably the mind-set we all have in school. We're in our own little worlds with our own group of friends. Anyone outside of our spheres basically doesn't exist, only when we need a quick favor or something."

"It doesn't seem right."

"It isn't. But, if you don't mind me asking, you've probably seen kids younger than you, sophomores or freshmen, getting picked on by someone in their grades. Have you ever intervened? You could handle a freshman."

"*Thanks.* I'm not a total weakling." Eric analyzed the question and conceded, "You're right. I usually just keep on walking. Fair point."

"I imagine you keep walking not because you don't care," Billy said. "You probably feel bad for the kid, even identify with him. But helping out the kid wouldn't stop the shit that Jason puts you through, so why bother?"

"Something like that, yeah."

"I'm curious. Why don't you fight back? Have you ever thought about it?"

Eric innocently chuckled. "I've never been in a fight in my life, Billy. I've never thrown a punch at anyone. I wouldn't know what to do. Punch first? Kick him in the balls? When it comes right down to it, I just don't want to fight. It's not who I am. Jason knows it and exploits it."

Billy nodded. "I've never taken a swing at anyone, either. Never really had a reason to. When you grow up like that, it becomes ingrained in you, and only reinforces your disposition against becoming violent. I know how you feel. I really do. Maybe next time if I see someone being an asshole to a smaller kid, I'll do something about it."

"Maybe?" Eric asked, knowing that "maybe" in all honesty meant "not likely".

Billy looked at his feet, realizing what Eric was thinking. "I promise I'll try." He clasped his hands, now hoping that if that opportunity ever presented itself he'd stay true to his word.

Eric coughed into his hand and then waved it in front of his face, squinting.

"Jesus, Billy, I don't mean to be rude but did you fart?"

"*Excuse me?*" Then Billy inhaled and became startled by the stench of decay that began seeping into the room. "No! That's not me!"

"Then what the hell?" Eric shouted.

Neither boy had ever experienced anything like it. Whatever emitted the necrotic aroma came from outside. They each stood to take an unwanted peek out of the window, neither of them eager to see what might be festering in the snow.

A deep growl distinguished itself from the rumbling generators and rattled the expansive front window. Billy and Eric approached the vibrating glass pane, expecting to look through it and see a hellhound bearing bloody fangs.

Neither boy moved. They did not want to see what was there.

And then it crashed through the window, spraying glass everywhere before landing in the middle of the family room.

Chapter Thirty-Four

The sounds of whooshing wind and distant generators couldn't obscure the sudden crash and thump heard from outside by the chief and Jack Halberstrom. Two high-pitched screams erupted.

They forgot about the ungodly stench and bounded back into the house. Gusts of snow and frigid wind whirled through the large, shattered window. The two men arrived to find Eric and Billy pressing their backs against the far wall of the family room, their bodies repelled by what looked to be a six-foot-long, muddy log in the center of the floor surrounded by glass shards.

"First the generator, now a fucking tree limb blows into the house? No fucking way!" Jack Halberstrom's face turned that sweaty shade of red made only by exasperated, overweight men.

The log groaned.

"Holy shit, it's him!" Eric spastically jabbed his finger at it. "It's Jason Nicholson!"

Jason's mud- and blood-covered face gasped for breath. Two bright-blue eyes appeared from underneath grimy eyelids. The rope enwrapping his body stank of wet earth.

The chief holstered his gun and grabbed his shoulder mic and called dispatch for an ambulance. He then knelt beside the boy and pressed his fingers to Jason's neck to check the strength of his pulse.

"Jesus, he's burning up! Hang on kid!" The pulse throbbed weakly. "Kid! Jason! Look at me! Can you look at me?"

The boy blinked and rolled his eyes toward the chief.

"Good job, Jason. Don't move. Keep looking at me. Who did this to you?" The chief figured it was worth a try.

Jason's mouth moved in slow motion, speaking nothing but wheezes.

The chief looked into Jason's eyes, which took on a blind man's dazed appearance. "Save your strength, Jason. Help's coming! Jack, talk to him!"

Jack Halberstrom pushed aside whatever resentment he normally would have felt toward his son's bully, for he didn't see a mean punk of a kid splayed before him. What gasped at his knees was a misshapen mass of bones and flesh molded by merciless hands.

"Just look at me, keep looking at me, kid," Jack told Jason, not knowing what else to say.

The chief sprang up and ran toward the breached window, peering through the incoming bluster, scanning yards and houses surrounding the Halberstrom home. It dawned on the chief that the rotting stench that'd so flustered him had dissipated. Seeing nothing, he turned to assist Jason, but froze upon hearing in the distance the sounds of deep-throated cackles slithering through the wind.

Chapter Thirty-Five

Police officers clad in black tactical gear and toting semiautomatic rifles stormed the Halberstrom cul-de-sac.

"I'm telling you, Dad! His body just flew through the window hard and fast!" Billy was almost nose to nose with the chief, who was trying to get his son and Eric to disgorge whatever they could remember. "It wasn't some lob job, either. Christ, look where he landed! I mean, he was practically a brick thrown through the window!"

Paramedics within the Halberstrom family room prepared to lift Jason Nicholson's body, freed from filthy cord that was in the process of being bagged as evidence, onto a gurney from the spot where he'd landed, fifteen feet from the broken window.

"My God, his body's nothin' but mush," said an older paramedic, who felt the broken bones shift below Jason's skin. "There's definitely internal bleeding, it's just a matter of how bad."

The rescue workers tried not to overly disturb the body as they stabilized Jason in advance of the walk to the waiting ambulance and intravenous lines destined to be plugged into his veins. They snipped through his winter coat and shirt to glean what might've happened to him.

"Look at that fuckin' bite mark." The older paramedic stepped back, pointing at Jason's arm. Two massive mounds of raised, punctured flesh oozed foul-smelling fluid.

"Jesus, he could be rabid, in addition to everything else. Let's go. Brace him, cover him and let's get him out of here," the older paramedic ordered a younger one, whose pained face revealed he'd forgotten the brace.

"Go get the damn neck brace! How could you forget it?" the older paramedic barked as the new kid on the squad hurried out to the ambulance to correct his rookie mistake.

Billy couldn't believe that the same clean-cut teenager he'd seen acting like a prick earlier in the day had been pummeled into something almost as lifeless as a scarecrow.

Jack Halberstrom stood behind his boy, next to Billy, a hand placed on Eric's shoulder for reassurance. "Son, you see anything?" Jack had anticipated the chief's question.

"We were both sitting on the couch, like, perpendicular to the window. The body just crashed through, but like Billy said, kind of in a high arch." Eric mimicked the trajectory by thrusting his hand outward into a swan dive.

The chief poked his head through the gaping window hole in a futile attempt to rule out what *didn't* ferociously hurl a teenage boy into the upper level of a two-story home. All he saw were special weapons and tactics officers traversing the snow.

"I don't see any catapults or circus canons outside," the chief said to nobody in particular after withdrawing his head from the cold. "And it's obvious Jason was kidnapped and bound by *somebody*. He didn't beat the crap out of himself and then tie up his own body. So clearly his abductor threw him in here."

"By hand?" Jack Halberstrom scoffed.

"Yes, exactly." The chief, still looking outside, slowly nodded his head. "Someone threw Jason Nicholson's body into your home. And then ran off on foot. I didn't hear any cars peeling out of here. Did you?"

"No," both Eric and Billy answered simultaneously.

"Jack, do you recall tires squealing through snow when we were outside?"

He agreed with a headshake that he didn't. "So whoever did it can't be far. And your guys are out there right now picking apart the woods looking for him. So you'll get him, Chief."

"That's a really ballsy thing to do." Schweitzer surveyed the scuttlebutt in the chilly Halberstrom family room. The busted generator's inability to provide electricity and heat fast became evident. Daylight was fading, so much so that emergency workers had borrowed police flashlights to scan Jason Nicholson's body, just to ensure they hadn't missed a bone poking through skin. Police officers from neighboring municipalities convalesced in the house while search teams fanned throughout the neighborhood, knocking on doors, looking for witnesses and venturing into Hancock's vastly wooded acres.

"Why draw so much attention to yourself?" The chief, deep in thought, paced the room, weaving his way around the people in his path. "I mean, he knows we're out there looking for him. He must've known I was in here before he threw Jason. Hell, my car's right outside. I'm assuming he knows the area and the proximity of the police station from here..."

The young paramedic who'd forgotten the neck brace interrupted the chief's train of thought upon returning and then gently fitted the brace around Jason's throat and neck.

Jason had earlier closed his eyes and they remained shut. He'd still said nothing. The chief pivoted his head to Eric Halberstrom, who hadn't notice he was being monitored.

He's enjoying this, the chief thought.

Eric's thin lips pressed together, forming a sliver of a gleeful smile. His eyes feasted on his vanquished foe.

The chief felt in his bones the only thing Eric desired more was for Jason to be conscious and aware of the bullied boy's quiet revelry— *How's it feel, you scumbag?*

"Hey, Eric," the chief called.

He jerked his gaze from Jason to the chief. "Yeah?"

Schweitzer ambled over to Eric, towering over him, hoping some intimidation might eke some useful information out of him. "Whoever did that to Jason wanted to make sure you saw his handiwork. That's why his body ended up in your house. You might not realize it, but this has something to do with you. What do you think of that?"

Eric nonchalantly shrugged his shoulders and then took one final gander at the bully-cum-gimp. Gusts of snow blew through the shattered glass, dusting Eric, but he paid the cold no mind.

There's no way he's getting out of the hospital anytime, soon, Eric thought. *Hell, he may die. And even when he does return to school, he'll probably be traumatized, mentally fucked. Even sweeter. Release the nightmares. Let him spend the rest of his life in agony.*

"If you find whoever did it, bring him by so I can thank him," Eric said.

Jack Halberstrom slapped his boy in the back of the head. "What the hell are you talking about? Look, there's getting even and then there's attempted murder, which is what this looks like to me. He might have roughed you up a bit, but you shouldn't be happy about *this*." He pointed to the paramedics carrying Jason outside.

Eric, shocked, turned to dress down his father on one side while simultaneously speaking truth to the chief on the other, "I've got a guardian angel in my corner, and I couldn't be happier that it's watching over me. I feel like I just won the lottery, Dad. Actually, if you were to offer me twenty-five thousand bucks or what happened to that jerk-off, I'll take the latter any day of the week. Now, if you think that makes me bad, fine, that's your prerogative. And on some level you might have a point. But you haven't experienced months of being the target of someone else's daily cruelty.

"You know what's almost worse than always being called a 'fat fuck' in front of a girl you might like? Or getting punched to the point where you can't move your arm? Waking up before school and knowing that at some point it's *going* to happen later in your day and not being able to do a damn thing about it. That's not getting roughed up, *Dad*. You get roughed up playing football. What I've gone through almost every day for the past three months is called getting dehumanized. Hell, I'm more upset that the window's broken and the power's out than I am over Jason Nicholson getting his ass justifiably kicked.

"But let me make things a little bit easier for you, Chief. If you really think I'm somehow complicit in all this, I give you complete permission to check out my computer. It's in my bedroom. I won't touch it. Just take it with you when you leave. Go look at my phone bill, my cell phone and my bank account, which has about ten bucks in it at any given moment. You can go all *CSI* on me and I won't kick up a fuss. Hook me up to a lie detector. Hell, I *want* you to hook me up to a lie detector. I'm not bullshitting you. There's nothing, *nothing*, to tie me to whatever happened to Jason. Just good fortune."

The chief, nonplussed by Eric's candor, turned to his father. "Your thoughts?"

"I believe my son," Jack said without hesitation. "And I have no objection to you doing any of the things he suggested. You can check me out too, just to clear up any thought you might have that I somehow oversaw this whole clusterfuck. And you know what should really help you close the book on us before you even open it? Your son's missing, Chief! Do you really think we'd put Tim through that kind of hell?"

That hit the chief hard. His disbelief upon finding Jason in such perilous shape had blocked any notion that Tim might be experiencing the same torment. *What if it's defiling my son as we speak? Or Travis, or Brittany, or Kelly? Jesus. He might be systematically torturing them all.*

"Dad, Jason's alive. Right?" Billy spoke up.

"Yeah, at least he is for now." The chief, somewhat dazed by reality, walked to the window and watched as the ambulance's lights blazed red and blue. "God, I hope that driver knows how to handle spinouts."

The vehicle carrying the best piece of evidence as to the whereabouts of the other missing children vanished into the white abyss, destined for arrival at Morristown Medical Center, forty-five minutes away. Passing the ambulance in the opposite direction were vans from the New York NBC and ABC news affiliates. Word had gotten out that something big was up at the Halberstrom house. The vehicles parked on the curb behind hastily tied yellow police tape strewn across the yard.

"Dad, listen! If Jason's alive, then that tells me that Tim is too. Whoever's out there could've killed Jason in a heartbeat. But he deliberately chose not to. You said it yourself: this is all being done by design. Jason's being alive is part of the plan."

The chief turned his attention from the encroaching broadcast journalists toward Billy and forced a half smile. "That's my boy. You're thinking logically. But I'm having trouble wrapping my mind around this: Jason was a bastard to Eric, right?"

Eric, off to the side, silently nodded.

Billy continued, "And Maria Flynn said her brother was a real jerk to a boy in his grade. I know what you're thinking. Who was Tim bullying?"

The chief didn't answer. He grabbed his shoulder mic and instructed dispatch to get one of the officers to personally drive Jason Nicholson's father from the municipal building to the hospital so he could be with his son.

There was little more the chief and his boy could do at the Halberstrom house. Investigative teams continued to pick apart the neighborhood as the whiteout conditions stymied their effectiveness.

"Let's go give the prosecutor an update," the chief told his son. "Jack, Eric. Why don't you come on down too? You'll freeze here. We've still got to process this room, and we can get official statements from you about what you witnessed here. We'll keep someone posted. Nobody'll get inside, promise."

"Fine by me," Jack mumbled and began looking for his keys.

"Do you want to take my computer along?" Eric reminded the chief of his offer.

"No." His answer carried finality. It flew in the face of any police training designed to eliminate suspects. He processed everything he knew, and while no investigator worth his or her salt would blindly let potential evidence sit in a cold, dark house, the chief took that option. And he did something else that police officers do after weighing whether someone deserves a ticket based on all the information at their disposal. He went with his gut. "I believe you."

Chapter Thirty-Six

The chief pushed through a pack of shouting reporters who greeted him in the municipal building's lobby.

"Not now, guys, give us a few minutes," he said. "Come on, Billy."

His son dutifully followed him, along with the Halberstroms. They all ducked into Schweitzer's office. "I'm gonna go get the prosecutor. Don't say anything to anyone outside."

The chief was about to shut them all in when Maria Flynn appeared in the doorway. Billy, standing in front of the chief's desk, took notice and became rigid with concern.

"What are you doing here? Is everything all right?" Billy beat his father to the punch.

"My mother and I wanted to be closer to where the action is, I suppose. We figure if there's a break in the case we'll find out about it sooner. At least I hope that's the case. Still no sign of Kelly?"

The chief quickly dashed her hopes. "No. However, there's been a development."

Morris County Prosecutor Vincent Di Renzo stormed past Maria into the chief's office. "What happened, Don?"

"Chief, can I please speak to Billy? Now?" Maria asked. "It's really important."

"Okay, wait!" The chief felt bombarded. "Billy, go talk to Maria in one of the conference rooms. You know the rules. Don't tell those jackals a goddamn thing if they come asking. Jack and Eric, you're staying with me and the prosecutor."

Billy scampered outside and pulled Maria's arm toward the empty chambers where the council members met when discussing things in closed session.

And then everything became blissfully quiet and warm. The municipal building's generator did a marvelous job supplying heat.

"Have a seat," he invited her. The two got comfy next to each other in padded swivel chairs seated around the council's wide oak table. Billy immediately disregarded everything his father had told him and recounted for Maria the attack on the Halberstrom household.

"Do you think he'll live?" Maria thought what she was about to say would've been the most upsetting piece of news, but Billy'd one-upped her.

"The doctors know to call my dad the second there's an update. I doubt the ambulance is even at the hospital yet, with the blizzard as bad as it is. Until then I'm thinking there's an EMT hovering over Jason with the shock paddles, waiting for the machine to give off one of those long beeps. By the way, what's so important that you needed to speak with me in private?"

"Okay, here's the deal, I did some asking around, like you suggested. Do you remember a student named Susan Weaver? She'd have been a senior like Tim."

"Can't say I do."

"Trust me, you've heard of her. Most of the high school's heard of her. She transferred at the start of the school year. Her parents put her in Catholic school. Morris Catholic High School, to be exact."

Uh-oh, I think I know where you found out what you're about to tell me, Billy thought.

Maria didn't want to use the word *boyfriend* due to her painful awareness of Billy's sensitivity over her burgeoning relationship, but also because she wasn't even sure if that's what they were yet.

"Chris is in her grade, and they're friends," she continued. "He gave me her phone number and encouraged me to call her. I did and explained to Susan that both Brittany and Travis went missing. She was worried I might be accusing her of having something to do with it, but I convinced her that my motives were totally innocent, and that their behavior toward her actually could've led someone else to become involved."

Billy stopped her. "Wait, Travis and Brittany? How do they know each other? You're losing me."

"It took some prodding, but there's a reason her parents are paying ten thousand bucks this year to transfer her for her final year of high school, and it has everything to do with Brittany Cabot," Maria said.

"How so?"

"Early last year they were all at Travis Reardon's house when his folks were out of town. You've seen that place, it's ginormous! Perfect for a long night of drinking, hanging out and sneaking off to various rooms to hook up, which is what a bunch of the guys on the football team did with the cheerleaders and hot girls. You know how they all hang out together."

"That's not exactly breaking news, and I'm certain Tim wasn't at the party because it might impugn his squeaky-clean image."

"Tim doesn't figure into any of this, if that's what you're thinking. Anyway, Brittany, Susan, everybody's getting smashed on Travis's dad's good whiskey. It's late, kids are crashing at the house because there's no fear of getting found out because Travis's folks were in the Bahamas. Keep in mind, this is before Travis and Brittany were officially a couple. They'd gone out on a few dates but it wasn't like they were exclusive. Brittany was *really* into him, though. That's why she flew into a rage when she walked in on Susan and Travis goin' at it in his bedroom."

Billy tugged at his already loose hoodie collar. "They were, um, you know, goin' at it, as in—"

"Sex? No. Susan said they were just foolin' around. Does it really matter?"

"No!" Billy's voice cracked. "Not at all. I mean, depending on what she walked in on, it might've riled her up even more, I guess."

"Well, I suppose so. But they're in Travis's bed, on the covers, and she rolls off of him, and Brittany's standing in the doorway staring daggers at both of them."

"If they weren't boyfriend-girlfriend yet, then what was the big deal?"

"Exactly! That's what I was thinking. And at first that's what it seemed like. Brit walked away and Travis and Susan got kinda red-faced, giggled and then started up again. About a month later Brit and Travis were officially together. Susan treated their one-night stand, if that's what you wanna call it, as a fun hookup, nothing more. Then the tweets started coming. Almost every day someone would create a new Twitter account with a fake handle and bombard Susan's Twitter feed, calling her a slut, whore, cocksucker." Maria covered her mouth with her pointer and middle fingers. "Sorry about the language."

Billy stayed serious. "No worries. I mean, if that's what someone wrote, then don't gloss over it."

"But it got even worse. She'd get text messages from numbers she didn't recognize that would say things like 'end it all, you pig'. Day after day she'd be called a 'skank', a 'fat, ugly whore' or, let's see, 'no guy would ever wanna fuck a loose slut like you', and, 'why don't you go and kill yourself so none of us ever have to look at your dick-licking face ever again'. It didn't matter how many times she'd block people, those vicious messages and tweets kept coming. And on Facebook too. Susan would post innocuous photographs of her and her friends, and then the comments underneath the photos were just horrible. They always centered on Susan's weight, her appearance."

"Look, if none of that was true—and I'm inclined to think none of it was—why would she bother to care?"

"Billy, girls are sensitive!" Maria slapped her palm on the glossy tabletop, loud enough to make Billy bounce in his seat. She said it not to scold but to educate him for future consideration. "How can you not know that? We're all super self-conscious to begin with. We obsess over whether people think some of those names or awful descriptions might be true. It doesn't help when everyone on the planet who you care about, or a boy who you might like, reads all of that crap.

"And it was all anonymous and never ending. Susan couldn't figure it out, but she felt so humiliated because all of her friends, her family members, they all saw the smears. How could they not? And it metastasized. Susan was helpless to stop it. Not only did she have to contend with all that nonsense about her on her own pages, but she constantly worried about the demeaning garbage kids at school began posting on their own Facebook and Twitter feeds, talking smack about her.

"This went on for months, from fall through the spring of last year, right before we got out of school for the summer. And all during that time, kids who didn't like Susan for whatever the reason, or kids who just wanted to be assholes, would start saying stuff to her whenever they passed her in the halls. Pretty soon it wasn't relegated to just being online. Some of the kids started to believe it. They hear all that stuff making the rounds in the hallways and pretty soon it's accepted as fact.

"Then people started taping construction-paper signs on her locker for everyone to see, like *Ugly Plus Worthless Equals Whore*. There was always a new one waiting for her every time she went back to her locker for a textbook or to get her coat to go home. She'd rip them down, one after the other, and they'd always reappear, waiting to taunt her.

"She couldn't sleep. Her grades started to slip. She started smoking pot in order to relax. She was a straight-A student at the start of last year, and by the end of it she'd turned into an unstable basket case. All because of some faceless, nameless creep."

"Wait, hold on." Billy drummed his fingers on the table, trying to conjure up a not-too-distant memory. "I remember hearing things like that last year about a Suzie Dunford. Hell, I remember seeing some of those signs. Wasn't she the girl who tried hanging herself from a ceiling fan in her bedroom last May?" He didn't wait for Maria to answer as clarity filtered through his mind. "But the fan was loose and she ended up crashing to the floor and blacking out."

"Exactly! *That's* Susan Weaver."

"My dad went to the hospital to talk to her as she recovered, met with her parents, trying to figure out why she tried to kill herself. She never said. But why the name change?"

"She was mortified! Wouldn't you be? You get tormented every day of your life for five or six months straight, try to off yourself and screw it up, and then realize you have another year left to attend school with the very same people mocking you? She knew it would only get worse, so she opted for a new start, took her mother's maiden name and took the more formal Susan instead of Suzie."

"So, Brittany was sending her all of that stuff?"

"No," Maria said in a hush. "Travis was."

"What?! *Why?* That makes no sense."

"Brittany made him do it. She orchestrated it. She went out of her way to befriend Susan after the party where she saw them hooking up, so Susan would never suspect her. And all the while she was playing the innocent babe in the woods, she manipulated Travis into taunting her online, telling him exactly what to type so it would emotionally cut her to the bone.

"And when Susan needed to be consoled or a shoulder to cry on, Brittany would be right there for her. When Susan said she wished she could escape all of this, Brit pointed her in the direction of some of her druggie friends, all the while saying she shouldn't do it, but making no effort to stop her from getting high. Brit didn't just want to get back at Susan for daring to get her hands on Travis; she wanted to literally destroy her."

"But why would Travis be complicit in any of this?" Billy said. "I've never heard Tim say anything about him acting like such a jerk."

"He did it for the same reason all guys do incredibly stupid things when a woman asks them to do it: sex. Brittany more or less told

Travis to do all that to Susan or else they'd stop being a couple, and he wouldn't get any of the benefits, if you know what I mean. And he'd be seen as being dumped by the coolest, hottest girl in school, and she'd spread word that he was lousy in the sack, to boot."

"What a vindictive bitch."

"I know! In a way she was punishing Travis, too, for hooking up with Susan at the party. Brit must've gotten it in her head that they were already a couple and felt betrayed when she saw those two going at it. So she hatched her plot and now Suzie's a Susan who's essentially restarting her life at seventeen years old. That sucks.

"She still lives in Hancock and takes the same bus as Chris. That's how they got to know each other. She eventually opened up to him about why she didn't bother going to Hancock High School."

There was no hiding this one from Billy. He'd have to man up and take it. "I think she confided all this in me because she knows Chris and I are seeing each other. Once she started talking, it all began gushing out. Both she and I cried at certain points in the conversation."

"It makes sense," Billy said. "Talking's the best thing to do, rather than dwelling on it. I guess I should take some of my own advice sometimes." Not wanting Maria to think that over too much, he refocused on Susan. "I hope she got help. Or at least is still getting it."

"She said something about counseling helping her. I'm really surprised she was as forthcoming as she was. Like you said, talking seems to relieve some of the anguish. I said I'd like to visit her after the storm blows through, maybe get lunch together."

"You absolutely should."

"She has no social media presence anymore: no Twitter, Facebook, Instagram, nothing. I don't even know if she texts anyone. I mean, can you imagine growing up without social media? What's the point of having an iPhone? What did our parents do to waste their time back in the old days when they were in high school in the 1980s?"

"Wait, but how did Susan realize any of this? Brittany wouldn't have just come out and told her."

"Travis got sloppy. Hancock High School has closed-circuit cameras placed in and around the building, but none of them center on that stretch of lockers. He posted the signs on Susan's locker when everyone else was in class. If there'd been cameras there, that whole mess would've been uncovered long before it got to the point that broke

160

Susan. But get this: the moron would keep the signs in a binder in his backpack.

"One day last spring he left a few in the pack, not in a binder, so that if you walked behind his seat in class and looked down at the floor where he'd placed his pack—opened, mind you—you could see what was inside.

"And that's just what Susan did. She was in the same chemistry class with Travis, and when they were all working on a project, she spotted one in his backpack when she went to get a Bunsen burner, of all things. It was made up of bright-yellow construction paper with purple lettering reading *I Take Two Cocks at Once.* I mean, disgusting, right? Travis's back was to her, so she squatted down to pretend to tie her sneakers and briefly leafed through his pack. There were five of them in there. She was shocked.

"She spent the rest of the class in a daze. She saw Travis ask to use the bathroom and he took his backpack with him. Right after class she made a beeline for her locker, and that same purple and yellow sign was taped on it. She tried hanging herself that night."

"Did she confront Travis or Brittany? Why didn't she tell someone?"

"She didn't tell anyone, probably for the same reason Eric Halberstrom never said anything to his dad until all this happened today: it's embarrassing when you can't defend yourself and have to admit it. You feel weak. And when it gets out that you blabbed to your folks or to the principal, you're a squealer and that makes you look even worse in the eyes of everyone else, or so you think. It's all bullshit, but that's how the world works in high schools and prisons.

"As for Travis and Brit, she confronted them both that day right after school. Travis clammed up. Susan could tell he was ashamed. I doubt Travis even knew the emotional damage he'd caused her, probably because he never bothered to find out. It sounds to me like he hit the Send button and then moved on to reading about sports, the coward. But it emboldened Brit. 'Next time keep your filthy hands to yourself, slut.' That's the last thing Brit said to Susan before she walked away, like nothing had even happened.

"It gobsmacked Susan, made her question her friendships and whether she could ever trust anyone again. She went home, found an extension cord and tried to end it all. I doubt Brittany even raised an eyebrow when she found out that her actions led to a girl almost killing herself. I bet you anything she blamed Susan for not having a thicker skin."

Billy rocked and twirled around in his chair, thinking.

"We both saw why Jason Nicholson was dragged through hell and back, and you were up front about Kelly's behavior." He dragged the tip of his sneaker on the ground to stop the swirling. "I cannot believe I'm about to say this, but Brittany and Travis have made it abundantly clear why Krampus paid them a visit."

"Kelly's just immature," Maria said. "Travis is an unthinking dupe, and we both know there's something seriously wrong upstairs with Jason and Brittany. Tim's no thug, Billy. Unless he's a brilliant sociopath who's fooled you and your family for the past eighteen years..." She did not know how to complete the thought.

"I have a theory." Billy became reserved. He'd let too much slip and literally waved away the thought as if it were a bothersome fly buzzing around his head. "Never mind. I'll go into it more if and when I think there's something to it—"

"Nope, spill it, Schweitzer." She was nonthreatening in tone, just curious. "You can't just throw something like that out there and reel it back. This isn't a reflection of how hard I think your dad and the rest of the force are investigating this—I think they're busting their butts—but we don't have much else to work with right now. Not that I'm deputizing myself or anything. So what's up?"

Billy's cell phone rang and signaled welcome relief when he recognized the number and felt assured that a much-needed distraction was forthcoming.

"Mike, I'm putting you on speaker with me and Maria Flynn. We're at the town hall. You're very well aware of what she saw earlier today and you're not questioning any of that, right?" Dead silence. Billy smiled and looked at Maria and borrowed her line, "So what's up?"

Maria and Mike Brembs exchanged pleasantries, followed by Billy's description of Jason Nicholson's dramatic reemergence.

"I don't think it's necessarily important news." Mike's voice sounded clear as it rose from Billy's iPhone placed on the table. "But I figure why not keep this whimsical conversation rolling with news that sounds more appropriate coming from a coffee klatch? And it'll really spice up my German report."

"Mike, please get to the point," Billy said with his usual waning patience.

"Did you or Maria or any of the other affected families get postcards featuring pictures of the thing that Maria absolutely, unquestionably saw today?"

Maria rolled her eyes. "That wasn't too condescending, thanks, Mike."

"All right, I'm sorry. But the question was serious."

"I haven't really had time to check the mail today, but there weren't any stuck to my front door or under one of my dad's windshield wipers," Billy said. "Maria, you?"

"Not a thing," she said. "And the mailman did manage to make it to my house before the thing that I absolutely *did* see today took my brother, smart-ass."

"Lesson learned," Mike said respectfully. "I keep forgetting what you guys are going through right now. I'm assuming none of the other families got anything, so here's why I bring it up. Krampus is an incubus."

"It's not exactly news that it looks like the devil," Billy said.

"Ah, but there's a difference between your garden-variety, pitchfork-wielding devil who'll drag you kickin' and screamin' to hell and an incubus. Somehow, and don't ask me how, Krampus in the early 20th century sort of made a resurgence in Europe in the form of Christmas postcards. And we're not talking any of that cutesy shit with prancing reindeer and smiling elves. Almost every single one of them that I've seen features your boy Krampus, tongue a wagging, harassing women in, well, let's just say suggestive ways."

Billy and Maria eyed each other with suspicion before both saying, "Go on."

"I mean, one of them has Krampus looming over some cowering girl who's on her hands and knees, like he's about to give it to her doggy style. Another has an equally terrified girl kneeling right in front of Krampus looking like he's about to make her polish his knob—"

"Jesus, we get the idea, Mike!" Billy cut him off.

"Hey, don't blame me for painting a picture. And I didn't say she was actually *doing* it. But that's what's online. Look it up for yourself. I'm not sugarcoating anything."

Maria immediately opened Google on her iPhone while Mike continued speaking.

"It's pretty smutty stuff. I'm surprised AC/DC hasn't written a song about Krampus," he said. "I can't quite see how that equates to spreading good Christmas cheer, other than to suggest you've been pretty damned naughty so you better literally watch your ass."

"He's not kidding." Maria showed Billy her phone, its screen now sporting a Krampus Christmas postcard.

"Sweet Jesus!" The misogyny left Billy agog. "A naked, hairy Krampus and a cute little girl are straddling the same rocking horse. Not only is Krampus pressing himself against her, he's also licking the top of her head."

"That's one of my favorites!" Mike chirped. "I'm thinking of getting one and sending it to my grandma. She'd get a kick out of it."

"I most certainly have never seen anything like that in my life!" Maria shouted at Billy's phone.

"Ditto here," Billy said. "I appreciate you bringing it to our attention, but it's looking like a dead end to me. No postcards. I can ask the other families if anything odd came in the mail, but I'm sure they would've said something."

"Hey, one more thing," Mike said. "What is a German monster doing in the United States? Like, did Europe suddenly run out of bad kids to punish?"

"I haven't even thought about that." Billy rolled his eyes so Maria could see.

"Seriously, how did your Krampus guy get over here? I mean, anything with a pulse can sneak across the Mexican border. That I understand. But it has to get to the physical continent first. I'm guessing it snuck onto some barge when nobody was looking, because short of airmailing itself inside a big box with holes poked through the lid, I don't see that thing getting on a plane."

A knock on the conference room's door interrupted the conversation. "Billy, you in there?"

"Just in time! Yeah, come in, Dad."

The chief opened the door and wiggled his pointer finger for his son to join him.

"Sorry to bust in, but the prosecutor wants to ask you a few questions about what happened at Eric's house before he feeds the press again. Just tell him the truth."

"I will, Dad. Mike, I gotta go," he shouted over his shoulder.

"Hi, Chief Schweitzer, I'm pulling for you and your family," Mike's disembodied voice said.

"I appreciate it. I'll let you guys finish up. Billy, meet me in my office." The chief left and shut the door.

"Talk to you later, Mike." Billy ended the call and motioned for Maria to join him. "I don't know if they're gonna let you sit in on this, but I'd like you to be there. We're all involved."

The two exited and walked toward the chief's office.

"Those postcards were freakin' insane," Billy said as an aside.

"Oh my God, *tell* me about it." Maria playfully smacked Billy's shoulder the way a buddy would. "I mean, what sick mind would even contemplate putting little girls in such depraved positions?"

Chapter Thirty-Seven

Brittany Cabot couldn't help but notice with great trepidation the candlelit gleam in the leering eyes of the monster towering over her.

She couldn't press her back against the cold ridges of the cave wall any harder, lest they slice through her clothing. Still constrictively bound and sitting like a letter L with her feet poking underneath the archway created by the creature's massive legs, Brittany played a daunting game of chicken with the thing over who would speak first.

She cracked. "What?! What do you want?"

It scrunched on its haunches, sinking its lecherous smirk nearer to Brittany, to the point where their faces were separated by mere inches. It deeply inhaled her faded yet flowery scent.

"You smell *gooooood*," it hissed.

Two plus two immediately equaled four in Brittany's now-frantic mind. "Gross! Back off, you fucking pig!"

She channeled a burst of adrenaline to flip-flop and wriggle away from the creature, which nonchalantly pressed its hand against her chest, steadying her against the cave wall. Her breath sputtered through her teeth, as her eyes glowered hatred toward her captor.

"Feisty!" The thing delighted in Brittany contemplating the worst. Its deep voice snaked around her like an extra layer of cord.

"I like them on the feisty side. What fun is it when they just lie there? Right, Travis?" Krampus called over its shoulder to Brittany's boyfriend, who kept quiet.

"I don't know what's twisting through your sick brain," Brittany said. "But I swear I will spit, bite, thrash and—"

It silenced her tirade by exhaling its torrid breath onto her face. The rancid gush burned into her nostrils and throat, deflating her animated rage.

Travis Reardon, sitting five feet to Brittany's left, fought the searing pain caused by his broken bones and used his legs and lower back to lurch away from his subdued girlfriend.

"How chivalrous," the still-hunched thing said without bothering to look at Travis, now fifteen feet away from Brittany. "A real man would demand to be untied and then ask to fight his rival to protect his woman's honor."

Travis let slip the unvarnished truth, "She's not my woman and you're not my rival. And you beat the crap out of me before to the point where I'd get my ass kicked by Betty White."

Tim Schweitzer and Kelly Flynn, to Brit's right, likewise scooted sideways on their butt cheeks to distance themselves from whatever horror awaited her. The creature disregarded their efforts as it examined Brittany, who regained some lucidity as the thing's toxic breath worked its way through her system.

"Girl, can you hear me? Look at me!"

Its shout startled Brittany from her grogginess. She mentally emerged and realized that her circumstances hadn't changed, but anger still welled within her.

"Miss Cabot, your beau over there was valiantly pleading with me to mete out the discipline on him that I originally contemplated for you."

Her face brightened for the first time in hours and she lavished praise on her boyfriend, all the while beaming at him. *Finally, I'm catching a break,* she thought.

"Honey, I cannot thank you enough for sacrificing yourself like that for me. You're so brave! I knew you couldn't stand the thought of this piece of—" she caught herself, "—this piece of work laying a finger on me. I knew there was a reason I chose you to be with me! We're so lucky to have found each other."

Dead silence elapsed as both Brittany and the monster watched for a reaction from Travis, who lazily stared at his relieved girlfriend and then directed a contemptuous gaze at the creature. Its toothy smile indicated unbridled pleasure in the mental havoc it wrought.

You son of a bitch! Travis thought, now wishing he could somehow channel more strength to move himself even farther away than he'd already managed. It was bad enough one churlish monster already had it in for him. Now a second one would soon sprout her talons and fangs.

The monster disgorged a deep and taunting *har har har!* laugh.

"Girl, two things," it snorted. "When I said your beau valiantly pleaded with me to spare you, let me revise that to say he made no such plea. Rather, he did not protest and he skulked away like the wincing weasel he is. And even if he had made a sincere gesture to protect you, it would have mattered very little. I crave your beauty. The despairing feelings you imbue in others, your masterfully concealed wretchedness and your physical grace embody a perfect creature. If only the Master would permit me to take a bride..." The beast's feigned wistfulness trailed off, and then its mouth unhinged like a boa constrictor's preparing to swallow its prey. Out rolled its red tongue, two feet in length and dotted with pustular blisters where it wasn't riven with slits.

"Get the fuck away from me!" Brittany screamed.

The thing launched its tongue, planting it with a sloppy smack against her right cheek. The slimy muscle smothered her skin and stiffened as the beast slowly licked upward, satiating itself just as a giddy child would upon receiving an ice-cream cone topped with three scoops. Her screams became panicked squeals as the force of the lick drew skin into the monster's reeking maw.

It repeatedly flicked its tongue to her cheek to sop up blood and swished it against the walls of its mouth before greedily swallowing.

Brittany continued her shrieks as the creature's saliva began festering on the raw wound. She turned her scraped cheek away from the monster.

"Thank you, girl! You save me the effort of twisting your head." Again its tongue with fishhook-sharp taste buds lapped off Brittany's other cheek, this time taking a ragged piece of epidermis with it. Appearing as if she'd garishly applied too much rouge, Brittany violently shook her head, sprinkling red droplets everywhere while screaming "no!" to prevent the beast easy access to the blood it craved. She heard nothing but the creature's laughs in between her wails.

"Enough! You made your point!" Tim shouted as Kelly buried his head against Tim's shoulder to hide. Travis, too, looked away from the thing ravaging his girlfriend and into the cave's endlessly dark exit, wishing he could somehow run.

"I have not even begun to make a point, Herr Schweitzer," the monster said as Brittany continued to head-thrash to rid herself of the acidic pain eating at her cheeks. She couldn't fathom the undiscovered diseases rooting into the pores of her shredded flesh. "It is incumbent upon Miss Cabot to convince me she grasps the point of her predicament. And that will require some not-so-deep reflection by her. Whether she is capable of that remains to be seen."

Now dizzy and tired, Brittany slowed her headshakes, and her screams devolved into husky breaths. She hunched forward to stare at her lap, veiling her face with blonde hair, hoping the savagery would end. She could not escape the sight of its tongue's tip lolling like a clock pendulum above her thighs.

The beast drew its tongue straight up Brittany's face and slurped back into its mouth the tips of her nose and chin, her eyebrows and a swath of her forehead.

Brittany's banshee screeches pierced the boys' eardrums, causing them to squirm at the sound of her agony.

Krampus savored her delicate flesh as much as he rejoiced in her pain.

"Needs salt," it chuckled, and then directed one of its razor talons at Brittany's face to get her attention. He slowly pushed the curved tip toward her face and she froze, her eyes crossing as they followed the pointy talon that came to rest on the ridge of her nose. It accepted that she'd continually cry, but decided she was quiet enough for the next phase.

It withdrew the talon, relieving Brittany because it did not stick it through her skull. He instead lowered it under her chin and let the point rest on the soft skin covering her throat. Her whimpers became rushed breaths.

How quick will I die after it slits my jugular? she thought.

Only it didn't. The beast drew the talon down without nicking skin and placed it on the top cord that bound her. It applied slight pressure to cut the top strand, and then brought its nail down, slicing through the second tier, then the third, and then the fourth until it successfully slashed the cord from the top of her chest to the final strand binding her bare knees. The rope unraveled and fell to her sides.

Brittany breathed more freely and jostled her body to get circulation going to her numb extremities. Blood trickled into her eyes from her brow and mixed with her tears, and she scrambled to wipe it all away.

The beast smiled throughout and waited for Brittany to speak, prompting her to do so with a few quick raised eyebrows.

Realizing that snark and disdain would perhaps be unwise, she tried playing nice. "Thank you for letting me go," she mewled.

"Letting you go?" It played feeling affronted quite well. "Could it be that you mistake my intentions? You see, for me to let you go would mean you have successfully expressed to me that you fully understand why I brought you here in the first place, and that I have deemed you sufficiently repentant enough to be freed. So, first, please tell me why the Master instructed me to seek out your company."

Brittany repeatedly rolled her eyes and finally provided a theory she hoped the beast would accept.

"Because you think I'm hot and I flaunt it?"

The thing's disgusted sigh indicated *wrong answer.*

"Then *what?!* I don't get it! What the hell do you want from me?!"

"It's always about you, right, girl?" The beast stayed comfortably hunched, its grin never ending. "Maybe this will convince you to begin thinking of someone other than yourself. So, let us begin. In case you have not noticed, my tongue can reach places you would probably prefer it not."

It seized Brittany's left ankle with one hand and pressed her against the wall with the other, stretching out her leg like corn on the cob. She blubbered as it began its lick softly, enough to spare her more ripped skin, above her ankle, and slid its tongue over her calf and then up her inner thigh.

Chapter Thirty-Eight

"Don't do it!" Travis Reardon sat upright, his face pleading for the monster to display discretion.

Krampus stopped to momentarily appease Travis. It left its tongue on Brittany's thigh, just underneath her tight outfit.

Despite being freed from the cords, she was too terrified to fight and trembled while watching the tongue throb in its place.

The creature gestured to Travis by widening its eyes and titling its head forward, as if to say *and...?*

"Don't do it because she absolutely doesn't deserve what you're about to do to her! Nobody does!"

It sucked back its tongue and shambled over to Travis in its still-hunched posture. "She does not deserve what you just momentarily prevented, but she *did* deserve every abhorrent thing preceding it?"

"That's not what I meant. She didn't deserve *that*, either."

"But she must deserve *something*, right? I have witnessed the domineering and insulting way she speaks to you like a man-child, and you simply accept it!" It backhandedly smacked Travis across the face, not hard but enough to knock him down. However, it caught him and propped him back upright. "*That* was for simply accepting it."

"All right, *fine!*" Travis shook his head to free the cobwebs. "You want me to say it? She can be a real bitch sometimes!"

"Is that so?" The creature mocked surprise.

"Okay, a lot of the time! She was getting under my skin while you were outside, busy doing whatever it is you do. Hell, she even berated that little kid over there for crying!"

Kelly, still sidled up next to Tim, regained the courage to watch the creature.

"She snapped at me because I didn't have the strength to untie her," Travis continued, looking at Brit, who catatonically wavered where she sat. "She was offended that Tim didn't drop everything to help her after I told her that I couldn't. So, yeah, Brittany can be a selfish bitch. But that doesn't make it right for you to violate her like that!"

"Now it sounds like we are getting somewhere," it said with genuine intrigue. "So she angers you?"

He thought about it. "Yeah, sometimes."

"Does she make you do things that shame you?"

A few seconds of quiet preceded his hushed answer: "Yes."

"But she rewards you carnally, so onward you go." The beast ogled Brittany, despite her taking on the appearance of a netherworld clown. "I cannot say I blame you, though. Where there is risk, there is also reward, a luscious one at that. My question for you, though, is whether the pleasure was worth the steady decay of what I can only assume was something once decent within you."

Travis took a pensive veneer. "Sometimes you start believing your own hype, or at least what others say about you. I'm a great high school quarterback, bound for a big college. My name's all over the local sports pages. So having a smokin' girlfriend comes with the package. It has to, right?" He eyed Brittany. She looked pitiful yet angry, always angry, especially due to the cave walls amplifying Travis's description of her as nothing short of reprehensible. Travis remained contemplative. "So in order to keep up appearances you remain a couple, even though..." He stopped, not certain where he was going with that.

"Even though what?" Tim Schweitzer asked. Krampus stayed silent and never broke eye contact with Travis.

"Maybe I wanted someone else but couldn't have her," Reardon said. "Not someone on the cheerleading squad, like you'd expect, but maybe the girl who tutors me in math after school."

"Janet Oshima? That Japanese girl?" Brittany barked. "You preferred *that* over me?"

"You see what I mean?" Travis told Krampus, who'd taken on the role of a commiserating bartender. "*That*. She can't even assign Janet a gender because Brittany and so many people with her world view see Janet as nothing but a nerd. Yeah, Brit, Janet!" He leaned forward and shouted at her, hoping his words would affect her, but doubting it, knowing her indifference toward anyone not in her clique.

"Janet's funny and sweet. She knows a lot about football, a lot more than you'll ever know, Brit," he said. "She's smart, obviously, top-of-the-class smart with the rest of the Asian kids. Maybe if you'd take the time to talk to her you'd realize it—but, no, you'd *never* think of lowering yourself to her level, even though by doing it you'd be elevating yourself and not even knowing it. So for me to ask Janet out, see her in between class by the lockers, bring her to parties? I'd be something of a traitor in the eyes of those phony assholes who I call my friends. Like there's something wrong with me, or her. What a bunch of horseshit.

"But who am I to talk? Even I treated her like some loser brainiac when we first sat down with my algebra book. But I saw who she was after our first lesson and I couldn't wait to go back. But I'm no better than any of those judgmental pricks because rather than ignore them, I stayed quiet. Even now, I don't really acknowledge Janet in the halls when we pass each other. She always has a nice smile for me, but I usually give her a quick nod and brush right past her. Why?"

Travis's jaws clenched. His eyes welled. He wanted to retain his masculinity, but realized he had to drop it in order to rid his mind of the pain.

"Because Simon Cowell with tits over there has some dumb sign she wants me to hang on a locker, or a mean message she wants me to post on a website about some girl she doesn't like! She has me do most of her dirty work, and I just blindly do it. Because I'm supposed to? Because I'm the dumb jock who can't think? Apparently, I am. Hell, there's nothing fucking apparent about it!"

His hysteria erupted.

"Jesus Christ, Brittany, that girl tried to kill herself!" The last word echoed for what seemed like ten seconds before it faded, and only then did Travis finish disgorging what had festered for so long within him.

"You wouldn't even let me apologize to Suzie when it's the only thing I wanted to do." His tears were steady, but he kept his voice composed, "'Just stay out of it, Travis'. 'Be grateful she didn't go the police and squeal, Travis'. 'She's not our problem anymore, Travis'.

"She was never my problem to begin with! She was never even a problem! Until we made her become one to herself."

He slouched back against the cave wall, his emotions depleted. Brittany refused to look at anyone, glancing harrumph-like toward the ceiling.

"I cannot believe I almost killed that girl," Travis said. "God, forgive me, because I sure can't."

Krampus had remained still as a cathedral's gargoyle throughout, so much so that Travis forgot the abomination still crouched before

173

him.

"Salvation seems possible for you, boy," it said, and then chided Brittany. "But not so for all of us. The young can be impressionable to the point of being irredeemable. You see, boy, you have a natural inclination toward decency, yet you suppressed it for the childish reasons you so accurately recounted. And you suffered greatly for it.

"The Master chose you due to a belief that your immorality might be fleeting. Me? I thought you were irreversibly corrupted the first time I spotted you jamming your tongue into Frau Cabot's authoritarian mouth. But that is why *he* is the Master. Now, *what* the Master saw in Frau Cabot, other than her being a wretched vulture that picks at souls, perfectly illustrates that even the Master can guess wrong sometimes. But he is correct most often. Relax now, boy. You need to."

The creature slashed off Travis's ropes without cutting the boy's clothing or skin. He oozed out of the cords, allowing his limbs to splay for circulation. He then flinched in pain, a reminder of what had happened to his arm earlier that morning.

Krampus stood, cartilage creaking, until it hulked over Travis, who couldn't see the thing's darkened face, but heard its ultimatum.

"Why should you trust me *not* to jam two of my fingers in your eyes and my thumb in your mouth so I can rip off your head and use it like a bowling ball?"

Travis figured if something like that was going to happen, it already would have, probably.

"Well, when you put it like that, and based on what I know you're capable of doing, I shouldn't trust you."

"Do you think you can find your way out of this cave, even if you did manage to steal a lighted candle?"

"It'd be difficult."

"Do you believe that I could not almost instantly find you by way of your scent or the sound of your breaths were you to run?"

"I'm not going anywhere."

"No, you are most certainly not. But both your body and mind need rest, I would advise you take it."

"What about Brittany? What about Tim and the kid? And Jason? Is he dead?"

"Jason's life is no longer my concern," it said while surveying the lot before stopping on his target. "Neither is Frau Cabot's."

It lithely swept down to Brittany and he smacked her splotchy face into the rock wall, instantly rendering her unconscious. It carelessly grabbed her bare legs, dangled her behind its back without looking and released her. She landed with a dull thump in the box.

"Now, before I dispose of Frau Cabot, here, let us have a chat, Kelly Flynn," it said.

Kelly uncontrollably shook next to Tim and shouted, "Please don't lick me!"

Krampus chortled. "I prefer licking girls, Herr Flynn."

It crouched a few feet away from Kelly, who began bawling. Tim didn't back away, trying to show the creature he would do what he could to spare the boy any of the torture inflicted on Brittany.

"You won't hurt him." Tim said it one step short of it being a command.

"Stay out of this, Herr Schweitzer, or you might make it worse."

Krampus let the child cry it out a few moments and shot Tim a glance like *hurry it up, already!*

"Herr Flynn, stop crying this moment!" it bellowed, waiting for Kelly to compose himself, which he did by sucking back sobs, almost sputtering to contain them.

"Are you gonna beat me up or make me look like her?" Kelly tilted his head toward the crate containing Brittany.

"Sometimes fear of pain and suffering can be worse than the pain itself. But only sometimes. Think about that as I am not certain of your fate. You will decide it later."

"What are you gonna do with her?" Kelly asked.

"Dispose of her, Herr Flynn, unless you know of another use for trash."

Kelly recoiled.

"Come to think of it, perhaps it is best if you do sleep like Herr Reardon." Krampus lifted up both its legs at once and his body came crashing down on his hooves, making him look like a big M with horns in front of Kelly's face. The boy acted like his face was destined for the insides of the creature's bowels, but Krampus did no such thing other than to exhale a devastatingly toxic breath all over Kelly, who slumped to sleep on his side. It ambled over to Travis and breathed heavily on him for good measure.

"That ought to keep them out of trouble for a bit—at least it will keep Herr Reardon from getting any ideas of untying you two. Even though it *will* be pitch black in here in a few moments."

"Do I get to take a nap too?" Tim said, hoping it would happen, as he didn't enjoy feeling alone in the dark.

"Not a chance." It spun around the cave and blew out the candles, making Tim feel even more isolated.

"You get to stay awake, Herr Schweitzer, and ponder why you might be the worst child of this bunch."

Chapter Thirty-Nine

She reclined on the carpeted floor and faced the fireplace, propping up her head with one of the sofa's end pillows, allowing the flames to layer their warmth over her chilled body.

The sun had set shortly after five o'clock, and a contented sigh escaped her as she watched the orange glow flicker on the ceiling and provide the only light in the family room.

If Hurricane Sandy taught me anything, it's that nothing's bone-chillingly colder than a house deprived of power in the winter, she thought. Even though the storm technically hit midfall, it may as well have been winter. A costly generator was out of the question, but a steady supply of chopped firewood on the porch was plenty to keep the family warm in case the electricity failed them again. Wool socks, flannel pajama bottoms and a New York Yankees sweatshirt served the purposes of comfort and warmth.

She closed her eyes, not to sleep, but to listen to the blizzard. As much as she despised shoveling the white stuff, she loved listening to it swirl through squalls. Her parents weren't home yet, and they naturally worried more about her than she did about them. But they were good drivers. Mom had called and she'd be home in twenty minutes. In the meantime she enjoyed her darkened home under assault by nature's wrath.

Roasted air pockets popped in the burning wood as the flames lapped up every inch of the fireplace. For once she felt calm, a serenity she'd not felt for a long while. She'd piled plenty of kindling wood and split logs next to the fireplace, negating any chance of having to venture outside into the storm. And if it came to that, her father would be the one called upon to do it. He'd be home by then, for certain.

The one thing she didn't like was when the wind overwhelmed the trees near the house. Sandy had tilted them uncomfortably close to falling. Her mother and father had to pay thousands of dollars to cut down the dangerous ones. But other wobbly ones still stood, for now, due to unforeseen but necessary expenses. The weathermen hadn't predicted the forty-miles-an-hour gusts that bent trees that had stood sentinel centuries before she was born.

She hated the way dying trees exploded into machine-gun fire as they fell. One had toppled earlier when she'd struck a match to burn newspaper underneath the firewood. It missed the house by fifteen feet. Too close for her comfort.

A cracking crescendo interrupted her trance induced by the firelight rhythmically dancing above her. A tree was falling toward the house, based on the approach of the sound. She just hoped it wouldn't land flush and rip through walls or the ceiling.

And though it made impact, the tree managed not to expensively damage the house, as she'd soon learn.

She stood, grabbed the lantern flashlight purchased specifically for power outages and walked to the back door that led to the deck, which was built a good way out from the two-story house. It was that spatial distance, combined with the high, thick wooden railing, that had blunted the force of the falling tree. Had it been planted farther back from where it was, the top would've smashed onto the deck like a flyswatter. Fortunately it had sprouted close enough to the house so that the deck railing was the first thing it hit.

She pushed open the storm door through two feet of powdery snow and held out the lantern. Squinting, she saw that the thick trunk karate-chopped the railing and wedged into the side of the deck floor. This slowed the top of the tree enough so that it merely smacked with its multiple limbs the rooftop near the gutter. The uprooted tree now formed a triangular side against the house.

It'll be the first thing they see if they come in through the back, she thought of her parents coming home. *Welcome back, Mom and Dad. Look on the bright side, at least insurance should cover this one.* Then again, she really didn't know if that would be the case. She hoped so. Everything was so damned expensive, especially with college beckoning next fall. She listened as the tree settled into place. There was nothing she could do about it.

She ducked back into the house to warm herself by the fire, and as she withdrew the lantern she heard a quick crunch and what sounded like a straining grunt. She turned the lantern's powerful light back to the tree and saw it slightly rolling from side to side, but still centered where it'd landed on the deck. She waited a few seconds more, hearing nothing but howling wind through bare branches.

She locked the door and returned to the family room, tossed a few fresh logs onto the steady fire and resumed relaxing on the floor. She thought about the work that would have to be done the next morning, the digging out and traveling to stay with her grandmother in South Jersey if the power wasn't restored. They'd lasted one night in the cold during Sandy, and one was enough.

What is it about that tree that bugs me? she thought, and then it hit her. She wasn't surprised that the wind would blow down a tree, but *that* specific tree? That oak had stood missile straight for eons. Sandy, for all of her might, hadn't budged it.

More crunching. Only this time muffled, and coming from above, rising and falling, like waves rocking a ship at sea. She stared at the ceiling and focused her eyes on where the noises were being made. And then it stopped, and she heard only the sounds of wind and fire.

She sat up and opened the fireplace's glass doors and spread the metal mesh curtains so that nothing stood as a barrier between her and the glorious heat. Her head nestled back into the pillow and her hands clasped across her belly, she watched the fireplace like a television, allowing the flames to lull her to sleep if they wished. And she welcomed sleep and the breaks from reality it provided her.

But a trickle of soot caught her eye. It began as a few black teardrops falling into the fire, but then steady licorice strands of blackness rained through the expansive fabric of flame. A torrent of plummeting ash overwhelmed the blaze, trailed by a swelling scream.

A gymnastic thrust of her legs brought her to a stand, never once taking her eyes off the fireplace. The howl spiraled down the chimney and soon revealed a horrifying face as its body collapsed into the logs, exploding swarms of embers. Two hands clawed through smoke and flames as if to pull the stunned girl into the pyre.

Chapter Forty

Vincent Di Renzo, his confidence bolstered, took his place behind the podium in the Hancock municipal building to update what increasingly appeared to be a snowbound press corps. It'd be a rush job, but he'd give the broadcast media enough time to slap together enough footage for the six o'clock newscasts.

"We can confirm that Jason Nicholson has been found and currently is undergoing surgery at Morristown Medical Center," said the prosecutor, this time flanked by fewer lawmen, but enough to fill the camera frames. "Additionally, Hancock Patrolman Dennis Pena, who was attacked by a person of interest earlier today, has been listed in serious but stable condition. I will not comment on their specific injuries. Kelly Flynn, Travis Reardon, Brittany Cabot and Timothy Schweitzer still remain missing and we are actively searching for them despite the storm. Needless to say we are encouraged to have recovered Jason."

The slick attorney blathered out the boilerplate "anyone with information is asked to call..." It mattered little to him that the people who'd benefit the most by seeing the newscasts were without power. The New York City market was king.

The chief opted not to be part of the second press conference and stayed in his office with Billy. The Halberstroms departed for the Holiday Inn off of nearby Route 15.

"How are they, really?"

"Pena's cheekbone was crushed and they operated on his face," the chief told his son. "If he'd been hit a few inches higher on the temple he'd be dead. At least that's what the doctor said. He'll pull through. He still hasn't been able to tell us a damned thing, and I doubt whatever he'd say now would make much sense since he's so drugged up. So we play the waiting game. You remember the rule, right?"

"I'm not telling a soul, Dad."

"Like you didn't tell Maria anything?" The chief rocked back in his chair, facing his son who sat before him like a job interviewee.

Billy decided not to lie. "Okay, she knows about how Jason came into the living room, but she swore up and down she'd keep quiet. And she will, Dad. Promise. She won't go anywhere near the reporters. In fact, she's waiting with her mom in that conference room where you got us before. She's isolated."

"Mmm-hmm," the chief sarcastically smirked.

"Jason?" Billy said it with a *moving right along* urgency.

The chief turned somber. "It's not looking good. Massive internal bleeding, broken ribs, and the doctors confirmed he was bitten on his arm by a large animal."

Believe, Dad. Believe, Billy thought.

"The doctors may have to put him in an induced coma, depending on how surgery goes," the chief continued. "They've been working on him for a while now."

Both father and son felt sick over not knowing whether Tim was suffering the same fate.

"How long are you gonna stay here, Dad? It's not letting up outside. Do you have some extra cots lying around somewhere?"

"We have empty jail cells with beds in them. They're uncomfortable, but they *are* beds."

"You're seriously going to sleep in your own jail?"

"I didn't say *I* was." The chief arched his eyebrow and smirked at his boy.

"Hell *no!* You're not putting me on one of those beds. Lord knows what kinds of things are living in those mattresses."

"Don't sweat it. We have some cots and blankets for just such an emergency. It looks like we'll be here throughout the storm, unless something pops up, of course. Is that all right with you?"

"Absolutely. We're useless at home. Although, what if Tim winds up there? I mean, based on what happened at the Halberstrom house, it's not out of the question."

"I've thought about that." The chief weighed the unpleasant option. "How would you feel about going home with police protection looking after you, just in case Tim does find his way back to us?"

"Based on how the police protected the Flynns' house today? I'm not feeling very confident. No offense to Officer Pena. And that all happened in broad daylight. You take me back home tonight, with nothing but a police flashlight to show your officer the way? I'd rather sleep here. Tim's resourceful. He'd go to a neighbor's house and ask to use a cell phone."

"That's if he can walk, Billy. If he's tied up like Jason Nicholson and winds up on the floor in our house, unable to move, and we're not there? He'll freeze to death."

"Can't Mom stay there?"

"I asked her when you were talking with Maria. She wants to stay here. She doesn't want to be alone in the dark."

"Good God! It's her child! She *can't* be that selfish!"

"Oh yes, she can. I didn't want to get into a big argument with her so I just dropped it."

"Can't you just give the house keys to one of the cops and ask him to stay there? I mean, police protection means they're going to be there anyway."

"We need a family member just in case someone tries the house phone to ask for ransom. I don't think that's at all what's going on, but we can't take a chance. And I'd have two officers there, not one, and they'll know to be on their game after what happened to Officer Pena."

Captain Jim Sherwood knocked on the closed door and opened it without waiting for the chief's permission.

"What's wrong?" the chief asked after reading Sherwood's cautious face.

"I just spoke to dispatch. You're not gonna believe this. I haven't told the prosecutor. I figure it should come from you."

"Is it Tim?"

Billy, too, sensed it and gulped.

"No. We just got a call from a Susan Weaver."

Billy tensed upon hearing the name. "What happened to her?"

"Nothing," Sherwood said. "Nothing to her. However she was crying her eyes out to dispatch, something about Brittany Cabot coming down her chimney and almost burning alive in her fireplace. The ambulance is already on the way."

"Let's go." The chief stood and yanked his coat off his chair's backrest. "Billy, I know her house is a little out there, but ours is on the way. I'm gonna drop you off with my guys, and I'll check back on you after we're done at Susan's. Depending on how things go, I may even sleep there."

Billy grabbed his book bag and left the office for the conference room where Maria waited with her mother. They both sat in the same seats earlier occupied by Maria and Billy, and both stood to greet him. He again exchanged pleasantries with Maria's mom before addressing something urgent.

"Mrs. Flynn, if it's all right, I'm going to wait at my house for a little bit just in case Tim shows up or calls. There will be two police officers there with me. Can Maria join me? If it's all right with her and you?"

That startled both Maria and her mother, who demurred.

"Well, I don' think—"

Billy slyly whispered to Maria, "Brittany's alive. I'll fill you in on the way."

"Mom, I'm going!" Maria commanded. "I promise I'll be fine. Strength in numbers, right? And it's close by our house. You can pick me up on the way home, if you want to stay there tonight."

"I'm not crazy about—"

"Mom! If it wanted me it could've taken me away with Kelly. If it wanted to kill me, it *would* have. I'll be safe."

Maria's mother had said she believed her daughter's description of what happened to Kelly, but she fell into the camp that believed it was some psychopath in a costume. But her daughter had a point. She was ripe for the taking and left unscathed.

Billy jumped in. "And my father will be checking up on me. He has to go out that way and is going to drop me off. I could use the company."

Maria's mother stepped close and hugged her daughter. "You will call me when you get to Billy's house. Immediately. It'll be the first thing you do."

"I promise I will."

"Billy, you take care of her."

"Don't worry, Mrs. Flynn, I want to." Billy winced. Maria flushed red. "I mean, of course. Two armed cops will be with us who are super pissed off that one of their own was attacked by this bastard. Maria *will* be safe."

"Billy!" the chief shouted from down the hallway.

"That's my dad. He's ready. I'm ready. Maria, grab your coat."

183

Maria barely got one arm through her winter coat's sleeve before Billy seized her hand and led her out the door. "Thanks, Mrs. Flynn. Maria will call you very soon!"

The commotion was unavoidable in the lobby. Policemen from an alphabet soup of forces hustled by each other, determining who would go and who would stay. Billy spotted his dad, who gave a *come on!* arm wave.

Journalists fruitlessly asked what was happening and bevies of "no comment" followed from the chief and the prosecutor's team.

Billy led Maria through the crowd and outside to his father's cruiser. He swept snow off the car with his hoodie sleeve to hasten their departure. Maria saw they were out of sight from the reporters and practically shouted to Billy through the wind and snow, "What happened?!"

Billy slathered his arm across his father's windshield to clear it.

"I'm not condoning it in any way." Billy, quickly winded, stopped to catch his breath. "But it sounds like Brittany got what she had coming to her."

Chapter Forty-One

A procession of fully illuminated police cars, windshield wipers squeaking away, hummed along Winchester Road, keeping enough distance from one another in case of a spinout.

The chief drove in the back of the line as he'd be turning off Winchester to deposit his boy at their home. The two officers who pulled guard duty rode in their separate cruisers in front of Donald Schweitzer.

The chief gripped the steering wheel while forty-miles-per-hour winds fought his car. Billy and Maria sat in the rear. None could conceive of the pain felt upon being dumped into a burning fireplace.

Billy held his tongue. He didn't want his father realizing he'd dished everything he knew about Brittany to Maria while they were waiting in the municipal parking lot. The trip was uncomfortably silent, save for the rhythmic rumbling of rubber digging through snow to meet asphalt.

"Dad, I don't know if it's occurred to you, but it'd probably be a good idea to get some of your guys to Bryan Welles's house," Billy said. "Jason Nicholson magically appeared at the Halberstroms'." He looked at Maria, again hedging his bets. "And then there's the reason why you're driving to your current destination."

"Son, give me some credit," the chief called over his shoulder, focusing on the road. "I know you told Maria where I'm going. Did you tell her mom?"

"No, Chief," Maria butted in, respectfully. "I know what Billy knows, and that's probably less than what you know. And that's all I know."

"Well, that didn't sound confusing." The chief's attempt at levity fell with a plop. He then addressed his son's main point.

"Billy, I'm way ahead of you, but I appreciate the suggestion. I dispatched one of my guys—girl, actually, Officer Amanda Fryer—to the Welleses' place. It's in the opposite direction from where we're going, not too far from the Halberstroms'. And the Welleses are home and know to expect Fryer. Hopefully your brother won't be making a dramatic entrance, Maria. And I mean that with all respect. Jason's still under the knife and I have no idea what Brittany's condition is. I won't even get to see her, probably, because the ambulance will be gone with her by the time I get there."

They traveled the rest of the way in silence until the three police cruisers pulled into the darkened Schweitzer driveway, the chief's entering last.

"I'll take care of firing up the generator, Billy." He parked his cruiser. "You two go inside and warm yourselves up. When the power comes back, see if there's anything on the answering machine, okay?"

"You got it." Billy, ever the gentleman, stepped out of the cruiser and scampered around to open Maria's door. He pulled the keys from his pocket and jerked his head toward the house. "Let's go."

They cut through unblemished powder, guided by the chief's cruiser's headlamps. He'd hoped to see Tim's footprints heading to the front door but knew it was fantasy. Tim would've made his presence known somehow. Billy simultaneously unlocked the front door and shouldered his way in. He unthinkingly flicked the hallway light switch, only to be reminded of their predicament when it stayed dark.

"Let me find some flashlights, just in case *our* generator mysteriously breaks," he said. "Please go to the family room, to your left, grab a blanket and get comfy on the couch."

Billy didn't need light to know his way around his own house. He strode into the kitchen to the refrigerator, reached up top and found two small flashlights. He flicked on both and did a quick scan of the house. No shattered windows or kicked-down doors. And most importantly, no older brother discarded on the ground in pain or dead. Billy returned to Maria.

"I can assure you the batteries are fresh. Changed them myself after Sandy." He stood in front of her. She'd already found on the couch the thick crocheted blanket knitted decades ago by Billy's grandmother and draped it over her shoulders.

"Here, please take this and keep it handy." He gave her a flashlight and she kindly accepted. "I'm not crazy about them, but I know we have some candles I can light, and we can build a fire."

"A fire would be lovely." Maria's breaths puffed through the flashlight beam she held in front of her face.

Billy went outside and finally did what his father had asked him to do earlier that day. He brought in two bundles of logs under his arms and loaded them into the small storage bin set next to the fireplace. He then reached under the mantel and pushed open the flue.

"You sure that's a good idea?" Maria cautioned. "I mean, based on what happened to Brittany?"

Billy stopped loading wood onto the black iron grate but resumed after a few seconds.

"That's not going to happen, not to Tim." He crumpled up some old newspapers and stuffed them under the grate. "I'm certain of it. I'll tell you why in a minute."

He stood and grabbed the small box of matches kept on the mantel and flicked a combusting match into the newspaper.

"Voilà! We have heat." Billy grinned. "Now if I did it by rubbing sticks together I'd really be proud of myself."

Maria welcomed the mounting flames.

Billy sat in what normally would be his father's easy chair next to the sofa. The microwave oven beeped and he saw the kitchen light pop on through the hallway leading from the family room to the kitchen.

"Dad got the generator going. I'll put up the heat in the meantime too." He stood and walked over to the thermostat on the room's far wall.

"I'll be right back." He went into the kitchen.

The chief and the two officers walked through the front door after scraping snow off their shoes on the welcome mat.

Billy returned and spoke to his father.

"Nothing on the answering machine. No sign anyone's been here since we left this morning. I didn't check but I doubt there are any footprints by the back door."

"I would expect as much," the chief said. "Billy, Maria, I'd like you to meet Officer Darby and Sergeant Crenshaw."

Both men raised their hands and waved hello in unison.

"They're going to keep an eye on things."

"You're not going to make them march a perimeter outside the house, are you?" Billy's tone sounded halfway serious. "That would be cruel."

"No, smart guy. They'll be in here with you." The chief then spoke directly to his officers. "Billy will get you whatever you need."

"Actually, if you don't mind, Chief, I wouldn't mind taking a quick walk around your home," said Darby, a six-foot-tall, stocky cop in his twenties. "Just to get the lay of the land. And I can check the back door for you."

"I'll go too," said Crenshaw, a veteran policeman a few inches taller and several pounds lighter than Darby, with salt-and-pepper hair poking out from underneath his hat.

"Yeah, all right, but please make it quick," the chief said.

The two men drew their flashlights and went to work.

Billy returned to his father's chair and then turned on the table lamp next to it. The generator's puttering was pleasantly quieter and soothing, compared to the Halberstroms'.

"Kids, just take it easy," the chief continued. "You can contact me for any reason. And I promise I'll call you if anything turns up regarding Tim or Kelly. I know you'll do the same for me. I'll be back sooner than later, I hope."

The chief left Maria and Billy, and all the talk about phoning one another reminded Billy of something.

"You should call your mom, Maria. Put her mind at ease."

She thanked him and held a ten-second conversation with her mother to reassure her. She ended it and then told Billy something that had been eating at her all day.

"I don't understand how you can stay so calm, both you and your dad."

"You seem to be doing all right."

"I feel like there's a volcano constantly erupting in my stomach, Billy. My mother's in tears whenever she's alone. Your dad doesn't crack. Neither do you."

"I wouldn't say that. I hate not knowing, just as much as you do. But based on what I saw with Jason and what I heard about Brittany getting flambéed, I think their punishments directly related to how brutal they were to their victims. What Kelly did to that kid in his school? Small potatoes."

"That's not very reassuring. Kelly might not get beaten to a pulp or set on fire, but that doesn't close the door on him, I don't know, having his kneecaps busted? And how come Travis didn't follow Brit down that chimney?"

"Because he didn't instigate all that cruelty against Susan, that's how. I guarantee you that if either Jason or Brit could switch places with Travis right now they'd do it in a heartbeat."

"Or Travis could be smoldering in a pile somewhere," Maria cautioned. "And I hate to be the bearer of bad news, but you seem to be forgetting someone."

Darby and Crenshaw completed their impromptu outside surveillance and brushed the snow off their shoulders as they reentered the house. They each gave headshakes *no* to Billy, indicating nothing had disturbed the outside.

"Feel free to wander, guys," Billy called to them, and that's what they did. He also realized he had to play host but needed to prepare Maria for something he couldn't bring himself to tell her, but had to give her a crumb as to his thinking. He looked across the family room at his book bag, which he'd placed with care off to the side of the front door when he entered.

"Tim hasn't left my mind since we first learned he was gone." Billy brought his attention back to her. "You're going to need to hear me out on this one. I have a theory about why he was taken."

Chapter Forty-Two

"Forget the whole idea that it's Santa Claus's mercenary. How about something more believable, like, what if it's some kind of military experiment gone haywire?" Tim Schweitzer said out loud in the cold darkness. "Picatinny Arsenal's right next to here, assuming we're still in town. Maybe they were creating some kind of supersoldier and things went wrong? Like they cross mutated a man with a, I don't know, crossed him with a, a—"

"A gorilla and a ram?" Travis weakly replied. He'd awakened from the thing's induced slumber. "I doubt it. They make munitions there. My dad works at Picatinny. The Army might play God but not in northern New Jersey. I don't think he could in good conscience as mayor stand idly by knowing a freak like that might bust loose and pillage the community of its young. 'What did you know about the kid-stealing monster, and when did you know it?' There goes any hope for reelection."

"That's assuming your dad knows everything that happens over there. It *is* the military. It's not like they're forthcoming about everything they do. But you're probably right. Based on the thing's accent, and unless Arnold Schwarzenegger volunteered, I doubt the Army's using German soldiers to create the perfect fighting machine."

"He's Austrian."

Tim chuckled, and summoning his best accent, recited the line from *Predator* after Arnold defeats the alien hunting him: "What da hell are you?"

Travis laughed but almost instantly groaned. Tim sighed, wishing he could do something for his friend.

"How much pain are you in?" He spoke across the cave to where he assumed Travis slumped.

"Not much when I don't move, talk or breathe. Or laugh. Maybe I ought to become used to it. I don't know, at least the thing spared my throwing arm. Although my left side's so broken, my mechanics have got to be shot to shit."

"*Wow!* We're tied up in some cave and witnessed what very well might be a double homicide of two of our schoolmates, and you're worried about football?"

"Right now it's one of the few things I can think about that makes me happy." Travis wasn't in the mood for Tim's *tsk-tsk*ing and decided to speak to the only other person in the room. "How are you doing, little man? Are you awake? Holding up all right?"

"Tim's next on that thing's list." Kelly spoke in a defeated monotone used by condemned men watching the clock tick to midnight before the needle prick.

"Well, your heart's in the right place. I wouldn't worry about Tim, little guy. He has a way of eluding bad guys, on the football field, anyway. And I think that will translate here too, but don't ask me how," Travis replied. "Now, if you'll both excuse me, I'm going to fantasize about being profiled on ESPN and not having to answer questions about some stupid imaginary girlfriend who I met online, who wound up being a dude. Although at this point, that might be preferable to Brittany."

"Not funny," Tim chided.

"I wasn't trying to be."

"What are you talking about?" Kelly's voice lost its hopelessness in place of confusion.

"Don't worry about it," Tim, still sitting alongside him, said. "Let him think about whatever can take his mind off of all this. You should do the same. Is there anything you like doing? Sports? Video games?"

"Playing with my dog."

"*Oh.*" Tim remembered that Kelly's dog, Casey, was winding its way through the beast's intestines.

"And I might end up just like him." Kelly's demeanor returned to morose.

"No. That thing sounded like it was going to let you go. And even if it changes its mind, I'll make sure that doesn't happen, kid. I mean it," Tim said.

"Really? *How?* None of us can fight that thing."

"I mean I'll reason with it. I don't think it wants to hurt you or any of us, for that matter. It's basically following orders, like what the Nazis said at Nuremberg."

"Do not *ever* compare me to that repulsive cult of murderers!" A single candle flame dotted the darkness to reveal the thing had been standing there. One by one, the creature stood before the candles and lit them in a manner Tim surmised must involve it rubbing its talons together over the wicks to generate friction and heat.

"Der Führer and his minions were no fonder of me than you are," it said after lighting the final candle.

"You'll forgive me if I say I find that hard to believe," Tim felt increasing confidence when addressing the monster. Perhaps it was Stockholm syndrome, but he felt they'd built a warped rapport, however tenuous it might be. "I think Hitler and the boys would give the stamp of approval to anything, human or otherwise, that persecutes and brutalizes innocent people. It's not like the Germans have ever shown a propensity toward violence, right? Oh wait, eleven million people disagree. Something like you was built to wear a swastika. Christ, you even speak the language."

"*Christ!* You just said it, boy!" the monster excitedly boomed. "Any holiday centering on the birth of a Jewish child destined to be man's savior could never be tolerated by the Nazis. So they cast out Christ in favor of some god named Odin, or conflated Nazism with Christianity, pilfered its symbols and perversely interpreted it to condone the rise of the Reich. Hitler was God—nobody else. And when those goose-steppers were not doing that, they attached false political motives to aspects of the religion with which they disagreed.

"Austria was the worst! They accused me of being aligned with the communists! Why? Because the Master is fond of wearing red? *That* was their standard? Even worse, anyone dressed like me was arrested in Fascist Austria! Boy, did those jackbooted thugs get a surprise when they slapped the shackles on me!"

It held up and swiveled its left wrist so they could see the thick, rusted ring encircling it. A few aged chain links dangled from the clamp. "I wear this as a reminder that I cannot be stopped by man. Herr Flynn over there learned this earlier today when he shot me with that firearm he took from the policeman."

The creature stomped toward Kelly, who frantically kicked his legs to push his roped body into Tim's side for whatever protection he offered.

"Leave him be!" Tim shouted.

"Quiet, boy!" It thrust its open hand like an arrowhead between the tiny gap separating Tim and Kelly, carelessly flipping Schweitzer across the cave, rendering him useless.

Travis watched Kelly cower before the beast, hoping it would spare the little boy.

"Tell me, Herr Flynn, where did a young child such as yourself learn to shoot a pistol like that? I would attribute it to you simply being a public school student—most of whom seem to need training to use firearms just to walk from lunch period to gym class, such is the miserable state of your society. And you say?"

"I mean, I just pulled the trigger and messed with the safety until it went off," Kelly stammered. "That's the first time I ever picked up a gun, I swear!"

The monster leaned in and glowered at Kelly, examining the veracity of the claim.

"Do not lie to me! You apologized earlier and Frau Cabot yelled at you for doing so! Why?!"

"I'm not lying!" Kelly cared not a whit that he'd flooded his pants with urine. Tim could not rescue him. Death smelled mangy. "I just did what they did on *The Walking Dead* and shot you! What was I supposed to do? You were going to kill my sister! That's why!"

"*No!* Why did you apologize earlier to that wench who screamed for you to shut up?!"

The thing flicked out its Freddy Krueger talons, preparing to strike.

"If you believe in God, boy, and I suspect by your last name that you feast on His flesh and drink of His blood, then I would begin to pray to Him! You are about to be in His graces!"

The thing in a sudden overhand swipe raked its talons on the uneven rocks above Kelly, showering him in sparks forged by unbreakable nails cutting stone. It raised its claws for a second slash but hesitated and screamed, "Unless!"

"Unless what?!" Kelly cried.

"Unless you convince me why I should spare you!"

"Because I'm sorry!"

"Why are you sorry!? And do not *dare* say 'I don't know' because it frustrates me to no end!"

"But, I-I-I d-don't!"

"*Boy!* One warning! That is all you get!"

Kelly huffed, practically hyperventilating without the brown bag. He formulated what he wanted to say, knowing that death by exsanguination awaited should he speak imprecisely. "Because I'm mean to kids and now I know how it feels to get picked on. That's why I'm here! I know it!"

"Mean to what kids?!" Its cocked claw trembled as if the snap of an invisible string would spring it forward like a mousetrap bar.

"Bryan Welles! I pick on Bryan Welles, he's in my class! I'll never do it again, I swear I won't!"

"You'll never do it again? Why? Because you are here in front of me and that is what you think you should be saying to me?"

"No! No!" Kelly panicked. "I thought it was fun at first, picking on him, but when I saw him laughing at me today after I saw you eat the bear I knew how I'd made him feel."

"And what did it feel like?! Answer!"

"Terrible! Awful! Everyone in the classroom was laughing at me when I was crying in my teacher's arms. I'd made Bryan cry in front of some of the other kids a few times. I must've made him feel like crap, but I didn't know what it actually felt like until today. That's what I meant! Look, you said you only like licking girls, but even if you somehow made an exception for me today and licked off my face, I swear I would still go back to Bryan and tell him I'm sorry, I'm so sorry."

"Enough of this!"

Krampus roared unholily and Kelly screamed as claws rained on him, cutting through ropes, coat and skin.

Tim and Travis both pleaded for leniency, but Krampus would have none of it.

One. Two. Three violent rakes and the creature finished its assault. It stepped back to fiendishly admire all it had wrought, shaking from its nails white fluff, tattered threads and drops of blood.

It sopped up a few moments more of pleasure and then said, "Okay, you can go."

"What?!" Tim propelled himself upward to look at Kelly's remains. Relief washed over him upon seeing the boy freed. The cut cords appeared to have exploded outward. Kelly, unmoving, had lost consciousness against the wall.

"I believe you." Krampus nudged Kelly with its hoof. "Boy, wake up. You are free to go."

"Is he bleeding?!" Tim struggled to obtain the full picture.

"Yes, but only a teensy bit," the beast said. "A scratch here and a nick there. Either he was fleshier than I had thought or my depth perception is off. Either way, he will need a new coat." It leaned in, unsuccessfully attempting to frighten Kelly from his slumber. "Boy! Awake! Now!"

"Just like that?!" Travis barked from across the cave. "After all the shit you put me, Brit and that other kid through? You're not going to actually pound on him for being bad?!"

Krampus gasped at the thought. His tone bordered on offended to emotionally wounded: "Herr Reardon, he is *just* a little boy."

Travis flopped backward and stared at the jagged rocks above him. "Can you please breathe on my face again? I need to mentally zone out for a while."

It ignored the request and continued to scold. "Had you come to a similar realization of your own transgressions earlier, perhaps you would not be in your current shape. But you did not. Chalk one up to Herr Flynn."

"Good job, Kelly." Tim didn't care if the boy couldn't hear him. "*Awesome* job."

He exhaled even more satisfyingly as Kelly's chest rose and fell with his breaths. He butt scooted toward Kelly, not caring what the monster thought, and confirmed the flesh wounds were perfunctory.

"But, you said you heard him apologize earlier." Tim didn't realize he'd seated himself next to the beast. "How could you hear that? That's impossible. And how the hell did you even come in here without us knowing?"

It picked him up, spun him around and placed him in his original spot next to Kelly.

"You hear me when I want you to hear me, Herr Schweitzer. You see me when it suits my purpose, and you smell me when I need fear to overwhelm you. And I have these!"

The creature reached onto one of the cave mantels, retrieved an old Sony cassette recorder and pushed the Stop button with one of its talons. It reached into the leather pouch that hung on the side of its crate and pulled out a second dusty tape recorder. It then proudly displayed two devices that Tim barely recognized.

"Picked these up in 1980 upon entering the bedroom of some thieving brat in Ohio. Very useful for monitoring conversations," it said. "I leave one here to record, take it with me when I am out, and before I leave I start the second one recording so the cycle begins anew. Finding new cassettes and batteries for them can be difficult, but not impossible."

"Way to get with the times, grampa," Tim said. "A wee bit hypocritical, don't you think? Looks like you rely on rectangular boxes of your own. By the way, one of those modern rectangular boxes you rail against us using might provide you clearer recordings."

"You mean iPads? Their screens scratch very easily," it said while fanning its talons. "I know what you children use to amuse yourselves. I have crept into many a bedroom over the years to see how your technology advances. Even I get curious enough to try them. As for my Sonys? I do not spend every waking hour of my day listening to them. I rely on them only one time during the entire year. And you are witnessing it."

It delicately placed the prized tape deck it took from its pouch back onto the mantel and pocketed the other one for later listening. Kelly then began stirring.

The boy sat up and held out his hands, scrutinizing them as if they were alien appendages. He hadn't seen them in half a day. His down jacket remained zipped but ripped, ragged on his left side; white stuffing jetted out from where the monster had slit it. He slid his fingers vertically along the congealing slash marks running from his pectoral muscles down to his belly.

"Good! You are awake," said the beast. "Now you have my permission to leave, on the condition that you remember why you are untied."

Kelly retraced the events in his mind and slowly bobbed his head in recognition. "I'll be good."

But before Kelly could stand, Krampus lightly poked one of its nails into Kelly's chest to keep him still.

"Not just yet, Herr Flynn. There were boys littler than you who were not so fortunate, who were not repentant, or if they were it was mere pretend. Keep that in mind. I never rule out extremes when it comes to discipline."

"I will!" Kelly gasped while watching the pointy nail skip along the goose pimples on his bare chest.

"You see, Herr Schweitzer, among many of the other things that separate me from the Nazis: You can be as religious as you want and it will not bother me. Additionally, I have discretion that I am willing to use. I do not just follow orders. I get my assignments from the Master and then the rest is up to both me and the subject, which brings me to you. I have been waiting for this all day."

It grabbed from his pouch the scroll that already bore the scratched-off names of Tim's compatriots. The beast unrolled it, admiring it like a *Playboy* centerfold, searching instead for the correct name and not augmented breasts.

Finding its spot, the creature thrust one of its talons straight into Tim's muscular shoulder and withdrew the bloody point.

"You goddamn coward!" Tim gritted his teeth to absorb the pulsing pain.

"Oh *please*. Such drama to precede our little waltz." It predatorily stalked back and forth before Tim.

"You are a bright one, boy. And you know what you must do."

"I have *nothing* to confess to you." Tim had mentally prepared himself for this reckoning. He puffed his chest to make himself appear bigger, but knew his own ample strength could not physically stand the ruthless barrage in the offing. Still, he expressed a brave air.

"You don't intimidate me." He followed the beast's thundering strides across the ground, never losing eye contact or cowering. "Beat me all you want, I won't cop to something just to make you stop."

"Then the question boils down to whether I believe you. You put on a good front. *Why* you did what you did will confuse me for all eternity. The Master likes to head it off whenever and wherever he can. So, enough foreplay, Herr Schweitzer. One more formality and then we begin."

It squatted and laid out the scroll on the ground. Tim's blood beaded on the point of its nail. A flick of its eyebrows indicated it'd found the name on the parchment, and then Krampus snarled at the boy before him and scratched through the letters.

"You are now accounted for, Billy Schweitzer."

Chapter Forty-Three

"What if I told you that I was supposed to be with my brother in the pickup truck this morning on the way to school, like I usually am?" Billy kept his voice low, not wanting to involve the wandering policemen in his personal drama. He leaned in his dad's chair toward Maria, to the point where he barely sat on it. Maria perched on the sofa seat closest to Billy.

"You tried skipping out of school because of what happened last night?" Maria understood him not wanting to be reminded of fresh rejection, although she still considered it childish.

"Yeah, I was pretty bummed, I confess." Embarrassed, he plowed through it to get it behind him. "I just wanted to lie in bed all day, feel sorry for myself. That's hard to do when your dad enforces laws for a living. Tim left without me and my dad brought me in. What if that thing was after me and not Tim?"

It worked. Maria spat out a "whoa" upon achieving her moment of clarity.

"*Exactly.* It took Tim thinking he was me. There was no other time today it could get me. I got to thinking about it after Jason got nabbed when we were both in the exact same spot. Even if it knew I was there and wanted to get me, I was surrounded by you, Eric Halberstrom, the bus driver and then my dad. It *couldn't* get to me without announcing its presence to more than a dozen kids and two adults. It would've blown its cover. At all other times I was with my father. Or I was locked in a police department with an entire squad of officers. It took out Pena, who I doubt even saw the chain coming, and then you were the only one there when it nabbed Kelly. It counts on adults not believing some wild story coming from a hysterical kid's mouth. Hell, you saw how my dad didn't believe you."

"I felt like an idiot," she said.

"It was easier pickings to attack my brother like it did Travis. It had darkness on its side. Maybe I'd have been knocked out, confused in the aftermath of an accident. Same thing with Tim. Chances are he was all groggy after crashing this morning. My abduction would've been a blur to him. It would've been a much easier snatch-and-grab. But to attack my dad's cruiser the same way with me in it? Too risky."

"Billy, then what did you do? If that's what this is all about, *why* does it want you?"

He held back the truth, but he did not lie to her.

"It's personal. About as personal as you can get, Maria. I can't tell you."

"Was it because—"

"I'm not playing that game." Billy waited for one of the officers—it was Darby, he thought—to amble through the room. All Darby needed to do was to twirl a nightstick and speak in an Irish brogue to complete the stereotype. Finally he shuffled off.

"I feel comfortable telling you it has to do with me and my dad more than anything," Billy said. "Don't try getting anything else out of me. I can't tell you."

He sensed her disappointment.

"You didn't bully someone like Brit or Jason," she said. "I can't believe you'd do that."

"Absolutely not."

"Okay, assuming you're right, and it's after you, how does that help us? It doesn't bring us any closer to finding your brother or mine. If anything, your neck's on the line now."

"It's just a theory of mine. Maybe Tim did something horrible, but I doubt it. I'm convinced it was after me."

"But, Billy, think about it. There's no guarantee that creep will figure out Tim's not you, and if and when it does, how will it know where to find you?"

"It seems to know where bullied victims live. That tells me it knows where to find the perpetrators. It won't be hard for that thing to find me."

"You'd be risking the lives of a lot of people. Do you really want to take the chance of being burnt to a crisp or beaten into a coma? Jason very well might die because of what happened to him. You're no match for that thing physically. A barrage of bullets from my brother couldn't stop it. So what do you plan on doing?"

"Outwit it. Get us to lead it back to its lair. Admittedly a lot of different pieces will have to fall into place for that to happen."

"Including that thing figuring out it screwed up," Maria said. "And if and when it does, based on what I've seen, expressing humility in the face of failure won't be its first instinct."

Chapter Forty-Four

"Boy, you are going to have to do better than *that*," Krampus said. "Do you know how many times I have heard you whiny brats plead 'I'm not him' or 'you've got the wrong kid'? I honestly expected better of you."

"No, *really*, my name's Tim!" He and the monster had been going around in circles like that for five minutes. "Leave my brother the hell out of this!"

"The Master never gets the names wrong. Not once in all of my days of doing this has there been a mistake."

"Maybe not on his part, but my name is Tim Schweitzer. Look at my driver's license!"

"You can stall me for only so long, boy." It slipped the ruten of its crate and beat the bundle into its palm, readying itself to pound a confession out of Tim.

"Hey, genius, he's telling you the truth." Travis, lying on his back and not looking at the creature, felt pleasure when needling his abuser. "Looks like it's amateur night at the Monster Mash."

"His name is Tim," Kelly meekly offered. "It's what I've been calling him all day. Why would he lie to me?"

"Because he fears retribution for his sins!" it roared to quiet the boys. Even though it never in its life felt ganged up on, a sliver of doubt trickled through its mind.

"Tell you what, fine, my name's Billy." Tim steeled himself. He was ready for the wrath. "You can have at me. I don't want my brother anywhere near your stupid ass."

Krampus suspected something was now genuinely amiss.

"Think about it, Einstein," Travis ventured back into the verbal fray. "You have your tape recordings, right? Go back and listen to them. You'll hear for yourself that we've been calling him Tim all day. Nowhere on those tapes will you hear us conspiring to give each other bogus names."

The creature grunted. Its eyes flitted back and forth, taking in all the boys and ruminating over their points.

"Go ahead and play one of your tapes, you'll see."

"Travis, shut the hell up!" Tim realized the thing had doubts. Billy would crumble under the beast's fists. It hadn't yet dawned on Tim that Billy had done something warranting a visit from the thing. He'd grown up with him and thought he understood his brother. But even the closest of siblings can never know for certain what dark things brew in the deepest recesses of the other's mind.

Krampus spoke under its breath, begrudgingly hinting something might have gone awry. "That name *is* familiar, now that you mention it. Where is your wallet, boy?"

"It's in my backpack in my truck," Tim said it too quickly, and with a slight measure of uncertainty that couldn't slip past the beast.

"Boy, you tell me where your wallet is, or else I begin cutting." The thing flashed its nails and stomped toward Tim. "And while I deliberately missed disemboweling Herr Flynn, I can assure you I will not hesitate to split open your chest cavity if that is what it takes for me to find your wallet."

It thrashed its claws across Tim's quadriceps, cutting to injure. Blood burbled upward as Tim yelled and cursed out the creature.

"I am not joking, Tim or Billy, or whoever you are." It brought its claws back, ready to swing them like a pendulum. "If you desire the continued ability to walk without a limp..." It let the notion linger in Tim's mind.

"It's in my right hip pocket," he conceded.

"Good, very good, boy."

It scrambled across the cave with its back to the boys. Candlelight illuminated the scrunched thing hovering over something and surgically moving its arms. The boys couldn't make out what was happening but heard indecent sounds of slitting and squishing. It lurched back to Tim, who felt sick upon seeing a femur bone dripping globular flesh that the beast had ripped from the deer carcass off to the cavern's side.

"What the hell are you doing?!" For the first time all day Tim felt terror.

The thing in four precise and successive licks of its tongue cleared the bone of its meaty remnants. "Open your mouth, boy."

"I won't do it!"

"Yes you will." It brought itself down to Tim's level and pointed a single talon above Tim's already bleeding quad. Slowly it inserted the nail through the frayed cord into the leg. Tim opened his mouth to scream, and in an instant Krampus wedged the bone sideways into Tim's mouth. "Bite down now! Make yourself look like the dog you are!"

Tim, confused, slowly acquiesced, keeping his tongue back and placing only the tips of his teeth on the bone.

"This *will* hurt, boy."

The beast bore its pointer finger into the general area surrounding Tim's right hip pocket. Tim grimaced and bit down hard on the bone, imprinting it with a dental outline he would never see, but sparing himself from biting off his own tongue. The beast crudely etched a square through rope, clothing and flesh, stepped back and then screamed at Kelly.

"Go find it! Pull out the wallet now!"

Kelly sprang to Tim's side and moved his shaky hands around the bloody rope, peeling back layers of cord and denim like a huge postage stamp, exposing a bleeding hunk of meat. He let the rope fall from the heavy swath of clothing and realized the wallet was weighing it down. Kelly literally clutched Tim's pants pocket in his fingertips and held it at arm's length. Sweat poured from Tim's brow as he panted through the bone clamped in his teeth.

"Now!" The beast's command jolted Kelly to fit his tiny hand into the pocket and pull out the wallet. He flipped it open and found Tim's driver's license.

"Show me!"

Kelly cried as he stood on his tiptoes and held up the license as high as he could, allowing Krampus to bend and examine the ID card.

A hardening scowl revealed the beast hated what it saw. Krampus raised both its arms and shook them as it roared.

Kelly ran back to the wall and clung to Tim.

It paced in a wide circle, shaking its head, wondering what went wrong. It stopped cold and reached into the leather pouch attached to its crate. It plucked out and unfolded a large rectangle of parchment, speed-reading it multiple times.

"I hate these last-moment assignments!" Krampus slowed and calmly began rereading. "Normally, I have time to scout, to prowl you worms so I can anticipate your every movement." It squinted and shook its head in frustration. "Why does the Master write so small?!"

It clumsily stuffed its hand into the same leather bag and retrieved a pair of spectacles without arms. It held the abnormally large frames between its thumb and forefinger, bringing the dusty, cracked lenses close to its eyes and then pushing them back to bring the cursive text into focus.

Tim, Kelly and Travis all leaned forward in unison and lowered their jaws. The bone fell out of Tim's mouth. *You've got to be kidding!* or a variation of that thought flashed through their minds.

Krampus felt their stares, and a bit of self-consciousness poked at him.

"Do you have any idea how hard it is for me to get an eye exam?! I cannot just walk into LensCrafters!" it barked while continuing to read. "You can get a pair of eyeglasses in less than an hour! I had to wait twelve hundred years just for someone to *invent* them!"

It pored over the entire contents of the letter and exhaled a lengthy "oh" when it came to a realization. It dropped the instructions.

"I got those orders last evening, Herr Schweitzer—late last evening." Its behavior devolved from confident to scatterbrained. It looked around the cave, hoping to somehow spot a better explanation in one of the cracks. "Had I enough time to properly plan, this oversight never would have occurred. I read about a Billy Schweitzer driving to school, Winchester Road. I missed the part about a brother operating the horse. A brother named Tim."

Perhaps it was the lack of food or his body continually trying to mend its pain that was making him woozy, but Travis couldn't help himself. "So, you've never been wrong?" He sat up to exact some revenge. "Guess there's a first time for everything, huh?"

Krampus strode toward Travis, building up speed, and gave a cloven-hoofed kick to the boy's forehead. Travis flopped backward, his skull cracking on the rocky floor. "Sleep tight, boy." Finally, for good measure, it pulled from its crate some more of its endless supply of rope and quickly knotted Travis's hands behind his back and tied together his legs.

It then tightly cocooned Kelly and placed him next to Tim.

"I do not need you trying to free my new friend named Tim, Herr Flynn. I would not want him going anywhere before he has the chance to see me drag his cowardly brother before him and make him listen to Billy's pleas for mercy." It glowered at Tim. "And by the end of this night, he will beg for it."

Krampus shot its necrotic breath throughout the room to make the boys sleep and to extinguish the candles before vanishing.

It eventually stood at the lip of the cave's exit, unmoved by the pummeling force of blizzard winds, and drew in several frigid breaths of air. Krampus's rage welled within, and its release would be heard far and wide.

Chapter Forty-Five

Chief Donald Schweitzer pointed his flashlight at Susan Weaver's fireplace and the mounds of soot that had exploded from it. The family room smelled of wet smoke. Susan, cheerleader pretty with a blonde pixie haircut, clutched the small, handheld extinguisher she'd used to douse both the fire she built as well as the pathetic, screaming creature that tumbled out of it.

The chief had pulled into the Weavers' driveway as the ambulance carrying Brittany Cabot sped by him en route to the hospital. The home's front and back yards featured miniature zigzagging flashlight beams searching in vain for anything that could explain what was without a doubt the weirdest case any of the lawmen had ever investigated.

"Did she say anything?" the chief asked Susan, who stood off to his side, keeping clear of the detectives constantly walking by her. She'd found whatever candles she could to bring light to the room.

"Yeah, 'It wouldn't stop licking me'," Susan replied.

"*It?* Not *he?*"

"*It*, over and over again, 'It wouldn't stop licking me'. And she would not stop screaming."

"Did she describe the 'it'?"

"I asked her what she meant but she made no sense, just that its tongue was sharp."

"*What?*"

"She asked me 'How do I look? How do I look?'."

"She was worried about her appearance?"

"Chief, you cannot imagine what she looked like. She even begged me to bring her a mirror! I got one from my bedroom, and when I held it front of her she went ballistic. 'My face! Look what it did to my face!'."

"I hope she said all of that *after* she stopped being on fire," he said. "What was it about her face?"

"Other than being sooty it seemed like pieces of it were grated away like cheese. That's what freaked her out. It's like she didn't even realize she had been on fire."

"Where was she burned?"

"On her shins. She landed feetfirst, so her legs got the worst of it. She wasn't in there that long. She managed to get out by herself and began rolling around on the floor. Stop, drop and roll, you know? I threw a blanket on her and then doused her just to make sure she was out. She wouldn't stop crying 'My face! My face!'. She's probably still saying it as we speak."

"Did you know who she was at first?"

"No. Not at all. I just saw a burning woman. It was only after I brought her the mirror and got a good, long look at her face. Then I realized it was Brittany."

The chief motioned for Susan to accompany him to another room void of police activity. Finding a secluded spot in the dining room on the opposite end of the house, the chief spoke softly to her, not wanting to embarrass her.

"I remember asking you why you did what you did last spring, and you never answered. But Brittany was the reason you tried killing yourself, right? It's okay, you're not in trouble."

Seeing that Brittany literally dropped back into her life not less than thirty minutes prior, Susan wasn't overwhelmed by his inquiry.

She answered by asking, "How could you know that?"

"A hunch based on some things I've seen today."

Susan had heard about the kidnappings from the radio on her iPhone, and by reading a few local news websites. She'd hoped everyone would be found, even Brittany. Part of her moving on from attempting suicide was to embrace talk therapy and religion. And to forgive—something she found difficult to do—and also to forget, to never dwell on the monster that drove her over the edge.

"But it's funny you should mention why I tried doing what I did a few months ago. Kelly Flynn's sister called me earlier today asking about Brittany."

"*Really?* How long ago?"

"I'm not sure, three or four hours maybe? Chief, I really pray that your son's not in danger. But if you think I—"

"Kidnapped Brittany Cabot, cut up her face and set her on fire? No. Not for one second. Although you have to admit, you do have a motive. And my detectives and a few other people are going to speak to you about what you were doing today. It's all procedural. I know you're innocent. You need to tell me what you told Maria Flynn about Brittany, and I suspect Travis too. But you can tell that to me, and just me."

"Brittany can also tell you herself, you know."

"Oh, I'm looking forward to speaking with her too. But I have no plans on bringing up anything related to you, unless she brings it up. It will be discreetly discussed, regardless. You have something to do with what happened today."

"Chief, I didn't even go to school today! My parents saw me here before they went to work this morning. They'll be home soon and can vouch for me."

"Calm down! I didn't mean it like that. I'm saying whoever threw Brittany down your chimney already knew what she did to you. So maybe you told someone—"

She cut him off. "The only people who know are me and my therapist and Maria Flynn and her boyfriend. I trust my shrink implicitly, and I wouldn't have bothered telling Maria but she said it could shed light on what happened to those missing kids. And I'm good friends with her boyfriend, so I sort of opened up as a favor to him. I didn't really think Maria might be on to something until Brittany appeared."

Susan sat with Schweitzer at the dining room table and she educated him about the hell Brittany had put her through.

"I won't tell a soul. And if I need to tell anyone about this, I'll talk to you about it first. But I don't think it will ever come to that. Now, are you sure you didn't see anything? Think hard. Even the littlest thing might help us."

"I'm sorry, Chief. I mean, I chalked up the sounds on the roof to the storm, not to someone who climbed up that tree against the house to get to our chimney. I saw nothing."

The roar stunned the chief and Susan and ended the conversation. Their faces communicated the same thought to one another: *What on earth can produce such a sound?* They made for the front door and opened it, allowing entry to an unending cry not bellowed to accentuate torment but to announce an unholy presence of vengeance.

Chapter Forty-Six

It didn't begin low and culminate into an *a-roooo* wolf howl. It could not be suffocated by the gales and snowfall. It exploded into being and lasted until the thing generating it felt in its bones that the townspeople were all cowering before their windows fearing the unknown.

Billy was no exception. He, like so many others whom he'd never meet, stood within his home, looking skyward, unable to stop his imagination from running wild.

Maria, however, reacted differently. She knew what was out there, and although she and Billy had no way of knowing it, they were a lot nearer to the source of the rage than the chief.

"It's coming for me," Billy said it to her in a way that reflected resignation without fear, but with preparedness. "It knows."

"Then let's get the hell out of here," Maria said. "*Now.* Tell the officers."

"You heard how close by that sounded. It's gonna be on us in minutes."

Billy's iPhone rang and he answered to hear his father, in whom the roar had triggered a parental instinct commanding him to return and protect his child.

"I'm coming back there right now," the chief said. "Are you okay?"

"We're all fine."

"Did you hear it?"

"Pennsylvania heard it, Dad. We're thinking we should meet you back at the department. You want your officers to drive us?"

"I've seen too many crashed cars today. I'd rather have you fortified there."

Fortified, Billy thought. *He's never off duty. But he could be right.*

"Lock the doors, stay alert and keep close to my guys, okay? I'm almost home. Just wait ten minutes. I'll be there, promise." And with that he ended the call.

Officer Darby and Sergeant Crenshaw tried not letting on that the howl had spooked them. Each now kept their gun hands closer to their holsters and converged in the Schweitzer family room to be near the kids left in their care. One would stay while the other would go from room to room to look out the windows or doors for anything amiss.

Billy needed to slip away from the three of them if his evolving and crude plan to track the creature had any chance of succeeding. He walked to the front door, picked up his book bag and returned to the sofa to sit with Maria. He didn't bother looking inside.

"I need it to store a few things," Billy whispered, knowing her curiosity had been piqued.

"What things?"

"Not sure yet. I just hope what I'm looking for is there. I think they are."

Darby had gone to make the rounds while Crenshaw drew aside the front door's curtains to have a look at snow piles illuminated by porch light.

"Billy, you have to warn them about what might be coming here," Maria insisted. "They could wind up like Officer Pena or killed."

He would not argue with that. He acted fast.

"Hey, guys!" Billy called out. Crenshaw wordlessly walked toward the couch as Darby entered somewhat jittery.

"What's wrong?" Darby said.

"Nothing," Billy cautioned. "Not yet, but, call it intuition, whatever took my brother and hers, and hurt Officer Pena, is on its way here."

Billy expected the cops to roll their eyes and dismiss him with a *stupid kid!* wave of their hands. They instead hung on his every word.

"Now, I know you heard the prosecutor describe what Maria saw, and you might have a hard time believing it, but do you honestly think that screech you heard before came from a man? I don't. It's not some guy in a monkey suit. Don't ask me how I know, but it's *not* human."

"It's a giant, bigger than the both of you combined," Maria added.

"And it's coming to this house because it wants to take me to wherever it took Brit and Jason, and where Tim and her brother are now. You heard it yourselves. It's pissed off." Billy spaced out his final three words to the officers for emphasis, "Just. Be. Ready."

The two lawmen processed the information and added it to everything they already had learned throughout the day.

"I'm gonna get my shotgun. Stay with the kids." Crenshaw, the ranking officer, took command and zipped up his coat.

"Can you bring mine?" Darby flipped him his keys. "Please?"

Crenshaw, both sets of keys in hand, left through the front door, into the storm toward the cruisers to retrieve the weapons.

Billy waved to get Darby's attention. "I need to go get something. I'll be right back. You want anything in the meantime? I can make coffee."

"I'm all right."

Billy vanished down a hallway. Darby grimly smiled at Maria.

"Everything's gonna be fine," he told her, but neither believed it.

"You sure you don't want anything?!" It was Billy's voice from afar. "It's not a problem! I appreciate you guys looking after us! Maria?!"

Darby shook his head no and Maria answered for both of them, "Normally I'd say yes, but not right now, thanks!"

Maria walked to where the family room ended and the hallway began, straining to hear what Billy was up to. Even though the fire Billy had built warmed the room enough to provide comfort, she felt cold and her hands had turned clammy. Not one of them had an appetite for food or drink. They all experienced the chill bred by shaken nerves. All she heard from Billy's end were zips of a book bag being opened one moment and then closed a few ticks later.

"All right!" Billy replied. "Here I come."

A heavy, booming crunch of metal came from outside, making all three jump to attention. A few seconds later an even louder sound of avalanching machinery rippled through the house.

Darby opened the front door and looked through the storm door window. Crenshaw's cruiser, which had been parked in front of Darby's in the driveway, was gone.

"Kids, hide. *Now.*" Darby drew his gun and walked into the storm.

Maria and Billy disregarded the order and kept watch over Darby as he trudged through two feet of snow toward the driveway, illuminated by the motion-detector light centered above the single garage door.

A shotgun rested in the outlined center of Crenshaw's missing car. Darby, looking all around as he moved, reached for the pump-action piece. He holstered his pistol and checked the shotgun for ammunition. Fully loaded. He turned 360 degrees where he stood, to get the lay of the mostly dark landscape.

The young officer came full circle and stopped upon seeing his cruiser begin to wobble. He heard an immense groan and pumped the gun when he saw the car's front tires slowly lift off the ground. The tops of two twisted horns rose into view as the cruiser began its ascent.

Krampus lifted the automobile and with an Olympic hammer throw hurled it toward the street, roaring as he spun and released.

The garage light illuminated enough of the background so Darby could see in the distance the cruiser crush onto Winchester Road. Crenshaw was gone. Krampus and Darby squared off with sixty feet separating them.

Billy wiped away layers of condensation he'd nervously huffed on his front window, to better see the animal in its entirety.

"Now do you believe me?" Maria, standing next to Billy, her face just an inch from the windowpane, said.

"I always did," Billy whispered, realizing that other fantastical things once thought impossible to exist must also roam the earth. *What else is out there?*

The beast's hulking frame rose and fell as it heaved cold air and snow. Billy felt a shard of fear stick his belly when the thing's black eyes, dimly glinting like ball bearings in the garage light, darted above Darby's shoulders and bored through Billy.

I seeeeeeeee you!

Krampus drew a link of chain from its crate in one hand and its ruten in the other. He held each at his sides and waited for Darby to make a move.

Darby had been taught multiple tactics about how to handle violent suspects, but this particular scenario had never come up. However inclined he was to pull the trigger, he reminded himself that the thing confronting him had kidnapped and attacked several children, some of them still missing, and that killing the beast might mean never finding them.

Darby aimed the shotgun at the beast's massive chest and said in his most authoritative voice, "Drop your weapons and put your hands up! Now! Or I *will* shoot you!"

Krampus snapped the chain toward Darby. The front link smacked the shotgun sideways as Darby fired, missing his target. He lost his grip and the gun helicoptered away.

The beast roared and charged the policeman, who pulled his Glock and pointed it, but not fast enough. Krampus swung the ruten and

212

cracked Darby's gun hand sideways, sending the piece in the opposite direction of the shotgun. The monster then took a backhand swipe with the ruten, cracking Darby flush in the chest, knocking him off to the driveway's side. He landed on his butt and had trouble catching his breath. He steadied himself to see Krampus strolling toward him. The monster gave the ruten a polo swing upward, smashing Darby's face and laying him on his back.

"I think it's time to go," Billy told Maria.

"Where?!" she screamed.

"To the garage. I've got the keys. Move."

The two stampeded down the hallway, past bedrooms to the door to the small garage, which held an old Nissan Pathfinder that his father was planning to sell.

"Grab those two gas cans!" Billy pointed to the two red plastic containers, one topped with five gallons of fuel, the other half-empty.

Maria grabbed them and yelled, "Open the hatch!"

"Just a second!" Billy opened the driver's side door, slid into the seat and started the Pathfinder in one smooth motion. He looked around the passenger's side and found wrinkly, coffee-stained road maps, a dozen greasy White Castle cartons and a long ice scraper with a brush on the other end of it. He then turned on the headlights and put them on bright.

"All right, Maria. Let's go!"

Krampus stowed the ruten but kept the chain ready. It turned to the garage door upon hearing the SUV's loud engine. The Pathfinder exploded through the panels, taking the monster by surprise. Blinded by the headlamps and splintered wood, it jumped to the side, landed on the Schweitzers' front lawn and watched the SUV barreling down the hilly driveway.

Crenshaw's cruiser, lying on its roof on Winchester, poked its fender in front of the driveway enough to create an obstacle that would require the Pathfinder to swerve right to avoid clipping it. The front left side of the SUV crashed into the cruiser, causing it to spin in the snow. The SUV plowed across the road and down a small embankment. The Pathfinder hit the ground and drove into a snarl of trees, which stopped the SUV. The rightmost headlamps still shone and the engine continued to run.

Krampus slogged through the snow, long-jumped across the street and landed next to driver's window. It easily popped its fist through the side window and grabbed for Billy but found nothing. It ripped the Pathfinder's front door off its hinges and flung it aside to see an empty driver's compartment, save for the long ice scraper that became dislodged from where Billy had wedged it against the front seat and on the gas pedal.

Chapter Forty-Seven

"Hold on!" Billy yelled but doubted Maria heard him.

His snowmobile glided over the tree-lined path leading to the rear of Mike Brembs's neighborhood. Billy pushed his Arctic Cat F1100 Turbo—a guilt gift from his mom after the divorce—to 70 miles per hour on the open trail. Maria followed him on Tim's Polaris 800 Switchback PRO-R. It didn't take them long to exit the garage through the rear door and tear the tarps off the two snowmobiles parked underneath the Schweitzers' deck.

The plan was to get as far away from Billy's home as possible. Maria, while not as accomplished on a snowmobile as the Schweitzer boys, grew up in the area and had gone riding a few times with her father. She preferred leisurely jaunts that didn't break 40 miles per hour but knew the thing was after them. Secretly terrified she might lose control or smash headfirst into a tree, she nonetheless kept pace with Billy's clip of speed. If need be, both vehicles could blow past 100 miles per hour. She didn't want to try it, given the hour of night and limited vision through the blizzard.

Had it just been him, Billy would be traveling in the triple digits. He knew the trails almost by instinct. But he couldn't lose sight of Maria, not yet. The main trail was wide and straight. Both kids wore the visor helmets always stored in the vehicles' rear compartments when not in use. Billy relished the transparent face shield deflecting the cold, stinging snow from his eyes. Each snowmobile had a gas canister now stowed in the exact same storage compartment should the need for refueling arise.

Another earsplitting roar exploded from behind them.

Guess it just found the SUV, Billy thought and smiled as a result. Turning serious, he knew the beast would deduce what had happened. And he was proven correct when a third furious howl erupted. Even though his helmet muffled the sound, he knew it was louder and closer. Checking his side mirror proved worthless. The beast would literally need to sit behind Billy and wrap its arms around him like a biker babe clinging to her man for him to see its reflection in the glass.

It can't run this fast, no animal can! Billy thought. *And if it can, it'll catch Maria first.* He shuddered and dropped his speed so Maria could catch up. They could barely see each other's profiles, save for the slight illumination provided by the vehicles' headlamps. Both riders crouched behind the snowmobiles' windshields to better reduce wind resistance.

Billy enjoyed the jolt of adrenaline fueled by the fast ride. This wasn't him drag-racing his brother—something they were told never to do, but screw it—this was outrunning some incomprehensible being. And he was winning. *Thanks, Mom. As much as I hated you divorcing Dad, I'm glad your new squeeze has deep pockets.*

He heard the clank and then immediately felt it. *The chain, it has to be the damn thing's chain!* Indeed, Krampus whipped the links and nicked the Cat's rear snow flap. Had it hit the running board, Billy would've lost control and crashed.

How the hell can it maintain its speed and lash a chain as heavy as that one! Billy thought. But he expected this might happen. The chain then rained down between the two snowmobiles and slithered away at light speed.

Maria saw it and locked eyes with Billy. It was time.

Billy maneuvered left to a side trail off of the main path. Maria agreed ahead of time to pull the exact same move but on the opposite side. She followed suit when she spotted a trailhead opening and veered right. The pair had given the beast a fork in the road, and would force it to choose one of them. It wasn't the smartest of plans, they knew, but it would trip up the creature, especially if it followed Maria.

But each now had to focus ahead on the trees that could come jutting out of nowhere by the slightest deviation from their smaller trails. Each vehicle's front headlamp provided inadequate light to guide them. But onward. And they had to slow down. Going seventy equated to a suicide mission. The deceleration meant the headlights could better act as beacons. Whether the plan to split would be enough to dissuade the creature from further pursuit? Billy reasoned they'd know soon enough.

No chain slashed through the air to knock him off his snowmobile. It would've tried by now, he knew. A sudden boom accompanied by a bright-orange flash to his right diverted his attention. Billy jerked his head to see the aftermath of an explosion in the distance, where Maria would be riding.

Chapter Forty-Eight

It was after her. She refused to tear through the woods like Billy. She *couldn't*. She'd die. *It's gonna catch me.* She was certain of it. *Does the beast think I'm Billy? How far back is it?* Trees whizzed by, one after the other. *How can it see with the snowmobile kicking up plumes of powder to shroud the rider from its vision?*

She felt the trail narrowing. It was barely large enough for two people to walk side by side in the first place. And the hills steepened the farther she rode. Her arms shook. The chain slashed horizontally from left to right above her head and then disappeared. She felt like a calf about to be lassoed.

She had to choose. Continue trying to outrun some unstoppable hellion? Or attempt to reason with it? It'd had her in its sights before and spared her. Perhaps she could negotiate her brother's release or quell whatever continued agony might await him.

She did not want to die, nor did she want Kelly to suffer the same fates as Brit and Jason.

So focused was she on how best to break bread with this brute that she assumed the trail would continue its beeline straightness. Had she been more familiar with the smaller artery of travel, she'd have known a severe dogleg-left turn awaited her.

The time to negotiate the turn and slow down had passed. Her path inclined 45 degrees. The turn would take her downhill. Her road of travel served as a quaint footpath for outdoorsmen, joggers or cross-country skiers. No sane person would travel 40 miles per hour on it. She had no idea she was preparing for launch.

She didn't even know she missed the turn until becoming airborne, looking down and briefly seeing the path before darkness swallowed it. She tilted backward and fell off the snowmobile, which continued its forward trajectory. She fell far enough to knock the wind out of her as she hit the ground and tumbled downhill. A fat pine-tree trunk stopped her momentum. The upper right side of her body hit it first, then her helmeted head, which softened the blow.

She vaguely remembered the snowmobile smacking front first into the base of a massive oak tree at the end of its rainbow arch. The sparks upon its impact didn't surprise her, but the thunderous blast, fueled by the red gas canister that cracked open in the snowmobile's rear, knocked her backward. The explosion compounded the pain in her head. The blast fired pieces of plastic, metal and fiberglass into the tree trunk that shielded Maria.

Powdery snow found every open crevice in her clothing and she shivered. She pushed herself up from the tree and staggered like a drunk through two feet of snow.

Her vision blurred through the visor. She thought the resulting fire would've raged, but she had the fortune of carrying the gas canister with the least amount of fuel in it. The wind worked to douse whatever fiery bits remained, rather than spreading the blaze through the trees.

A wind gust caught her from behind and pushed her down the hill. She rolled a few turns but managed to stop herself from becoming a cartoon snowball. The hill was steeper than she thought. She again stood but felt a rush of blood to her head that immediately plopped her right back down. She sat against the nearest tree and waited.

It stood uphill.

The smoldering wreckage and its dispersed flaming pieces, along with the burning wood that'd sustained the impact, allowed her to see Krampus, still grasping its chain, shuffling through the storm. It reminded Maria of some bipedal mountain goat gingerly making its way down the Himalayas.

Centuries-old rocks jutted sidelong out of the ground, giving the appearance of steps poking through the hillside. Maria didn't think she'd taken that big a spill, but as her mind regained focus she understood she'd wound up in a quasi valley. She looked behind her and saw she still had farther to fall.

The beast trekked through the snow and stood underneath one of the cliff-like stones to take whatever shelter it could from the storm.

The dwindling firelight shone only enough for Maria to see the monster's outline subtly shifting through the darkness. She sat curled in a fetal position, both to preserve warmth and to cope with her fear.

Krampus leaned forward and plucked off her helmet to look at the quivering thing in front of it. The monster dropped the helmet and disgustedly grunted upon recognizing the facial features of something too beautiful to be a man.

"We both know I am not after you!" it yelled. "Certainly I had hoped you to be Billy Schweitzer, and on a clearer day, perhaps I would have realized I was chasing the wrong person! But here we are! And truth be told, I do not mind settling for you! Because he *will* want to find me all the more once he realizes I have you! And we both know why that is! I have an insatiable lust for redheads too!"

Maria concocted gruesome images of the creature defiling her.

"Where's my brother?!" Kelly remained her top priority, and not her own fears about the sexual torture that might await her.

"The same place where I am keeping Billy's brother. Perhaps you would like to go there? In fact, I insist that you join me!"

"Take me and let my brother go!" Her voice strained as she shouted. The cold air rejuvenated her lungs.

"Very well! I actually freed your brother not too long ago! He declined to leave, I imagine, because he would die attempting to find his way home! But I give you my word Kelly can abscond whenever he pleases! I have a sneaking suspicion he will not when he sees you bound so tight that blood vessels will freckle those luscious cheeks of yours!"

It went against every gut instinct she'd ever had, but Maria believed what the beast said. *Kelly had managed to escape, or at the very least make amends!*

"Take him to where he can be found safe! I don't care what you do to me!"

"Yes you do! You had better, girl!" It stepped closer toward her, revealing itself from underneath the rocky outcropping. "I have not had the best of Krampusnachts, young lady. You might equate that to having better Christmas mornings than others. For instance, you desired a certain doll but instead you got, I do not know, a spinning top or a jack-in-the-box. That is my equivalent this year, for it has not been my finest hour, so perhaps I deserve a little consolation prize while we wait for Mr. Schweitzer, and you will provide it quite nicely!"

It unleashed its wormy tongue and waggled it at her.

"But I'm innocent!" Her eyes followed the snakelike slab of meat that ached to touch her. The monster then slurped it back to speak.

"But I'm *not!*"

It reached for her but rather than hide from it, she summoned the courage to face it and keep her dignity. She locked eyes with it. She meant to remain in a stare-down as long as she could, but something

219

moved in the background, in the distance, framed in between its twisted horns.

At first she thought a Navy SEAL was standing on the rock above the beast. Its telescopic mask made the wearer look like it was hunting Osama bin Laden. The dark figure held what appeared to be a piece of luggage in both its hands and then tilted it up and over the rock.

Liquid splattered on the beast's head and shoulders. Maria smelled it immediately. The beast turned to look at the source and roared in pain as the fluid doused its eyes. The figure standing above tossed aside the bulky thing that sloshed when it landed and flipped up its mask. And then Billy Schweitzer revealed his face as he popped a road flare and threw a sizzling fastball at Krampus's head, igniting the gasoline he had poured on it.

The creature unleashed a guttural howl as fire consumed its upper body. Billy sprang from his stone perch and landed on his feet in a crouch in front of Maria.

"Grab your helmet, come on!" He took her hand, and led her up the hill, digging deep to move fast. She cradled her helmet in her other arm, the way a running back would with a football. The creature flailed its arms and ran to try to escape the flames that engulfed its head and licked the tips of its horns.

She didn't care where the creature ran, just so long as it wasn't following them. *It's probably easier to run downhill than up when you suddenly burst into flames,* she thought. The fire behind her was bright enough to illuminate Billy guiding her to the trail she'd failed to navigate.

The continued roars pushed them to run harder until the landscape flattened and they were back on the trail, with Billy's ride waiting for them. Almost all snowmobiles are two-seaters and his was no exception. His backpack and helmet waited for him on the snowmobile's seat. He sealed his pack in the rear compartment and fastened his helmet.

Billy started the snowmobile's engine. Maria, sitting behind him, slipped on her helmet, wrapped her arms around his chest, squeezing tight, and nestled her head gently against his back.

The Arctic Cat rocketed into the snowy abyss and Billy would not lose control. The next part of his plan required an Internet connection. And if all went well, Billy would be by his brother's side within thirty minutes.

Chapter Forty-Nine

The sight of two police cars scattered like debris along Winchester Road, as well as his SUV in a ditch, sickened the chief. He didn't have to see his house to know he approached disaster.

He stopped his cruiser in front of his ruined garage door and charged into his house with his gun drawn.

"Billy?! Maria?!" He repeatedly shouted their names as he cleared each room, Billy's bedroom being the final one on his list. The desk lamp provided the only light in the room. He tugged the string to the overhead light and saw the place empty of anything living. He checked the closet for good measure and found nothing. He glanced at Billy's desk as he walked by it and paused. He recognized the numbers on a curled sheet of paper and picked it up just to make sure he wasn't wrong.

"He knows he's not allowed, he *knows* it!" the chief yelled as he crumpled the paper, the same way Billy did with the piece containing Maria's phone number, and threw it on the floor. He rushed to his already cleared bedroom and into its walk-in closet that contained a gun safe.

Donald Schweitzer breezed through the safe's combination, infuriated that Billy had the numbers. He deliberately never wrote it down for fear of his sons finding it.

"Why wouldn't he just ask me?" he said while spinning the dial. *Clearly he didn't want me knowing.*

The chief turned the handle and swung open the door. The Remington Model 870 pump-action shotgun and a lever-action Marlin 336XLR remained secure. They rested in the bottom center of the tall safe. The Heckler & Koch P8 semiautomatic handgun was missing, along with a clip of bullets, from its shelf above where the long guns stood. He never left his guns loaded. All that remained of the pistol was its trigger lock. He picked it up and disgustedly flicked it back on the shelf.

He hadn't opened the safe in days. He kept his service weapon locked and unloaded on his nightstand. One son gone, the other armed with a pistol he has no clue how to use.

Or does he?

The chief had taken his sons to the shooting range when they each turned thirteen, just to get it out of their systems. Each had had a natural curiosity related to firearms, based on their dad's profession. He was relieved when neither had taken an interest in them. He wouldn't have objected if they had. He'd have simply been more vigilant of their behaviors, making certain a shooting hobby never became an unhealthy obsession.

The boys had gravitated toward sports, and that was fine with him. Because that was the case, he repeatedly stressed to them that the gun safe was off-limits. *Don't go near it.* The chief could recount more examples than he'd prefer of kids, usually with their friends over, sneaking into their parents' closet to check out the supposedly hidden arsenal, and someone accidentally ending up shot dead. His boys were past that irresponsible age, but the rules of his house were carved in stone, and the chief knew that no matter how smart or trustworthy they may seem, teenagers never outgrew irresponsibility.

How long have you been coming in here? Did you get the combo all at once or over time? All he could think was Billy must've somehow spied on him, either by hiding in the closet or setting up a concealable camera. He reached around the closet, slapping aside business suits and uniforms to see if one was there. Nothing. He had no time to check the whole place.

"What else did you take?" The chief stepped back from the safe and his eyes darted over the compartments holding different sorts of police paraphernalia. Two pairs of night-vision goggles and the corresponding headgear—gone. However, a Post-it note now rested in their place.

"Dad, got the GPS trackers, keep checking."

The chief had insisted his boys always wear personal trackers whenever they went snowmobiling, in the event of an accident. When activated, the little device would email the chief Billy's or Tim's coordinates. Even turning one of them on meant the locations could be found by going to the company's website, entering the device's serial number and then using Google Maps to home in on an almost-precise location, within a matter of feet.

The chief opened his phone's email browser but nothing from Billy waited for him. He put the phone on buzz in his hip pocket to make sure he'd feel it if Billy called. He dialed his son but it went straight to voice mail. Then it hit him. *Billy escaped! He must have! Otherwise, why raid the gun safe and forewarn his old man?* He hoped he was right.

Somewhat relieved, but still simmering over his son's flagrant disregard for what the chief considered his most nonnegotiable rule, the chief took one more look-see and noticed a couple of road flares were gone too. He shut the gun safe, sick to his stomach, and it only worsened when he remembered what else was on Billy's desk.

He returned to his son's bedroom and turned on all the lights before swiping out of the way loose-leaf papers bearing scribbled measurements and calculations. Underneath the notebook pages littering Billy's desk was a 30-by-42-inch architectural rendering of Hancock High School. He marveled at his son's sketching prowess but now feared Billy had channeled it for ill purposes. The main entrance, the fire exits, all circled. His son had penciled in a route from the parking lot, to the principal's office, and then to two classrooms, and then to the exit the chief had used earlier that day to access the football field.

Oh God, the gun! When did he take it? When did he draw this?

The chief scanned the sketch for a date, to try to figure out when his son might have worked on it. He found a *12-05-13* circled twice for emphasis above the block-lettered name of the school. There it was in front of him, a blueprint, but designed for what?

He didn't want to go to school today. Maybe he was having second thoughts?

Yes, he'd noticed his son seemed down, depressed at times, but he'd chalked it up to the usual blues any teenager goes through. The chief recalled how Billy had been clutching his backpack close to him all day, always making sure he possessed it.

The gun's in that bag. It was right in front of my face all day. Why else would he insist on bringing it everywhere with him? He said that Maria girl rejected him. Could that have pushed him to the brink? Kids get turned down all the time but they don't kill people over it. Do they?

The chief despaired upon realizing that, *yes*, some kids *do* kill for reasons beyond comprehension. Even run-of-the-mill jealousy and rejection can trigger irreversible madness in kids desperate for help but unable to find it.

Billy, not you. Please, God, not you. Not my son.

Another sickening realization hit him.

"My guys!" He ran from Billy's room and fled the house through the garage. "Darby! Crenshaw!" he shouted through the wind and snow.

The cruisers! He started to run past his car but noticed a raised mound of snow strangely shaped in the form of an angel with broken wings. A small hole yawned where its mouth would be. The chief dove into the pile and felt around, first grasping an arm, then pushing against a jacketed chest. He pushed both hands into the snow, gripped the jacket and pulled up Darby, snow tumbling from his head, face and shoulders.

"Holy Christ, hang on, kid!" The chief called dispatch to get the nearest ambulance and police cruiser to his house.

"Bring the whole fuckin' force if you have to!" the chief screamed before tending to Darby.

Schweitzer embraced Darby's right hand. "Darby, if you can hear me, squeeze my hand!"

He yelled the command a few more times and gasped in relief when a weak but detectable bit of pressure wrapped around his hand.

"Now how 'bout your feet, can you move your feet?!" The chief softly laid his hand on Darby's foreleg and felt muscle movement, and then saw the tips of the officer's black boots wave back and forth.

"I'm not a doctor, but I don't think your back's broken. I'm gonna move you," the chief said.

Darby groaned as the chief positioned his head under Darby's armpit, holding the young officer's forearm and opposite shoulder, and stood. "Come on, son, stand up. Help me out here."

Darby, whose smashed face sported a mean gash running up his forehead, tried getting his legs under him. His head throbbed in pain. *Concussion* was the word that kept flashing before the dark of his eyelids.

The chief dragged Darby into the house through the garage and laid him on the family room couch. The fire built earlier by Billy had reduced itself to a few glowing embers.

"Crenshaw? Have you seen Crenshaw?" The chief tried making the officer comfy until help arrived. His guess was that being buried in the snow actually protected him from the wind and frostbite, but he couldn't be certain.

"I don't know," Darby whispered. He never opened his eyes.

The chief grabbed from the back of his favorite easy chair a thick yarn blanket stitched by his mother and then draped it over Darby.

"Help's coming, kid. Just rest. You're safe."

The chief then did what he originally intended and charged toward the police cruisers. He first looked at the empty SUV. Instinct told him the two had managed to escape. Not one blood speck could be found.

He then returned to the street bearing the wreckage and started screaming for the sergeant by his first name. "Bruce! Bruce! Can you hear me?! Bruce Crenshaw!"

He walked around the upturned cruiser closest to him, uncertain of whose it was, and used his hands to dig through the snow next to one of the windows so he could better see inside. He found an empty backseat in car number one. He repeated the process for the front seat and again found it bare. He rose to see four mounds of snow had accumulated on the tops of the exposed tires.

The chief stepped back and panoramically viewed the roadway adrift with snow and mangled vehicles and felt he was the last living soul in some dystopic Ice Age.

The chief shook off the gloom to check the second vehicle ten feet down the road from the overturned cruiser. This car had landed upright, but the force of its impact had bent the wheels, crushed the frame inward and shattered all of its windows, and there wasn't a sign of anyone inside.

He felt on the verge of defeat but was buoyed when he passed the upturned cruiser to return to Officer Darby. He heard a voice.

It was muffled but clearly human, and sounded like "help!". The chief then heard thumping accompanying the pleas. The cruiser began to shimmy and rock.

"Help! Is anyone out there?!" The voice grew louder and the chief realized the person it belonged to was stuck in the trunk. He did a squat thrust to the ground and banged on the side of the cruiser's trunk.

"Bruce, you in there?!"

"Darby?!"

"No, it's Schweitzer! Are you hurt?" The chief pressed his ear against the metal.

"Shoulder's dislocated, I think!"

"What the hell are you doing in there?!"

"Jesus Christ, Chief, you think I planned on ending up like this?! I'd just gotten Darby's shotgun when I opened the trunk to get mine and then someone grabbed the back of my head and slammed it into the well of the trunk! All I remember was my shotgun being yanked from my hands, being pushed inside, someone slamming the trunk shut and then becoming airborne! My head also hurts like a bitch!"

"Did you see who did it?!"

"No, but he was fucking strong! Happened real quick too! Where's Darby?!"

"Inside! He's inside!" The chief sat in the snow next to the trunk, pressing his face close to the side when he spoke, his voice hoarse from screaming through the din of the storm, "He's resting! Not doing too good!"

"The kids?!"

"They're not inside!"

"Chief, I'm sorry!"

"It's not your fault, Bruce! It's not!" he yelled to make sure the sergeant knew he wouldn't hold him responsible for this gigantic shitstorm.

"Hey, Chief?!"

"Yeah?!"

"Can you get me the hell out of here?!"

"Hang tight, Bruce! I'm pretty sure I can't flip over a police car all by myself, but help is on the way! In fact, I can see it coming!"

The chief hopped up and saw, fast approaching in the distance, flashing red, white and blue lights emitting from any number of rescue vehicles. He called out one last time to Crenshaw.

"Bruce, we're gonna take care of Darby first and then get to you, so just hang tight! I won't forget you, I promise!"

He flagged down the oncoming vehicles to make sure they didn't plow into the broken police cruisers. They soon began lining up on the side of the road.

First up was a rookie officer. Bennings? Or Jennings? The chief wasn't sure of the name but explained the situation. He ordered him to have the ambulance park in the driveway and then get the paramedics inside to where he'd be waiting with Darby.

"What's he doing in the trunk?" the young patrolman asked the chief when he got to that part about Crenshaw.

"Long story, just keep him company. Make sure somebody brings the Jaws of Life. Crenshaw's been in there long enough."

The chief headed back to his house to make sure Darby hadn't died. The high of discovering that both of his officers had survived evaporated when he reminded himself he had no clue where his sons were, and whether they were dead or alive.

He held his front doorknob and waited a few breaths before going inside. *If they weren't in the SUV, and I don't think they were, then where...*

The chief pulled his flashlight from his belt and walked around to his deck and discovered their escape route.

He tempered his burst of elation with the knowledge that Billy couldn't always keep beating the odds.

Keep checking, he thought, and fished out his cell phone from his jacket pocket and brought up his email.

Nothing.

Chapter Fifty

Right about the same time Krampus discovered the SUV was a ruse, Billy called his best friend and had to be quick with him.

"Mike, gas up, bring extra fuel, and be ready to go."

"Isn't it a little late to—"

That was the extent of the call. Hopefully he'd be able to bring Mike up to speed if and when they rendezvoused near his house.

Setting fire to the monster had not been preplanned, but the decision to grab the night-vision goggles and the GPS trackers was spawned after hearing the roar that stirred the entire town of Hancock. It had stayed with Billy not because it frightened him—it did, in spades—but because it sounded so close to home. His mind raced to recall the caves and abandoned mineshafts in the vicinity, and which could be more easily accessed than others.

"Right before I poured the gas on it, I tossed Tim's satellite tracker into its crate." Billy appreciated not having to yell every word he spoke over the metallic purr of snowmobile motors. "Assuming the thing hasn't taken it off, it should lead us right to Tim. And I have a hunch where it is. There's a cave my father took me to, both me and Tim, when we were small kids, to go exploring. It's a few miles away from our home, and not far from Maria's. Winchester ain't far from it, either."

He sat with Maria and Mike in the Brembses' darkened man cave of a refurbished basement. Unlike the Schweitzers, the Brembses lacked a generator and relied on candles and kerosene-fueled floor heaters for vision and warmth. Only a few concrete-block-sized windows offered anyone a glimpse of the place from the outside, and whoever wanted to look would have to dig a path to clear the snow-obscured panes.

Even so, the three kids sat with their backs to a cold wall away from the windows to ensure nothing could see them. Two jars of pumpkin-pie-scented candles burned on each end of the family's billiard table in the center of the room. Maria sipped a bottle of iced tea. She was hot and parched from the excitement and had sweated her clothes to an uncomfortable stickiness. Billy continued to effusively thank Mike for the shelter. He and Maria needed this breather.

They'd emerged from the woods facing the Brembses' gated backyard but knew it'd be a dead giveaway if they left their vehicles by the fencing.

"I'll meet you at Miss Madsen's place," Mike told them over the phone. "Look for my mom's car out front and I'll drive you to my house."

Billy didn't want himself or Maria making footsteps near Mike's home, so they stayed on the snowmobiles in the woods until receiving further instruction.

"It's the home with the fancy greenhouse in the backyard. It's unfenced, so just park under her deck," Mike had told them. "She and her husband are already in Florida for the winter, and she's a real harpy, so screw her if that thing sees the snowmobiles and rips up her place looking for you."

Billy and Maria did so and discreetly walked in a single file from underneath Madsen's deck, literally clinging to the side of her home, to the street, where Mike waited for them.

"And the reason the police haven't already descended upon this cave of yours is...?" Mike didn't doubt that Billy and Maria had fled from something. More than anything, Mike wanted to see the thing that had shaken the sky with its fury.

"Probably because they're spread throughout Hancock, especially at the Halberstrom and Weaver homes," Billy opined. "And what am I supposed to do, tell my dad to send his men at eight at night to a place where I *think* Tim might be, based on a hunch of mine? That's why I grabbed the trackers. Just to make sure. By the way, that reminds me."

Billy punched up his father on his iPhone.

His dad couldn't get a word out before being interrupted.

"Dad, we're fine...I can't hear you, reception's terrible...I don't know if you can hear me, but I know you're worried...Don't be...I'm at Mike Brembs's house. My phone's dying...I'll talk to you soon...Worry about Crenshaw and Darby...and Tim."

Billy ended it.

"You can call him on my phone, you know." Maria offered Billy her iPhone.

They all sat next to each other—Mike, Billy and Maria—talking out loud and looking straight ahead. All each of them needed was a beer and they'd look like relaxed college kids attempting to divine the meaning of life, rather than feeling ragged and spent from fleeing a horned monster that was fluent in German.

"My phone's fine. It's probably best to let my dad cool down a bit. He's mad at me right now. I just wanted him to hear my voice to let him know I'm alive. And I've got another way to reach him, just in case." He held up a personal GPS tracker. "But this isn't the one I'm worried about."

Billy went to the tracking company's website on his iPhone and entered the serial number that corresponded with Tim's device.

"I put it on unlimited tracking, so I'll get automatically alerted every ten minutes of its location."

An overhead Google Maps image appeared on the iPhone screen.

"There we go: 41 degrees north, 1 minute, 23.2 seconds, and 74 degrees west, 33 minutes, and 4.7 seconds," Billy said, satisfied.

"What the hell does any of that mean?" Maria said.

"It means I'm right. My dad kept the coordinates of that cave, in case we ever wanted to go back and couldn't find it. He gave them to me and I've kept the numbers in my email account for years."

Billy left the map and went to find the saved digits.

"Between the two ten-minute intervals, the coordinates have gotten closer to the numbers my dad provided."

"Then your dad's getting the same emails," Mike said.

"No, he's not. These are pretty brand spanking new and Tim hasn't had a chance to use his yet, with football going on. The team would be pretty pissed if he hurt himself snowmobiling, so he's been holding off until after the season. He hasn't even programmed his yet. I just did tonight, so I can check on him. But my dad will get my emails and locations all the time after I turn mine on."

Billy held up the small lifeless gadget that looked more like a computer mouse than a potential lifesaving device.

"I have a feeling you're gonna end up using that too. I know how you work," Mike said. "You get something in your head and obsess over it."

"I'm going there tonight. I can't wait until tomorrow or when the weather finally cooperates."

"And you can find it in this?" Mike waved his hand upward toward the snowed-in windows.

Billy unzipped his backpack and held up the night-vision goggles.

"Now I know why you snuck off before," Maria said. "Clever. What else you got in there, other than road flares?"

"Don't worry about it." He stuffed the gadgets back in his bag.

"All right. Then let me worry about you and this hunch of yours," she said.

Worry about me? Billy thought. *By all means.*

Indeed, Maria's admiration for him had grown, especially for the way he'd handled a situation that made minced meat out of two trained police officers. He'd plotted the escape and skillfully executed it under unrelenting duress. And, most importantly, he'd rescued her. She'd felt an aura of protection around him the second he took her hand and led her to safety.

But then there was the book bag he guarded with a junkyard dog's vigilance. While every girl likes a little mystery in a man, Billy wanted no part of anyone knowing what else he had planned, and that she found more scary than intriguing.

"So what, you went to a cave a decade ago and because of that you think your brother's there now?" Maria said. "Respectfully, it's kind of flimsy."

"It was more recently than a decade. It's as recently as a few weeks ago. I actually go out there by myself to just be alone."

"Why haven't you ever taken me to this place?" Mike seemed hurt. "It sounds like a great spot to drink beer."

"Because it's *my* place. Sort of my dad's discovery, then mine. Everything comes full circle, you know?"

"No," both Mike and Maria answered.

"Since I'm the one the Krampus is after, it makes sense that it personalizes locations. It probably has an idea where we all like to escape to, and mine provided the most cover for its actions."

"Guess you're right," Mike said. "I mean, it can't really hide on Brittany's bedroom mattress without getting found out in a nanosecond."

"That's disgusting," Maria scolded Mike before talking to Billy. "But there's some truth to your theory. Kelly's favorite spot is in front of the television with the Xbox. It's not an ideal hiding spot." Maria slapped her own thigh. "Billy, that reminds me! That thing told me it freed Kelly!"

"What?"

"Right before you turned him into an Olympic torch, it said it had freed Kelly!"

"Then he's out there in *this*? I'm outta here, thanks for the rest stop, Mike."

"Wait just a minute, I'm going with you." Maria sprung to her feet to prevent Billy from leaving.

"No way. I'm not risking you."

"You brought *two* pairs of goggles, Billy," Maria said. "That was by design. If you're right, then there's every reason for me to believe that Kelly's still in there with Tim. He's smart enough not to go wandering around in this. *Both* of our brothers are part of this, or did you forget?"

"She's got you there, Billy." Mike also stood.

"Zip it!" Billy said.

"You can't deny Maria's got a legit point."

"To go in the cave to rescue Kelly? Yes, she does. But not to confront the thing that took him. That's all me. And it's bound to be even angrier at me for burning him up. And I don't want her or you in there with me if and when it gets me."

"Me?" Mike's ears perked up. "I wasn't even planning on going in the first place. You brought two pairs of goggles, not three. But let me amend my statement. I don't mind going *to* the cave with you, though. Not in. After all, what are friends for?"

Billy quietly laughed. "I don't blame you. And I must admit we could use an extra hand, if for no other reason than it catches you and gives us more time to run."

"Not funny. You know I'd go in there if you needed me to."

"I know, I'm playing with you."

Billy got the next ten-minute alert and confirmed the coordinates. "It's there."

Chapter Fifty-One

"You smell that?" Tim asked Kelly, who was regaining consciousness. Travis's snoring filled in the gaps of silence.

"Why did it tie me up again?" Kelly twisted on the ground. The crown of his head brushed the side of Tim's injured leg.

"Because it messed up. Don't worry, you're not in trouble again, I don't think." Tim felt grateful to finally have someone else to listen to, other than Travis's nasal buzzing. "What does that smell like to you?"

Kelly no longer got spooked upon waking up to total blackness. He sniffed.

"Like a wet dog." Kelly paused to better distinguish the aroma. "Like a wet dog that smokes cigarettes. Do you think it wants us to smell that? Like, when it said it could make us smell it in order to scare us?"

The scent of burnt mustiness seemed to hiss into the cave, soon followed by faint, harrowed roars.

"I don't think it wants us to smell that, but I don't think it can control it, either," Tim said. "Each time it's come in here with someone it just slipped in and didn't bother making a show of it."

The howling seemed to erupt from the belly and escape through its gritted teeth. Then pounding, six consecutive thuds of something smashed against stone, followed by full-throated bellows.

"It's hurt," Tim surmised. "It's not just hurt. It's in a lot of pain."

He whispered to Kelly, not putting it past the beast to be able to hear them from afar. "You ever try to hammer a nail but miss and hit your thumb?"

"Yeah, once or twice," Kelly followed Tim's lead and answered in a barely audible voice.

"What did you do right after?"

"I don't know, I think I pounded the table."

"That's right! You pounded it with your hurt hand to help divert the pain from the thumb. And you probably groaned or yelled."

"And swore up a storm. Son of a bitch!" Kelly said.

"*That's* what happened to our friend out there. And I doubt it was hammering anything. Billy must've hurt it. That's why it stinks like someone just put out a fire. He burned it. Why else would it be punching walls?"

"Maybe it's smashing its head against them!"

The pounding stopped and the hoofsteps grew in strength.

"Okay, Kelly, here's what I want you to do. Pretend to sleep. No matter what you do, pretend like you're snoozing like Travis. Just don't snore, because you don't. I've heard you. It'll know if you're faking it."

"But I just woke up."

"Kelly, you don't want to be awake for that thing when it's injured and pissed. Let it take it all out on me. You've suffered enough. So has Travis."

Hooves crashed against solid ground. The bones and skulls strewn about the cavern rattled with every stomp.

"Tim, thanks for everything. I mean it. Billy's lucky to have you. I don't mean to be rude, but good night."

Kelly shut his eyes and rested his head against the rumbling cold wall.

Chapter Fifty-Two

"I'm sorry, I thought they were downstairs, Don." Melissa Brembs returned to Donald Schweitzer, who patiently waited for her inside the home's front entrance. The onslaught of snow had turned a typically five-minute trip into one that instead took twenty.

"They were in the basement not fifteen minutes ago," she said, confused. "I heard them all talking."

The chief explained the choppy phone call and that Billy and Maria had cut through the woods on their snowmobiles to get to the house. He kept coy on the details, to spare Mike's mother from plunging into a world of worry over her son. Turns out he didn't have to.

"He must be with your son and that girl looking for—" She touched the tip of her forefinger to her lips. "Is it true what that prosecutor said? There's some pervert running around out there dressed like a Sasquatch? I thought Mike had invited Billy over to help keep him company. I didn't mean to lose track! Is Mike in danger?!"

"Don't get ahead of yourself, Melissa." He felt comfortable calling her by her first name, as she did with him. The boys had been lifelong friends, and the families constantly stayed on great terms.

"I have no idea where they went," she continued. "Mike didn't say anything about leaving. I mean, where the hell would they go in this?" She paced around the chief, wringing her hands together. "I was upstairs resting my eyes. I didn't hear them leave, Don. I'm so sorry."

"Don't apologize. Just try to remember, were Billy or Maria talking about anything when they got here?"

"Mike was waiting for them to arrive. Like I said, I was upstairs, but I could've sworn I heard my car leave the driveway. I didn't think anything of it. I mean, there was no reason for Mike to take it, which he's not allowed to do anyway if I'm not with him. I decided to check on it a few minutes later and the car was right where I'd parked it, and there they all were, standing where you are now. I offered each of them a bottle of iced tea—the girl took one—and then they rushed downstairs. All hush-hush."

"They were on their snowmobiles, Melissa. That much I know. Where does Mike park his?"

"Under our deck but—"

"Thank you, excuse me!"

The chief turned on his flashlight, left through the front and ran to the rear of the Brembses' house. It felt odd standing beneath the deck on hard dirt when he'd been trudging across snow for what felt like days. A snowmobile rested dormant underneath a large swath of plastic blue tarp, its sides and corners weighted down by cinder blocks.

A second sled, the chief presumed Mike's, was gone, its tarp sloppily balled up and tossed against the house amid six clustered concrete chunks. Schweitzer couldn't miss the freshly made parallel lines weaving through the whiteness toward the rear of the yard and an open gate. But only one set of tracks existed where there should've been three. He found no signs that Billy or Maria had parked anywhere near the deck.

"Don, is it there?" Snow fell on the chief in clumps through the deck slats where Melissa had walked when she went outside looking for Schweitzer.

"No, nothing!" he called up to her. "It's gone."

He trundled through the storm to the gate, which stayed open and in place. His flashlight followed the trail left by Mike's snowmobile, leading off the premises to the left, and then he noticed another trail joining it from the right. Either Mike was leading Billy or vice versa.

"Don! Whaddya see?!"

The chief jogged up the deck stairs and led Mike's mom back indoors.

"They went back into the woods, that much is obvious. Now, *where?* I can follow them on foot. That actually might be quicker than waiting for one of my officers to bring by one of the department's rides to chase them down."

"You have *police* snowmobiles?"

"Snowmobiles and ATVs. We sure do. We've just never had to use 'em. Melissa, can I trouble you for a glass of water?"

He figured it best to hydrate himself before embarking into the mess.

The jarred candles reflected brightly around the kitchen that led to the back door. She reached into the fridge and grabbed a bottle of water. "I'm sorry I can't offer it cold. Power's been out since, well, you know the story."

He twisted off the sealed cap and gulped it down, making satisfied-man noises.

"You want me to call anyone, Don? I feel silly asking the police chief if he wants me to call the police."

He downed the entire sixteen ounces without once letting up for breath and wiped his mouth with his jacket sleeve when he finished.

"Nah, I'll take care of it." Then it occurred to him that it'd been a while. "Excuse me a second."

The chief pulled out his phone. A surge of energy coursed through him when he saw that Billy had activated his beacon.

"Melissa, something just occurred to me."

Chapter Fifty-Three

Billy's world shifted into shades of glowing and grainy green and black.

He guided Maria and Mike single file through the woods, aided by a pair of night-vision goggles, although to describe them as *goggles* was to offer them the kingliest of compliments. It was a head-mounted, dual-eye unit with two sleek scopes jutting out six inches. A chin strap kept the contraption still, and Billy had the ability to flip the scopes ninety degrees upward in a pinch.

The chief stored two pairs in the house should duty ever dictate he need them. They came in useful when catching kids sneaking into the popular, wooded Hancock spots to smoke pot, drink beer or make out, all of which could just as easily be busted up without the goggles, but they looked so goddamn cool online that the chief couldn't resist budgeting six thousand bucks to buy two of them for the force. Billy mentally thanked the good townspeople for their tax dollars.

There were enough geographical landmarks to help Billy navigate his way to the cave, despite the snow weighing down tree branches and altering the landscape. He rode the main trail back toward his house from Mike's. Two huge granite boulders, at least seven feet tall and twelve feet wide, stood next to each other along the trail to Billy's left. Snow could not hide these boulders, and directly opposite them ran a side path that Billy and Mike followed deeper into the forest.

A hard-right turn waited for them one hundred yards in, and then a winding left before one final straight stretch to the fork. Mike and Billy parked the snowmobiles two hundred feet away from the cave as the terrain became hillier and rocky.

They stayed tight and shunned the use of flashlights, which Billy carried in his backpack. Maintaining the element of surprise meant no noise and no light. Enough natural light existed to allow Billy sight. Maria followed him, her arm outstretched, her hand on his shoulder, and Mike did likewise behind her so they all remained linked while trudging through the relentless snow.

They walked downhill from where the fork split. From there, the forest became a dense tangle meant only for hikers.

The whipping snow forced Maria and Mike to close their eyes and tuck their heads into their collars like turtles for warmth. Billy, undeterred by the storm, slowly shepherded them into a valley containing three expansive, flat basalt formations spread like lily pads across the forest floor.

If the cave's entrance had been covered by two wooden panel doors with flaked red paint it would've resembled a storm cellar instead of a rocky gash leading to a subterranean pit. The endless snowfall couldn't conceal that the area before the cave's maw, and it became obvious to all three of them that the greatly disturbed snow meant someone had been in and out of it all day. The mouth normally opened inconspicuously between two of the three massive basalt formations. The uninformed might think it to be the remnants of some uprooted, rotted-away tree and simply move along hoping a rabid raccoon wouldn't pop out of it. Billy had no clue how his father found it but he'd always been pleased that he did because of the solace it provided, allowing him to escape from the outer world.

But Billy knew serenity no longer dwelled within that black hole. Maria's and Mike's eyes adjusted enough to the dark so that they could see slightly ahead of them without a flashlight. Still, they both desperately wanted to turn one on to have a better look, but Billy forbade it.

He let his backpack fall from his shoulders and he caught it by a strap before it could hit the ground, where he then delicately placed it and unzipped one of Mike's old winter coats that he'd borrowed for the trip. Now stripped down to his black hoodie, Billy handed the coat to Mike and retrieved the second pair of night-vision goggles from his pack, and two small red lights that looked like bicycle reflectors to attach to the headgear.

"Why weren't you wearing that on the way here?" Maria examined the head and tail of the battery-operated light, figuring out where to attach it on the headpiece Billy had handed her.

"Because we already had some natural light. These goggles work by amplifying light thousands of times, and there'll be none of it down there." Billy moved his fingers around his head to ensure everything was in place, and then activated his light and continued the crash course. "Red works best because a bright headlight would overwhelm the sensors. And the color of the screen is deliberately green. The human eye can differentiate shades of it better than any other color. So, it's gonna be like you're looking in binoculars. In a way I guess you are. You're not going to have any peripheral vision; you'll be looking through a circle."

Billy fished a police flashlight out of his backpack, which had now decreased considerably in size, and gave it to a relieved Mike. He then handed Maria a small standard-sized one.

"Just in case your headlamp goes out," he told her. "Don't lose it. Ideally I'd have brought along the bright headlamps too. They didn't fit. Oh, don't freak out if you flip up your goggles, turn on the flashlight and can't see anything. Your eyes will need to adjust to the dark."

"Good to know. And I'm assuming you have a flash—"

He didn't let her finish. "Yeah, I have one in my pack." He slipped his arms through the bag's shoulder straps. "Maria, you stay behind me. If we catch any sight of that thing, you run."

"What about you? You're not *staying* down there, right?" She adjusted the chin and side straps to make certain the headgear fit snugly. A red glow then emitted from her forehead.

"I have to. Otherwise, I'm assuming it won't stop until it gets me. Better have it happen here than in my bedroom at three a.m." Billy sat down to inch himself into the hole the way he might an in-ground swimming pool. "I don't remember reading that this thing buries itself in the earth the moment December fifth or sixth ends, only to be let loose during the same time the next year. I think it finishes whatever its mission is, and then it goes to wherever the hell it lives."

"I'm guessing that would be hell," Mike said.

Billy scooted himself into the cave the way he'd done countless times before. He didn't drop straight down. It was more of a 45-degree dip.

Once in, he poked out his head like a prairie dog to instruct Maria.

"Just do like I did and you'll be able to stand up about twenty feet in. Can you see all right?"

"This is unreal." Maria slowly rotated as she took in the night, sporting a bumpkin tourist's gawk upon seeing New York City skyscrapers for the first time.

"Can I see?" Mike felt left out. "And what the hell am I supposed to do? What if that thing's over the next ridge and is making his way back here while you're playing groundhog?"

240

"Well, if it doesn't yank your head off, just tell it where I went," Billy said as he and Mike both safety-spotted Maria as she crept into the hole.

"I don't think it's gonna just thank me and be on its way," Mike said.

"Here's what you do," Billy said. "Wait inside the entrance for shelter."

Mike waited a few seconds for a bit of elaboration but heard none.

"That's it?! You want me to keep dry?"

"I do, and I also want you ready to help whoever comes out of this cave. I don't care if it means carrying someone uphill and laying them onto a sled to get them back to civilization. We're gonna need your help, Mike. You're not just along for the ride. I'm really thankful you're here."

Mike leaned in and gave his buddy a fist bump. "Be safe. And get going. I want to get out of this crap."

Maria thought the Disney *Alice in Wonderland* cartoon made falling down a rabbit hole appear so fun and elegant. *Clearly Walt's never been underground,* she thought. Her butt slid easily along the smooth ridges leading into a horizontal drift through limestone bedrock.

It was as she expected: a flat floor with an arched ceiling about nine feet high. She extended her arms sideways and couldn't quite touch the walls. She guessed the span to be six or seven feet. She expected to see timbering erected to stabilize walls, but none existed.

"How do you know it's this way?" she asked, looking at the green-and-black wormhole that Billy'd shunned in favor of another.

"Cave-in's back there. It's been that way forever. This is the only way to go."

Maria, out of curiosity, lifted up her goggles and experienced total darkness. "There's no way Kelly could find his way out of here on his own," she said while lowering her goggles.

"Odd as it sounds, flashlights wouldn't be that much of a help, either," Billy whispered, hoping Maria would catch on that he preferred silence. But he needed to remind her of something.

"It's easy for me to say, but try to stay calm," he said. "The air's not the best down here. Don't hyperventilate is what I'm getting at."

"I'll be fine." Maria was thankful the floor didn't require hopscotching around gaping holes. Millenniums of rainwater and snowmelts and God knows what else had worn the borehole smooth. Was she walking through a passage pounded and crushed into existence by some ancient underground river, or was this some prehistoric sea cave carved by an ocean? She ran her fingers along cool crevices as she walked.

They'd gone about fifty yards from the entrance when the tunnel opened into a cavern where stalactites dangled high above like octopus tentacles.

"I thought this'd be it," Billy said dejectedly. "I mean, this is my spot."

Maria couldn't believe tunnels and this cavern—she estimated it to be thirty feet by thirty feet—and others like it sprawled for miles below her Hancock home. She scanned the cave walls and admired the bumps and bulges. But she didn't need to look hard to understand the path ended here without any trace of life.

"Billy, what do you do down here when you're alone? Make a scary face with the flashlight under your chin?"

"I relax. And I don't need a flashlight all the time. If you look upward you'll see a circle in the middle of the ceiling." Billy stood in front of the walls and shuffled sideways, feeling the frigid stone with his hands, looking for a nonexistent lever that might reveal a secret passage. *How could it not be here?*

"Yeah, so?" Maria said while looking upward.

"It's a manhole, but not man-made like you'd think. My dad noticed it not long after he first found this place. He eventually located the opening aboveground and laid an iron plate over it. Don't ask me where he got it. I'm guessing he creatively acquired it before becoming a cop. Like him, I keep it covered when I know I'm not gonna be here for a while 'cause I don't want anyone else falling in and figuring out what's below it."

"Or accidentally killing themselves?" Maria added the part she felt more relevant.

"Yeah, that too. They'd have to go out of their way to find the cover. I take it off to let in sunlight before coming down here. It's worked so far. Enough light gets in for me to chill out during the daytime."

Billy completed his orbit around the cave as Maria gradually came to understand why he'd wall himself off from the world in such a lonely yet beautiful place.

"I mean, you saw the entrance, someone's been through here,"

Billy said while pacing back and forth before stopping and waiting for Maria's take.

"When was the last time you looked at the cave-in?"

He stayed silent.

"I mean, if there's a cave-in, that means there's a cave, right?" She spoke in a *well duh!* tone to state the obvious.

"It's been a while." He then began to double back.

Maria followed.

He turned and put his finger before his lips to remind Maria they should keep quiet. And it was. All she heard and felt were soft footfalls and her heartbeat, which elevated with each step she took upon passing their original secret entrance.

She wanted to ask him how much farther because they'd walked for what seemed like two hundred feet along a path on a gradual decline. However, the deeper they went, she noticed the walls didn't seem so confining and instead expanded in circumference. Billy's cavern wasn't too far in, and the way he'd described the cave-in made it sound like it was right there, don't even bother looking at it.

Billy held up his hand to pause their progress. And then he turned and lifted his goggles so she could see his wide eyes awash with confusion and fear.

"It's gone," he mouthed.

Maria saw not a speck of debris or rubble in the drift.

Billy broke his no-talking rule.

"There was a freakin' Indiana Jones boulder back there and a bunch of other smaller rocks blocking the way. You'd need dynamite to clear the path, or you'd have to chisel the shit out of it," he whispered.

"Or you could be inhumanly strong," she replied just as quietly.

An alien grumble breezed through the dankness. They focused on the black hole ahead of them and knew the rumbling wasn't being made by shifting stones but by something hostile, the unpredictable warning produced by a guard dog standing still, its eyes never leaving the foolish thing invading its space.

And then the sound quieted and seamlessly melded into the void awaiting them.

Billy spent his time in silence, contemplating their next move. He'd seen the damage done to Jason Nicholson, and had heard about the scorching Brittany Cabot was forced to endure. He surmised neither of them likely had laid a hand on the monster that tortured them, whereas he managed to simultaneously set it on fire and humiliate it. Surely things worse than horrid were in store for him should he fall into its clutches.

His goggles still up, Billy's eyes adjusted to the blackness enough to see a glow that bathed Maria's face in red. *I might die tonight,* he thought.

Billy mouthed to Maria *"lift up your goggles"*. He mimicked the action he wanted her to take.

He couldn't see the confused look in her eyes, but she did as he asked, and watched his face vanish.

She'd later deduce that in those few moments of blindness, Billy was staring her in the face and building up nerve, all of which led to the delicate touch of Billy's lips pressing against hers. A startled "mmm!" escaped her, and despite instinct prodding her to yank back her head and take a slap at a cheek she couldn't see, she ignored it and gently returned his small display of affection.

Billy didn't know how long he and Maria shared the kiss, which he would remember on his deathbed, providing he lived long enough to lie on it. It could've spanned an hour but Billy would always recall his first kiss lasting mere seconds. He did his best to savor her softness and scent as he reluctantly withdrew from his moment of glory.

Maria remained still, wrapping her mind around the brazen yet tender kiss, and heard through the darkness not sappy platitudes describing one kiss's potential to define the rest of his existence, but something reassuring and spoken with confidence: "I won't let anything bad happen to you, Maria. I promise. Follow me."

She hoped there'd be time enough later for introspection surrounding the kiss's meaning for *her* life—like, for instance, momentarily forgetting her boyfriend's first name. Now, though, she listened to Billy and trusted him.

He lowered his goggles, as did she, and they saw each other in different lights for the first time. He jerked his head forward to signal *let's go.*

He led her into the abyss and to the thing lurking deep within.

Chapter Fifty-Four

Mike Brembs sat against the cave wall that allowed him the most shelter from the snow, while still permitting him to keep his ears to the world both inside and out.

He had draped around his shoulders the extra coat he'd lent to Billy to provide an additional layer of warmth. He wore a ski cap and winter gloves and, all things considered, he couldn't complain. He kept the perspective that he had the freedom to leave the cave whenever he wanted and wasn't confined without sight.

"Wish I'd brought my earphones," he said while holding his fully charged iPhone gorged with an array of rock music recorded decades before he was born. He pocketed the phone in his coat and zipped it shut. He grabbed the flashlight beside him and directed the beam into the center of the black hole, hoping to see his friends making their way back with the missing kids.

"That would be easy. Too easy." He clicked off the flashlight.

"Hey, Mike, why do people talk to themselves when they're in dark, isolated places?" He waited a beat before answering himself. "I don't know, Mike. It's either craziness, loneliness or an attempt to calm your nerves, or a mix of all three. That sounds about right. Wait, what the hell is that?"

The nonrhetorical question prompted him to slowly pop out of the hole and survey the landscape. *Oh, that's right. I can't see shit.*

The rumble had built up a distance away and then halted. Had he actually heard something? Maybe he *was* going crazy. He was alone, and now his nerves begged for calm.

He kept to himself this time. *Only a fool would turn on a flashlight to look around and announce to the world his position. Only a fool would stay in the entrance to a cave frequented by a hairy European creature with hostile tendencies. Get your ass out of here.*

Mike attempted to conceal his exit by Marine-crawling out of the cave through the two feet of snow that carpeted the forest. He controlled his knee and elbow pushes to keep from kicking up plumes of snow and blowing his cover. The blizzard made his getaway all the more feasible because no man could see through the snow without the goggles worn by Billy. But by all accounts it wasn't a man out there.

Keep going. Don't crash your head into tree trunks, he thought.

He slithered counterclockwise around the rock to his left. He hugged its perimeter and figured he was on the two hand and would slowly emerge when he hit the nine. Mike had no way of knowing how he would measure it. His goal was to retreat a safe distance and then adjust to the changed circumstances.

Mike tried distracting himself from worry by thinking he was a goofy gopher screwing up a golf course fairway by leaving a bumpy trail. But he wasn't fully covered. Each movement through the snow brought it down on him. And he wore two bulky coats that crested through the snow like a whale breaching the ocean. He never doubted the thing's ability to see through the impenetrable mire. He could only make out whatever was literally a few inches ahead of him and even that caused eyestrain.

Sweat stained the ski cap covering his brow. He corrected his course whenever a tree obstructed his path. He began to pant and wanted to burst up for fresh air and then find a downed tree for cover.

Enough! He sat himself against the rock. He didn't bother looking around, but rather listened for labored breathing or something massive crashing through the woods. He hugged himself into a ball for warmth and remained like that, eyes shut, ears honed.

Nothing but wind gusts that dislodged clumps of snow from branches high above, sending them to the ground in intermittent plops.

Only a fool would go back the way he came, Mike thought. *So complete the circle and approach from the back of the opening.*

The rock formation stood high enough to conceal his tall frame, so he rose and cautiously walked a few feet before stopping to see if he could hear anything suspicious. He repeated this process until he rounded the stone. As much as he dreaded it, he needed to turn on the heavy police flashlight he'd grasped in his right hand the entire trip. He quickly directed the light from his feet and sent it outward, never sending it skyward for fear of becoming an easily spotted searchlight. It worked. He saw the entrance's hump and killed the light.

So now what? Sit inside the cave again? It's Russian roulette. Bears are already hibernating, I think, and there hasn't been one confirmed mountain-lion sighting in New Jersey since the Pleistocene, and if the Road Runner can handle a fuckin' coyote, then so can I.

His eyes came in line with the darkness before he continued his roundabout. The final leg was ninety feet away and he'd made it halfway when the foot stomps thundered from behind.

He spun and clicked on the flashlight, but caught only a glimpse of the dark mass crushing into his chest, launching him backward into the storm.

Chapter Fifty-Five

"I thought we'd see more bats," Maria whispered.

The beastly rumble had yet to stir again, and each had tired of the monotonous lull.

"They're dying out," Billy rushed back, blurting the rest of his answer in short clips. "White-nose syndrome. Some weird fungus killing them. Bad for nature. I don't care right now."

"Good point." She welcomed the dearth of hundreds of potentially rabid creatures roosting above with little eyes gleaming to remind her they could swarm in an instant. She'd counted three bats since they'd begun their descent. "What else lives in caves?"

Billy stopped and waited for Maria to do likewise. He listened for signs of anything and heard not a peep.

"Salamanders, maybe," he answered. "Cold-blooded things."

"That's comforting." Her voice rose in exasperation because their surroundings had remained the same corridor. Maria's frazzled nerves made her sweat profusely. She ignored the cold, unzipped her coat and let it fall to the floor.

Billy heard the rustling and glanced behind him.

"I'll get it on the way back," she continued their hushed repartee.

"That's the spirit!" He smiled at her, a genuine one fostered by the closest thing to afterglow he'd felt up to that point in his life. She knew what he was thinking, and grinned when recalling his unexpected sweetness.

Billy guessed they'd walked somewhere between five to ten minutes. He had no concept of how many hundreds of feet they'd descended. He blocked out any thought of a cave-in, other than the one that Krampus apparently had pulverized. He brought his attention back to the moment and was thankful that he did.

"Oh *wow!*" He'd seen pictures of places like this in documentaries chronicling faraway places. But here? *In New Jersey?*

The tunnel walls dissolved to reveal a chamber the size of a football field. Stalactites met with stalagmites to form grand columns—

some forty feet tall! Where they didn't meet, they dangled or sprouted, respectively, in varying lengths to give the impression that Billy and Maria stood in the jaws of some gargantuan fanged horror. Their steady footpath remained true and halved the chamber. A closer look revealed the formations in essence guarded an underground lake to their left. They both weaved through the spires of calcium carbonate to a bank overlooking dark water.

"I betcha anything there are translucent fish with no eyes swimming in there!"

"Billy, *quiet!* We're not alone down here, remember?"

His eyes followed what appeared to be water flowing under their defined path and it fed into a second concealed lake on the other side of the trail. A loud plop shattered the silence and he saw ripples of water extending toward him. He looked up and saw a hefty dripstone hovering over the center of the lake. Every so often a thick water droplet would detach from the tip, plummet and disappear, leaving a resounding echo in its wake.

They continued onward, crossing the stone footbridge to the other end of the cave. Not only did a continuation of the trail flow into another tunnel ahead, Billy noticed similar cavern openings leading into other parts of this undiscovered world. "Should we split up? Or do you want to check them out together?" Billy asked in an excited whisper.

"Stick together! Strength in numbers, right?"

"Agreed. But I want to see how many paths lead from this place, just to get an idea."

He counted four. The chamber was closer to being a circle than a square. Whatever its odd shape, four archways separated themselves by roughly the same seventy-yard distance. There was the one from which they'd entered, and the second straight ahead. A circular footpath formed around the lakes and the lawn of jagged mineral deposits, the way a running track wreaths a football field.

Billy ignored the entrance before them and focused on the far-left cavern opening. He looked at the rightmost one but immediately discounted it, doubling back as if to leave the chamber but instead taking the round footpath toward the one that intrigued him.

"What's so interesting about that one?" She followed him.

"You don't see it?"

She assessed the four passageways.

"They're all empty, Billy."

"I agree, but they're all not as dark." He pointed to the archway in his sights. "Look hard, you'll see it."

The profile of blackness pulsed with accents of green. Billy couldn't discern a timed pattern, only that the shade would blip lighter one second and revert to blackness before flashing again on a whim.

"I see it." Maria, like Billy, searched for an explanation.

"The only thing that could cause that is a different light source," he said. "It can't be ours."

"A flame moves like that, Billy, with the wind."

"It's not a raging fire, not even like the one I built earlier tonight," he said, dialing down his volume. "But you're right."

He eyed Maria. "You ready for this?"

"Yes," she whispered, and then waved him to escort her back to the entrance that'd led them into the chamber.

"What's the plan?" she asked when the tunnel wall concealed them.

"I was just gonna go in there. I mean, I'm not going to make a spectacle out of it. Just kind of sneak forward, see if I can spot anything, and hopefully Tim and Kelly will be in there, alive."

"And our friend?"

"I'm ready for whatever happens."

His response worried her. He spoke not to impress her with bravado, but with a sense of finality.

"Billy, it might kill you. You *cannot* be ready for that."

"You can, if you've had enough time to think about it, prepare for it and accept that it might be in everyone's best interest."

"What are you *saying?*" She scolded him like a mother disciplining her child during church. "I sure as hell didn't come down here to die, Billy. And I refuse to believe you did, either."

He spoke slowly to convey his point.

"I never said *I* prepared myself to die. Nor did I ever say me getting killed would be in *anyone's* best interest." He paused. "I can understand, however, how people can arrive at that decision. That's all."

A young man's cry ended the conversation. Billy slipped off his backpack and unzipped it. Maria gasped and stepped back when he pulled out the Heckler & Koch, slapped the magazine into the grip and pulled the slide to chamber a round.

He ignored Maria's shock and rushed ahead of her so she couldn't deter him. He turned left onto the circular path and kept the gun by his hip.

Maria kept pace from a distance, her eyes monitoring the firearm rather than ensuring her path was free of obstacles. Billy slowed about sixty feet from the cavern's entrance and pushed his open palm in back of him to stop Maria, who rose on her tiptoes to see what might lie ahead.

She contemplated the scream. It wasn't Kelly's, based on how he behaved at his school after first seeing the thing. It had to either be Travis or Tim. She cast them out of her mind upon catching a whiff of it and knew that's what made Billy stop. They were far enough away so that divining something from the darkness proved daunting, but they could both smell the gasoline.

"He's gonna kill Tim!" The shout came from a child.

Billy looked back at Maria and they both nodded in agreement for they both knew.

It's Kelly!

Their worry compounded because Kelly's shriek came from behind them. They both faced the rightmost cavern that portrayed no light.

"My brother's in there," Maria said, not looking at Billy. She turned to get his take on what to do next.

"Billy, drop!"

He didn't need to see what had appeared in Maria's sights. He collapsed just in time to feel the chain sizzle through the air above his head and smash into the wall next to the path.

Krampus, his wooden crate gone, charged from the passage that sporadically glimmered and snapped his chain toward Maria, who dodged it and ran in the direction of her brother's cry.

Billy rolled on his back to see the monster bearing down on him. He pushed himself up into a sprint and broke left toward the passage opposite the one that'd led them into the chamber. The beast roared and whipped the chain sideways at Billy, cutting through columns and stalagmites, whose tips popped off like champagne corks.

Krampus ignored Maria and pursued Billy, again whipping the chain, hoping to ensnare him, but instead snaring a column. It snapped back the chain and brought down the column's midsection.

The beast roared at its miss and saw Billy escape through the passage.

Maria ran through the entrance she hoped would lead to her brother and slowed her pace when her path became windy, about twelve feet high and wide. The trail formed an S pattern, and when she rounded the final bend her vision became dotted with two pairs of glowing eyes sitting next to each other against the wall of a round cave about an eighth of the main chamber's size.

Travis had no clue who'd burst into the cave with a glowing red lamp on her forehead, but next to him sat a kid who, seeing familiar waves of hair highlighted by the light, did.

"Maria! That thing wants to kill Tim!" Kelly bounced on his bottom, happy to see his sister. "He's not far from here. I heard him before! You have to free him!"

"With *what?*" she said. "I don't have anything to cut him or you loose!"

Then she noticed their hands were free. Both sat with their legs jutting outward, their hands clasped in their laps.

"We're already loose!" Travis sensed freedom for the first time in more than twelve hours and was desperate for it. "That thing brought us in here and cut our ropes. We can't see shit. But you apparently can!"

The thing's howl wormed into the cave but sounded distant.

"It's chasing Billy," she told the two. "He told me if I saw that thing that I had to get out of here, and that's what I'm doing, but you're coming with me. Can you stand?"

"I can!" Kelly said.

"I need help getting up," Travis said. "My arm and sides are all messed up, so be gentle."

Maria held Travis's right hand and pulled while Kelly grabbed him by the belt of his jeans to help him stand. She retrieved from the back of her pants the small flashlight Billy had given her.

"Kelly, don't turn this on unless we become separated." She handed him the tube. "In the meantime, just hold on to me."

She stood and turned away from him. "Hook your hands into my back pockets. I'll walk slow, promise." Kelly did as she said, and then she addressed Travis who stood behind him.

"Same thing, you hold on to the back of my brother's collar, we'll all move as one, understand?"

"Let's go," Travis said.

"We're not leaving without Tim," she said. "I know where he is, so, literally, hang on."

She led the three-person conga line into the primary chamber and scanned the breadth of the room for any sign of Billy and the beast. She explained the makeup of the place to give them some bearings and continued to the cave that originally drew Billy's attention.

"It's got a bunch of candles going in there," Kelly told her. "I think it was planning on doing something to Billy in there in front of Tim, like it made all of us watch when it tortured everyone."

"You got off easy, little man," Travis said.

"Quiet, both of you," Maria snapped. "Billy's keeping that thing away from us on purpose. I don't want to jinx it and make it change its mind."

They shuffled onward. The slow pace made the chamber seem twice as long as when she'd originally entered it. She knew they were making progress when she caught whiff of gasoline fumes.

"Kelly, you said there were candles in there," Maria said. "Do you smell that? What did it do to Tim?"

"Don't know. But it came back all pissed off with a big jug."

"Was the jug red? Could you tell?"

"Yeah, I think so."

"Wonderful, that's the jug Billy used to pour gasoline on Krampus."

"*Who?*" Travis said.

"Krampus. That thing. Its name is Krampus," she said. "Billy burned the hell out of it before. Now I know what it's planning on doing to Tim. Pick up the pace, gentlemen."

"That's why the monster was screaming," Kelly burbled with satisfaction. "We all saw what happened to it but it wouldn't say *how.*"

"How long was the monster screaming?" Maria asked as she halted the caravan at the opening they would take to exit the earth.

"A long time," Travis warily spoke. "He kept punching the walls like a boxer. Why are we stopping?"

"You can't see it, but we're right next to the tunnel we took to get down here," she said. "Tell me, do you think Tim can walk without help?"

"I think so," Travis said. "His hip's all carved up but he should be able to make it."

She first grabbed her brother by the shoulders. "Walk backward, Kelly, I'll guide you."

Kelly did as she commanded until he stopped against the base of the tunnel wall. Maria repeated the process with Travis.

"You two sit down and wait here. I'm going to get Tim. If you see Billy or that thing, yell. I'll come right back."

"How are we supposed to see them?" Travis said.

"Sorry, force of habit. Just keep quiet. I don't want to send you guys up there and risk getting lost. I'll be as fast as I can, promise."

Maria zoomed into the flickering tunnel. The light brightened and the stink of fuel peaked when she completed walking an L pattern into the cavern. Her vision became dotted with multiple glowing beads scattered all over the walls of a round cave about the same size as the one holding Kelly and Travis.

"Jesus, *Tim.*" She first caught sight of the blood staining the rope by his hip.

He rolled his bound body from side to side on the floor and squeezed his eyes shut to prevent gasoline from burning them. A red five-gallon container had been tipped on its side next to Tim and had gushed gas into a puddle that had drenched the ropes.

"Who are you?! Where's Billy? Is he all right?" Tim gasped, and then coughed as some of the fuel trickled into his mouth.

Maria made a quick introduction and set about freeing Billy's brother.

"Last I saw, he was fine, but he's busy running from that thing right now."

She scanned the cave for anything that could possibly pass for a cutting tool. She grabbed a cracked bone, she knew not whether it was human or animal, and pressed down with all her might and snapped it over her bent knee. Jagged edge in hand, it was worth a shot.

Maria started at the rope that knotted Tim's feet together. She rubbed the bone against a big jumble of thread and carved faster as some strands frayed and snapped. She intensified her makeshift hacksawing, hoping one cut would unravel the whole mess.

"Why didn't it burn you?" It seemed like a logical question to ask. "I mean, I'm glad it didn't. But why go through the trouble?"

"My guess? Torture." Tim expanded his legs to put pressure on the ropes to make them snap. "Billy burned it somehow and I was supposed to be payback."

"He sure did." She explained how Billy had rescued her.

"Yeah, well, wait till you get a look at the thing," Tim said. "On second thought, I hope you don't have to."

"It's that bad?" One more determined swipe of the bone and she cut through the knot. Fiber shreds rained to the ground en masse as Tim kicked apart the ropes. From there it was easy to free him. She helped Tim to his feet and made like he was a Maypole, circling around him to unwind his bindings. He was knotted by his collarbone, but simply lifted off the remaining length when enough slack freed his arms.

"It's gonna get real dark out there real quick." She instructed him to hang on to her the way Kelly and Travis had and started her trek back to the other two boys. Tim caught on and moved with her into the chamber.

A flashlight beam briefly crossed her face and caused her to flinch. "Turn that damn thing off!" Maria hissed as she closed in on Travis's and Kelly's position. "You're gonna blind me with that!"

"Sorry!" Kelly blurted. "I heard footsteps and wanted to be sure."

Reunited, she came to a decision Billy would bless.

"We're going. All of you, get in line."

"What about Billy?" Tim said in a panic. "You can't just leave him here."

"I know it doesn't make sense, but Billy wants to stay down here with it. He did something wrong, but I have no idea what, and he intends to sort it out tonight and hopefully wind up like Kelly in the process, unblemished."

"But, Maria, I didn't light the thing on fire," Kelly said it like she'd forgotten. "I'm sure the monster will take that into consideration."

"Cheerful thoughts, Kelly. Think cheerful thoughts," she said.

The boys lined up behind Maria—Travis first, so he could better support himself by holding on to her, and Tim in back of him in case Travis lost his footing and needed to be caught. Kelly brought up the rear and clung to the back of Tim's varsity jacket. He carried the flashlight for good measure.

She stood in the center of the tunnel and took the first step.

"Tell me if I'm going too fast; I'll slow down," she said. "I'm only going to stop to put my coat back on. I dropped it not too far up ahead. If you lose grip and become separated, speak up, I'll find you. There aren't any tunnels branching off from the one we're in so you won't be able to wander."

They began ascending. Maria looked behind her and saw the chamber disappearing from view, and as she did, a roar shook the karst.

Chapter Fifty-Six

Billy controlled his breathing. Short, silent breaths, in and out. His path split three ways one hundred feet into his escape tunnel and he banked right without even thinking why. He'd gotten enough of a jump on the creature so it couldn't possibly, Billy hoped, see which of the three passages he'd taken.

His path revealed a small cave no bigger than a standard high school classroom, with no other exit. Billy backed himself against the wall at the entrance's side and craned his neck left to see if the thing would storm into view. He held the gun over his heart sideways as if saluting the flag, waiting. He'd be toast if the monster followed him. He stood rigid and then closed his eyes to let his ears sense what they could.

I doubt a five-hundred-pound thing with hooves can tiptoe on rock and not make a sound, he thought.

He waited and heard nothing. Billy had chosen wisely and needed to be certain his movements wouldn't tip off his pursuer. He squatted, placed the gun softly on the ground in front of him and then slid off his backpack to slowly unzip it.

One by one he slipped off his sneakers and with equal caution placed them into the bag. The cave flooring was blissfully smooth and free of rubble. Still, even the soft soles of his sneakers could betray him by making noise as he walked in the deathly quiet environment. Billy's socks now gave him the best chance at being stealthy. He adjusted his backpack to fit tightly and not shift or make much noise. Billy wasn't a ninja and knew he couldn't stay completely quiet, but he needed any advantage he could muster.

He rearmed himself with the pistol and took long, exaggerated steps out of the cave and into the tunnel. It took fifty steps for him to feel comfortable with his feet padding against cold rock. Billy had zero traction should he have to run in an instant, but the socks provided useful cover.

He made it back to the three-way fork and became flooded by

many thoughts at once.

Was Maria all right? Where'd she go? Kelly said Tim was on the verge of being killed. I didn't hear anyone else scream. Now what do I do?

Pretty soon the monster would check all three passages, Billy knew. He needed to explore. He took the middle tunnel and grinned when he heard the monster's roar of frustration upon again being outmaneuvered by this irksome child.

Onward!

Chapter Fifty-Seven

"You sure you're all right?" the chief asked Mike Brembs. "I swear I didn't know it was you until I was on top of you."

"Please stop asking about it, Mr. Schweitzer. Like I said, the rocks on the ground broke my fall."

"I thought I heard a crack, that's all." The chief sat with Mike in the cave opening, wishing they were huddled over a fire as they watched the snow fall. "For all I knew, you could've been a kidnapper and—"

"Chief, please!" Mike scolded and then laughed. "I've had worse falls off my sled. It's too bad I didn't hear you riding in on my dad's. I can spot the sound of his motor anywhere."

"I parked it where you and Billy put yours. Your mom said it would be okay if I borrowed it."

"He'll understand why. He's staying in a hotel somewhere tonight, anyway, and will come home tomorrow when the roads are clear, *if* they're clear."

"I seem to remember there being two snowmobiles under our deck," the chief said. "But I only saw one of them back there. Should I ask what happened to the other?"

"It's probably best not to, but don't worry. Nobody got hurt. And now they're down in the cave. I know that's not what you want to hear."

"No, but I figured as much." The chief readied himself to delve into a cave he'd not seen in years.

"Are you sure that's gonna be bright enough?" Mike eyed Schweitzer's flashlight, a shorter one, not as bulky as the kind he figured police typically carried.

"It's ten watts LED." He flashed the beam into the darkness and it cast an impressive light. "How long they been down there?"

"At least an hour, probably more."

"And you didn't hear anything?"

"Not a sound."

The chief groaned. "I don't know whether that's good or bad." He mulled various scenarios before remembering what had worried him the most about Billy. "Mike, does Billy have a gun with him?"

The question flummoxed Mike. "No!"

"You sure? He has his backpack, right?"

"Yeah, sure does. But he took a whole bunch of stuff out of it and I didn't see a gun, bullets, nothing."

"It doesn't mean it's not in there," the chief grumbled. "One more thing, has Billy seemed down to you lately?"

"You mean, like, moping around?"

"Yeah, something like that."

"He seems a lot more quiet, keeps to himself," Mike said.

"He hasn't been talking about hurting himself, has he?"

"No. Not at all."

"No defeatist talk?"

"*No.* If there is a gun in his pack, it's to defend himself down there."

"Okay, I appreciate it. I had to ask."

"Now you're worrying *me*," Mike said. "I didn't see it, but he apparently risked his life before to save Maria, and he didn't use a gun. He's with her and is trying to get three missing people up to the surface. Those aren't the actions of someone who's given up on everything."

"That's comforting. It really is, Mike. Thanks."

The chief delved into the cave.

"You're welcome." Mike pointed his own flashlight through the dark to help guide the chief. "Look, don't get disoriented. Leave a trail somehow."

The chief answered wordlessly with a smile that Mike caught in his beam, and then he was gone.

Well, this was a bad idea, the chief thought as the darkness enveloped him. He wielded his flashlight like a white lightsaber with a never-ending tip and stood where the tunnel leading from the outside intersected with the drift.

His light ping-ponged off the walls and revealed nothing but rocks of different shapes and sizes, nothing that would allow for him to recall where he'd been.

Just like riding a bicycle, he thought as he began walking through the drift where he'd led his boys way back when.

The LED flashlight provided enough light to guide his way into the cavern. And like Billy, he felt defeated upon seeing it empty. He returned to the base of the cave's exit and remembered the cave-in. He walked a short distance and focused the beam down the gradually sloping path once blocked by rocks and heard an "ouch!" in return.

"Who is it?!" the chief yelled.

"Turn off your light!" came a girl's voice.

"Maria?!"

"Chief?!"

The chief shined the beam at his feet, saw a hovering red light coming into view and recognized the pair of night-vision goggles just below it. He slowly trickled the light forward so as not to distract the wearer and saw four sets of feet trudging in lockstep.

Mike Brembs, too, became momentarily blinded when the chief's flashlight beam smacked him in the face a few minutes later. He stood and scooted out of the cave to give the chief room to exit. Mike's stomached fluttered when his flashlight picked up the people trailing Schweitzer.

"Billy?!" he yelled.

"No, I wish that was the case," the chief responded as he rose from the hole. "But I've got Tim and the others! And now I really need your help."

Everyone stood outside of the cave and lined up in front of the chief, who barked out the orders.

"You're all going to help Travis get up that hill." The chief directed his flashlight through the swirling flakes up the ridge.

"I can make it, Chief." Travis felt a much-needed adrenaline rush upon tasting real freedom.

"All the better. You're going to ride with Mike back to his house. Tim, you're riding with Maria, and I want you to sandwich Kelly in between the two of you. It'll be tight but you should be all right."

"Wait, why can't I ride my own snowmobile?" Tim said. "Is it here?"

"Yeah, about that..." Maria started, but the chief stopped her.

"Tim, no arguments! You've been through hell. Maria's way more alert than you right now, and she can handle herself, right?"

Matt Manochio

"Yessir," she answered.

"Okay, good. Now, Maria, hand over your gear."

She promptly did as he asked and described the layout of where he'd soon be headed. The chief slipped on the head mount and then did something he'd wanted to do all day. He wrapped Tim in a giant bear hug, lifting him off his feet.

"Your brother was right," the chief said.

"Dad, you can put me down now," said Tim, ever the self-conscious teenager.

"No, listen to me. Your brother never doubted you were alive. I'm so glad he was right."

He felt himself getting choked up and didn't want to cry in front of the kids, but couldn't help it, the sides of his eyes squeaked out tears as he put down his eldest son.

Maria hugged her brother from behind, knowing how the chief felt, and she couldn't wait to deliver Kelly to their parents.

"All right, get going," the chief said. "Mike, you call the station the second you get home. Hell, do it before you leave, if you have reception."

"I'm coming back, Chief." It was Maria, and she wasn't up for a debate. "When we drop them off I'm coming back."

"So am I," Mike said.

"I'd expect nothing less. Only this time bring some backup with you."

The kids made for the hill.

"Wait!" the chief called, and they all turned. "Is there anything else I should know about what I'm dealing with down there?"

The kids all glanced at each other, and their looks didn't give off vibes of hope.

"Dad, you can't stop it." Tim expected his father to say something but he didn't. "But I don't think it'll hurt you."

Tim then reflected on his own encounter with the beast. "Well, I don't think it will hurt you that *much*. The thing said Billy might be the worst one of all of them in the cave. I don't know why, but this is all up to Billy now."

"That's why he stayed down there," Maria added. "He wants to put an end to all this. And I'm worried because I don't think Billy cares what might happen to himself in the process."

262

The goggles in place, the chief clicked on the red light and descended into the earth to try to prevent his son from fulfilling a death wish.

Chapter Fifty-Eight

The middle passageway of the three that Billy'd found led after fifty feet to a small cave with *four* tunnel openings.

This could be an SAT question, he thought. *One path leads to three paths, and one of those three paths leads to four paths. If one of those four paths takes me to a set of seven paths, how many paths will await me after I take one of those seven paths? Answer: Fuck the SAT.*

He took the leftmost of the four. It opened into a large cavern, smaller than the main chamber, but large enough to house a basketball court. Stalactites dripped from a ceiling forty feet above him. The ground, too, featured the assortment of jutting formations that also might seem at home on a dinosaur's back. He ran his hand up and down one of the cold columns and marveled over how many hundreds, no, *thousands*, of years it must've taken to form.

He knew they were fragile—the thing's chain had shattered the column in the chamber with the ease of breaking porcelain—and didn't function as a means of support. It was simply beautiful. The slender formation he held was no thicker than the barrel of a baseball bat, and it vibrated.

Billy took his hand off it for a moment and then placed the fleshy pads of his fingertips against the limestone drip. The tiny vibrations ceased. Instead, the column trembled, as did the ground.

He didn't panic. He first stuffed the gun in the front of his pants and quickly slipped off his backpack to retrieve the remaining signal flare and his sneakers. He needed traction. He slipped the flare in his pants next to the gun, and zipped up and refastened the now-empty pack to his body.

Where to hide?!

A lake didn't occupy the center of this cavern, only a misshapen floor that rose and fell in spots. The only feature of the cave that might help Billy was its most obvious one: a round rock—almost like the Indiana Jones boulder that once had blocked his way to this world— settled in the corner. It was big enough to provide him high ground, maybe fifteen feet at its topmost point, hopefully with enough space to hide where it sloped to meet the wall. Now he just needed to find a way to climb it.

The wall to the right of the stone featured enough nooks and crannies for him to slip in his fingers and get some footing. He'd never climbed one of those faux-rock walls he'd seen at fun centers, but imagined they worked the way he was now attempting. He couldn't maneuver his head with much freedom due to the goggles poking out so close to the wall. So he focused on the boulder to his left and felt around for a crevice.

Up he climbed as the trembling persisted. His fingers became slick with sweat and jeopardized his grip. All he could think of was a sledgehammer rhythmically crushing the floor as the thing stomped its way toward Billy.

Does it even know I'm here?

He examined the boulder and found no grooves that would allow him to latch on. He reached for a ledge that spanned the entire length of the wall, and which hung over the boulder, but it jutted outward one foot higher than he could grasp.

Billy needed an adrenaline rush so he thought about what he'd almost lost that day, what he'd gained that he hadn't expected and all that was still possible.

Billy got the best footing he could and grabbed the highest slivers of rock that allowed him a firm grip. A fall wouldn't kill him, but would force him to think on the fly of something else that probably wouldn't work.

On the internal count of three he simultaneously pushed with his legs and pulled himself up with every ounce of strength he had, doing his best to jump. He became slightly airborne, no part of his body touched the wall for an instant, and he reached as high as his arms allowed and grabbed the ledge with both hands. He gripped tightly and shimmied himself sideways until he dangled over the boulder. Careful not to break his goggles, he descended by finding a few gaps below for his hands and feet. The rock's round top made for a clean slope down to where it melded with the wall.

Billy lowered himself like a setting sun until he was completely hidden behind the boulder's zenith. He adjusted his goggles and headgear to remain unseen as the thing entered the cavern.

It surveyed the cave and dragged its chain where it walked.

Billy reached for the gun tucked in his pants as the hoofsteps approached. He thought better of it and instead retrieved the road flare. Quietly he removed the cap to expose the red tube's button. He ran his right thumb over the coarse striking surface on the cap top. He pointed the rough side at the flare's combustible end that he held in his clammy left hand.

The thing halted to sniff the air and take in its environment. Billy's pulse rushed through his throat. He couldn't see a thing while tucked behind the rock's topside, but the solid hoof clops neared. Again it stopped and smelled what it could, and then it withdrew; its steps grew fainter.

It can see in the dark, he thought. *I'm certain it can hear a flea burp. Maybe its weak sense is smell?*

Billy wouldn't let relief take hold yet, but the beast clearly had retreated from the rock and him.

It stopped again and the cave went silent. No more sniffing.

Come on! Get the hell out of here! Billy closed his eyes to say a prayer, something he'd been doing a lot lately.

The next thing he heard was the chain, but only for a moment.

The links crashed down on Billy's spot, hitting the top of the stone. He had huddled with his head down and his arms and legs tucked underneath him. His back, fully exposed, absorbed the brunt, the end links smacking his rear ribs.

He screamed as the chain whipped back.

The beast roared and then grunted for some extra oomph to bring down the chain with more force. Billy backed up as far as he could, figuring the beast would aim for the same spot, and avoided a second iron lashing. The chain rapidly shot back.

"I surrender!" Billy shouted before the next barrage. "You got me!" Billy rearranged his goggles so he could climb down. "Give me a second so my eyes can adjust!"

"You either get down here in five seconds or I beat that rock until it breaks!"

"Okay! Just wait!" Billy sat on top of the boulder, his feet facing the beast. "I'm gonna slide down."

You can't surrender yet, he thought. *Not until you're sure Tim's free.*

The beast cautiously moved closer to the rock while Billy's brain raced for yet another escape plan.

266

"I think I can do this," he reassured the creature. "Let me just get my legs ready for when I land."

Krampus stood ten feet from the boulder. The beast had flicked the chain back and held it, ready to strike again if need be.

Billy balanced himself on his butt and stretched out his legs.

"Get down here now!"

"Okay! Here I come!"

Billy pushed himself forward and began a downward slide. The decision to wear his sneakers paid off. At the last second he planted his feet against the rock, gained traction and pushed off, leaping at the beast.

He struck the rough cap against the flare in midair, igniting a bright-red flash. He focused on the creature's face and closed his eyes, holding the flare like Norman Bates would a knife. He plunged it forward, hoping a meaningful strike would buy him some time.

The sizzling tube struck the beast's left eye. Billy, still holding the flare, smacked against the beast's chest as it howled. He used his free hand to push off its furry torso and brought the flare with him.

Billy landed on his feet and backed away from the beast, which held both its hands over its damaged eye and continued its tortured yowling. He held the burning flare in back of him to maintain his night vision and ran toward the cavern's exit.

Don't look back!

Billy backtracked and burst out of the passageway that was one among four. He knew the middle of the three openings before him led to the main chamber, and that's where he ran. But before doing so he turned and threw the flare into the entrance next to the tunnel he just exited.

Maybe that thing will get distracted and follow it, he thought as he bounded toward the chamber. The fading screams reminded Billy that he'd probably just signed his own death warrant.

Chapter Fifty-Nine

Hancock Police Captain Jim Sherwood and a second policeman helped the paramedics load the gurney holding Travis Reardon into the ambulance that was waiting by the snowy curb in front of the Brembses' household. Mike had called the cops the moment the group left the chief.

Two police cruisers were parked behind the ambulance. All the vehicles' lights were flashing.

"Son, we need you to get in there with him," one of the paramedics told Tim Schweitzer while examining the gruesome wound on his hip.

"My dad and my brother are still back there!" He was sitting on one of the two snowmobiles parked on the Brembses' front lawn. Mike and Maria hadn't gotten off their vehicles and impatiently sat, waiting to unload and get moving. Mike's mother, awkwardly attired in snow boots, pajama bottoms and a thick blanket, stood next to her son.

"Kelly, go with the policeman, he'll take you to Mom," Maria instructed her brother, who scrambled for the safety he hoped Sherwood could provide.

The other officer shepherded Kelly to his cruiser to return him to his waiting mother at the police station.

Sherwood took Tim by the shoulders.

"Your father would want you taken care of, so please, for both our sakes, go ride with Travis to the hospital. That cut on your leg needs some serious treatment. Go on."

He guided Tim toward the rear of the ambulance to end any discussion. Two waiting paramedics grabbed Tim's hands to help pull him into the ambulance. One of the EMTs sat him down and began addressing the wound. The rear doors closed and the ambulance barreled into the storm.

The cruiser with Kelly followed. Sherwood and another officer, who had originally ridden with the cop who now drove Kelly, remained.

"If one or both of you wants to see where we found them, get your asses over here," Mike said.

Sherwood couldn't argue with that. "I'll go," he told the other officer. "You stay here and wait for the others. Sheriff's officers are on the way with that dog."

"Bring all the flashlights you can!" Maria called to them and took off, she was done waiting.

"And flares!" Mike added.

The officer handed over his flashlight to Sherwood, who retrieved from the cruiser's trunk an LED lantern, five emergency road flares and a black tote bag containing dozens of glowsticks left over from a police-sponsored Halloween safety promotion. He stuffed everything in the tote and climbed onto Mike's sled.

"Please take care of them," Melissa Brembs told Sherwood as he straddled the sled. She also knew there'd be no debating her son.

"And you be careful, Mike," she said.

"Ma'am, I think they're the ones who are gonna be taking care of me," Sherwood said.

Mike's snowmobile chased Maria into the woods.

Chapter Sixty

The more he explored the chamber and its branches, the more he regretted not discovering the labyrinth earlier. What these dripstones and stalagmites must look like when backlit with colors of red, green, yellow and blue!

None of the smaller caverns that branched off from the chamber could match its majesty, but each had their own unusual charm.

Well, except for the one littered with skeletal remains and candles— that's just creepy, he thought, gripping the pistol tighter as he kicked through the cut ropes that reeked of gasoline.

He'd heard the beast's continuous roars from within the tunnel of forks, but they soon died down. He thought for certain it would enter the chamber, but it didn't, and this allowed him a fuller exploration of the area. The leftmost and final of the three tunnels did a large loop around the skull cave, past its entrance, and led back into the chamber.

How long has it lived here? he thought. *Long enough to know every crevice and hiding place.*

The distant rumbling might have been soft, but he easily detected it and knew what created it. The plods grew in magnitude and quickness of pace. They were coming from the cave of forks, as he'd come to think of it. He took refuge between two huge stalagmites that had sprouted in front of one of the cave's thick mineral columns, this one off to the right of the skull cave, close to the underground lake. The spires rose four feet from the columns' bases, which provided a nice place to scrunch into a ball and hopefully go unseen.

The monster, should it enter the chamber from the cave of forks and head for the skull cave, would not pass him unless it decided to walk straight from the chamber opening, across the makeshift stone bridge dividing the lakes, and then make a right to follow the path to the skull cave.

A metallic slithering joined the pounding of each hoof on stone.

The stomps ceased upon it breaching the entranceway, and it

exhaled to spread its rank breath around the chamber.

"I know you are in here, boy." It spoke in a low growl that became amplified due to the chamber's makeup. "The air smells different."

He peeked out from behind the column and saw the thing beginning a clockwise patrol of the chamber, along the outer rim. A scent of charred fur and flesh lingered around the beast. It would first pass the cavern on the far wall before reaching his hiding place. He looked at the gun. His best chance was a quick face-to-face confrontation.

Aim for its eyes, he thought.

"I have not had a challenge like you in almost half a century," it said. "Usually the bad ones are all cowards, easy to snatch and pummel. But every now and then a cretin such as yourself comes along."

It then took a deep sniff and continued on its trajectory.

"I must admit I was not expecting you to put up such a fight, but I appreciate the struggle. Sometimes the animalistic instinct to survive never appears in my prey, and if it does, they do not properly channel it. They attack without thinking of the next step, believing a boost of strength can stop me. But not you, boy."

It disregarded Kelly's cave and rounded the bend to pass the chamber's exit leading to the outer world.

"You seem to be forgetting one thing, however. Perhaps it will come to you in a moment." It slowed its gait. "Think quickly, boy. You are running out of time."

He jogged his mind, trying to come up with what the thing might be talking about.

"Ah, well, you will figure it out soon enough." It picked up its pace and strode by the exit.

It would be in his green sights in moments.

"How about a fairer fight? I'll drop my weapon, and you can use whatever you wish. I am ready for it this time."

The chain clanked to ground.

He closed his eyes and said a prayer.

It stopped walking a few feet from the stalagmite that shielded him and then the beast roared to shake the foundation.

Do it!

He stood, whirled and pulled the trigger five times. Into nothing.

The bullets ricocheted around the chamber until clinking to the ground. Gunshot echoes faded to silence.

He walked to the spot where he figured the beast would be and held out his arms. The chain looked like an anaconda that had died midslither on the floor. *What the hell?*

A sickening hawk broke the quiet, followed by a gooey spit.

A glob of phlegm splattered on his head and seeped into his eyes. He squeezed them shut, dropped his gun and flipped up his goggles to clear away the gunk. He heard a mocking laugh from above and then the earth-quaking impact of the thing landing on the ground.

It grabbed him, pinning his arms to his sides, lifting him in the air.

"Well, not quite what I was expecting," it said. "Hello, Billy Schweitzer's father. At least, that is who I am guessing you are based upon your name tag." The creature scanned the small gold plate, above the jacket's breast pocket, that read *D. Schweitzer*.

The beast held the chief with one hand on his jacket while using the other to nimbly crush the upturned goggles between its forefinger and thumb. It then dropped the chief, who now helplessly stood in front of the creature.

The chief rubbed his eyes but it didn't matter. He was blind without the goggles.

Oh shit! The red light! The chief gave a *how could I be so stupid?* groan.

"Ah, you figured it out!" the beast crowed. "It helps that I can see in the dark. But it helps even more when a red light leads me right to someone who forgot he left it on. Your son thought of that before. He must have derived his smarts from his mother, ja?"

"Where's my son?!" he yelled while waving his arms in front of him.

The thing rolled its eyes and pushed the chief's chest, sending him on his butt.

"Billy Schweitzer has remained out of my reach all day. But I imagine that is about to change. I was upset when I saw your other boy had gone, but you also fit the bill, very nicely, I might add. Now, how about we find your little boy?"

Chapter Sixty-One

Billy Schweitzer imagined a colonoscope's unenviable journey as he explored the tunnel of forks. He'd yet to formulate the best way to escape New Jersey's suffocating bowels while remaining intact.

He'd confront the monster at some point, but human nature prevented him from sauntering up to Krampus to turn himself in. He kept thinking there had to be an easier way. None materialized.

He returned from the middle passage of the three-pronged fork and began scouring the final tunnel on the left. Billy wound around the loop and knew where he was headed when he caught sight and smell, respectively, of flickering light and gasoline fumes.

"Boy?"

Billy turned off the red light after hearing the beast's call and remained motionless.

"Billy Schweitzer?! How were you going to do it?! Pressed against the roof of your mouth?! Through the heart?!"

His stomach sank. *How can it read thoughts?* On a day when nothing made sense, Billy accepted it.

"I am not the only one here who is curious! Speak!"

He heard a swift whack followed by a man's scream and then the creature: "Speak, damn you!"

"Billy, I'm in here!"

Dad?

"How will this work, Billy Schweitzer? How much pain do you want your father to endure before you come crawling to me, begging that I stop?"

Krampus made the chief sit against the skull-cave wall. Before entering, the beast had crushed his pistol in its hands before ordering the chief to toss his belt and its accessories into the lake. His eyes had adjusted to the dimly lit domain, and his nose detected something different on the beast that the gasoline fumes couldn't hide: the sickly smell of roasted skin.

The monster stopped in front of one of the candles near its head, and the flame cast a glow on scorched, flaky flesh covering most of its face. Much of Krampus's brown, furry mane had burned to ash. The chief didn't know how the beast had snuffed the flames, but they'd burned long enough to blacken Krampus's horns halfway up from their base.

"What was the plan, boy?! Walk into the school and shoot yourself before that delicious girl?! Were you going to take her with you?!"

Krampus again swatted the chief with the ruten, resulting in another pained cry.

"Pretty soon I will start swinging to break! Do you want your father receiving disability for decades?! How would you like to be tasked with caring for him for the rest of both of your lives?! What a father-and-son moment it will be when you place your dad's naked body into the bathtub to scrub him! Better still, you burned me, twice! I still have some fuel left in this container. You will never again recognize your father!"

The beast grabbed the red jug and dumped the remaining gasoline on the chief's face and body. It then heaved the empty container against the cave wall. The creature stalked to the far side of the cavern where a deer carcass festered. It ripped away a femur and licked it clean of remaining muscle and ligaments. Krampus then reached into its crate, the top half of it burnt, resting against a wall below shelves of candles, and pulled out some fresh rope, but then stopped.

"Even better," it told the chief. It dropped the cord and picked up some of the cut, fuel-drenched strands of twine that had bound Tim. It knotted a few pieces around the femur's ball joint and held it to a candle's flame.

Billy had removed his goggles and saw from outside of the cavern the glow of bursting firelight.

"I imagine you are plotting how best to proceed." The beast began its discourse civilly but elevated its voice so it could be heard from beyond the cavern. "So let me hasten your decision!"

Krampus stepped toward the chief and waved the torch over him. Schweitzer averted his eyes from the flame. He felt the heat and knew one falling ember would kill him.

"Either Billy Schweitzer presents himself immediately or else his father burns!"

A single bullet slowly twirled through the air and landed softly on the chief's belly before rolling off and clinking to the ground. The clip with the remaining ammunition followed and plopped softly on the chief's lap, followed by the empty pistol, which Billy slid across the cavern floor before it stopped just shy of the chief's upturned boots.

Billy ambled into the light holding his hands aloft to show he carried no weapons.

"Let him go." His best poker face stared at the beast.

"Or what, exactly?" said Krampus, impressed by the boy's bravery in the face of annihilation.

"My father's clean and you know it. By the looks of him you've exacted some measure of revenge or pleasure—I'm not sure which."

Billy recalled the people who'd previously sat in the cavern.

"I'm assuming you did what had to be done to Travis, and I think it's safe to say Kelly's painlessly learned his lesson because I've yet to hear of him bleeding all over Bryan Welles's living room floor. It's done."

"Ah, but not completely. You see, they all witnessed what was done to the others. Why should it be any different for you?"

"Leave him alone!" Donald Schweitzer snapped.

The beast jabbed the ruten's tip into the chief's chest to hold him at bay.

"Because I'm sorry! That's why it should be different!" Billy tried holding back the sadness but it erupted when he looked at his father. "I'm sorry, Dad. I'm so sorry."

He was glad Maria was nowhere in the vicinity because his tears rolled freely as he spoke. "I took the gun last night after I hung up with Maria."

"Billy, I know about the gun." The chief didn't care if the beast hit him for speaking out of turn. "But you didn't do anything with it; I don't think you even shot it. That's all I care about right now."

"I did it on an impulse, I swear! Please believe me."

"I do."

"I was in my bedroom, just looking at the gun. I never seriously thought about it! And the second I realized what I had done and how nuts it was, I went to put it back in the safe but heard you coming and had to go back to my room to hide it in my bag. You made me go to school this morning and I brought it with me. I could've tried putting it away when you were waiting for me in the car, but I thought you'd walk in on me trying. And I kept it with me today because I thought I'd need it against him!" Billy pointed at the creature, who listened as intently as the chief.

"I wouldn't have done any of that, Dad, but I've been so sad! I'd never turn a gun on myself! I can't! I just want this sadness to go away and it won't and it's driving me *crazy!*" he screamed the final word.

The release cleared some of the fog from Billy's mind. The chief's eyes flitted back and forth from the beast to his boy, wondering what he should do. Krampus withdrew the ruten.

"That blueprint on your desk," the chief said. "You had today's date on it."

"So *what?*" Billy panted and wiped away tears. "I wrote December 12 on the bottom corner too. I got an extension. But what the hell does that—"

"You weren't going to shoot up the school?" the chief said.

"What? *No!* Where on earth did you get—"

"And *that* is why the Master thought you might be the most terrible child of them all," the beast interrupted, jabbing a pointy finger at Billy. "The Master knows what you *might* do, not what you *will* do. A child beating another is cowardly. A child who ends its own life? Selfish. But a child slaughtering many innocents, at the root, is evil. The signs usually manifest themselves but go ignored by those who foolishly reason away the behavior. Your school might not have been in your plans, but you thought about killing yourself, boy, however fleetingly. Your father failed you."

"That's bullshit!" The chief became livid. "I've always done what's best for him."

"Naturally you would say that," it shot back. "Maybe if you tried focusing more on your children than brooding over that ex-frau of yours, you would have realized your boy's suffering long before it reached this point."

Billy kept his hands raised, trying to urge calm.

"So you know my kid better than I do?"

"Not *me.* The Master. He realized your boy was troubled years ago."

"I doubt that. And how exactly could your so-called master possibly be aware of my boy's problems, whatever they are?"

"Hmm? How does that carol of yours go? Ah yes, 'He knows if

you've been bad or good, so be good for goodness sakes'." The monster warbled the tune in a singsong voice, dumbfounding the chief over what the beast had implied.

"You can't expect me to—"

"Believe? Yes, I do!" it roared. "Because there you sit before me. You see the bones, the flames, this cave. The gun. Do you think you are hallucinating?"

"No."

"You know what else you saw? A worthless shred of human debris now linked to your fancy medical machines, allowing him a lingering life irrevocably altered by his debauched humanity. That all happened today. You bore witness to the aftermath."

"Like you had nothing to do with Jason or any of the others," the chief said.

"I had nothing to do with making them reprobates. I tried setting them on a righteous path."

"Oh *God*, spare me the hyperbole. You're insane! For all I know, Jason's dead, Brittany's got third-degree burns, and do you honestly think Kelly is going to get a normal night of sleep for the rest of his life? And Travis? Jesus, you broke I don't know how many of his ribs, and his arm—"

"*Not* his throwing arm. I took care to leave that one be, just in case he proved sufficiently repentant. Fortunately for him, he did. Or so it seems."

The beast suspected the chief's confusion.

"Do you not realize that I have corrected the paths of thousands of young men and women who have gone on to live decently?"

It slowly circled Billy, who locked eyes with the thing.

"Doctors. Teachers. Judges," it continued. "A president of the United States—have fun figuring that one out. But the occupations need not be glamorous. Everyday insurance salesmen and women. Taxi drivers. Firefighters."

It looked away from Billy to Donald Schweitzer. "Police chiefs." Krampus let it hang in the air. "Tell me, Billy Schweitzer. How do you think your father became familiar with these caves?"

"Impossible!" the chief shouted. "Don't you think I'd remember you?"

"No," it said matter-of-factly. "Some remember me, some do not.

But they all tend to refrain from speaking about me. I tell them, like I told Jason Nicholson, that I will never stop watching. *That* usually keeps them quiet. But I am realistic: kids are going to gab. But it plants that extra germ in their minds that I might return through the bedroom window.

"You were young, Donald Schweitzer, younger than Kelly Flynn, even. The young more easily repress bad memories. And I conditioned you well enough to break your habits."

The chief shook his head at his son. "He's crazy, Billy."

"You were a bully, Dad," Billy said. "You must've been something along those lines. What else could it be?"

"Correct, Herr Schweitzer! Your father had all the makings of Jason Nicholson, only worse. He was merciless to Paul Reardon when they were in kindergarten. The Master dispatched me all those years ago to see if you were receptive to corrective action. You blubbered worse than your boy as you sat before me. But I believed you were sorry, just as I believe your boy now. Not everybody gets that benefit, especially the ones who I know are liars, as you can see around you."

Billy and the chief scanned the skulls among the wrecked skeletons.

"Fortunately for Jason and Brittany, the Master now frowns upon child consumption as the ultimate punishment. A pity, if you ask me. But I suppose it would sully Saint Nicholas's image if word got out that he turned a blind eye to the devouring of children in his name.

"So now I beat them to the brink. Survival usually means they will behave in ways more beneficial to society. Death? Perhaps it is for the best for everyone."

"Why Hancock?" Billy asked. "Why this place?"

"Herr Schweitzer, why *not* this place? Over the course of two thousand years I have visited many lands. Other than the number of people, Hancock is no different than Berlin, Copenhagen, Vienna, what have you. When did Hancock corner the market on purity? Human nature ensures my ability to unearth the deviants from wherever you cluster.

"And the Master has many dark servants. Knecht Ruprecht, for instance, in Germany, he's a bearded man not unlike the Master, but who wears brown robes. The Master rewards the deserving children with candy, while Ruprecht flogs the brats with a sack of ashes. Now, if it was me, that sack would be filled with hammers.

"Those children should thank the heavens for the ashes because Frau Perchta, an old Bavarian hag, on the other hand, stalks the countryside during Christmastime to assess the decency in children. Good behavior means a shiny penny in their shoe. Badness means she'll slice open their bellies, scoop out the innards, replace them with hay and sew shut the stomachs!" It pondered what it'd said, reminiscing, "I always liked Frau Perchta."

"The last time you were here, it was for my dad, right?"

"And a few others. Very perceptive, boy. As you can see, my coming to town does not go unnoticed, as hard as I try. Outmaneuvering the authorities proved so easy decades ago. There was none of this email or Internet. Knocking down your telephone lines crippled the town long enough for me to do my work and allow for confusion and rumors. One of your newspapers even ran a headline, *Did The Jersey Devil Do It?* Ha! What sophists! I do not even have wings! But one thing remains the same now as then: Enough time needs to pass before my return. As will be the case after tonight."

It turned to the chief one final time, but spoke to both Schweitzers.

"Why did you become a policeman, Billy's father? Was it your lifelong dream to protect this little town for twenty-five years before taking an obscenely generous pension? Or did something else motivate you? I know the answer. Do you?"

Without warning it blew out the candles and the torch. Billy turned on the red light and lowered his goggles. Both he and the chief heard the chain piling into the crate.

"Billy?" The chief spotted the red light on his son's forehead.

"I'm all right, Dad."

The beast slowly approached him as his eyes adjusted to the night vision. Krampus wore his crate, with the tail end of the chain dangling over its side. The beast held its ruten. Billy thought he'd destroyed the beast's eye with the flare, but only the skin surrounding it seemed burned. Strands of new hair poked out of regenerating flesh, veiny and glistening pink.

"Children have constantly racked my body with pain while trying to defend themselves, Herr Schweitzer. Fire has been the constant method available to them throughout the ages. Do not flatter yourself, thinking you are the first. I have had maces crushed against my face, swords skewering my ribs, axes to my spine, throwing stars that one time I went to Japan—yes, Christians live there. I exist to dispense and

279

receive pain. And, like you, I detest being its subject."

Krampus cracked the ruten twice against Billy's left arm, shattering it. He screamed and his father called for him.

"That, Chief Schweitzer, was for your boy burning me," it said. "After all, it *did* hurt. I think your son can accept one broken arm as payback, ja?"

"Yeah, I'll take it!" Billy groaned and doubled over, trying to figure how best to cradle his fractured limb.

Krampus refocused the boy's attention by placing the ruten under his chin and directing his head upward for one final look at the beast.

"You will heal, and so will I."

The creature slipped the ruten into its sheath and loped out of the cavern toward the main chamber.

Billy made sure Krampus had disappeared before tending to his father.

"Dad, I'm standing in front of you, hold out your hand."

The chief did, and Billy used his good arm to pull him upright, receiving an unexpected bear hug from his father.

"Dad, that hurts!"

"Whoa, my bad!" The chief loosened his grip and gingerly held his son close.

Despite wearing the goggles, with only a soft red light for guidance, the chief recognized his boy's cheeks and chin, and the smile that formed when Billy saw his father's face expressing gratefulness in grainy shades of green and black.

"I didn't know how bad you were hurting inside, Billy. I just thought it was the blues, you know? I never knew. I should've picked up on it and for that, *I'm* sorry."

He'd put his father through enough, and there'd be time later for lengthy personal conversations.

"Don't be," Billy said. "Let's get out of here."

He started leading the chief out of the cave when an echoing voice stopped them.

"You cannot kill evil—only its host. I assure you those candles will burn again."

Hoof clops soon faded into silence.

Chapter Sixty-Two

Maria, Mike and Captain Sherwood lit up the cave with every method available to them.

Sherwood carried the LED lantern while Mike and Maria each wielded a police flashlight as they made their way down the long drift into the limestone chamber. Sherwood cracked a glowstick and dropped one every one hundred feet to create a trail.

Billy held his broken arm close to his chest as he and the chief began their ascent. Billy insisted on wearing the goggles and leading them.

The chief walked behind his seeing-eye son, his hand resting on his boy's shoulder. He also wore Billy's backpack, which contained the unloaded gun, ammunition, and ruined night-vision goggles attached to salvaged headgear. He held by his side the flashlight Billy had brought with him, and kept it on but away from his son's line of sight.

"I'm gonna get you help, and I'm not just talking about your arm," he told Billy. "There's no shame in talking to someone."

"I know. I can't say I'm looking forward to it."

"We'll think of something to tell Tim and your friends about why that thing wanted you."

"Let's tell them the truth, Dad. Enough hiding. I almost did something I would've regretted. They can infer what they want, and we'll tell them I'm doing something about it. Anything beyond that is none of their business. Oh, whatever money I have is going toward buying you a new gun safe, with a combination I won't know. I don't want you worrying about me."

"Save your money. I'll take care of that, but I appreciate the offer."

"If it's all right with you, I want to come back down here, Dad. To explore."

"I hate to break it to you, but it's a crime scene. We've got to identify those skeletons down there. We'll close some very cold cases."

"I get that. I mean when you're done with this place."

"Well, I don't mind you going to that small cave I took you to. If anything happens, like a cave-in, there's an opening and we can hear you. I'm not sure how safe it is down here the deeper you go. Other people will have to find out about it."

"You don't have to release the coordinates to the press, you know. Keep it behind the blue wall."

"For now, we will, no doubt."

"What are you going to tell that gasbag prosecutor?"

"That it was some crackpot in a Halloween disguise."

"But it wasn't."

"We don't know that for certain. At least I don't," the chief said. "Or, maybe I will tell him a woodland creature was working for Santa Claus to punish bad children. I have a feeling Hancock's going to be in the news for a little while, regardless of what I say. Honestly, I'm not sure what I'm going to tell that gasbag prosecutor. I'll worry about it after your arm's set and Tim's stitched up."

Billy had been aching to ask him and Maria, and the first chance presented itself.

"So, do you believe in Santa Claus, Dad?"

"I can't even think about that right now. Do *you*?"

"Let me answer you three weeks from now. Just disable the burglar alarm before you go to bed."

Billy then asked what he knew would keep both him and his father up for many nights to come. "Where do you think it went?"

"Not this way. Probably through one of those other tunnels leading to God knows where. Someplace we'll never find it, and it's probably best that we don't. But I believe what it said about not coming back here for a while, if ever, since we know about it."

"Go ahead and bag those candles down there as evidence, Dad. It'll figure out how to get new ones. You saw it yourself, some things can't be stopped. So you accept it and fight it and survive it however you can. It *will* come back."

The chief's anger at his son evolved into pride. "You saved those kids, Billy."

"Travis and Kelly saved themselves. I can't say the same for Brittany or Jason. And Maria helped as much as I did, probably more."

The chief didn't respond. He appreciated the modesty.

Billy stopped to focus on something. His father bumped into him, not expecting the sudden halt.

"What is it?"

"There's light up ahead, Dad. I can see it."

Acknowledgments

Thank you to my editor, Don D'Auria, for giving me the opportunity to write books and for his continued faith in my ability to do it. I hope to one day meet Samhain Publishing's publisher, Cris Brashear, so I can personally thank her for investing company time and money in me. This will have to suffice in the meantime. Thanks!

Lorraine Ash, a former colleague from my newspaper days and a published author herself, provided encouragement and advice to a young writer who sheepishly approached her to ask for help with a different book I was writing back in 2007. It is not an understatement to say that without her support I would not be published today. Thank you, Lorraine.

Thank you to Paul E. Mussman, Esq., for his sage legal advice, and for being a great brother-in-law.

I cannot express enough love and thanks to my mother and father, Carol and Lorenzo Manochio, for their support in areas of my life too numerous to mention.

And, of course, thank you and "I love you" to my wife, Tehani, for not only proofreading my writing, but for also noting inconsistencies and suggesting ways to improve my work—even when our toddler son, Nathan, is running around wearing nothing but a diaper and figuring out how to dismantle the cabinet locks underneath the sink. She's the best wife/mother/editor out there.

Do check out www.krampus.com, "Home of the Christmas Devil", as it is one of the most resourceful websites to chronicle Krampus throughout the ages. I highly recommend www.toplessrobot.com, which has an informative and hilarious post titled "10 Fun Facts about Krampus, the Christmas Demon". Both of those websites helped shape my understanding about the creature and its exploits. The text from the Wikipedia entry written in German is indeed what you'll see if you search for it. The English version and its associated sources also helped to shape my knowledge. Among them: *Time* magazine, the *New*

York Times (which chronicled Austria's shunning of Krampus during the Third Reich), *Reuters*, *Der Spiegel*, the *Vienna Review* and *National Public Radio*, among others.

About the Author

Matt Manochio, a recovering journalist, is a supporting member of the Horror Writers Association. A University of Delaware graduate, he lives in New Jersey with his wife and son. He can be reached through his website: www.MattManochio.com. Or follow him on Twitter: @MattManochio.

It's all about the story...

Romance

HORROR

www.samhainpublishing.com

CPSIA information can be obtained
at www.ICGtesting.com
Printed in the USA
BVOW03s2338171116
468262BV00001B/10/P